Return to Sad Hill

ARMANDO RODERA

RETURN TO SAD HILL

1ª Edition

ISBN: 9798860641150

Author's mail: info@armandorodera.com
Author's fanpage: www.facebook.com/ArmandoRoderaAutor
Author's Web: www.armandorodera.com

ABOUT THE AUTHOR

Armando Rodera (Madrid, 1972), an avid reader since childhood, is one of the pioneers of digital publishing in Spain. He studied Telecommunications and worked for ten years in the technology sector until he found another occupation that allowed him to devote more time to literature.

Thanks to his success on Amazon, he published in 2012 his debut novel *El enigma de los vencidos* (Spanish Version) with Ediciones B. His successful novel *El color de la maldad* became the best-selling police thriller on Amazon.com for three consecutive years and caught the attention of the American publisher Thomas & Mercer, who published the English version in 2014, *Color of evil.*

He also published *La rebeldía del alma*, an intimate thriller that was number 1 on Amazon.es. His historical work *La posada del viajero* was the 3rd bestselling ebook on Amazon.es the year of its publication. Other works of his on Amazon are the thrillers *Juego de identidades*, *Caos absoluto* or *El Pastor*, without forgetting *El aroma del miedo*, a detective novel set in the Levantine coast with the same protagonists of *El color de la maldad.*

Throughout these years several of Rodera's books have been number 1 in digital format in Kindle stores in Spain, France, Italy, Brazil, USA, UK, Canada or Australia.

THE GORGE

Santo Domingo de Silos (Burgos), August 1966

He would never have guessed that this would be the last night he would visit his favorite hiding place, a small cave hidden in the limestone rock that served as a watchtower for dozens of birds of prey to build their predator-proof nests. Under the immense mass of stone perforated by time and erosion, a few meters above the dangerous access to the gorge of La Yecla, Juanito kept the fruits of his plunder.

The boy, a peasant from the nearby town of Contreras, traveled throughout the region to earn a few bucks with his shady dealings. After they had started shooting the film in the Arlanza valley, a couple of months before, he had managed to increase his haul with objects that an acquaintance of his, a black marketeer in Burgos, paid him a good price for - a pocket watch belonging to one of the protagonists of the film, stolen in a moment of distraction while its owner was having a coffee in the sun in the main square of Covarrubias, a silver dollar he had stolen from the production assistant, or the rolling tobacco that the

American actors smoked during their breaks and that he had craftily taken. Small trifles that could go unnoticed as they vanished as if by magic, but that earned him good money.

Juanito was a slim young man with long legs and a boyish face, a smart kid who was sometimes too smart for his own good. At that moment, however, something made him hesitate. A bad feeling made his stomach churn for a few seconds as he thought of all the misdeeds he had done in recent times. He did not want to worry too much; he had not committed any serious crimes. He thought that the Americans would not miss those inconsequential objects seized because of their carelessness and his skill, but anguish began to take hold of his guts when he thought he saw a strange shadow on the rocky wall, by the entrance of the gorge.

"Who's there?" the boy cried out in a trembling voice, more to bolster himself than expecting an answer.

Silence hovered in the summer night typical of the Burgos region, more than a thousand meters above sea level, where the 'cool' was a daily occurrence. Cold sweat ran down the back of Juanito's neck, an unmistakable warning that something bad was about to happen. The creaking of wood, a few meters from his position, alerted him to the danger and made him hurry. The lack of light in the area, illuminated only by a full moon almost obscured by clouds, did not exactly help him in his task, but he had to move fast.

Once the cache was safely stored, with the objects carefully wrapped in newspaper to better preserve them inside the small damp grotto, Juanito left the base of the ancient watchtower.

He skipped carefully between the rocks and reached the central part of the gorge of La Yecla. The gorge, chiseled over millions of years by the waters of El Cauce stream, could be crossed little over half a kilometer further away thanks to a series of bridges and wooden walkways raised over waterfalls and pools. A route with rock ceilings that could be pleasant in broad daylight, but which in the dark, and with his heart pounding, became a lot more threatening.

Juanito approached the route along the middle, just where the path was leaving the gorge and he was free from having the limestone mass above his head. He then noticed a ray of swaying light filtering through the nooks and crannies of the gorge, just from the entrance closest to Santo Domingo de Silos. After hearing the sound of hurried footsteps and labored breathing, together with the sight of a round silhouette outlined among the rocks, the young man from Contreras was finally convinced: he was in trouble and had to get away fast!

The unstable wooden walkways built over the pools were not the best way to escape from his pursuer, but his youth and knowledge of the area gave him a small advantage. He had to be careful at certain bends so as not to plunge into the void and break his neck on the rocks below, especially in those tight angles of the path that had no railing. He had little more than a hundred meters to go to reach the end of the gorge when a deep voice froze his blood:

"Stop right there, you bastard! I'm going to beat the shit out of you".

The young man had guessed long ago who his pursuer might be, but after hearing the unmistakable sound of his voice, he had no doubt. That man would keep his word if he caught him, he would skin him alive and leave him at the mercy of the carrion birds.

He could not stop to think about it, least of all try to talk some sense into the man who was chasing him. The boy then remembered his innocent reflection of a few minutes earlier: he had come to think that his petty stealing from the Americans could not be considered such a serious crime, without realizing that he was really facing a much bigger problem.

Juanito jumped between two catwalks and slipped on a damp ledge. The stumble threw him off balance and he hit his side against the edge of a sharp rock, moments before falling and bruising his face on the ground. He was petrified and groaned in annoyance, but he knew he could not wallow in his pain. He hastily tried to sit up, but the fall had left him more winded than he had expected, he had lost precious seconds which his pursuer seized to catch up with him.

"Got you, you son of a bitch!" he heard next to him.

The newcomer pointed his flashlight directly at Juanito's face and dazzled him. The young man tilted his head to get out of the powerful light, while he crawled along the catwalk and looked for a spot where he could safely escape to the mountain where no one would find him. But the man did not let him go and kicked Juanito in the side with a forceful rage, unloading all his accumulated anger. He screamed in pain as he curled into a ball.

"You deserve to be beaten to a pulp, you bastard. What am I going to do now? You've ruined my life..."

The man stopped hitting him and remained distracted for a moment, staring into the void while he leaned the flashlight against a rock. The beam of light lit up the side of the narrow cave next to them. Juanito seized the chance to get on his knees and sit up slowly, while he looked in fear at an attacker who seemed to be thinking of something else.

The boy could not let the opportunity slip away; he might not have another. But his pursuer was not as distracted as he seemed to be, and as soon as Juanito stood up he blocked him, trapping him between his huge body and the small railing that was the only thing separating them from falling into one of the deepest chasms of the gorge.

"Where are you going, smartass? You think you're going to get away after what you've done to my family?"

"I'm sorry," the boy stammered, dizzy from his enemy's foul breath. "I couldn't do anything, sir. I tried but..."

"Couldn't you do anything, you bastard? You explain that to your maker when you meet him. Or better yet, to Satan when you burn in hell with all your kind."

Then he grabbed him by the neck with one strong hand, calloused after a lifetime of hard work in the fields. Juanito felt the pressure on his throat and tried to pull away without success; fear had practically paralyzed him. The young man had the feeling that his eyes were going to pop out of their sockets and for a few moments he did not even struggle to survive, he let his arms fall at his sides as he realized that his life was worthless.

His last thought was for his family, while hatred gripped his soul knowing that he would die right there, at the hands of his neighbor, with no one coming to his aid. He did not want to leave this world with the image of his murderer in his mind, so he searched for something pleasant to think of as farewell.

But he did not succeed. The only thing that came to his mind, was of that same afternoon, he had stolen a trinket from the camp set up by the film production company in the Mirandilla Valley, between Contreras and Silos, right next to the fake graveyard that had been built as a set for the film. An accursed place to which he should never have returned to, but greed had overcome reason. He had left that graveyard in the direction of La Yecla and, in a paradox of life, he was now going to find his own grave in the damned gorge.

He was considerably surprised when he recovered his senses and because of it, it took him longer than necessary to realize what was happening: the air was trying to enter his lungs again after a few seconds, in which his throat had remained closed, and his body was struggling to regain normality.

He coughed and cleared his throat at the new situation before gasping like a fish out of water unable to breathe normally. He leaned against the railing and tried to get out of there, but the massive frame of his attacker prevented him from moving. While the beating of his heart returned to normal, he heard his rival's lament, regretting his actions, from what he could guess through the annoying ringing that had settled in his ears.

"What am I doing? I am not a murderer..."

The man grabbed Juanito by his shirtfront and in spite of being afraid, he no longer saw fire in the eyes of that damaged man, but he would rather escape from his clutches before he changed his mind. He tried to redirect the situation, but his body did not respond as the moment required and his voice barely echoed inside the grotto.

"I..., I'm sorry, I'll sort it out. I'll take care of it, don't worry."

"You'll take care of it? A little punk like you couldn't do anything even if he wanted to. Don't make me laugh."

"I swear I'll make it up to you, you have my word. My mother is ill and needs a lot of care. Let me go back to the village. No one has to know about it and I..."

"What do you mean nobody has to know about it, you jerk? We're already the talk of the whole town, not to say the whole region, and you're to blame for everything!"

Juanito tried to break free and pushed hard at the man, but could not make him budge. The only thing he managed to do was to prove the effect of action and reaction. His movement caused his opponent to push him in turn against the wooden railing, more out of pure instinct than to cause him real harm, but fate had prepared an ending for them that neither had foreseen.

The railing gave way at the exact spot where Juanito had hit it with his body and he plunged through the resulting gap. Juanito screamed as he fell backwards while contemplating his attacker's stupefied face in the shadows, unable to react in time to grab him. The sound of a skull cracking was the prelude to a thunderous silence, not even stifled by the wind howling through the gorge or the flapping of the vultures taking off from the top of their crag.

The man picked up the flashlight and carefully peered over the edge of the catwalk. He saw Juanito's motionless body at the bottom of the chasm. The boy had hit his head against the rocks and his body looked like a broken puppet, his neck bent in a position incompatible with life. There was nothing he could do for the poor wretch, all that remained was to get away so that no one could connect him with the event.

The bed of the stream that ran through the gorge was not too deep in that area, but he hoped that Juanito's body would not be found until a few days later, half-hidden as it was between two rocks. The only clue to what had happened there was the damaged railing, so he ended up tearing it all off and hurling the pieces into the void. The path built along the gorge had no such safety element along the entire route so no one would have any reason to suspect anything

Regrets invaded his mind, but he pushed them away as best he could as he hurriedly left La Yecla. He had to look after his family, that was the important thing, and to find a solution to all his problems. Although the first thing would be to convince his wife, a woman of formidable character, to provide him with an alibi if he ever needed one: he had not moved from his house all night, and he knew nothing about that poor wretch if anyone asked him.

He had left the mule-drawn cart on the other side of the tunnel dug out in the rock, so he retraced his steps and set out to return to Contreras. It was already late and he had a long way to go, so he prayed that he would not run into any early risers that might spoil his plan.

SUMMER PLANS

Madrid, July 2016

Having just turned nineteen and after finishing my first year at the School of History of Art with good grades, all I had left was to enjoy the summer. My grandparents were delighted and wanted to celebrate it with me at a special place for us: the apartment my family had in Sancti Petri, in Chiclana de la Frontera, next to the spectacular beach of La Barrosa, one of the most famous on the coast of Cádiz.

I enjoyed a relaxing fortnight - beach and snack bars, where I could forget about books at last. I even got a healthy tan, my skin was too white for my taste, thanks to the Andalusian sun and the Levante wind blowing on the Costa de la Luz. Although, of course, spending the vacation with an elderly couple was not the best plan for a girl of my age.

"I'm going back to Madrid this weekend, Sandra," my grandfather remarked one day. "Would you like to join me or would you rather spend a few more days here with your grandma?"

"Oh, I'll come with you. Next week I want to meet Ana before she goes on vacation to her village. Besides, I'm a little tired of so much sun."

My grandfather's name is Adolfo and he is a renowned psychologist who retired some time ago. He had turned seventy-five that summer, looking great by the way, and he was still driving his old-fashioned Mercedes. My grandmother Matilde is five years younger and always picks on the two of us because we are thick as thieves, so she would not be surprised if we left her alone in Cadiz while we returned to the capital.

I had grown up with them in their renovated apartment on Toledo Street, in the heart of the Arganzuela district of Madrid, a neighborhood that I have always loved. My parents had died in a traffic accident when I was very young, after leaving me with my grandparents one evening - my mother and father had gone out to celebrate their fifth wedding anniversary so I do not have many memories of them.

I want to believe that I took my parents' death extremely badly which was the reason why I became a rebellious child and a troubled teenager, so my grandparents had to fight to 'straighten me out'. Perhaps, at the time, I was not very aware of the real reason, but I quickly realized that I was not like everyone else. There was always some charitable soul who labeled me a 'freak', and some jerk I had as a classmate at school, and they laughed at me because I was always accompanied by my grandmother.

Thanks to my grandfather's training and experience in psychology I was able to manage while growing up and maturing. I studied at the Instituto San Isidro, almost at the end of Toledo Street, next to the collegiate church and very close to the Plaza Mayor, mostly to continue the family tradition. My mother and grandfather had studied there, a mythical academic center of the city where many illustrious scholars had studied throughout its history.

Right before the end of middle school I still had some confrontations with students and teachers, but I managed to get my act together in time for high school. I did not really believe I had any problems - all teenagers consider themselves misunderstood and I was no exception - but I only managed to grow up when I came to terms with my true situation.

Deep down I was not really behaving that badly. Yes, I had sneaked out on occasion, mostly to sleep over at a friend's house, and I had gone binge-drinking like any other young person my age. But I had not tried drugs and was not planning to, nor had I been too much of a problem when it came to boys either. Some passing fling or hook up, but nothing too serious.

When I turned sixteen, I became fully aware of what would happen to me in the near future. My mother had been an only child and so was I, no siblings, uncles, aunts, or cousins on that side of the family. On my father's side I did have more family, but the truth is that I had not had any contact with them for many years. So there was really only an elderly couple who, by the law of life, would leave me alone in the world rather sooner than later, so I had better get my life on track before that happened.

Yes, my parents had passed away many years ago and my grandparents had spoiled me. Or so my grandmother claimed when she saw how her husband treated me. My grandfather had lost the apple of his eye when he lost my mother, Sara Millán, and had made me his new favorite person. He was sometimes a hard and inflexible man, but he adored me, and I used to take advantage of that to wrap him around my little finger to get whatever I wanted.

For example, we had had our quarrels about my studies for as long as I could remember. Since I was little, I had always argued, whether it was about school or extracurricular classes. They wanted me to learn languages, study computer science or become a virtuoso violinist or pianist. But I preferred to sign up for athletics -my long legs and my capacity for sacrifice predicted a great sporting future, according to my coach , and ballet -again, the length of my limbs gave my movements greater flexibility, but I lacked the necessary qualities to be a *prima ballerina*, I dismissed any other activity simply to antagonize them. Although in the end, I had to rule out any high-impact physical exercise, as I developed a small chronic knee injury which did not interfere with normal life, but enough not to aspire to high goals in sport or dance.

The biggest argument came when I chose Humanities as my College major. My grandfather wanted me to study medicine or psychology, and my grandmother wanted me to follow my mother's career, a young lawyer who had died just after opening her own law firm. But it was not for me and I chose the path that would later lead me to the School of History of Art, a decision that was not at all well received at home, although in the end I got my way.

"At least choose the Autónoma, like your mother!" My grandmother had said, shocked that I had signed up for the Universidad Complutense of Madrid.

I answered that the UCM option was a better one for me, both because of the good transport connections: train and subway, from our neighborhood and the fact that almost all my friends and acquaintances would be studying at the same Campus.

My grandmother had shaken her head, not understanding why I preferred to use public transportation. She was used to getting around by cab, or in the family Mercedes when the two of us went anywhere together. They had even bought me a car to get around Madrid, a cute Mini to show off with, but with so much studying I had not even had time to get my driver's license. Perhaps next year...

"I knew it! It's all those gutterpunks you hang out with who are to blame, the same ones who drag you to demonstrations and all that anarchist stuff."

I smiled to myself and preferred not to argue with her. My family had always been quite conservative, but I had my own ideas and I was not going to change no matter how much they insisted.

My grandparents had given up because I was impossible, although they never missed an opportunity to remind me that I would be just another unemployed graduate when I finished my degree in History of Art! I told them I would not, that I would have several possibilities: getting a PAC (Professional Aptitude Certificate) and then become a teacher at some high school or look for a job in an art gallery or even in a museum. And, of course, that shocked them - those professions were unworthy of their granddaughter.

Anyway, I was not losing any sleep about what to do with my life when I finished my studies, there were still three long years to go, but at some point, I would have to consider it if I really wanted to secure a future before my grandparents were gone.

A few days later I was chatting about this with my friend Ana, at her house, in Doctor Esquerdo Street. She was telling me that I was not going to have any money problems when my grandparents left this world.

To my embarrassment, I had to agree with her. When my grandparents died, I would inherit everything as the only living descendant of the Millán family: the big flat in Arganzuela, next to the Pasillo Verde, the apartment in Cádiz, the house in Donosti and the chalet in the mountains. Not to mention the cars, money and shares. Grandfather had sold his clinic in Ríos Rosas, which had been working very well for decades and had a select clientele, for a very large sum, and the family savings were considerable. No, I was not going to lack anything, but I wanted to lead my own life away from the Millán inheritance.

"You can always share it with us. You know that Julián has been crazy for you ever since we were kids and even more so now, so we would be sisters-in-law, think about it!"

"I've already said no, Ana, don't insist. To me, Julián is just a good friend, apart from being your brother, nothing else. And why do you say 'more so now'?"

"Jesus, girl! It's obvious! Have you looked at yourself lately?"

"What's wrong with me?" I asked, checking myself in the mirror.

"You're getting hotter by the day, you bitch, I don't know what you're doing. Between your long legs and the curves you've got, there's not a student at the Complutense whose head doesn't turn when you walk by on campus. Not to mention that Caribbean tan you've come back with from the beach..."

"You've got to be kidding me!"

"Okay, whatever you say. I wish Alberto would look at me like that, but I think he's a little too fond of you. You hoarder!"

"Who, Julián's friend?" I asked, pretending, knowing perfectly well who Alberto was. I had also looked at him favorably in recent times, although I had preferred to focus on other things. "I doubt it, they consider us just kids, you know."

"Oh sure, that's what it is... Good thing it doesn't upset me. I was going to show Alberto what a nineteen-year-old girl can do. It's his loss."

"But, Ana...!"

I pretended to be shocked at her, but I wanted to change the subject. Julián and Alberto were two years older than us and were going to start their last year at the Complutense after the summer. They were both studying on our campus: Ana's brother was studying Law and his friend Criminology, both at the same college, located very close to ours, also in Ciudad Universitaria.

Ana and I had been friends and classmates since we were twelve years old, when we started our first year of

E.S.O. (Secondary Obligatory Education) in San Isidro together, and then studied in the same class in high school and now at the University. I had also met her brother in high school and later at her house when I went to study with her, or just to pick her up to go out.

"And what would you say if I invited you to spend the summer with us at the house in the village?" Ana blurted out.

"What do you mean by 'us' " I asked curiously.

"You know my family has a house in Carazo, near Silos, right?"

"Yes, of course, you've always told me what a good time you have, when you go on vacations to your grandparents' village in Burgos."

"This year my parents have other plans and won't be coming. My mother's sister may come with my cousins, I'm not sure yet, but what I do know for sure is that my aunt Menchu -we all call her aunt although she's actually my grandmother's cousin- will also be there with my cousin Raquel"

"I still don't follow, honestly."

"Well, we have plenty of room. My grandparents' house is huge, it has six rooms since the renovation. And Menchu's family bought the house next door and renovated it to their liking, so we have two houses to sleep in. My parents are away, my relatives will not control me that much and I've already told them that I'd like to invite some friends to spend the summer in Carazo."

"Really?" I said more interested. "That would be great, but I don't think my grandparents would let me go."

Ana tried to win me over to her plan. According to her, I should not have too much trouble getting my grandparents to grant me permission: I had finished everything with good grades, I had nothing better to do that summer, and they had known Ana for years. The fact that her relatives would be keeping an eye on us could be something positive if it came to that, even if it was just a little lie. I lost nothing by trying.

"What about your brother? I seem to remember that he was very fond of the local festivities, I've already heard more than one story about his summer conquests."

"My brother's an asshole who's never scored with anyone. Oh, hang on, that's not entirely true, I think he scored once with a girl from Barcelona who was spending the summer at a relative's house. Although maybe this year, by partnering up with the handsome Alberto, he will have more success, you know, hunting in pairs."

"I don't understand a thing," I said nervously hearing the name of the future criminologist. Is this how you want to persuade my grandparents? If they know we're going to be with boys all day long, they won't be too happy."

Ana promised that my grandparents did not need to find. Apparently, Alberto and Julián would be spending a few days at a country house in a nearby town, as they were planning on attending some convention or other.

"I'm not too sure about the details, they'll explain it to us later. Don't you like the idea?"

"Yeah, sure, it would be great," I said without thinking too much about it. I could persuade grandpa to let me spend a few days with Ana, especially if I let him believe that we could not travel about since we had to sleep at her aunt and uncle's house every night. Then I took in something else my friend had said, "What did you say before about them telling us about it?"

"Oh, yes, that. Nothing, we're meeting the boys at eight o'clock at Tribunal for a drink. You're coming, aren't you?"

"Jesus, girl! I need warning!" I said annoyed. I had not planned on meeting Alberto that afternoon and I was not dressed up enough. No make-up, no eye liner, and I had my hair in a ponytail to be more comfortable. "I was just coming to your house, that's all. I can't go out looking like this!"

I had put on a pair of cut-off jeans that left little to the imagination, and a white T-shirt to show off my tan. Apart from sneakers and sunglasses, I was not wearing anything else.

“Don’t be stupid, seize the opportunity and show off that body of yours! Come on, get a move on, we're going to be late.”

I could not refuse, and so I went with Ana to meet Alberto and Julián. I preferred not to think about my looks and concentrated on preparing the strategy to persuade my grandfather.

On the way to the subway Ana continued driving me crazy with her plans. She came up with another way to persuade my grandparents. It was not a bad idea. In my second year I had a couple of subjects about medieval art, and what better way to prepare for them than by visiting the famous monastery of Santo Domingo de Silos?

“That’s all there is to it, then. We'll have a good time, we'll enjoy the festivities and if possible, I'll get a nice tan. My cousins know the bathing areas, so bring your bathing suit even though it's dry land. And I hope to hook up with some hot-looking guy, of course.”

“Sure, but remember that neither of us has a car. And if the boys are going to be on their own, I think it’ll be difficult to move around.”

“Forget about that, we can always hitch a ride, everyone knows everyone there. And don't worry, my cousin Raquel has a car and knows the Arlanza region well, you'll see how much fun we'll have! Look… speak of the devil, here come Alberto and Julián”.

When I greeted my friends, I did not know what to do with myself. They were both eating me up with their eyes. Julián was blunter, after all we knew each other better, but Alberto was not far behind. He was staring but pretending not to although obviously, my summer outfit had impressed them both.

"What the …, Sandra, you look fantastic!" Julián said after giving me two kisses more affectionate than usual and giving me a good once over. "The beach tan suits you, not to mention other things..."

His sister slapped him on the shoulder when she sensed where Julián was going, whereas I did not know where to hide. Then I greeted Alberto and he was a bit more restrained:

"Yeah, honestly, Sandra, you look amazing. How was Chiclana?"

"Good, thanks. Although I was getting bored there, spending all day with my grandparents. I knew some of the girls at the condo, but they left last week and time was dragging on forever."

I then took a closer look at the two of them. They could not be more different even though they were great friends. I had known Julián for years and he would always be my friend and Ana's brother. Of average height, he seemed shorter because of the muscles he had developed lately at the gym. He could spend hours pumping iron, an activity which, to tell the truth, I was not too interested in.

He was a cute boy, there was no denying it, but he was not my style. His hair was not as blond as his sister's and his eyes were not as light, although they looked a lot alike. But I had never fancied blonds, even if they were named Brad Pitt. With his fashionable haircut and his toothpaste-ad smile, I could picture him at a casting for models or in any of those reality shows that proliferate on television.

I could not say that I was an expert on boys or romantic relationships, but I was more drawn to intelligence and curiosity in a man. That is why I noticed Alberto, apart from the fact that physically he was more my type: tall, dark and a little gawky, but with style. His face had the look of someone who has never broken as much as a plate in his entire life and, at the same time, a roguish look that attracted attention. A strange but quite attractive mix that had been winning me over gradually.

The four of us headed for a tavern we knew in the Malasaña area and once there, ordered some beers. Alberto also ordered some *raciones* for snacks and we continued talking about our plans.

"I've already half persuaded Sandra, to come with me to the village this summer. Isn't that great?" said Ana as she attacked the plate of *croquetas de jamon.*

"To Carazo?" What a pain, you'll be bored to death there".

"Well, well … the master finds the village boring now? You didn't use to say that when you lost yourself with some girl in the fields and I had to lie for you at home. Hang on, that only happened once and it was because the girl in question had a sight problem."

"I'm not listening to you, smartass," Julián said to his sister before addressing me. "Seriously, there's not even a fucking bar there, it's a very small place. Okay, I'll grant you that it gets livelier with the *fiestas*, but it's like the desert there: hot during the day and cold at night."

"How can there not even be a bar? That's impossible in a town in this country, isn't it?" I asked, looking at Ana.

"Well, let's see, this idiot's right. The town is small and doesn't usually have a bar, but it changes a lot during the holidays. Besides, we'll go around with my cousin Raquel, I don't know what you're thinking. And it's not a desert, I've been told that the Arlanza is amazing this year. I've also been told about a bathing area near Covarrubias that is awesome in summer."

"We'll be staying in Salas, and there are bars there. In fact, there's even a movie theater in the Casino, although I think they're having the movie convention there, aren't they?" Julián said while looking for his friend's confirmation.

"What movie?" I asked interested.

"It's the fiftieth anniversary of the shooting of *The Good, the Bad and the Ugly* in the area, and a convention is being held at the end of July there. It's going to be really interesting. I know some of the organizers and I'm already looking forward to all the events."

Alberto spent a long time talking about the movie and the activities he had prepared for the weekend. He sounded enthusiastic about the whole idea, although many of the things he told us were like Greek to me. In fact, not even Ana knew that the movie had been shot in Burgos, as our friend assured us.

"I don't think I've ever seen that movie. Is it with Clint Eastwood?" I asked.

"That's right, Sandra. It's a *spaghetti western*, the end of Sergio Leone's famous *Dollar Trilogy*. I thought it would be a great opportunity to attend this event and paid for the pre-registration months ago. If you haven't seen the movie, you now have the opportunity to enjoy it in a unique environment."

At home I had watched some 'Westerns' when I was a child, but only because my grandfather liked them. I had become fond of classic American comedies because of my grandmother, who had a small collection on VHS and DVD that we would occasionally watch together.

Alberto went on to tell us about some of the activities of the festival that had been organized throughout the region, with events in various towns. Apparently, many young people from the area had acted as extras in the movie, the shooting of which had caused quite a commotion in the Arlanza valley during the summer of 1966.

"You've got to see Sad Hill Cemetery, it's awesome," Alberto said.

"I don't know much about that sort of thing, to be honest," Ana replied. "At most I've visited some Anglo-Saxon romantic cemeteries and little else. They sort of give me the creeps,"

"I'm not talking about a real cemetery, it's a recreation. The association that organizes the symposium has been restoring the famous graveyard that was built near your village, in the valley of Mirandilla, to shoot the illustrious and acclaimed final scene of the movie".

Ana and I looked at each other blankly. Neither of us knew what Alberto meant by the acclaimed scene and he realized it right away.

"Really? You don't know what I'm talking about?"

"Well, no, not really," I said.

"The three-way duel with Morricone's immortal music, the *triello*: a scene included among the most famous in the history of cinema. Not to mention that IMDB users have listed *The Good, the Bad and the Ugly* as one of the most important masterpieces, always placed among the hundred best films in history."

"It doesn't ring a bell. I don't really like the genre either," said Ana.

"I swear that if you haven't seen the scene somewhere, you have surely heard Morricone's tune a thousand times."

And having said that, Alberto began to whistle the melody he was referring to, at which point my friend and I nodded emphatically. He was right, we had heard those notes many times, but had not linked them to what he was telling us.

I was silent for a few seconds, while Alberto showed me on his cell phone some Youtube videos on the subject: the famous scene, with the original cemetery in the background and the shootout in that kind of stone coliseum surrounded by thousands of graves; and then, current videos with the efforts of dozens of volunteers rebuilding a set that had been buried by time, vegetation and neglect.

"I don't know, now I'm curious. It doesn't sound bad at all. It must be a peculiar place. Although what a spoiler you've just made of the movie" I joked.

"That's the way to go! There's still a lot of work to be done, but they're on the right track. If they get more involvement from the Junta de Castilla y León or other organizations, the Arlanza Valley can become a reference place when it comes to preserving this kind of scenery and creating a different type of tourism for the region."

"I don't know how long you'll be in the area, but we weren't planning to go to Carazo until the last weekend of July," said Ana.

"We're leaving this Wednesday morning by car. I've managed to get my mother to lend us the Focus. The official reception in Salas for those registered for the convention is not until Friday afternoon, but I want to see some of the exteriors, where the most important scenes of the movie were shot. Why don't you two come with us?"

Ana and I looked at each other for a moment, and I felt my friend pinching my leg under the table. She always picked on me because she knew that her brother liked me, although Julián would make a pass at anyone who came his way, and so I took it with a pinch of salt. But Ana sensed, since I had not said otherwise, that perhaps Alberto might have a chance with me. That was what the pinch had been for. I thought then that my friend wanted to play at matchmaking and that she thought we had a good chance."

"Man, that would be nice, although first I'll have to persuade my grandparents, and tell them I'm leaving earlier than planned,"

"Yeah, you do that, we can bring the trip forward if I get organized. That way you can take us to Carazo and we don't have to rely on my cousin. And I can give you guys better directions to find those places, my brother has as good a sense of direction as he has a funny bone."

Julián showed his sister his raised middle finger. They were always messing with each other like kids. I knew it was just a pose because they both adored one another and Julián would have done anything for Ana.

"I want to visit the San Antonio Mission, whose interior was shot in the monastery of San Pedro del Arlanza and to find the location of the Betterville Fort, which was near Carazo. Not to mention the battle of Langstone Bridge, between Hortigüela and Contreras and, of course, do the route around Sad Hill Cemetery!"

Then he took an informative brochure out of his pocket. It was folded in three, and it had more information about the routes of *The Good, the Bad and the Ugly* throughout the region, whether by car, bicycle or on foot. Alberto showed it to Ana, emphasizing some points on the map drawn on the brochure, and my friend pointed them out accurately as he went along.

"I've decided that you need us to visit all those places." She told the boys seriously, "I'd heard that someone from the village had been an actor in a famous movie shot in the area, but I hadn't realized until now that it was *The Good, the Bad and the Ugly*. The monastery is easy to get to, in fact we also wanted to visit it although it's in very bad condition. But the other sites won't be so well signposted, so you have no choice but to take us with you."

Ana had spoken for both of us, but I had not put up much resistance either. She winked at me in a complicit gesture and I think I blushed pretty obviously.

"Well, I've had enough of the subject for today," Julián cut us off. "Another round of beers?"

IN SEARCH OF SCENERY

Arlanza region (Burgos), June 1966

Sergio Leone wanted to finish his *Dollar Trilogy* in style and was sparing no expense. The Italian filmmaker already knew the Almeria desert and the different locations he had used in the two previous films of the saga, *For a Fistful of Dollars* and *For a Few Dollars More*, so for the moment, he did not need to visit the region again. Although he would also shoot some scenes there, as well as in the vicinity of the mountains of Madrid and other places, he needed something special to finish off his trilogy and close the circle: a different place that would transport the viewers to the past and take them to the high plains of Arizona and New Mexico during the American Civil War.

Assistant director Giancarlo Santi was the original Location Scout for the film. Leone wanted something very definite: locations around a river that had a similar environment to New Mexico, or at least landscapes that could resemble it. The Spanish authorities, with whom they were in constant communication to obtain the different shooting permits, had already suggested some locations in northern Spain, but the filmmakers were not too sure.

Sergio Leone's interest was sparked when José Antonio Pérez Giner, one of the professionals he had worked with on the two previous Spanish-Italian-German co-productions of the saga, told him about a region of Burgos that could serve as a perfect location for the most important scenes of the film.

Pérez Giner had already shot *The Castilian* in the area, a film starring Espartaco SAntóni and directed by Javier Setó, which told of the birth of the kingdom of Castile. The production manager and Setó himself recommended the Arlanza Valley to Leone because of its similarity to the landscape of Arizona and New Mexico: the type of vegetation, with the Burgos junipers and other native species, its limestone rocks and steep hills would be perfect for what the Roman director had in mind.

Then Leone called Carlos Simi, scenographer and set designer, to accompany Pérez Giner and check the suitability of the area in person. They toured the region and chose different locations where some of the most important scenes of the film would be shot later.

The director wanted to climb a small mountain that had a sort of plain at the top. And he instantly fell in love with Peña Carazo: a vast space, completely empty, that would serve his purposes. There were no constructions to be seen, no power lines in the area, so the location would be perfect for the movie.

They already had the first location on the outskirts of the town of Carazo, on a hill known as Majada de las Merinas. A place where Carlos Simi could build the imposing fort he had in mind, to recreate the Betterville concentration camp.

Then they found other perfect locations for shooting. For instance, the half-ruined monastery of San Pedro de Arlanza, between Hortigüela and Covarrubias, could serve as the interior of the Mission of San Antonio, a religious convent converted into a military hospital during the American Civil War. And the Arlanza River itself would emulate the famous Rio Grande for a scene in which Leone intended to put all the meat on the grill.

Leone urged the producer to use his contacts in the army and the Spanish authorities. He finally had a budget to match and wanted to take advantage of it to shoot scenes worthy of Hollywood cinema itself.

* * *

In the region there had been no talk of anything else for a few weeks. In Salas de los Infantes and other towns in the region, advertisements had appeared in which extras were requested for the shooting of a big movie. All the young locals wanted to sign up to find out firsthand the makings of a movie production of such caliber and, incidentally, to be able to earn a little money.

The area was devoted mainly to agriculture and livestock, so working as extras attracted the attention of many young people who could change their routine for a few days if their tasks in the fields allowed. And of course, the news also reached the neighboring Contreras, which was very close to some of the locations where Sergio Leone's team planned to shoot.

"Stop this nonsense, Juanito, you have to help me with the sheep!" said Venancio Burgos to his son when he told him about the movie.

"I'll help you afterwards, Father, don't worry. But let me go down to Salas to sign up with the other lads from Contreras. They say you can earn good money."

"Agh, do what you want!" Venancio had replied, tired of arguing with his son, knowing that Juanito would do whatever he wanted. "But I want you here at lunchtime without fail."

Venancio was trying to get the boy back on track after dropping out of school. He was fifteen, had never done too well in school, and in the end had ended up leaving his books. Juanito was a free spirit and preferred to spend the whole day wandering about, especially now that the good weather had arrived, and this drove his father crazy.

The young lad had already committed some petty theft that had earned him more than a slap on the wrist when he was caught red-handed, so he had learned not to do his stealing in town or from acquaintances and, of course, to be more careful when it came to actually doing it. He believed that the arrival of the movie people could bring him good profit, either by working as an extra in the movie or by using his skills to take advantage of the carelessness of others in order to cheat the foreigners who would be visiting the Arlanza Valley during that summer.

Juanito borrowed his older brother's bicycle and pedaled at full speed along trails he knew well. First to the nearby town of Barbadillo del Mercado and then, along the road to Soria, until he reached Salas. He arrived at the Bar Infantes and there queued up to sign up for the list of possible extras, as other young people from the region were doing, although he was not given much hope when it was his turn.

"You're still too young," he was told, "I don't think they'll choose you. Apparently, they're looking for young men to be soldiers, but you haven't even got any hair on your face yet."

The locals laughed at the wit of the person in charge of the list of registered participants, but Juanito was not discouraged by their impertinence. The boy looked older than he was, due to his height, although he didn't have much flesh on his bones and his baby face gave away his true age.

"We'll see, you sign me in and time will tell. Is it true what they're saying about the pay? I've heard that you can earn more than two hundred pesetas for a day's work."

"Hey kid, go home and let the grown-ups do our job, we still have a lot of work to do."

The man dismissed Juanito with a look of contempt and the young man left the place ruminating his defeat. He had been about to answer the man as he deserved, but he restrained himself in time. It would not be the first time that his big mouth had got him into trouble, so he decided to go back to Contreras and not piss off his father as well. If he punished him or hit him with his belt, he would not even be able to show up for the casting if the movie people finally called him.

On the way back he fantasized about what he could do with two hundred pesetas, and even more if he managed to work there for several days. And, if in the end he was not chosen, Juanito was already thinking of becoming a regular at the shoots and helping out in any way he could, even if he did not get paid. That way it would not be suspicious to see him always hanging around the set, ready to take any valuable object that could make him some profit.

He made his way back to Contreras at a slower pace, so as not to get tired pedaling, but still fast enough to reach home by noon. When he entered the town, he thought he caught a glimpse of a familiar figure in the distance, so he pedaled a little faster to make sure. He had not been mistaken, it was the daughter of the Mediavilla family. Maybe he could talk to her for a while before going to lunch. He got off the bike and left it lying on the side of the road. He ran until he caught up with the girl and walked next to her.

"Hello, María!" he greeted her cheerfully, "Are you going to the fountain?"

The girl nodded, although it was obvious since she was carrying two large buckets to fill with water. A weight too heavy for her puny arms, so Juanito wanted to take advantage of the opportunity.

"Do you want me to help you? I still have a little time before lunch."

María was sparing with words, everyone knew that. She shrugged and allowed Juanito to carry one of the empty buckets, although it would be when filled that he would really be of help. The lad thought he might have time for something else. He slyly made his way to the back of an abandoned house, an unnecessary detour if they wanted to get to the fountain as soon as possible. But Juanito had something else in mind.

The girl did not seem to be paying much attention to the path they were taking, she was just walking beside him listening to his chatter. Juanito told her about the shooting of the movie and commented that he had signed up in Salas to work as an actor. Maybe the girl would come with him one day if she felt like it.

María made a vague gesture because they both knew that her mother would not allow it. Doña Pura did not fool around and Juanito tried not to cross paths with her in Contreras. She was a woman of character and her daughter was sacred to her. He was not afraid of her, but if she found out his true intentions, there would be nowhere to hide from her wrath.

"Come on, hurry. There's something I want to show you," said the boy, trying to appear interesting.

Juanito left the bucket on the floor and went into the abandoned house. It was a place known to all the kids in town, even if none of the parents in Contreras liked the idea. María left her bucket on the floor too, but delayed following him inside. Juanito knew the girl was hesitating, so he had to offer her an incentive.

"I've taken tobacco from my brother, if you want, we can share it."

Months ago, they had taken their first puffs on a cigarette together, secretly, choking with cough as they inhaled the smoke. Neither of them knew how to smoke properly and they did not even like the taste tobacco, but it had made them feel all grown up and they liked to break the rules imposed by their parents.

Juanito had met the Mediavilla girl at school, neither of them had had much of a future with studies. She was a nice girl, well-liked by everyone, even though some neighbors could not stand her mother. In any case, the two of them had always been friends, and María trusted him.

He stared at her figure, tall and slender but with incipient curves that did not go unnoticed. María was looking very pretty, with her copper hair shining in the sun and those curious little freckles that speckled her whole body. The boy felt a whiplash of lust and insisted that María accompany him inside the half-ruined mansion.

This would not be the first time, but Juanito still felt guilty. They were both kids just starting to experiment with their own bodies, and the young Contreras boy wanted to go further with his neighbor. They had kissed and groped each other over their clothes, nothing else. And he thought that maybe this time María would let him go a little further.

After sharing a cigarette inside the abandoned house, sitting on the floor with their backs against one of the walls that were still standing, Juanito wanted to make the first move. He approached María and kissed her on the lips. She let him do it, even though neither of them was enthusiastic about the taste of nicotine in the other's mouth.

Juanito thought his chance had come and continued kissing her with the passion and inexperience of youth. He began to caress her and María did not protest, so the boy's audacity grew by the minute. He then slipped a hand under her clothes and moved tentatively closer along her chest, taking pleasure in caressing the incipient mounds of her small breasts. The girl moaned, he did not know if from pleasure or because he was hurting her, but Juanito was not deterred. He then wanted to put his other hand under her skirt, but María stopped him. He had been too daring and she pushed him away abruptly, before getting up from the floor and leaving the house.

"My mother will kill me if I take too long. Are you going to help me or not?"

Juanito smiled and nodded before getting up. At least María had not been too angry with him and had let him touch her tits under her clothes. She had even seemed to like what they were doing and on the way to the fountain she did not tell him off. She actually seemed more forthcoming and was even teasing him.

They filled the heavy buckets and Juanito offered to carry both of them back. María did not let him so they carried them between them, one each. At least as far as the vicinity of her house before going in different directions so they would not be caught together. The boy waved goodbye to his friend, contentedly, and walked away. He could not consider María his girlfriend, but he had gotten further with her than with any other girl in town. And perhaps, over the course of a summer that was looking quite different, he might do other things so that his friends would not laugh at him and tease him about his amorous exploits.

He returned to the crossroads where he had run into the girl, picked up his brother's bicycle and headed home, just in time for lunch. Juanito was happy after a very profitable morning and made two wishes for that summer: to work in the movie or at least earn some money with the shooting and to enjoy more of María Mediavilla's warm and tantalizing body.

But sometimes wishes turn against us…

THE SIERRA OF LA DEMANDA

Carazo (Burgos), July 19/20, 2016

In the end I had had no major issues persuading my grandparents to let me go to Burgos for a few days with my friend Ana. I had not even had to use the excuse of cultural visits to prepare subjects for the next course.

I gave my grandmother an affectionate kiss, thanked both of them for their trust, and went to my room to pack my suitcase. That night I was going to sleep at Ana's house so that we could all leave early in the morning.

The following day, around eight in the morning, the custodian of the farm was warned of our arrival. We got up extra early so as not to waste time, but Julián had gone to bed late and was not in the mood to wake up early. He had protested from under the covers when his sister called him earlier. Anyway, Alberto was already waiting downstairs, with his car double-parked while Julián was still having breakfast in the kitchen.

"You go downstairs so Alberto doesn't get nervous," Ana said to me just as our friend rang again. "I'll finish cleaning up around here, I'll get my brother and we'll be right there."

Ana winked at me and motioned for me to hurry. Perhaps she intended for me to spend a few moments alone with Alberto in the street, although it did not seem like the best time, just woken up and with dark circles under my eyes.

I met Alberto on the street, who immediately came to greet me before putting my suitcase in his car, a blue Ford Focus with some scratches, but in generally good condition. He greeted me with two kisses and asked me about our friends.

"They'll be down in a minute. Ana's finishing putting everything together and Julián got up late."

We chatted about nothing specific while waiting for our friends, who still took another ten minutes at least. We put everything in the trunk, quite tightly packed due to the volume of luggage of the Castro siblings, and got ready to start the journey. Julián wanted to ride in the back for a little nap, so Ana almost forced me to ride in the front with Alberto. I did not mind much though, that way we could chat while we headed to Burgos.

We crossed the province of Madrid and shortly after we took the exit of Aranda del Duero. From there Ana directed us, so we had no problem finding the national road that went to Santo Domingo de Silos. We decided to stop for a while at the cradle of Spanish Romanesque architecture to stretch our legs and have a drink before continuing our journey.

Half an hour later we were back in the car, we took the bypass that circumvented Silos so as not to cross the village and entered the regional road, towards Salas de los Infantes, to reach our final destination: Carazo.

We found the winding road a bit heavy. Luckily Alberto was driving prudently and without too much aggressiveness. Although we had to put up with cars from the area overtaking us at quite dangerous places, perhaps more used to a route they knew by heart. A few minutes later we left behind the worst stretch of road and soon arrived at Carazo.

"Don't expect much, guys, it's a very small town," Ana warned us.

Alberto slowed down as he entered the town and turned left following Ana's directions. He parked the car and the four of us got out, greeted by a stray dog that sniffed at us curiously. Immediately a woman came out of one of the houses and addressed us with great fuss.

"Long time no see, Ana!" she shouted before giving my friend a big hug, "Oh my God, Julián, I didn't recognize you with all that muscle!"

Julián could not help blushing a little while Alberto and I stood apart as we watched the family members greet each other. At that moment I noticed that Julián was wearing shorts and a tight T-shirt that really showed off his biceps and pecs, Alberto had opted for a pair of summer jeans and a light blue polo shirt that looked great on him.

Ana introduced us to her cousin Cristina. She must have been in her forties, and looked nothing like her cousins. She had dark skin and jet-black hair, but what was most striking was the great figure that could be guessed under those tight jeans that suited her so well.

"Hi, guys, nice to meet you," she greeted us with two kisses.

"I thought you were coming to Carazo alone with a friend, Ana, I didn't know she would be accompanied by her boyfriend."

"No, no, I..." I stammered.

I did not want to imagine what color my cheeks must have turned, especially with the hot flush that came over me. And I was not the only one, apparently. Alberto looked like a tomato while his friend laughed at the situation, until Ana straightened things out and explained to her cousin who Alberto and I were. But she did it with a certain irony.

I just squirmed and pretended to look at the trees, while Alberto kicked at a stone, frightening the poor dog as it was dozing in the sun. Ana's cousin must have seen something to mistake us for a couple; maybe the chemistry between the two of us was more evident than we thought.

"Oh, I'm sorry. Sorry for the misunderstanding, I have such a big mouth. You two certainly make a cute couple, though," she said before winking at us.

Julián held back the laughter that was about to come out of his mouth. It appeared he was amused by the embarrassment his cousin was putting us through. Better that than for him to be pissed at me for thinking there was something going on between Alberto and me, when I had always ignored his clumsy amorous approaches. Julián stepped in and gave his friend a hand.

"Well, Cris, we're going to Salas, but we'll be coming back another day with more time, won't we, Alberto?"

"Yes, I told the owners of the lodge that we would arrive before lunch. We'll come back another day with more time."

"I'm taking you up on it, guys."

We agreed that we would talk later to see what we could do that afternoon and also the following day. Alberto had told me on the way that he had found a bathing area, on the internet, with waterfalls and deep pools in a part of the river located near the monastery of San Pedro del Arlanza. It could be a nice excursion for the next day, which was forecast to be very hot.

The two friends got back into the Focus and honked at us in farewell. I stood gawking for a second as the car pulled out onto the road again, a moment that Ana seized to mess with me a bit.

We went into the building and found a small living room where a huge dining table, flanked by a long bench against the wall and four or five chairs on the other side, occupied almost the entire space. On the back wall there was a fireplace that would do a good job in the cold Burgos winters. And to the left was the kitchen, Ana went in there to greet a short woman who was fiddling with the pots and pans.

"I thought it was strange that you didn't come out to greet us, Aunt Menchu."

From what she had told me previously, Menchu was actually Ana's grandmother's cousin, and Cristina was her daughter, although for my friend they were her aunt and cousin.

"I could hear you from in here child, but I couldn't leave the stove you know."

I stood at the kitchen door, next to Cristina, while Ana greeted her aunt. She was in her sixties, with short, ash-blonde hair, almost white. Behind her horn-rimmed glasses she had lively little eyes that were happy to see her niece, whom she squeezed in her arms while she covered her face with kisses.

"I hope you're hungry, lunch is almost ready. Won't you introduce me to your friend?"

I was half hidden behind Cristina, who just at that moment stepped aside so that I could enter the kitchen. Menchu dried her hands before grabbing a glass of water she had on the counter and I stood next to Ana, waiting for introductions.

Before my friend said anything, I noticed the astonishment in the woman's eyes as she looked at me as if she had seen a ghost. The glass in her hands fell to the floor and broke.

"Oh God, how clumsy of me!" she apologized as she bent down to pick up the pieces without taking her eyes off me.

Cristina hurried to help her. We went back to the living room and Ana introduced me properly. Menchu watched me with hawk-like eyes, although I could no longer detect the impact I had seen a little earlier in her pupils.

I then accompanied aunt and niece upstairs to the upper floor. There were several bedrooms, and as the house was not full, I was to have a room to myself. Menchu pointed out my room, which she had already prepared, and I thanked her for the trouble she had taken before my arrival.

“You’re welcome, sweetheart. Go on, unpack, freshen up a bit and then come down, lunch is almost ready and I've also prepared a pitcher of fresh lemonade, it's very hot today.”

I thanked her again. Menchu waved it off. I placed the suitcase on a chair and set about putting the clothes in a closet that had been left empty for me. I then noticed Menchu's curious glance at my back, so I turned to her again but I was not quick enough, the woman was already going downstairs and I heard her voice in the distance:

“If you need anything else, don't hesitate to ask.”

I was left alone in my room, trying to understand what had just happened. Why had Menchu been so startled when she saw me? Why had she looked at me like that, even though she had tried to hide it? I would have to ask Ana in case she had also noticed something strange in her aunt's behavior. We would all have to live together under the same roof for the next few weeks and I just hoped there would be no bad feelings of any kind.

Once I finished putting everything away, I freshened up and went back down to the main living room. Cristina was already setting the table and Menchu was still in the kitchen, finishing the preparations for the meal. I took a deep breath and told myself that maybe it was just my imagination, I was not going to think badly of the good woman.

What I did not know was that it would not be long before I found out why Menchu had reacted the way she had when she met me.

THE ROAD TO DEATH

Salas de los Infantes (Burgos), July 20, 2016

At the same time that Julián and Alberto were arriving in Salas de los Infantes to stay in a rural lodging in the town, Arrigo Ambrosini was leaving the 'Gran Casino' Auditorium Theater of Salas, next to the Plaza Mayor. The man, an Italian living in Barcelona, had just turned sixty-nine years old. He was a former assistant cameraman who had taken his first steps in the cinema in a blockbuster shot fifty years ago in the Arlanza Valley and its surroundings: *The Good, the Bad and the Ugly*.

The organizers had tried to locate as many people as possible who had worked on the film, for its 50th anniversary, but this man's whereabouts had been uncertain. Ambrosini, had been away from the cinema for some time, and it was only by chance that he found out about the event through a journalist. He phoned the organizers and they were delighted to invite him, although he did not guarantee his attendance but he told them that he would do his best to be at the event.

In the end, he was not going to participate as a speaker in any conference because he had not given any advance notice, but he did not mind. He had brought his own car with him from Barcelona. He did not like airplanes and preferred to use his own car rather than renting one, so he trusted his old Renault 19 to make the whole trip.

He went straight to Salas de los Infantes and looked for accommodation, but the hotels, hostels and rural houses in the surrounding area were full. He was then given the details of a hotel in Santo Domingo de Silos where there might be rooms available, he had phoned and managed to book a room until the weekend.

He was also told that most of the anniversary activities would be held at the city's Gran Casino, so he went to there to find out more. The official reception for those registered and invited to the celebrations would not be held until Friday, and a previous pre-registration was required to be part of the list of participants in the symposium. He would have to talk to the organizers to fix that. He was also not too concerned about not being listed as an official registrant.

Ambrosini then decided to go to his hotel to rest; Silos was only a few kilometers from his current destination and he would arrive in time for lunch. He reminisced about some past banquets in the area, such as the typical *asados* of the region, and his mouth watered. Arrigo had already made up his mind and he thought he deserved a good meal after so many kilometers on the road.

The Italian left Salas in his vehicle, took the N-234 towards Burgos and turned off at Hacinas. He did not find it strange that a black SUV was following him at a short distance, until a couple of kilometers later when he realized that the driver was almost on top of him and braked just in time to avoid a collision.

"What the hell are you doing, you asshole?" Arrigo exclaimed out loud as he looked in the rear-view mirror, alert to the movements of his pursuer.

The old man, unnerved by the situation, did not know what to do. The powerful SUV was gaining ground on him at a high speed, coming at him as if it were going to ram him, and then would brake sharply before touching him, although on two occasions it came within inches of grazing the bodywork of the old Renault.

"Va *fan culo*!" exclaimed Ambrosini quoting his ancestors.

He was about to stick his "little driving finger" out of the left window to give the suicidal driver a piece of his mind, but thought better of it. Before his saintly wife died, he had already had arguments with her for confronting other drivers and once they had almost assaulted him. So he tried to calm down and remain attentive to the road, which was already complicated enough without that added pressure.

He sighed with relief when he spotted a small town they were about to pass through. From his earlier days there he remembered that it was Carazo, just the last village before coming to the dangerous curves that separated that town from Santo Domingo de Silos.

Arrigo did not think twice, he was not willing to risk his life. He had already lived a long time and his youth was far away, that was true, but he did not feel like dying there because of an imbecile who thought he was a Formula 1 driver with a brand-new car. He slowed down, put his right indicator on - which could well mean that he was going to swerve soon or that he was indicating to the driver who was chasing him that he could overtake him safely - and did not wait any longer.

He had to swerve sharply to the right as the SUV almost ran him over when he took the turn. Not only did the suicidal driver not slow down, but accelerated when he saw his maneuver and almost rammed into him. Ambrosini lost himself in the narrow streets of Carazo, stopped the car between two houses and opened the door to breathe. He retched and thought he was going to throw up on the spot, but he managed to contain himself.

He exited the car, locked the door and walked around a bit to calm his nerves before he had an anxiety attack. The psychopath's behavior had really got to him, but fortunately he was out of danger now. He had lost sight of the SUV, he exhaled a sigh of relief and thought he no longer had to worry about it.

Since he was still rattled, he decided to wait a little. He thought about having a drink to calm down, but he did not want to lose any reflexes for the road, besides the fact that he could not find a bar in the whole town. It was thirty-five degrees in the sun at two o'clock in the afternoon, there was not a soul in the street who he could relay his woes to.

Arrigo was tempted to return to Salas, but he was no coward. Besides, the SUV would already be in Silos at the speed he was going along those roads, so he breathed in deep and prepared to continue his journey. If he did not do it now, he might not be able to face the trip later, when twilight fell on the Arlanza Valley.

He went back to his old car and started it up. He sat still for a moment, trying to concentrate on regaining the feeling and normal rhythm in his old heart, before getting back on the road. He knew that treacherous curves awaited him on his way to Silos now, a route that demanded attention even when it was clear. He prayed he would not run into any other lunatic, kamikaze drivers who overtook you at every turn, or head-on trucks at some stretches where there was barely room for two cars to pass each other.

Ambrosini accelerated, re-entered the road that split Carazo in two and left the town in search of his destination. Just as he was leaving the town, he thought he saw a group of girls chatting in the cool air in an orchard next to a magnificent house. By instinct he raised his arm and greeted them before leaving the limits of the town, without even noticing that the young women returned his greeting.

He picked up a little more speed and regained control almost completely, ready to face the first curves of the route in better spirits. The curves themselves were not that dangerous or tight, but they had to be taken slowly and with all five senses alert. Arrigo deftly negotiated several curves and headed towards Silos, just a few kilometers away.

Halfway there, more or less, he thought he saw a black silhouette in the rearview mirror. It could not be true, he hoped it was just a similar car. But the image of a black SUV grew larger and larger in his rearview mirror and he knew he had not been mistaken: his enemy was back, stalking him, ready to spoil his journey.

What does this beast want? Ambrosini wondered. It was clear that the driver had tricked him and not the other way around. He had probably swerved as well, and had hidden in the village until his victim rejoined the road. And now he was there again, like a sinister hunter in search of his prey.

Arrigo knew there was nowhere to turn or stop, unless he wanted to be run over by the huge vehicle. No other car was visible on the road and there were no other witnesses, so he sensed that his only way to get away would be to get to Silos before his stalker. There he would be safe and sound, he did not think the driver would dare to go after him and beat him out of whatever bar he would be hiding in.

But for that he had to reach the next town and those few kilometers were going to take forever. The pursuer began to toy with him, cat and mouse-like, accelerating until he was next to him in the curves and then slowing down and leaving him some space on the straight stretches. And all over again, all to make the Italian nervous while he held on tightly to the steering wheel.

Arrigo tried not to panic. His reflexes were not those of his youth, but he considered himself a good driver and he was less than four kilometers from his destination. He did not want to accelerate too much so as not to spin out on a curve, but he knew that in about five minutes he would be safe, so he tried to concentrate on that thought so as not to drive himself crazy.

At that moment he felt a metallic bump against the back of the Renault and a slight whiplash in his body. It was a warning, a small touch to scare him, but he knew that this man was not going to mess around. He did not know who he was or if he owed him anything, but it was clear that he was out to get him.

The blows were getting stronger and more frequent, causing Arrigo to almost lose control of his old Renault. He accelerated on the next straight stretch to get away from the maniac, a stranger who seemed to be laughing at him, hiding behind the dashboard of the huge Range Rover SUV. He tried to catch a glimpse of his features, hidden by large dark glasses, but the distance, his nerves and the reflection of the sun on the windows prevented him from distinguishing the mysterious driver's features.

Ambrosini felt more and more harassed and on the next double curve he did not calculate the distance well. Zigzagging left and right he swerved too much and the wheels lost grip on the asphalt. The Renault swerved to the right, bounced off the rocky ledge as Arrigo swerved again to correct the trajectory before going off course, just in time to see the dangerous ravine on the left side of the road approaching at high speed.

The wheels were still skidding on the tarmac when he felt a bump on the back of the driver's side. The momentum of the car after the crazy escape, the bouncing against the rock and the subsequent energy transmitted by the powerful off-roader when it hit him, were too much for the old Renault. Arrigo could no longer control his vehicle, unhinged after his adversary's touch on the bodywork, he knew that this was where it was all going to end.

The Renault went off the road on its way to the abyss and fell into a ravine. The right wheel then hit a ledge, burst, and Arrigo let go of the steering wheel, unable to control the vehicle. The Italian lost consciousness from the brutal blow to his head as soon as his car began to summersault and he was no longer aware of anything else, while his fragile body was tossed from one side of the car to the other, a wreck at the mercy of the enormous forces that were tearing his vehicle apart on the way to his metal tomb.

The driver of the SUV did not even stop to check if the driver of the wrecked vehicle had survived the accident. He continued on his way, without bothering about anything else, ready to lose himself in the ancient streets of Silos. He had no regrets about what had happened, at least for the moment, although causing the accident had not given him any special thrill either. Rather, it had left him with an inner emptiness that he did not know how to fill.

There would be time for regrets, for now the game had to go on.

LANDING IN THE LAND OF *EL CID*

Covarrubias (Burgos), June 1966

The shooting of *The Good, the Bad and the Ugly* in Spain was almost thwarted because of bureaucratic issues, even though Leone had already shot in Spain the first two films of a trilogy that, many years later, would come to be considered a cult saga for many film lovers.

For a Fistful of Dollars and *For a Few Dollars More* had been shot under the international co-production format, with an equal percentage of Italian, German and Spanish crew. But after the unexpected success of these two films in the transalpine country and the cascading word-of-mouth effect, there were big changes when it came time to shooting *The Good, the Bad and the Ugly*.

Sergio Leone initially considered the possibility of shooting in the United States with Hollywood blockbuster status, but with an all-Italian crew. They ignored the previous work done with the Spanish production company of Arturo Gonzalez and the German company Constantin, so the Italian production company PEA, with the approval and financial backing of the all-powerful United Artists, took on the task alone.

The Roman moviemaker had gone from being a misunderstood genius to a director and auteur, acclaimed worldwide thanks to the unexpected success of his westerns. He went so far as to move to Los Angeles with Luciano Vincenzoni to look for locations with the intention of shooting in the usual places of classic American westerns. They even had a provisional title for the film, *Two Magnificent Rags*, which was later discarded.

The Italian director, Mediterranean and excessive but with a special charisma, obtained an initial budget of 1.2 million dollars for his new film, a budget that would increase as production progressed. In the end they decided not to shoot in the United States and opted again for Spain, with locations in Almeria, Burgos and Madrid, although they would start first in Rome before coming to Spain.

Leone had put behind him the range of obstacles, especially logistics and of lack of budget, of his first two installments of *The Man with No Name.* Or so he had thought when preparing the end of the trilogy. In truth, the complications had only just begun and the film was on the verge of being put on hold. They already had the locations in Burgos and Almeria, but the obstacles of Spanish bureaucrats and the excessive prices that, in his opinion, were being asked for carrying out his project in Spain, almost put an end to the shooting.

At the end of April 1966, they requested shooting permits from the General Directorate of Cinematography and Theater, which were granted in mid-May. They also obtained the approval of the show business syndicate and the Commission of Script Censorship, which gave the Italian production 120 days to work in Spanish territory, always under the supervision of Franco's authorities.

Leone's bad temper was legendary and his outbursts were notorious on the set. Aside from his bureaucratic and production problems, Leone also argued with actors and subordinates during long shooting sessions.

He had had his ups and downs with Clint Eastwood during the shooting of his first two films, and the end of the trilogy was to be no different. The Californian actor had been paid fifteen thousand dollars for the first film, on an approximate production cost of two hundred thousand dollars, and had raised his fee for the next production to fifty thousand dollars on a total cost of six hundred thousand dollars.

When it came time to negotiate for the last film, with the Californian actor having already become an international star thanks to the success of his two previous films with Leone, Eastwood wanted to be firm and asked for a salary of two hundred and fifty thousand dollars, plus 10% of the profits generated in the United States.

Leone was furious at what he considered a small betrayal by Eastwood, an unknown actor who had achieved fame thanks to him, in his opinion! He even went to Los Angeles with his wife to convince Clint, in tense and difficult negotiations that finally came to fruition.

The tension between actor and director went back a long way, to previous shoots. Eastwood hated tobacco and Leone forced him to always have a cigar in his mouth which he was supposed to chew with relish, an element that gave more life to an actor who was too hieratic, according to Leone. In any case, the problems between them did not come to an end after the signing of the contract for the end of the trilogy. Eastwood saw the poster for the new film and protested at having to share it with two other American actors. And, of course, Clint exploded.

For the role of the bad guy Leone had first considered Charles Bronson, but this did not materialize because of the actor's schedule. So, the Italian filmmaker returned to the figure of Lee Van Cleef, as in his previous film. He liked his look, the way he had of crossing the screen and making the general public feel threatened by his presence.

But in this film the duel was not only between good and evil, since Leone wanted to add a third leg to the stool. The circular structure would become an unexpected three-way duel, as it included a third party in discord, the *ugly one*. This character, Tuco Benedicto Pacífico Juan María Ramírez, played by Elli Wallach, was a Mexican rogue, a highwayman with no decency whatsoever, a brazen scoundrel with a funny side that ended up stealing a lot of Eastwood's limelight.

After finishing the work in Almeria, Clint Eastwood and Eli Wallach became great friends. One was quieter and shier, a quiet man who hit it off perfectly with the actor from Brooklyn, a much more affable and friendly guy than the character he would play in the film.

Clint did not trust Spanish planes for internal flights, so he preferred to travel by road to the different locations, always accompanied by good old Eli. They had already traveled by car from Madrid to Almeria on endless roads that made their journey an odyssey, but that did not matter to them. They decided to head to Burgos from the south of Spain the same way: by car through the dusty roads of a country still dominated by Franco's regime.

To do so, they once again counted on the collaboration of the Fernández family, the drivers they already trusted after several epic journeys across the Iberian Peninsula. They talked to Juan, the son of their former driver, who had set up business on his own with his brother Diego, to take them to Burgos. But Juan's wife was pregnant and he did not want to leave her alone, so in the end she joined the group as well.

The actors stayed at the Arlanza hotel in Covarrubias, but Wallach wanted to do some sightseeing and even visited the monastery of Santo Domingo de Silos in the company of the Fernández couple. Sometimes Eastwood or Wallach slept in Burgos capital, and sometimes the driver would take Clint to Madrid during the weekends, since the Californian actor had friends there from his previous visits to Spain.

Most of the film crew also stayed in the Burgos town of Covarrubias during the last third of the film, although the logistics were handled from Salas de los Infantes. A stage of the shooting that involved a lot of production design work, so they needed the help of hundreds of extras, figurants, workers and soldiers of the Spanish army to carry out everything Leone had in mind to finish his masterpiece.

* * *

When the movie makers arrived in Covarrubias, they revolutionized the whole region during a summer that the locals would never forget. Like the young Juan Burgos, better known as Juanito, who was awed to see the American actors up close in the town's main square.

The main crew of the film stayed at the brand-new Hotel Arlanza, inaugurated a few months earlier after rehabilitating a historic house following the guidelines of the traditional architecture of the area. A hotel with thirty rooms that was occupied in its entirety by personnel working on the movie. And the rest of the crew, assistants and friends, settled as best they could in guesthouses, inns and private homes of neighbors in the area that housed them during that summer that went down in history.

Three languages were spoken on the set: Italian, English and Spanish. Leone and his main crew, as well as many of the supporting actors he had used on other projects, were Italian. But almost all of the support, logistics and crew were Spanish. And the three main actors, the stars of the movie, were American. A curious hodgepodge of languages, which did not understand one another, but that managed to carry the ambitious project forward. Between translations and mimicry, they always managed to solve any misunderstanding that arose.

In the end Juanito, after much insistence, managed to be included in the list of possible candidates to work on the movie. Hundreds of extras were going to be needed, but also workers to prepare the large sets that the director planned to set up in natural scenery in the region.

"If they choose you to shoot as an extra that day, you can earn two hundred pesetas or more per day of work," assured Domingo, a neighbor of Silos a little older than Juanito, whom he had befriended after his adventures in the region. "And if there is no opening, we can always sign up to dig ditches, carry lumber or whatever they need to build the sets."

"And how much would you earn then?" asked the boy from Contreras.

"They say about forty or fifty pesetas a day. That's not bad. Between one thing and another, if we work all summer, we'll earn a good day's wages."

Juanito did not feel like digging ditches or hauling logs for the constructions that were being built in the area. It was hard work, too much sacrifice in the sun, with temperatures that were too high for what they were used to in Burgos. He preferred the winter and was not afraid of the snow, but the torrid summer was too much for him.

Anyway, that would be much better than staying in Contreras, helping his parents at home or in the fields. He would have more freedom, earn more money and meet interesting people for his other businesses. He would have to bring in some money at home, but his parents would never know what he was really going to earn working on the film.

Domingo and Juanito were dumbfounded when they saw the stars of the movie coming out of the Galín restaurant, located in the Plaza Mayor of Covarrubias and in front of the Hotel Arlanza. They had not managed to learn their names, so they called them by the nicknames or nicknames they had heard from other people who worked with them.

Clint Eastwood became, for them *El Rubio*, a lanky guy almost two meters tall and with a steely gaze that could melt anybody. The kids had listened, paying attention to one side and the other, to some of the characteristics of the protagonists of the film. And from what little they could see with their own eyes, the person who described the American actors was right.

Eastwood was a quiet, taciturn, shy man, although very polite. Sometimes he would be seen walking around the area with his golf club on his shoulder, or he would go out to exercise. According to the women in the area he was a very handsome man, although Juanito did not think he was particularly so. Perhaps it was because of his height, his enigmatic aura of classic ladies' man, his unintelligible words or his blond hair. It did not matter, for whatever reason he attracted the attention of waitresses, sales clerks and any young woman who had anything to do with the shooting or the administration.

Then there was Lee Van Cleef, another big man with a look that was impossible to forget. The youngsters heard *El Rubio* call him 'Angel Eyes' and Van Cleef had stuck with the nickname throughout the film set.

They could not prove it, but rumor had it that this Yankee even drank the water from the flower vases, so the moviemakers brought his wife from North America to keep him under control. The plan worked: after his wife's arrival he began to behave better and in Covarrubias he was considered a serious and very gentlemanly man. A man Juanito had seen smoking a pipe in the plaza and knew he would have to get closer to him in order to steal some tobacco.

The third protagonist was Elli Wallach, better known as *Tuco*, which was the name of his character in the film, a Mexican gold digger. He was a nice New Yorker who had made great friends on the film set, although he sometimes had a bad temper and got into fights at the hotel or wherever he felt like it. Juanito had met him a couple of times and they had even exchanged a few words, since *Tuco* was the only American who spoke a little Spanish.

Throughout that summer, Juanito heard all kinds of rumors in the region about the Americans. Some said that their binges were brutal, as well as the rampages through the corridors of the hotel in the small hours of the morning, with nude men and women coming in and out of the rooms. Others said that a fellow townsman had beaten up *Rubio* playing billiards. Some even claimed that from time to time they organized great parties with Spaniards in the gardens behind the Covarrubias pharmacy.

The young man from Contreras had been wandering around the square, hiding behind the columns of the arcades while he watched the actors. The group that had just left the restaurant had taken refuge on a terrace, in the shade, to have coffee or something stronger to wash down the meal, oblivious to the expectation caused among the locals.

The next day, very early in the morning, the bulk of extras had to be ready in Covarrubias for a marathon day of shooting. Juanito borrowed his brother's bicycle and got up early to arrive on time from Contreras. It took him just over an hour to pedal the fifteen kilometers that separated the two towns, but the effort was rewarded.

Minutes later they all left together in buses for the monastery of San Pedro de Arlanza, located less than ten kilometers from Covarrubias. There they would shoot inside the semi-ruined monastery.

Juanito was very jealous of his friend Domingo, who was taking part more actively in the scene of the Mission of San Antonio. The young man from Burgos appeared inside a vat of water, next to a one-armed man, in an instant that he would remember all his life. And even more so when he learned that he would be given a thousand pesetas for a single day of shooting.

The boys had a great time, although the day was longer than expected due to some technical problems. The crane that the director wanted to use to shoot some scenes from above could not be used and he had to improvise. Leone ended up climbing on the shoulders of an assistant, camera in hand, to try to shoot those scenes he needed while the boys applauded.

Juanito was surprised by the director's display of energy when shooting the different scenes. He did not understand a word he was saying, but his angry gestures and the scolding he gave the crew were a warning. The Italian was a man of strong character and if things did not go his way he would fly into a rage.

In any case, it had been a very productive day. Aside from his salary as an extra, Juanito managed to sneak a silver coin that someone had dropped next to the director's chair. He stepped on it slyly when he saw that no one was paying attention, bent down to put on his shoes and took the opportunity to pick it up and put it in his pocket. Another piece to add to the small cache he had hidden. He would not get rich, but thanks to the film he thought he would have a good supply of funds to help him face the long winter.

The only thing Juanito missed during those marathon days was the presence of María, his neighbor and friend, although perhaps he would have to start calling her something else. The girl also seemed to be comfortable with him, although neither of their parents would have approved of the kind of relationship they had.

He wanted to keep earning money and the next few days were going to be just as hard, but Juanito hoped that María might come to the shoot one day to keep him company. He got along well with Domingo, but he preferred a thousand times to get lost with his red-haired neighbor and fool around somewhere with her during breaks in the shooting.

THE DISCOVERY

Carazo (Burgos), July 20, 2016

The meal was very pleasant, but I could not get the feeling that Menchu kept watching me. I tried to dismiss it and ignore her stares, but anxiety did not leave me. I was tempted to tell my friend about it, but it did not seem appropriate.

We retired to rest, at that time the heat was pressing and the best thing to do was to take a nap. We had gotten up early, gone to bed late the night before and on top of that Menchu had stuffed us at the table, with the consequent drowsiness after such a big meal.

We woke up in the middle of the afternoon, still drowsy, and watched our hostess fiddling in the kitchen. Menchu was preparing coffee, something that would come in handy to wake us up. Menchu added some delicious tea pastries to have with the coffee, for which some new arrivals joined us. Ana's mother's sister, her aunt Monica, suddenly appeared in the house with her daughter Raquel after leaving their car in the driveway. The two women also asked Menchu for a cup of coffee while Ana caught up with the new arrivals.

“We meet the famous Sandra at last," said Raquel. “My cousin’s always talking about you.”

“I well, I hope...”

Raquel was a little older than us, but not too much. I liked her the moment I saw her and I knew we would get along well. However, her mother was eying me strangely, perhaps because she had caught Menchu looking at me that way.

Suddenly Menchu got up from the table, apologized and said she would be right back. A few minutes later she returned with something in her hand, made a sign to Monica who got up. The two of them whispered quietly, a few meters away from the table, while they looked closely at something Menchu had in her hand. I started to get annoyed, because now there were two women staring at me in a weird way. I was about to jump up when Menchu sat down opposite me, on the bench, and told me straight out:

“Forgive me for staring at you so rudely my dear, you must have noticed that I'm not too subtle. It's just that you remind me a lot of someone.” I tried to dismiss it with a smile. “You look just like a childhood friend of mine. At the time I lived in Contreras, my parents' town, and I used to play a lot with the Mediavilla's daughter, María.”

Having said that, she handed me an old black and white photograph of a group of kids next to what looked like a huge graveyard. Ana moved closer to me to take a look at the photo and was as stunned as I was, although I had actually turned white: the girl looking back at me from that photograph was almost identical to me. In fact, it could have been me back in my high school days.

“My goodness, you’re the spitting image of each other”

Ana's statement did not make me less bewildered, as I continued to stare at the faded edges of an old photograph that returned my image as if it were a magic mirror. Next to me -well, next to the main subject of the photograph-, several boys and girls were crowded together in different poses.”

"This is me," said Menchu, pointing to a spritely girl with pigtails. "Here's my friend Lourdes and other neighbors from the village."

"Are you at Sad Hill Cemetery?" asked Ana.

"Indeed, the photo was taken in the summer of 1966, just when they were shooting the film *The Good, the Bad and the Ugly* in the county. Do you know the story?"

"Well, we'd heard something, hadn't we, Sandra?"

I did not even hear my friend's words, lost as I was in a kind of fog that floated around me, I could only focus on that photograph and how destiny, mocking as always, was smiling at me from an image taken fifty years ago in a valley very close by. Did I have anything to do with that girl?

I cleared my mind in time to hear Ana explaining to Menchu our fleeting and recent knowledge about it, thanks to Alberto's explanations and his participation in the 50th anniversary of the shooting. I was still numbed, not letting go of the photograph, and taking in every little detail.

"So, Sandra, are you sure you don't have family in Burgos?"

"No, I don't think so," I replied before even thinking. "My grandparents are from Madrid, although I think my grandfather's family came from Huesca. My mother was also from Madrid and my father from a town in Badajoz, so I don't think I have any relatives in the area."

No one in the room mentioned that I had used the past to talk about my parents, so I assumed that Ana had already filled them in on my family situation.

"It's funny, really," I added. "I'll have to talk to my grandparents, maybe there's a lost branch of the family from Burgos which I don't know about."

They were all looking at me as if they had seen a ghost and I did not want to keep feeling so uncomfortable. Ana seemed to notice and came to my aid, changing the subject. She got into a conversation with Menchu and Cristina about friends and distant relatives they knew in the area.

And I tuned out of their talk, still a bit dazed after seeing that old photograph. What had become of that girl?

Then a strange feeling took over my stomach but I did not want to pay attention to it. I should learn to listen to my body, since it was warning me of something very important and at that moment, I was not aware of it. How was it possible that we were so alike?

SAD HILL CEMETERY

Arlanza Valley (Burgos), July 20, 2016

Meanwhile Alberto and Julián, after also resting for a while in their room at the rural lodging, decided to head towards the epicenter of the film's 50th Anniversary celebrations: the iconic Sad Hill Cemetery. After checking a map for the best way to get there, the two young men hopped back in the car. They left Salas de los Infantes on the N-234, on the way to Barbadillo, before turning off to Contreras, from there, along a dirt road, was the access to the cemetery.

The path ended at a long wooden fence, which seemed to be the outer limit of a private estate. They parked the car and walked the few meters to the gate that gave access to the property. And there, as soon as they entered the beautiful valley of Mirandilla, they knew for sure that they had found the famous graveyard.

They came across some wooden plates nailed to a dry tree, with *Sad Hill Cemetery* written in them along with the names of the three actors starring in the movie. Underneath was the title of the movie with the name of the director and the dates 1966-2016, which reminded them that this year was the 50th anniversary of the shooting of *The Good, the Bad and the Ugly*.

Next to it there was a stone monument, a tribute to the movie with the figure of Clint Eastwood, an outline of the Sad Hill cemetery and Sergio Leone's signature. As soon as they walked a few meters towards the cemetery, they came across the imposing metal silhouette, made to scale, of the main protagonist of the film. And next to it, welcoming them to the site, they also found a metal post with a Sad Hill sign and two crossed pistols. They had reached their destination.

They crossed a beautiful expanse of land carpeted in green, flanked on both sides of the valley by the imposing peaks of Peña Carazo and San Carlos on one side, and the mountain of Los Cuetos on the other. Alberto was thrilled to be visiting in person what he had so far only been able to see through YouTube videos of the graveyard.

"I thought I knew about the Mirandilla valley. I was here years ago, when I was a kid, but there was no trace of graves."

"Of course, the people from the association have been restoring the graveyard only recently, I think since last year. Apparently, there were about five thousand graves at the time of the shooting, and they've already managed to put up more than a thousand. They've made a crowdfunding campaign and have another interesting initiative underway: for the modest price of fifteen euros, you can put your name, or the name of the person you want, on a grave. I think several celebrities have already signed up."

"Freaks! I would never put my name on a grave!"

They left behind the metal effigy of Clint Eastwood behind and entered the rows of burial mounds. After crossing several rows of tombs, placed in concentric circles, they finally reached the hanged man's tree. They were just a few meters from the beginning of the central cobblestone square that, like an amphitheater or coliseum, was part of the final scene of the film, the three-men duel in that round stage.

The two young men stayed a while longer in that place, but they did not want to be late, so they returned to the car immediately. The drive to Silos was going to be a little more complicated than from Contreras, but the views would be much more spectacular. The vehicle suffered less than Alberto had expected and, after skirting the plateau on the side closest to the valley, they came to a sharp bend to the right.

"Stop the car here, Alberto. Look at the view!"

The driver was paying more attention to the road than to the view down the hill, so he had not noticed the scenery. But he obediently pulled to the side so as not to block the path of other possible drivers, and pulled the handbrake since they were in the middle of the slope. They got out of the car with their cell phones in their hands and looked over the cliff to take in the impressive view.

More than 1400 meters above sea level, they were able to admire the serene beauty of the Mirandilla Valley, with the massifs of the Carazo and San Carlos crags right in front of them. Down below, where minutes before they had been walking, they could see the circle of stones in the shape of an amphitheater although the rows of tombs were not visible to the naked eye and it was necessary to zoom in with the phone camera to see them from the heights.

They left the valley behind and minutes later arrived at Silos. They entered the town by a different road, not the main one. The distance between this town and the cemetery was shorter than from Contreras, and also with panoramic views that were worthwhile, but it was worse to travel in a conventional vehicle.

"Why don't you call your sister again and see if she answers the phone for once?"

Julián tried his sister's phone again, but only heard the typical message "Off or out of coverage". They left Santo Domingo de Silos ready to face the dangerous stretch of curves that separated them from Carazo. But they soon had to stop because of an inconvenience they could never have imagined.

"Is that a car down there?" Julián asked when he spotted something metallic glinting in the sunlight, several meters below the level of the road, among the trees.

Alberto thought that maybe his friend was right and stopped the Focus.

On a country road like that, with two narrow lanes both ways and no proper shoulder, it was difficult to park the car in a safe place for fear of being hit by another vehicle. In the end, the young man braked a hundred meters ahead, at a small bend in the road with better visibility. Alberto put the hazard lights on the Ford, but ignored the positioning triangle and the reflective vest. If a Guardia Civil patrol arrived, they might be fined, but time was running out and they did not know if there were any seriously injured people in the crashed car.

They walked back, as far as possible from the roadway, along the rocky terrain, and always keeping an eye on that lane where the vehicles were coming at them head-on. A few meters further on, they spotted skid marks and shards of glass on the road, in front of a rocky outcrop where the marks entered the undergrowth, towards the inside of the ravine and among the trees.

"This way, Julián," Alberto shouted to his friend, who had fallen behind.

Alberto went carefully down the hillside, stumbling forward through the brush, rocks and bushes that grew wild everywhere. He spotted the wreckage of a gray car, upside down. Most likely it had run off the road for whatever reason, thought the criminology student, and had flipped over several times before ending up there. A total wreck that he hoped would not have resulted in fatalities.

"Is there anyone inside?" Julián asked, still a few meters behind.

"I don't know, I'm on my way. I hope the car doesn't explode."

The young man hesitated between going closer or calling the emergency number 112 first. He did not want to make a fool of himself if it turned out that the remains of that old Renault had been abandoned there for years, although his instinct told him that it had not been that long since the accident. He then faced the last few meters of terrain over an area of sharp rocks and reached the small depression where the vehicle was stuck, wedged between two rocks and some trees that prevented it from falling further down into the ravine.

Alberto could not see anyone inside the car from his position, but he had to go around the Renault and get to the driver's side, in case anyone was trapped in the wreckage.

Alberto threw his hands to his head as soon as he had full visibility of the driver's door. There was a man, or what was left of him, and he looked dead or very badly injured. The driver remained restrained by the seat belt but the position of the body, lying upside down, looking like a broken puppet, did not give him a good feeling.

"Shit! Julián, call 112!" he shouted.

Alberto arrived at the car at last and saw that there was nothing he could do for the poor man. The driver's head was a bloody mass after repeatedly hitting the walls of the car and not even his features could be distinguished. Alberto overcame the ghastly impression and checked to see if the injured man still had a pulse. He placed two fingers on the jugular vein, in the least bloodstained place he could find, and made sure of the sad reality: the man was dead.

Meanwhile, Julián was trying to call on his cell phone, but down there among the trees, with rock formations all around, he had almost no reception. He decided to climb back up to the roadway to call 112 and gestured to his friend to wait for him by the road.

Alberto stayed for a few more minutes next to the lifeless body, an elderly person as it seemed to him at the time. He did not want to push his luck any further and moved away from the vehicle, in case the Renault had a gasoline leak and ended up exploding. Then his foot stumbled over something that did not look like a rock. The young man bent down and picked it up. It looked like the dead man's wallet.

He knew he should not touch anything at the accident site, but his curiosity overcame his prudence. He opened the wallet and saw the man's papers: Arrigo Ambrosini, his identity card read. Alberto was surprised at the discovery, but he decided to leave the wallet where he had found it and climb up the hill to meet his friend and wait together for the Guardia Civil.

The patrol arrived minutes later and the boys explained what they had discovered. The civil guards took charge of the situation, thanked them for their help and urged them to leave the scene, as their vehicle was still badly parked and they needed room to work, given the imminent arrival of ambulances and other official vehicles.

"Will we have to go to the station to make a statement?" Alberto asked the officer.

"There is no need for the moment. My colleague has taken note of your license plate. If we need anything you will be contacted."

Alberto nodded and walked away with his friend. The conversation with the civil guard seemed strange to him, but he did not want to think about it. With so much coming and going it had gotten very late and they had not even reached Carazo yet.

"Come on, dude, let's go. We can do nothing more for that poor man, let the authorities handle it."

Julián was right, but Alberto was left with a bitter aftertaste in the pit of his stomach. They got back in the car and continued their drive, just as they heard the ambulance arrive. The paramedics would only certify the man's death, although perhaps Alberto had been mistaken in his first assessment and they could revive him.

Minutes later they finally entered Carazo and parked next to the old orchard of Ana and Julián's family. The girls were there, in the cool air, having a drink while chatting with a woman Alberto did not know.

"Well, well... at last!

"Jesus, Ana, I've been calling and texting you all afternoon."

The girl was taken aback by her brother's abruptness. But then she looked at her cell phone and remembered that there was bad reception there. Sandra also glanced at hers, but it was just as dead as her friend's. Their smartphones did not even notify them of missed messages or missed calls.

Julián greeted his cousin Raquel and then introduced her to his friend Alberto. He noticed that she was also looking at the young man with a hint of interest. *Fucking Alberto, he drives them all crazy*, thought the law student, more surprised than angry.

"We thought we would have arrived earlier to fetch you, but we were delayed, weren't we, Alberto?

The young man told them about their itinerary and visit to Sad Hill. Alberto did not want to elaborate too much on the impression the monumental place had made on him; he would rather have his friends see it with their own eyes. Besides, he wanted to tell them what had just happened to them on the road, a few kilometers away.

"You also know the valley where the cemetery is, Ana. We were there, drinking, during the San Roque festivities a few years ago. Wasn't that when cousin Pedro threw up all over himself?"

"Come on, is that where it is? You can walk from Carazo, it's not that far. I've heard so much about the cemetery and I didn't know we already knew the place. But back then there were no graves."

"That's right," said Alberto, "the association that has organized the 50th anniversary has been restoring the graveyard for some time. It was abandoned for decades. But that was not the highlight of the afternoon."

"What happened?" asked Sandra. "You do look rather pale."

"I'm going to ask Aunt Menchu for a couple of beers, to see if the shock goes away. Go on, Alberto, you tell them"

While Julián went inside the house, Alberto told the girls what had happened at the local highway, a few kilometers away. The three women were dumbfounded as the young man recounted what had happened. Although they were quite used to more than one accident on those bends every summer.

"A classmate or ours was killed there five years ago," said Raquel, more affected than the rest as she remembered the tragedy. "It's a shitty road, always the same."

"I don't know what happened, it seems to have been in broad daylight. It was an older man and I don't think he had been drinking at that time of day, he might have been distracted for a second.

"I'm sorry you had to go through that ordeal," said Menchu, who joined the conversation at that moment. "I've never liked that road and these crazy girls have been on it thousands of times in worse conditions."

Ana and Raquel took the hint and bowed their heads, not wishing to take the bait. They did not want to agree with Menchu, but she was not exaggerating; they had been in the car of some acquaintances when the driver had had a few. The young people of the area passed through there in the summer, during the various festivals of towns in the region, in circumstances that could make the hair on the back of any sane parents' neck stand on end.

"You'll stay for dinner, won't you?" asked Raquel.

"Yes, of course," Julián answered before Alberto could say anything.

The Criminology student nodded and sat down next to Sandra, a detail that did not go unnoticed by the rest of the group. The girl then looked him straight in the eyes and said:

"Great, so let's talk about tomorrow. What are your plans then?"

"I don't know, all this about the accident has left me a bit shaken. Let's see, the official reception of the symposium isn't until Friday, but tomorrow afternoon they're opening a cool exhibition about the set designs of the movie with original sketches by Carlo Simi himself. And I think there is also something else with photographs and documents of the shooting, although it's not until eight o'clock in the evening."

None of those present knew what Alberto was talking about, but no one interrupted him until Raquel intervened.

"Well then, we have the whole day off. Shall we go to the Blue Fountain?"

"And what's that?" asked Julián.

"It's a very cool area in the river for swimming," added Ana. "It's next to the Monastery of San Pedro de Arlanza, so you can also check that out."

Sandra and Alberto agreed. Their friend had also hit target by adding a visit to the ruined monastery to the plan, because he could visit one of the original locations where the movie had been shot, and for her, because her artistic curiosity encouraged her to get to know this peculiar enclave. Perhaps it would be a good way to spend the day.

"Well, let's have dinner," Menchu interjected. "You'll have plenty of time to talk about tomorrow's plan."

It was late in the evening, and the coolness of the Burgos night took over. Almost everyone was dressed in summer clothes, with shorts and T-shirts, so they immediately noticed the drop in temperatures. One by one they went into the house to mitigate the cold, until only the four friends were left on the improvised terrace: Ana and her brother, Sandra and Alberto.

"Julián, come inside with me for a moment. I want to show you some photographs that my cousin has, you're going to flip."

Julián grumbled a little, but followed his sister into the house. Sandra made a gesture to her friend which Alberto did not know how to interpret. Perhaps they had spoken before. He certainly was not going to protest; he was grateful to Ana for leaving them there alone, even if it was only for a few minutes.

"Now that Ana's mentioned photographs, I wanted to ask you for a favor."

"Of course, tell me...."

"You see, it's a story … a bit odd".

Sandra then told him about the strange feeling she had had the moment she had met Menchu, the way the older woman had looked at her and the whisperings that had gone on with Monica. When Alberto heard the real reasons for this behavior he was surprised, but his astonishment was even greater when he saw what Sandra showed him.

"Menchu showed me this old photo and I sneaked a photograph of it with my phone. What do you think?"

"What the …. But... this girl looks just like you."

"Yes, that's what I said. And, of course, it's only natural that they were all surprised when they met me."

"Is she a relative or something?"

"Not that I know of, and that's where I need your help. I know that the girl's name was María Mediavilla Castroviejo, or is called because I don't know if she is alive or not. And her parents, Purificación and Eusebio, I don't know much more."

"What do you need?"

"You brought your laptop, didn't you? I don't know if you have Wi-Fi in the cottage, but I'd like to know more about this family."

"Yes, there's Wi-Fi, although not very powerful. I'll see what I can do, don't worry, and if I don't find out anything, I can always ask Adolfo."

"There's no need, I don't want you to get into any trouble because of me."

Neither of them wanted to mention it out loud, but Alberto knew what Sandra was referring to. Everyone in the group of friends knew that he knew a former hacker who now worked for the Computer Crimes Unit of the National Police.

"Don't worry, I won't go into the Deep Web or anything like that. I'll do a little research on social networks and I'll access some databases I have, but everything will be legal. I'll let you know as soon as I can."

"Thank you very much, see what you can find out. The truth is that I've been turning it over in my head all afternoon, ever since they showed me the photo.

"No wonder..."

BETTERVILLE FORT

Carazo (Burgos), July 1966

The shooting of the movie progressed, with some problems, but little by little Leone began to see the results. The enormous work of the technical, logistical and production team, helped by hundreds of locals and soldiers who arrived from the San Marcial barracks in Burgos, succeeded in meeting the requirements of the Italian director.

Leone was enthusiastic about Carlos Simi's fantastic designs, but it was not easy to translate the sketches by the set designer into the real world. The leitmotif of the play was based on three outlaw characters, very different from one another, who set out in search of a war loot, a treasure of two hundred thousand dollars that none of the three outlaws would be able to locate without the help of the other two.

The movie was supposed to recreate the American Civil War, in New Mexico, in particular General Henry Hopkins Sibley's campaign. One of the most impressive settings for the movie, which Simi had been working on for some time, was to be the fort at Betterville. Leone and his team chose the outskirts of Carazo, in a place known as Majada de las Merinas, to set the immense enclosure. Under the guidelines of Carlos Simi, an imposing fort was built with a huge rectangular palisade of one hundred and twenty-five by one hundred and ten meters, deep moats and several annexed constructions where the most lurid details of the war would be depicted: tortures, executions, etc.

Leone's representation was based on real photographs of the Civil War, specifically of the Andersonville (Georgia) camp. A macabre enclosure where, apart from the overcrowding of prisoners, there were other unpleasant events such as the mass execution of prisoners or scenes of cannibalism among the prisoners, concentrating all the horrors of the war in that location.

For this purpose, numerous workers were hired, who excavated over marathon days in order to have the stages ready on the scheduled date. Workers from the area were hired to help in these tasks, among them the young Juan Burgos, who took part in the construction of the fort together with his colleague Domingo. The Contreras resident had been working at a good pace for weeks, either as an extra or helping in the construction of sets.

In addition to what he earned honestly with the salary paid to him by the producers, Juanito continued with his deviousness. Stealing from here and there he was gathering a small booty that he would have to hide better. He had already located an ideal cave next to the gorge of La Yecla, but he had not had enough time to get close enough to hide it.

The hard work building the fort took its toll on the workers, unaccustomed to such long days under the torrid sun of a particularly hot summer, with temperatures close to 40° Celsius. In one of the breaks Juanito went to cool off, just before eating the chorizo sandwich his mother had prepared for him. His mind drifted to his home, the town of Contreras and the local people, among them his friend María, whom he had not seen for days.

The two teens had continued to be intimate throughout the summer, whenever they found a moment, without their parents being none the wiser. Juanito had taken the girl to the fields one evening when they were able to get away, after dinner, and there they had experienced feelings unknown to either of them until then. María was becoming more and more daring, and did not mind Juanito caressing her, even in places where she had never even allowed herself to think about. Together they discovered the pleasure of kissing, caressing and the touch of skin on skin. Her expertise increased with the passing of furtive encounters, but guilt troubled her thoughts with the threat of hell.

The two teens wanted to go all the way, but they knew it would be wrong, they could not let themselves be carried away by lust. María had it engraved in her subconscious, accustomed to her mother's harangues, a devout, God-fearing Christian. For her mother, any matter related to sex was a sin, and the girl would bow her head before Doña Pura's sermons. She would not be able to admit in her presence that she felt like a cat in heat and that her belly throbbed with desire whenever she met the Burgos' son.

So Juanito was looking forward to finishing work on the Fort and have a few days' rest. He knew that the movie people would not be in the area forever and he might be wasting the opportunity to continue earning money, but he had decided not to keep working on other sets. If he was hired as an extra for another scene, he would not mind spending all day in the sun shooting, it was not that tiring either. But digging or hauling heavy logs did not suit him at all. He had committed himself to the construction of the palisade and the pits and he would keep his word, but he would not accompany Domingo in any other physical work.

In any case, he would continue to hang around the film set, whether or not he was working on the scenes that were being filmed, looking for other objects he might steal. His presence was already known to the Italian film crew, who tolerated him, and for the Spanish crew he was just another kid who would help in anything and did not get in the way too much.

He also needed more free time. The demands of the filming schedule were high and the days were short, so they needed almost every hour of the day, either to record scenes or to make progress in the building of sets that would be used in the following days. Juanito wanted to dispose of his time more freely so could devote it to his chores. And, of course, to resume what he had pending with María, who seemed to be just about to fully give in to him.

The Contreras boy did not want to get overexcited, but he saw his goal in sight. He did not intend to force the situation, but he sensed that María wanted it too. He wanted to lose his virginity and dreamed about having sex with María, knowing that he would be given a beating if anyone found out, since they were both still under age.

THE BLUE FOUNTAIN

Hortigüela (Burgos), July 21, 2016

I stayed up all night. I could not get the image of those teenagers in the photo out of my mind, happy in their escapades during the summer of 1966. That photograph taken next to Sad Hill Cemetery had upset me more than I thought it would, and a strange feeling of anxiety had been gripping my stomach since the previous evening.

It did not seem to be mere coincidence: the appearance of that photograph had to mean something. I did not know if this young woman was a distant cousin of mine, but I knew myself. If I did not manage to find out something, I would soon become obsessed by the subject and it would be bad for my sanity.

I was tempted to call my grandmother to tell her about it, but I decided to be cautious and wait to see if Alberto could get some information. Maybe my grandparents had a relative in Burgos they had never told me about and that girl belonged to that branch of the family. I only had an old photograph, and maybe the looks of that girl were not that much like me, but I would not rest until I had exhausted all the possibilities.

In fact, what bothered me the most was Ana's family's reaction. Anyone can find a more or less reasonable resemblance to someone by looking at a photograph. But comparing a two-dimensional image with someone in the flesh is not the same as comparing two flesh-and-blood bodies. And that was what kept my mind from resting.

Menchu had reacted very strangely when she saw me for the first time. She had looked as if she had run into a ghost and for sure, if we were to go by what we saw in the snapshot, I looked just like her old friend. I was a few years older than that girl, but the resemblance had caught Menchu's attention. And if the three-dimensional memory of María Mediavilla had struck Menchu that way after seeing me, it was for a powerful reason and I had to find out why.

Thinking of my grandmother brought another image to mind; the mind sometimes makes strange associations. Years ago, when I was still in school, my grandmother had gotten very angry with me and scolded me in a way she had never done before. And all because I had happened to look in her room, for the present she was supposed to give me for *Reyes* (Jan 6TH, the equivalent in Spain of Santa Claus).

When she caught me rummaging through her drawers, she had yelled at me with such emotion. After enduring her swearing, she strictly forbade me to enter her bedroom without permission. I had bowed my head and nodded, before going to my own room, remorse about what had happened.

Why had she told me off and what did that have to do with what was going on? I tried hard to remember my grandmother's exact words, but my brain was not up to the task. Especially after a bad night and no caffeine in my body.

I took a shower to clear my head and went down to the kitchen, where Ana was already having breakfast with Menchu. She was pretending better than the day before, but I knew she was still watching me out of the corner of her eye, perhaps to try and catch some gesture or movement that reminded her of her old friend.

Menchu left us freshly brewed coffee and bread.

“In a little while we are all going to Salas," she said.

I did not know what she was talking about and set about preparing my toast while I took the first sip of coffee, a strong and forceful brew I needed to start the morning off with.

“What did your aunt say about Salas?”

“Menchu and Monica are going down to Salas to do the shopping, because now there are so many of us and the poor woman doesn't have enough food for everyone. She prefers to shop there because it's cheaper. We are going with them in my cousin's car, and that way we save the boys the trip. They are waiting for us at the gas station at the entrance of town.”

Ana's cousin came with us to spend the day, so the house in Carazo remained empty. Alberto and I wanted to visit the ruins of San Pedro de Arlanza first and then we would head to the bathing area we had talked about.

The two friends were already waiting for us with the car when we entered the town. From the outside it looked like a much larger town than the ones I had known so far in the region, but I did not have time to see much more. Menchu left us there and went to do her shopping, while we packed our backpacks with everything we needed for the day.

“Come on, let's get going.” Alberto said while looking at me in an enigmatic way.

Was he planning to tell me something? Maybe he had found out something about the girl in the photo and did not know how to tell me without drawing too much attention to himself. I would have to talk to him alone later, I did not want the others to find out about our search, for the moment.

“I think you know the way, Alberto. We get to Hortigüela and there we take a detour to the damn monastery. I don't know what the hell you want to see there, it's in ruins."

"I told you that it's one of the key scenes of the film, you moron. I want to see where they shot it, even if the monastery is in ruins. Besides, it won't take long and the bathing area is very close".

"And I want to see it too," I said. I had been reading some information on my cell phone earlier: apparently the monastery is considered by many scholars as the "Cradle of Castile". According to legend, it was built by Count Fernán González to honor the promise made to Saint Pelayo, no less than in the year 912.

I had read about this curious legend in a tourist blog. Apparently the good Fernán González, before becoming Count of Castile, had gotten lost in this area while hunting wild boar, and had ended up in a lost cave where a hermit lived. The man had predicted a successful future for him and when Fernán became a Castilian Count, he returned to that place to build a hermitage in honor of Saint Pelayo, the name of the hermit who had predicted a great destiny for him.

"What a pain in the ass!" exclaimed Julián. "Well, I'll go with my cousin to the Blue Fountain, she's the only one who knows how to get there. Are you coming with us or are you staying with the scholars, Ana?"

"I already know the monastery and I don't really want to visit it. It might even be dangerous in that state of ruin, even though I should be interested, because next year we have medieval subjects, but I think I'm going to pass for now." She replied.

I then caught Alberto looking at me in the rearview mirror, because I was behind with the other girls. I nodded slightly, thinking he was sending me some kind of signal, although maybe I was wrong. Anyway, I was going to find out in a few minutes because we were going to be alone and we could talk calmly, away from prying ears.

I was not expecting the immensity of the monastery, which appeared out of nowhere as we rounded a bend. We left behind the village of Hortigüela and soon arrived at our destination. There, in the vicinity of the Arlanza, sheltered by the canyon formed by the river and among the thick forests of junipers that surround it, stands the majestic silhouette of San Pedro de Arlanza, today less impressive than it must have been in its prime. But, even so, the site was overwhelming, and I did not regret having wanted to visit it.

We passed the monastery and parked a few meters further on, in a wide plain on the right, halfway to the mountains, flanked by some trees where we could park in the shade to protect it from a sun that was beginning to be intense.

Our friends left us alone and I headed towards the monastery with Alberto. We crossed the road, a fallow field, and arrived at the foot of the immense limestone mass, a semi-ruined building that still caused awe even in its pitiful state.

Alberto pointed out an access from which we could descend from the plateau where we were, several meters above the lower level of what must have been the refectory. The remains of the imposing columns greeted us in the early morning and I tried to imagine the true magnitude of that enclosure in all its splendor.

San Pedro de Arlanza had been an important abbey in the thriving Castile and from its church had come some of the most important miniature books of the tenth and eleventh centuries. Unfortunately, however, the majesty of the monastery had passed away and many of its most outstanding remains were now scattered halfway around the world: in the Archaeological Museum of Madrid, the National Museum of Art of Catalonia or Harvard University, among others.

Alberto told me that several restorations in recent years had put a stop to its deterioration. Visitors could find an amalgam of walls, arcades and columns of different styles, from the more classical Romanesque of its bell tower to the Gothic of its central nave or the Herrerian of its cloister.

While we talked about art, we continued touring the parts of the monastery that could be accessed. Alberto had brought a brochure about the building that he had been given at the rural house where he was staying, so I took the opportunity to demonstrate my architectural knowledge as we deciphered the different parts of the building described in the brochure.

"My goodness, I did not realize! You must forgive me: here I am going on about the monastery and you being so patient about it."

"What exactly do you mean?" I asked.

"What we talked about last night! I was so excited about Clint Eastwood that I didn't remember to tell you what I found out about the mysterious photograph you showed me."

I did not want to get excited, especially when I learned that Alberto had not found any reference to María Mediavilla Castroviejo either in social networks or in other databases to which he had access. The disappointment had to show on my face, because Alberto immediately took me by the arm and tried to cheer me up as if it were not all over.

"Don't give up so easily, Sandra, I won't. I did not find any marriage certificate, death, studies or any other detail that could lead me to any record to draw from. And that does seem strange to me, because it isn't only that there's no trace of her on the Internet, it's that she seems to have evaporated from the face of the Earth. And yet..."

Alberto cut the sentence short and I was confused, had he discovered something important and the asshole was just making himself sound interesting? I could not stand it any longer and asked him to continue.

"And yet, what?"

"Nothing, but I found data of a certain Purificación Castroviejo Rojas, born in Contreras, Burgos, in 1930."

"Don't tell me you've located her mother?"

"Exactly, Sandra. The woman's mother is alive and well. Or at least she appears to be, in the current patient records of a nursing home in Burgos."

"Are you serious?" I jumped in disbelief. "That's fantastic!"

"I don't know the situation of the good lady, but she is a boarder in the residence of Nuestra Señora de la Luz, in Burgos itself."

The news took me by surprise; at last, I had a thread to pull. I tried to convince Alberto to take me to that residence as soon as possible and he weighed the idea. The following afternoon, the activities of the movie convention were to start and he would be very busy, but maybe we could go there in the morning.

I did not want to insist more and walked away from Alberto while I turned the idea over in my head; I had a lot to think about. I walked at leisure through the place with a strange feeling while he resumed his inspection of the monastery. Seconds later I glanced in his direction and saw him absorbed in his thoughts as he contemplated a fixed point on the floor. He even bent down and began to look around as if anxiously searching for something. What could have come over him, I wondered to myself.

"I would swear that this is where the bed Clint Eastwood lay on during his convalescence scene at the San Antonio Mission was located. And I distinctly remember that through the window of his room you could see another building. It's that one up there, the hermitage of San Pelayo, according to the brochure I have about the shooting in the region.

He then began to manipulate his smartphone and showed me an image of a frame from the film. Alberto was right: that was the exact spot from which that shot had been taken, or at least it looked practically the same. It was a curious feeling, almost as if we were traveling back in time.

I went on listening to his passionate explanations about the San Antonio Mission, the convent converted into a military hospital where Elli Wallach's character had taken Clint Eastwood so that his cinematic alter ego could heal from his wounds. The interior scenes of the supposed mission were shot in those ruins and to recreate the exteriors the production company had chosen the Cortijo de El Fraile in Níjar (Almería). I did not want to interrupt him, but we had been there for quite a while and the others would be waiting for us by the river.

"Shall we go now? It's late and they're waiting for us. If you want, we can come back another day."

Alberto nodded and we walked up the hill, looking for the local road that would take us to the Blue Fountain. We followed Raquel's instructions and soon found the place she had told us about. We left aside the two columns that limited the access to a private property and entered a stony path that went downhill, on the way to the river.

After crossing a grassy area where some kids were playing ball, the unmistakable sound of water told us where to go next. We had to dodge some fallen trees, perhaps felled by the supernatural force of lightning in some summer storm, and then we entered a lusher area. Our friends' shouts pointing us in the right direction ended up leading us to our final destination.

Before getting together with the gang we prepared a strategy that we hoped would sound credible, in order to escape to Burgos, the next day. We did not think anyone would want to join the excursion, especially if we had to get up early, so we had the perfect ruse.

We spent a great day in that place, surrounded by nature and with lush trees to shelter us from the sun in the middle of the day. The water was very cold, something I had already guessed at, but the place was worth it. The river flowed violently in some areas, with a current that did not exactly invite swimming, but it also formed small coves between rocks, natural pools of water where you could swim at ease.

"And why do they call this place the Blue Fountain?" I asked after devouring the tortilla sandwiches that Aunt Menchu had prepared for us.

It was Raquel, Ana and Julián's cousin, who told us that we were above the deepest underwater gallery in Spain. She told us that it measured one hundred and thirty-five meters and was a famous cave for speleo diving lovers. That cavity was called the Blue Fountain, which had later given its name to the whole place.

THE LANGSTONE BRIDGE

Surroundings of Contreras (Burgos), summer 1966

Sergio Leone was still very worried. Problems with the shooting were coming thick and fast and the logistics were playing tricks on him when it came to facing a major challenge: the battle of Langstone Bridge. It had to be the most impressive scene in the movie, on a par with the best Hollywood production, but it was all setbacks.

They had chosen a site in the Arlanza valley, about three and a half kilometers from Hortigüela and also in the vicinity of the village of Contreras. The small river from Burgos would have to pass for the mighty Río Grande in the fiction, and that was the first of their concerns: to create a dam more than a hundred meters long to provide the Arlanza River with a greater flow.

A short distance from the monastery of San Pedro de Arlanza they wanted to build an immense stage for the great battle. The imposing northern camp would be set up right there, once they finished felling dozens of trees and digging hundreds of trenches around it, on a small hill near the river.

Leone had the invaluable help of the Spanish army and other people from the various towns of the region, willing to work on the great project. More than a month of hard work to meet the demands of the Italian director, determined to shoot a majestic scene that would go down in the annals of the seventh art. Leone needed Eastwood and Wallach's characters to blow up the sturdy wooden bridge to get rid of the threat resulting from the two armies fighting in an area they needed to clear, so they could cross the river and reach their destination: Sad Hill Cemetery, where their loot of two hundred thousand dollars was hidden in a specific grave.

In fact, it would end up becoming the most expensive scene in the movie and would involve more than two thousand extras, a complicated exercise to manage for all involved. In it the Yankee troops and the Confederates had to face each other in a cruel and bloody battle for the control of the wooden bridge, one hundred and fifty meters long, located over the river that would take place before the intervention of two of the protagonists of the film.

The initial set designs turned out to be more complicated to execute than originally assumed. The work on the dam was joined by the construction of the gigantic bridge and the positioning of the troops for the shooting. More than five hundred men were working simultaneously on both tasks to satisfy the demanding Italian, in a hard effort that lasted for six weeks. Although the real difficulty arose when it came to blowing up the bridge in a risky exercise that almost ended in misfortune.

The specialists placed the explosives in different strategic points of the enormous bridge before blowing it up. But the scene did not go right the first time, or the second...

The first attempt was discarded by Leone as it lacked the spectacle the filmmaker was looking for in one of the film's climactic scenes. For the second attempt, the Roman director wanted to thank the Spanish army for their immeasurable work throughout the production, so he gave the privilege of the detonation to one of the officers in command of that regiment of extras. And then disaster struck. Leone shouted in Italian to warn the whole crew. But the Spanish army lieutenant was not familiar with shooting orders and misunderstood the Italian director's 'watch out' gesture. The soldier then proceeded to blow up the bridge to the astonishment of all present since no camera had been able to capture the moment live!

Sergio Leone started shouting and swearing at the sight of the mess the lieutenant had caused. Rocks and timbers had flown through the air in all directions, without warning, and smashed one of the team's vehicles, although fortunately there were no injuries.

The Spanish military man rushed to apologize to the Italian director for his unfortunate mistake and assured him that his men would rebuild the bridge in less than a week so that they could shoot the scene again. Leone calmed down a bit and decided to return to Almeria to finish shooting other scenes before returning to the already cursed Langstone Bridge, (deep inside he was fuming).

Days later, after many reversals, the final moment arrived. In the scene, the characters played by Clint Eastwood and Eli Wallach had to place the dynamite charges on the pillars of the bridge and flee before the imminent explosion. Leone wanted to do it this way to give veracity to the scene, and placed the actors in positions very close to the bridge at the moment of the explosion. But his opinion clashed head-on with Eastwood's more prudent view.

The actor wanted to know where he and Eli should stand. Sergio Leone instructed him to stand near the first camera. Then they were to climb up to the next camera so that the bridge would explode behind them.

Eastwood stood surveying the terrain, gauging distances and potential problems before the dangerous scene. His calm demeanor seemed unperturbed, but Leone knew he was ruminating on something he was not going to like. Eastwood wanted to know where the director was going to stand and Leone assured him that he would be by the second camera, waiting for the actors to arrive. But Eastwood demanded that he be near them when the bridge blew up.

Leone had to swallow his pride and agree with his star, so he called his crew and they agreed to use Eastwood and Wallach's doubles to shoot the most dangerous part of the scene.

When the bridge exploded in spectacular fashion, this time captured on camera in all its splendor, the actors sighed in relief to be out of harm's way. Rocks and wood fragments fell relentlessly and almost hit the assistant cameraman standing closest to the bridge, just where Leone had originally intended the actors to stand.

Wallach quickly realized the danger of working with Sergio Leone. His friend Clint had already warned him. And it was not the only time that the New York actor would experience the Italian director's recklessness in his own flesh.

At the beginning of the film, Wallach's character fell into the hands of the authorities on several occasions, who sentenced him to hang without a second thought. The trick consisted of *El Rubio* shooting from a distance, so that *Tuco* could flee before breaking his neck or asphyxiating himself with the noose. But sometimes these scenes became dangerous.

Leone expected that when Eastwood fired, a small charge of dynamite would explode on Wallach's back, who was awaiting death on the back of a horse. That explosion was to break the rope and make the animal run wildly. The American asked the director for earmuffs for the horse, Hollywood style, so that the animal would stay calm. But Leone refused and, of course, more than one problem arose due to the horse's restlessness when shooting such scenes.

The sequence shot on the train tracks in La Calahorra was even worse. *Tuco* remained handcuffed to his jailer, who was already knocked out, and decided to place the handcuffs on the rails so the train would free him as it passed over them. Wallach huddled on the small slope that bordered the rail, waiting for the train. When the wheels of the convoy broke the chain, Tuco freed himself and quickly moved away, but the metal plates that some of the cars had on their underside almost decapitated him.

Wallach breathed a sigh of relief after seeing death so close and when Leone wanted to repeat the scene he flatly refused. He did not want to stick his neck out again, even though he still had to shoot other dangerous scenes throughout the film. If he had listened to Clint when he warned him at the beginning of the shooting...

A THREAD TO PULL

Burgos, July 22, 2016

The day before had been a long one by the river, and we had arrived in Carazo in the middle of the afternoon, eager to rest. We said goodbye to the boys, who left us in the village on the way to Salas, and I agreed with Alberto that he would pick me up the following morning, around ten.

Just as we were leaving the Blue Fountain, Alberto commented that the next morning he wanted to go to Burgos to visit the site of the old San Marcial barracks, the place from which many of the soldiers who had taken part in the 1966 film had come, as we had previously agreed on. We knew that our friends would not want to join the excursion and even less if we had to get up early. So, without hesitation, I volunteered to accompany him. But I imposed a condition that I thought would be credible in the eyes of others: I wanted to visit the Cathedral in Burgos.

Our friends ignored us while we arranged our date, although apparently the conversation did not convince Ana. That same evening, she pestered me with questions, claiming that I had been fooling around with Alberto all day and that I was hiding something. She even thought that the Burgos thing was a vulgar excuse to go to a motel with my supposed lover in broad daylight. I denied it, but her insistence forced me to tell her the truth.

I explained to her the uneasiness that had settled in me after the discovery of the photograph and the reaction of her relatives upon meeting me, and also the selfless help Alberto had given me. I needed answers and perhaps I would find them in that residence. She seemed surprised, she had not thought that the incident would have affected me so much, but I assured her that it was something important to me. I did not manage to persuade her, but she assured me that she would cover for me in front of the others and that she would not tell Menchu about my inquiries.

I thought I heard a hint of annoyance in Ana's words, but I did not quite understand why she should be upset with me. This had nothing to do with her, apart from the fact that I was involved in this story because of her relatives' reaction when they had met me.

The following morning Alberto came to pick me up at the agreed time. Only Menchu was up when I left, so I said goodbye to her without giving her any real explanation. The good woman looked at me with suspicion, even though she did not know the real reason for our visit to Burgos.

On the way to the capital of the province I brought Alberto up to date and told him what I had talked about with Ana. He assured me that she would get over it, it was of no great importance in his opinion. A few minutes later we parked near the residence, and my stomach churned. I did not really understand the reasons, but I thought that this visit would be important in order to find out if there was a reason for everything that was happening to me during those days.

I had never been to an old people's home before and I found it a depressing place. I only saw a small room where some ladies were quietly watching television and, in a corner, some men playing cards. We went over to one of the nurses who were there and I let Alberto speak. He asked for Doña Purificación and explained that we had come to visit her.

"Are you family?" The nurse asked us.

"Yes, well, you see... Her parents are Doña Pura's cousins and since we were in the area visiting other relatives, we wanted to take the opportunity to say hello to her." Alberto said.

"Well, this is a bit irregular, but since you've come this far...."

The nurse warned us about Doña Pura's condition so that we would not be caught by surprise: the old lady suffered from advanced senile dementia and had few moments of lucidity. Perhaps Ana was right and we had made the trip for nothing, but now we would not turn back.

We went into the pretty spartan room with only a bed, a bedside table and a small closet. The old woman was in her wheelchair, her back to the door, so she could look out on the small garden that was visible through her window from a distance of about two meters.

"You have a visitor, Doña Pura," said the nurse as soon as we entered. The old woman did not even flinch, so our companion guided us to the patient's side.

Alberto encouraged me to speak and I had to clear my throat to be able to address the old woman. Doña Pura was a very old woman, with completely white hair and a face lined with wrinkles. Her gaze was lost and, although her eyes were pointed outside the window, I doubted that she was actually seeing anything. I regretted then that I had come to the residence, but I was already here so I had to take advantage of the opportunity, if I could get anything out of the woman.

"Good morning, Mrs. Pura, how are you today?"

"She's a little deaf in this ear, now that I remember," the nurse said. You'd better stand in front of her so she can see you. But don't stand right in front of the window so as not to take away her view of the garden, it's something that sooths her a lot.

“Of course, don't worry," Alberto answered.

The nurse moved the wheelchair back a little further, so that we could pass through the gap between the bed and the old woman. We stood on either side of the window, facing the good woman, although Doña Pura did not seem to notice and continued to look outside.

“If you will excuse me for a moment, I have other things to attend to. I'll be right back. I'll leave you alone for a few minutes.

Alberto thanked her, then motioned me to approach the old woman. I had not even thought of what I wanted to say to that woman, and least of all now that I realized I was facing the imposing wall of a senile mind.

Then I took out my smart phone and enlarged the image of María Mediavilla, although I did not think that Doña Pura would be able to see the details on such a small screen. I stood in front of her and squatted in an attempt not to obstruct her view of the garden.

“Look, Doña Pura, I have a picture of your daughter María here. Do you remember her?”

I held the phone right in front of her eyes. The old woman seemed to grunt as I blocked her view of the garden, but she quickly calmed down. I thought she might be staring at the photograph and searching through the haze of her memory, but I could not be sure.

I sat up and stood next to her, while I kept the photograph in front of her eyes. The old woman changed her attitude and even looked like she was about to speak.

“This is your daughter María in a photo with her friends, many years ago. Do you know where your daughter is now? I would like to talk to her.”

The woman had stopped looking at the garden and her eyes remained fixed on the screen of my phone. I felt terrible and even more so when I saw that she was about to get upset, but Alberto motioned to me to persist before the nurse returned.

“You see, I need to talk to your daughter, it's very important to me. A friend of hers from the village showed me this photograph and I...”

Doña Pura then followed my voice and looked up for a moment. I could see the movement of her pupils and the astonishment reflected in them when she saw me standing there. Her eyes widened in surprise and she began to mumble nonsense.

I did not know what to do when I saw the old lady getting so agitated. At that moment the nurse came in again and reprimanded us as soon as she noticed the situation.

“What's going on here?” She blurted out as soon as she entered the room, just a moment after I had put my cell phone away.

“Nothing, we just wanted to say hello and she started to get nervous for no apparent reason," said Alberto.

“Excuse me, but you have to let her rest. She's very upset and that's not good for her blood pressure.”

We both nodded and left the room, but first we said goodbye to the old woman. I do not know what I was trying to accomplish, but I did not lose anything by trying, so I insisted as I said goodbye.

“See you soon, Doña Pura. We will come back some other time to talk about our dear María. Rest and take care of yourself.”

-Ma… Ma… María….” She mumbled with difficulty. “No, I didn't want to... Sleep, my pretty girl, the Virgin is with you.”

The last words were uttered almost without stammering, as if she had regained control of her lost mind for a moment. I did not understand the meaning of those words, but I knew that my presence had caused that alteration in Doña Pura's state.

"I'm sorry, but you have to leave. I'm going to call the doctor just in case, I don't want any problems with Doña Pura."

We left with a heavy heart and, without saying a word, we walked down the corridor until we were out of the residence. We had not even said goodbye properly, embarrassed by what had happened. I feared that the state of nerves in which we had left the old lady might cause her some problem, so I felt even guiltier.

On the way back to Salas we remained silent for several kilometers. I was in my own world, thinking about what had happened and turning it over in my head. Maybe I should have behaved differently in the woman's presence, or maybe it would have been better if I had forgotten about it. Stirring up the past sometimes has consequences, and I was not even prepared for everything that might happen around me.

"Are you alright?" Alberto asked after a few minutes.

"Yeah, well, I don't know... I feel terrible for upsetting an old lady like that, for stirring up her memories in such an abrupt way. It must have been a shock for her to see me. Maybe I reminded her of her teenage daughter and her mind went completely haywire".

"Don't worry, take it easy. Doña Pura will be fine, you'll see. I saw how her face changed and her pupils were fixed on you, that's good for her. Her eyes gave off something special, a mixture of joy and relief, almost as if a great weight had been lifted off her shoulders."

"I don't know, I feel like an idiot. I haven't found out anything and we're worse off than before. The nurse won't let us go back there in a million years and I still have a knot in my stomach, I even feel like throwing up."

"Come on, calm down. Take a deep breath, we are already in Salas. By the way, I found her last words very odd."

"Yes, she even seemed to regain her sanity for a few moments."

"Maybe she took you for her daughter and that's why she called you María. And then she says "No, I didn't mean to... Sleep, my pretty girl, the Virgin is with you". Does it have any meaning?"

We stopped in Salas and had a quick lunch in a cafeteria, before Alberto drove me to Carazo. He was going to be busy all afternoon with the symposium activities, I could not abuse his trust so much. The following day he also wanted to attend the official inauguration of Sad Hill and the lunch with the congress registrants, so I preferred not to bother him. The poor guy had done enough already. But I did assure him that I would be happy to accompany him to the Sunday pilgrimage in the Mirandilla Valley, with the screening of the film in the open air and what not, which seemed to please him.

I knew that Alberto had come to Salas that weekend to participate in the 50th Anniversary activities of the movie and I felt guilty for taking up part of his time for my detective nonsense. The worst thing was that Monday was around the corner, Alberto would be back in Madrid and I would not have achieved any of my goals.

I was at a crossroads, or rather at a dead end. On the one hand, perhaps I ought to forget about my investigations, leave the Mediavilla family aside and continue my life as I had been doing. Although in my inner self I knew that while I was in Carazo, surrounded by Ana's family, the matter would continue to haunt me and would not let me rest in peace.

On the other hand, there was my incipient relationship with Alberto. Not that anything had happened between us, apart from the improvement in trust between the two of us, the complicity and his generous help in my particular odyssey, with no signs of anything else. I did not even know if the nurse at the nursing home would allow me to visit Doña Pura again after what had happened. Maybe I would call that afternoon to see how the old lady was doing.

Alberto had told me about the rest of the weekend's activities and I knew I would not see much more of him until Sunday afternoon. I was looking forward to seeing that mysterious cemetery with him and attending the pilgrimage, although I did not know if I could stand the three-hour western screening, lying on the floor of a Castilian valley as night fell upon us. Maybe snuggling up together under a blanket when the cold set in would make the experience more digestible.

THE BLINDNESS OF YOUTH

Contreras (Burgos), August 1966

At last, he was free of the heaviest tasks, those in which they had been spending more than ten hours a day for weeks. Juanito had had enough of helping in the construction of the Betterville concentration camp and needed a break after working long days under the terrible sun of the Castilian plateau. Digging ditches, hauling logs and building walls was not something he wanted to do again in his life that was for sure.

The young man did not want to say goodbye to the shooting yet: he had made good friends during the summer and he needed to remain part of the crew in order to go unnoticed at certain times. His loot was increasing steadily, although he knew he could still get some more trinkets before the film crew left the Arlanza valley. He already had his eye on a couple of objects, he just had to find the right moment to take them without drawing too much attention.

He knew a marketeer in Burgos with whom he had already made deals in the past, and he would soon contact him again. It was not that he had managed to steal the crown jewels, but between the proceeds from the sale of the stolen goods and his official salary, he would have a good cushion to get through the winter and not have to ask his parents for money.

Maybe he should be more ambitious and think bigger. He had more than earned it after a summer in which he had worked his fingers to the bone, sometimes literally, dealing with nails and wooden pallets. Firstly, he had to figure out the exact amount he needed to achieve it, but a far-fetched idea then began to form in his brain.

What if he invested all the profits in something for himself? Maybe it would be enough for a dream he had had in mind for a long time: a motorcycle. He hated getting tired and sweaty everywhere on his bike, and a motorcycle would be great for his commute. Yes, he was decided, that would be his goal. Although he had two equally complicated problems ahead: to attain the minimum amount for an expense of such magnitude, even if it were a second-hand motorcycle and, on the other hand, to convince his parents to let him make such a purchase of something they might consider unnecessary.

That summer he had spent little time at home, although his parents did not blame him either. The young man from Contreras contributed to the family economy with part of his earnings and his parents could not complain. He did not help in the fields or at home, but that money would do the family a lot of good.

Besides, his father had seen the condition in which the boy arrived after the very long days of working outdoors, so he could not even object. On the contrary, he was glad that the boy finally seemed to be focusing and behaving responsibly, sacrificing himself for a reason instead of wasting his time like every other summer. Venancio was proud of his son, perhaps he would become a man of means after all. And all thanks to the movies, who would have thought.

Juanito decided to put aside his little dream for a while and concentrate on another equally important one: his relationship with María. During the last few weeks, he had not been able to take proper care of the Mediavilla girl and he feared that some other boy in the region might want to take her away from him. Not that they were in love, or that they were formal boy and girl-friend or anything like that, but he would rather María did not fool around with anyone else.

Especially when he was so close to another of that summer's goals. They had not talked about it clearly, but it was obvious that they were both on the same wavelength. Excitement and desire overflowed every time they were together alone, and the only thing left to do was to consummate their passion. He knew that María was dreading the moment, especially knowing her mother, and he was not a hundred per cent sure himself either.

He did not like to talk about it with the older boys because they always made fun of him since he was still a virgin, so meeting Domingo that summer had served as an escape valve. The older boy from Silos had a bit more experience than he did and without mocking his situation, gave him some clues that he hoped might help him if the need arose.

For the moment he had to regain María's trust, as they had not seen each other for days due to his exhausting work schedule. He had told her on several occasions during the month that he would love it if she came with him on a shooting day, although in the end those days were the fewest, as he was almost always busy with other tasks.

At last, he was able to see the girl one afternoon, but María could not stay too long so as not to upset her mother; she had chores to do at home. Juanito had to restrain himself and hide the excitement that filled his body, prisoner of adolescent horniness. He decided to invest the little time he had in convincing her to accompany him the following day, which was a free day and he could show her the sets and show off his friends on the film set.

"Don't worry, your parents don't have to find out, we won't be going far," the boy promised.

"If my mother finds out I'm going with you, she won't even let me leave the house. I don't know why she's got such a grudge against you."

"We won't even leave the village as the filming is nearby. They're going to shoot a scene with two of the main characters on the outskirts of Contreras, near Alto de San Juan.

María nodded knowing that it would not be so easy for her to escape from Doña Pura's clutches. But the following day, her mother seemed to have other concerns on her mind and her father was in a good mood, so they did not put up too many impediments when she said she was going out for a few hours. The girl was very happy and also pleased to see Juanito's delighted face.

The teens joined other neighbors who had the same idea: to witness the magic of the cinema from up close. Juanito was in his element and was greeting everyone, known or not, to impress María. She noticed his magnetism and felt proud of her friend, who strutted around like a peacock.

They were able to watch the shooting of a scene between *Rubio*, already famous throughout the region, and the actor everyone knew as 'Angel Eyes'. María smiled and applauded when the director stopped the sequence, which had to be repeated many times to the delight of the audience and the annoyance of the actors.

"Would you like to go for a walk?" asked Juanito. "They're going to spend a long time repeating the scene here. If you want, I'll show you some of the sets I've worked on."

"I have to go home soon, Juanito. If it doesn't get too late, maybe...."

The boy smiled at his friend's hesitancy and took her hand to guide her. He decided to take María towards the area where the palisades and trenches of the northern camp had been erected, right next to the Arlanza River, where an impressive bridge was being built and where a bloody battle was to take place.

But their plans were thwarted in the face of an unforeseen situation they could not have foreseen. The young couple were frolicking in the fields, happy and oblivious to the rest of the world, when they spotted a group of people in the distance. María had not even noticed them, but Juanito became alert when he saw the strangers.

"Too much of a woman for you!" shouted one of the young men before crossing paths with them.

Juanito realized they were three boys older than them, he thought they were also from the region but not from Contreras. The one who had spoken was cross-eyed and he thought he had seen him before, he did not know whether it had been at some fiesta or maybe on one of the movie shoots.

María became nervous and moved closer to Juanito. She motioned him to be quiet and hurry up. She preferred to leave them behind rather than face the group; they had not given her a very good feeling either. But the hot-blooded boy could not let it go when he saw they were embarrassing his friend. Least of all when he heard what else came out of the mouth of one of those unprepossessing strangers, seconds after they crossed paths at close range.

"Son of a bitch, what tits the little redhead has, come with me, beautiful, I'll show you a good time!"

María squeezed Juanito's hand tighter as she feared the boy's reaction. Juanito tried to hold back, but his temper got the better of him. They had already left the group behind, going in the opposite direction, but there was still time to catch up with them. He let go of María's hand, bent down to pick up some stones and prepared to throw them.

"You're a bunch of assholes!" he shouted as he threw several pebbles at them.

The first two missed, but the third hit bull's eye. The cross-eyed man had turned when he heard Juanito and received a brutal blow in the middle of his forehead. Immediately blood began to flow from the wound, the man was stunned and dropped to the ground while his friends rushed to help him. Juanito and María had already run away, but they had time to hear the wounded man's imprecations:

"You'll pay for this, you bastard! I swear you'll regret this."

The couple ran away laughing, although their escape made them take a detour away from their original path. María then decided to return home and not continue with Juanito's plan, even though they were bothered no further. They were late and her body was not in the mood for playfulness after the scare.

The boy understood all right and walked María home. He could not be angry with her, even if those idiots had spoiled their fun. He, too, had been left with a strange feeling in his gut from that encounter. He only hoped he would not have to regret his actions in confronting those guys.

A NIGHT OUT

Covarrubias (Burgos), July 22, 2016

I tried to take a mid-afternoon a nap to relax after all the emotions I had experienced. But my head kept going in circles and I could not fall asleep. And even less when I realized that Menchu and Monica were still talking quietly, interrupting their conversation as soon as I appeared. I greeted them in the kitchen before going up to my room, although Ana followed right away to talk to me. She wanted to know if I had plans for that evening. I told her I did not.

"Well, we've been invited to a party in Covarrubias, at Julián's friends' house. He will be there, although I don't know if Albertito will join us later."

My friend winked at me, but I knew she was just messing with me. And she still had not asked me about our adventures in Burgos. I took the opportunity to tell her what I knew. Alberto was going to attend a conference that afternoon given by a journalist who had written several books on cinema, among them some about Sergio Leone. I hoped that it would not end too late and that he could come to the party afterwards.

We left Carazo early with the idea of having something to eat before the party. We ended up sitting down to a full dinner on a terrace, right on the famous main square of Covarrubias. Next door was the hotel Alberto had told us about, where apparently the actors and part of the film crew of *The Good, the Bad and the Ugly* had stayed. I could not imagine Clint Eastwood walking through those narrow streets; it must have been something to behold.

Once we finished eating, a while later, Julián introduced us to some of his friends and we immediately joined the party. I forgot about my problems and only cared about having fun. I danced like a crazy person to the summer hits and I think I drank too much. Or I mixed too much, it could have been either or both. Ana glared at me, since I had gone from mojitos to gin&tonics, and the alcohol was starting to take its toll on my body. I had to sit down for a while to rest, with a soft drink in my hand, to try to prevent the drunkenness from going too far and ruining my night.

Ana sat next to me for a while, to see how I was feeling. I did not want to make too much of a fool of myself, because sometimes when I drink too much, I do silly things. My friend knew that so she was keeping an eye on me, just in case. I thanked her silently, but fortunately the dizziness had passed and I felt a little better.

Half an hour later Alberto showed up at the party, looking handsome as hell. Either the alcohol was still doing its thing in my mind or I was more hung up on him than I wanted to admit. He greeted Julián and the rest of his friends, though he quickly became aware of my presence, sitting in the corner next to Ana. My friend stood up immediately, nodded to him and allowed Alberto to take his place next to me. I planted two resounding kisses on his cheeks, near the corners of his lips, and enjoyed the moment as I absorbed the scent on his neck, which smelled of expensive cologne.

"A soda?" he asked me with an ironic air as he looked at my glass. "Either this party is a pain in the ass and you're a saint, or you've had too many mojitos, you must've had one too many and you're trying to recover sitting here."

"Well, a bit of everything, I won't deny it...."

"Well, I'm here to liven things up. Shall we dance? You're about to discover my legendary flow," he joked.

I really wanted to dance with Alberto, but my dizziness was not completely gone. I shook my head at his offer, at least at first, but he insisted Of course he convinced me with his mischievous smile and those lively eyes that seemed to speak to me in whispers. The truth is that I remember that evening a bit in a haze and perhaps, with time, I have idealized it in my memory. But I will never be able to forget it, for many and very different reasons which I will tell later.

"I have something very important to tell you," he said as we danced.

"Okay, I'm all ears."

I looked like I was freaking out, or so I thought at the time, as I waited like an idiot for Alberto to propose to me or something like that. But what happened was something very different, the spark that would ignite into something so strong that it would change my life forever. I will never know what would have happened if we had not gotten involved in that way, but I have never regretted anything that happened. And, of course, I will always be grateful to Alberto for helping me in something so important to me.

"I found out something about your mysterious friend...."

"What friend are you talking about?" I asked like an idiot, more absorbed in those lips I longed to kiss than in his words.

"The one in the photo, who else? I think I found a clue about the famous María Mediavilla."

My alcohol-soaked brain was trying to process the information, but my raging hormones won the battle. I looked at him spellbound, smiled and took his hand, ignoring what he had just told me.

"Okay, tell me about it calmly, Alberto. Dance with me to this song! It's my favorite and I want to cheer up a little."

"But I..."

I overcame Alberto's reluctance with a pout that I hoped was funny, although in my state it might have been pathetic. My friend ignored me and agreed to dance with me in the center of the improvised dance floor. I moved to the beat of the music and moved closer and closer to him. I think he noticed.

We danced, laughed and enjoyed the evening, although by Alberto's body language he was not as relaxed as I was. Maybe he needed to release what was inside him, but at that moment I was ignoring him and was only focused on one thing. We moved around the dance floor and ended up on the side, a little away from the main group of the party. Alberto looked at me with sheepish eyes, and I did not know if it was because he felt sorry for my attitude or for some other reason. Anyway, I said to myself, I have already made a fool of myself enough and a little more will not matter. Although the uninhibited state produced by alcohol sometimes produces the opposite effect to what you are looking for, still I was not going to back down.

"Come on, don't be prude," I said in his ear. "The night is young, dance with me."

And at that moment, something happened. I do not know if it was chance, fate or whatever, but that is what happened. I looked up at the starry sky above our heads and I thought I could make out the dizzying passage of a shooting star. Alberto stared at me for a moment, very fixedly, and then the pounding rhythm of the music gave way to a slower song, which invited us to dance much closer together.

Alberto held out his hand and I accepted his offer. We danced body to body, close together, with my head resting halfway between his chest and his shoulder. I abandoned myself for a few moments there and sighed, happy to find myself in a place where I felt safe and at peace with myself.

We were barely moving our feet, although we were trying to keep up with the music, but we were both more aware of other details.

I thought I felt Alberto bury his face in my hair and I knew we both felt the same. Or at least we were on the same page, or so I wanted to believe. I'm not going to say that we were in love or anything like that, but it was obvious that there was chemistry between the two of us and someone had to make the first move.

I decided to be the first, I have never understood why men have to take the initiative in such matters. I withdrew my head a little from its particular shelter, raised my chin and looked directly into his eyes, wanting to get lost in his pupils. I am not short, but Alberto was a good twenty centimeters taller than me. I raised myself a little on tiptoe, smiled and half-opened my lips as my gaze moved from his eyes to his full lips, the ones I hoped would take notice of mine.

Alberto then crossed the distance that separated us and kissed me gently, but also firmly. It was a short kiss that gave way to other longer and wetter ones, while our tongues also began to get to know each other in depth. I feared that the dizziness produced by the alcohol would play a trick on me by having that kind of intimacy with him, but fortunately my system behaved and the endorphins won the battle.

I thought I heard a murmur accompanied by whistling, far away, almost in another world. At that moment I was not even there, my body had been transported to a higher plane where only the two of us were, oblivious to all the problems of the universe. I felt orphaned from his mouth when Alberto separated from me, but what I glimpsed in his eyes filled me with joy. Then he took me by the chin, gave me a little peck on the lips and whispered:

"On the way from Salas, I must admit that I was thinking of you, but for another reason."

"You didn't like it?" I asked between alarm and anxiety.

"No, yes, I mean... Of course I liked it, I rather loved it. And I don't want to be a spoilsport, but I do have to tell you something. I don't want you to get angry because I didn't tell you before."

"Are you a virgin?"

Maybe my joke was out of place, but alcohol sometimes plays tricks on me and loosens my tongue more than usual. Had I overdone it? I hoped he would not hold it against me, and take it the wrong way.

"No, but that's not the point," he replied more seriously, which put me on my guard. "Seriously, Sandra, we need to talk about what I found out about María. Let's go outside for a moment, it's noisy in here."

I nodded in embarrassment, I had behaved like an idiot. It was true that he had told me about it before, but I was thinking about something else and had not paid enough attention to him. At least I had not scared him off completely, as he took my hand and led me through the party guests toward the exit.

We then crossed paths with Ana and her cousin, who apparently had been looking for us for a while to say goodbye. It did not escape my friend's notice that Alberto was holding my hand. She assured us that Julián was going to stay the night in Covarrubias and asked Alberto with some embarrassment to look after me. She gave me two kisses and whispered something in my ear, although I do not remember it well. It might have been "Have a good time" or "Be careful", although deep down she was a little envious of me for having hooked up with Alberto.

A few minutes later we were also leaving the party. It was already early in the morning and it was cool, so Alberto grabbed my shoulder with his arm and pulled me close to him as we strolled through the lonely streets of Covarrubias.

"You see, this afternoon I was thinking about what the old lady said to us at the nursing home. You know, 'I didn't want to, my beautiful girl... the Virgin and blahblahblah...'".

"Me too, to be honest. It seems like something very intimate, something a mother says to her daughter when she puts her to bed or something like that. I think she mistook me for María when she was little and the little sanity left in her mind drove her to say those words."

"Yes, maybe, I thought so too. In fact, it's natural for people with dementia, Alzheimer's and other types of degenerative diseases to remember events that happened many years ago better than any current details, such as what they had for dinner the night before, for example."

"And what did you find out? I thought you had been busy all afternoon with the symposium at the Salas Casino."

"That's right, it's been a very interesting afternoon, I'll tell you about it. But before that, I was resting for a while in my room after leaving you in Carazo at noon. I turned on my laptop, did some random searches, then something more specific in a different search engine than the world famous one and *voila*!"

"What's that?" I asked when I saw the image Alberto was showing me on his cell phone.

"This is a picture I took from the laptop screen. I didn't have much time because I was late for the opening of the event. It is the header of a private blog I found, which refers to the same words."

"I don't understand..."

"In the list of search engine results, I found an interesting reference. It only showed part of a paragraph that included the phrase and belonged to a Blogger blog: *Memories of a life*. It was a post, an entry from December 2006, but the blog is private."

"And you can't access it then?" I asked confused.

"No, not at the moment. I don't know if at the time they configured that blog only for the author or guests who wanted to access it. It may be abandoned or inactive, or it may still be up and running, no idea."

"We don't even know if it has to do with María or someone in the family. It's not a very common thought, but we can't rule out that it may be just a coincidence.

"That's what I thought too," he said annoyed at not being able to access the blog. "Maybe my friend can give me a hand with access, although I'm going to owe him too many favors already. Besides, looking at the picture that's the main image of the blog, you will agree with me that it would be too much of a coincidence. This blog has something to do with this family, for sure."

Alberto showed me the image again, somewhat grainy as it was taken from the laptop screen with his cell phone. The details could not be appreciated well, but the main environment that formed the image could be seen.

"Don't tell me it's..."

"It is, Sandra. It's an image of the Carazo rock, an iconic place for the inhabitants of this region. It's one of the hills that surround the Mirandilla Valley and apparently the locals know it as *El Fuerte*," (The Fort).

"But that's fantastic! You were right, you're the best."

And having said that, I kissed him on the cheeks without hesitation. Alberto took me at my word and wanted to prolong the kiss, something I did not oppose. But then something sparked in my mind and I remembered that I also wanted to tell him something. I broke away for a few moments, he looked at me with desire and I knew that my intervention could cut off our relationship, but I had to tell him.

"By the way, I'm sorry, but it slipped my mind. I've also been thinking about our visit this morning. And then it occurred to me to call the residence..."

"You did what?" he asked in alarm.

"Nothing, don't worry. I just wanted to make sure that Doña Pura was feeling well after the shock of our visit, nothing else."

"I would have kept quiet, but okay. And was the old lady well?"

"Yes, that's what I was told. Although it seems that in the middle of the afternoon another relative came to visit the patient and they didn't let him see her because she was taking a nap and they didn't want to upset her again. A rather strange guy, I was told, who didn't take the refusal very well."

"Well, that's curious..."

Alberto took a step back for a moment, looked me in the eyes and I saw concern in his face. A gust of cold air crossed our path and I shivered. We left the historic area of Covarrubias and headed towards the parking lot where Alberto had left his Focus. We sat in the car, he started the engine and put the heater on for a moment, at least until we warmed up.

He then told me what had actually happened when they came upon the crashed vehicle near Carazo. He explained to me how he had come across the deceased's wallet while trying to help him and other details, such as the presence of glass on the roadside, just where the car had left the roadway before plunging into the ravine. He had learned that the deceased's name was Arrigo Ambrosini and later found out that the man was an assistant cameraman during the shooting of the movie in the summer of '66.

"And why didn't you tell me about it before?"

"I don't know, I didn't want to think more about it and I didn't want to involve you. So this afternoon I spoke to the organizers, I mentioned the death of the Italian in a car accident on a nearby road and no one knew anything. Apparently, he was not a fixed guest for the 50th anniversary, but they had spoken to him weeks ago and the Italian had assured them he would try to come by. And of course, after learning that he had passed away in tragic circumstances, he was the talk of the meeting for the rest of the afternoon."

"Well, it's not so strange either. I don't think that the authorities, once the body has been identified and the relatives have been called, will have to contact the organizers of the convention. I imagine they have other concerns on their minds."

"Yes, but this is not Madrid. In such small towns you find out about everything and people tend to be gossipy by nature. And the news of a seventy-year-old Italian who died in strange circumstances, a few kilometers from where the 50th anniversary of the shooting of an Italian film in the region is going to be celebrated, should have caused a bigger stir."

"You can't do anything else for this man. Leave it to the Guardia Civil, there is little we can do."

"That's not really what I'm worried about, I don't know whether to tell you."

"Come on!" I protested. "Now you can't leave me hanging."

Alberto then turned his gaze away from my face and looked at the dashboard of the vehicle. The clock read 1:22, I remember that perfectly. His worried face when he told me next:

"Someone at the symposium found out that I've been asking questions. Or maybe they saw me next to the accident site, I don't know exactly. When I left the event this afternoon and went to my car, I found this note on the windshield."

Then he handed me a sheet of paper, folded in two. Inside, in a common typeface, was the following text: *Don't butt in where you're not wanted. Stop asking questions or you may find answers you are not prepared for.*

"Jesus Christ! That's a full-fledged threat, Alberto. We have to go to the police, this is getting out of hand."

"No, I don't want to involve the authorities for the moment. I want to find out something else. Let me remind you that I am studying Criminology."

"Yes, but you're not Sherlock Holmes and I'm not your Dr. Watson. Let the professionals do the work; we already have enough investigations underway."

Then I realized how selfish my attitude was. Alberto had become involved in my story, had taken me to Burgos and had put up with my nonsense about María Mediavilla and her mysterious past. And I, on the other hand, reacted that way when he told me what was happening to him, something that could be considered a real problem.

I apologized awkwardly.

"Don't worry, I understand you. And don't think I haven't been thinking about it all afternoon. Especially after the other message I received" he replied.

Alberto handed me his phone and I could read the message on the screen. A shudder came over me again and my whole body trembled, from my feet to my head.

If you really want to know the truth, investigate the crimes that occurred in the region in 1966. Tonight, at 2:00, you will find more answers inside the monastery of San Pedro de Arlanza. Do not call the police or you will regret it. I will be waiting for you there, don't miss it.

"No way! You're not thinking of going, are you?"

"Well, not at first, but I've been thinking about it for a while now and I think..."

"Are you even listening to yourself? If you don't want to call the police, at least take me with you so you don't go alone."

"No, Sandra, I'm not going to put you in danger too."

"Me too?" I cried out in horror. That meant that I had sensed correctly that he might be in some danger. "You see, you have two options: either you take me with you or I call the police right now and we forget everything."

I crossed my arms and looked at him with a surly gesture, hoping he would take me seriously. The haze that had settled in my head minutes before had almost completely dissipated and adrenaline was coursing through my body, putting me on my guard. Alberto shook his head for a moment and tapped the steering wheel before answering.

"Damn it!" He cried, "All right, we'll go together. But you will do what I tell you, no exceptions, no buts.

"Okay, perfect. Let's go now, we're not there yet."

Our starting point was ideal to reach San Pedro de Arlanza in a few minutes, since Covarrubias was only a few kilometers from the monastery. It was also true that it was not the same to travel those roads at night and without knowing them well as in broad daylight, but I trusted Alberto's expertise; he always seemed to me to be a prudent driver. Prudence and, perhaps, cold blood, could be decisive for the adventure we were getting into.

Why did we do it? Over time, after analyzing the situation calmly, I have thrown my hands to my head at our reaction that night. Who could have thought of such folly? The situation in which we had been unintentionally involved, the threatening messages and everything that surrounded us at that time cried out for other solutions. But no, we heeded the platitudes about young people and went wild and oblivious as hell.

My heart was pumping at full speed and threatened to burst out of my mouth. There was no trace of alcohol left in my blood, or at least I did not notice it. The adrenaline that coursed through my veins was the only fuel I needed at that moment, without it, I would never have been able to go on.

Alberto, however, seemed much calmer. He had always struck me as a calm, almost pragmatic man. He kept his eyes on the road to avoid problems with the treacherous curves, but otherwise there was nothing about what we were going to do which he seemed unprepared for. Only his frown and concentration gave me a glimpse of what was really going on in his head.

I felt guilty because I sensed that Alberto was more concerned about my safety than his own. Yes, I know that we women are strong enough to take care of ourselves, but I understood what my friend might be thinking. All that about the stronger sex and other bullshit that fortunately, society was trying to change little by little, sometimes with a lot of suffering.

A few minutes later we arrived at our destination. We parked on the same esplanade as the last time, a few meters from the monastery, and prepared to wait. Alberto turned off the engine and did not turn on any lights, so we remained in the dark, under a leafy tree, to hide as much as possible.

We did not even roll down the windows in case the sound of our whispering escaped. I knew that those freakish precautions were foolish. If there was anyone nearby, they would have seen and heard us coming with total clarity, especially since it was a dark and lonely night, with no living thing for miles around, apart from the birds of prey that flew over the sky of Burgos, something I had become accustomed to during those days.

Alberto opened the glove compartment and took out a flashlight that he carried there for emergencies. I would have to make do with the light of my cell phone so as not to break my neck as we entered the ruins of the monastery. I was afraid of what we might find down there, but if it had all been a bad joke or a false alarm, I'd rather come out if it with everything intact.

"I'll lead the way. Stay close."

I nodded seriously and followed Alberto. We left the vehicle behind, crossed the road and headed towards the area where we could access the ruined site in the easiest manner. The full moon of a few days before had partially withdrawn, but at least visibility was not zero in the area. Despite the poor light, we managed to get there without much trouble and without needing our flashlights. Fear was drilling into my temples, but I could not lag behind. I was not going to abandon Alberto in such a situation, least of all after forcing him to take me.

Alberto put a finger to his lips for silence, although terror had taken hold of me and I did not think it would let me utter a word. If anything, a bloodcurdling scream, which stuck in my throat when I saw the dark, rock-strewn pit in which we were going to lose ourselves in the next few minutes.

Our previous visit to the monastery had been curious and interesting. But at that moment I was appalled to find myself there. My bad head had played tricks on me. And all for acting brave, when any reasonable person would have called the police while staying well away in a safe place, preferably many miles away.

I thought I heard a sound behind me, just as we were about to go down to the monastery grounds from the grassy plateau that surrounded it from the far side of the road. I gasped, but Alberto reassured me. The forest might harbor other living beings that might have caused the noise .The idea took root in my mind and did not help to temper my mood.

Alberto made a sweep with the beam of his flashlight, but we did not distinguish anything special. Fortunately, there was a kind of stone staircase that allowed us to reach the level where, what had once been the floor of the monastery was located. We looked around, always focusing with our flashlights, and found nothing threatening. Nor any sign that there were any other visitors in the abandoned monastery.

"Is anyone there?" shouted Alberto.

I was shocked, I was not expecting it, especially since we had been in silence for several minutes or speaking in whispers - Alberto's powerful voice bounced off the walls of the millenary building and caused a curious echo effect as the sound waves crashed against the solid walls in the background, but no one answered his question.

I could not reproach Alberto either; I did not even have the strength to tell him that he could have warned me before announcing our arrival at the top of his lungs. In any case, there was nothing else we could do. If someone had wanted Alberto to go there at two o'clock in the morning, it had to be for a reason, and he had only cried out loud so that someone would know what to expect.

Was it a trap? My feverish mind began to rave and told me that this was a bad idea. My legs wanted to go back up the stairs and run at full speed to the safety of the car, but my brain was not up to the task and issued contradictory orders to the rest of my body. Under that pressure I was not much help to Alberto, but I did not want to be far from him either.

Panic overcame me during those anxious minutes, but I had to keep going. I could not afford an anxiety attack under those circumstances, so I clung even closer to Alberto's back and we began to move forward with small steps.

That part of the monastery, without walls and exposed to the weather, looked clear. So we continued our mission to the back, the best preserved part of the building. We then heard a kind of buzzing and flapping sound, but we immediately distinguished its origin. A flock of bats, an animal I did not like at all, flew by a short distance from our heads. I did not want to think about one of those critters latching onto my hair because then I would have screamed at the top of my lungs.

My mettle was not adequate to withstand all those scares, I even felt the pulsations in my head. I could not back out halfway or abandon Alberto to his fate, but I swear that in those moments I prayed that we would not encounter anything else. But providence did not want to relieve my night, it had other plans for us.

Alberto called again, but there seemed to be no one there. Apart from the vultures that hovered above us, hundreds of meters high, perhaps waiting for a reason to abandon their nocturnal flight and approach the earth. A shiver came over me and I knew I would have nightmares for the rest of my life about that ghostly monastery, whose shadows and gloom were about to give me a heart attack.

"What's that?" Alberto asked me in a low voice.

I looked everywhere, but saw nothing. I wanted to ask him, but Alberto signaled me to be quiet and pointed to the left, just behind a thick wall that blocked our full view of the room. I tried to listen more carefully and I thought I could make out a rhythmic sound, like a tapping. Alberto pointed in that direction and we found more birds, in this case a crow and a pair of magpies that were hopping around, without flying, while moving in a small space and pecking here and there.

"Stay here, I'm going to take a look."

"Don't you dare leave me alone! We'll go together to see what's there."

I could have listened to Alberto and stayed put. We walked the few meters that separated us from the birds and soon discovered why they were so interested in that particular area of the monastery. They had discovered something to eat and had to take advantage of the opportunity before the vultures and other scavenger birds came to snatch their booty. Alberto illuminated the area with the powerful beam of light from his flashlight and I stifled a scream before clinging tightly to my friend. The unspeakable sight of that human wreckage, deprived of its essence as a person, would accompany me in my most terrible nights until the end of my days.

"What the fuck...! But what the hell have they done to this man?"

I did not want to go any closer, but Alberto approached to check what was obvious to the naked eye. The man was dead and there was nothing we could do about it. The body appeared dismembered, completely mangled. At that moment I did not know if he had been run over by a truck or had been subjected to terrible torture, but his humanity had been taken away until he was a wreck.

"Don't touch anything!" I begged him. "I'm going to call the police, let's wait for them to arrive in the car."

"We're not going to do that, Sandra. We would have to answer a lot of questions that we don't have answers to. For example, what were we doing here at this hour?"

I considered his words for a moment. We would have to be there all night, or worse, answering a lot of questions at the Guardia Civil headquarters. We had not done anything, nor did anybody know we were there, unless some camera had captured the presence of the Focus in the area.

"Please, let's get out of here. And stop pointing the flashlight at the poor man, I'm sick to my stomach just looking at him. Not to mention the putrid smell he's giving off."

Alberto nodded and accompanied me out of the monastery grounds. As soon as I got into the car, a shudder took hold of me and my whole body began to tremble. Alberto hugged me and tried to reassure me, although that experience would be engraved in my mind forever.

"Who could have done this savagery? Poor man, we don't even know who it is."

"I'm an idiot," Alberto replied. I could have taken a picture of him with my cell phone to try to find out more. With all that blood I couldn't make out his features, maybe I knew him".

"But are you listening to yourself? It's better not to have anything in our possession that might link us to the corpse. Since we haven't done our duty calling the police, you won't be such an idiot as to leave clues about us."

"Relax, I'll make an anonymous call in a little while. But first let's get out of here, that's enough for today."

"All right, that's fine with me. I hope the Guardia Civil arrives before the vultures attack that poor bastard."

CERTAINTY

Contreras (Burgos), August 1966

María thought about Juanito often, even though she did not want to call him boyfriend or anything like that. The things they had done together could be considered boy-girlfriend rather than just friends - or so her friend Carmen kept telling her. She was more expert in these matters - but she preferred not to think too much about something her mother would have considered a mortal sin.

Doña Pura was a fervent Catholic, very religious and devout, and she was furious about her daughter running around with a young man. María was young and had just discovered her body and her sexuality, a whole host of new sensations she wanted to explore with Juanito. He might not be the man of her life, nor were they going to get married or have children, but that summer she just wanted to explore with him and learn new things together. At least for the time being.

The first few times Juan had tried to touch her she had felt dirty; her mother's teachings were very present in her head:

"Men are evil, they only want to use your body. You have to stay away from sin or you will burn in hell. Temptations are evil, you know that. And you must remain pure until you meet the one who will be your husband and father of your children."

For Doña Pura it was insane to have sex before marriage; or to even think of sex for pure pleasure. For her, the carnal union between a man and a woman should only be for procreation, as dictated by Holy Mother Church. María did not understand this, least of all after exchanging opinions with her friends and with other older girls who had already tasted the sweetness of passion.

For the moment, María felt sufficiently satisfied with the kisses and caresses she was giving Juanito. She shivered just thinking about his hands on her skin, and her body reacted involuntarily without her being able to help it. She remembered their encounter in the abandoned house, and her nipples instantly became erect, causing her a mixture of pleasure and pain as they rubbed against the coarse fabric of her dress.

She did not know if she was ready to have sex yet, but she liked Juanito very much; in each furtive encounter in which they explored their bodies the feelings of pleasure had grown a little more and the excitement of both threatened to sweep them away.

The young woman had been very surprised to discover Juanito's erection for the first time. A mixture of disgust and youthful curiosity gave way to another state. She then began to feel powerful, she knew that it was she who provoked that arousal in him and she used that newfound power to take the reins in their encounters.

María did not understand very well everything her friends told her, but she had learned to know her body and intended to use that wisdom. She had come across that moment almost by chance, one morning when she was washing herself, but ever since she had discovered the sources of pleasure in her own body, she had longed for Juanito to recreate those areas for her delight.

One afternoon that summer, the fieriness of their kisses and caresses made Juanito insist on going further. María had been thinking about it for days, but did not dare to take the final step. Her mother's teachings had taken strong root in her head and Christian guilt was very present in her life. Although her youthful, lush body demanded other things, she could not succumb to the devil's temptations.

Kissing and fondling could be considered a venial sin, or so she wanted to think, but if she allowed Juan to deflower her, her world would collapse instantly. And her mother would be able to banish her from the village or beat her to death for allowing such infamy in the Mediavilla family.

So, María refused to continue and turned away from Juanito. The young man was not surprised, he had expected this, but continued to insist.

"You can't leave me like this, María. Look at the state I'm in."

The boy took María's hand and brought it to his crotch. The girl felt the hardness of his member and became excited as she felt it throbbing, but she could not lose control.

"Come on, I'll teach you. That's it, very good..."

That was the first time María had masturbated a man and she could not deny that she enjoyed the experience. She had the power in her hands again and Juanito was at her mercy. She became even more aroused as she watched her companion's face as he climaxed and the wetness she felt inside herself proved to her that they were both on the same page.

But, of course, Juanito wanted more. And with each encounter the excitement increased, until it reached heights that seemed unbearable to both of them. When she felt his inexperienced fingers inside her, she knew that she could not last long without surrendering herself. She thought she was ready, although she was very afraid.

"You have to be careful, María," her friends told her. "You can't let him come inside you, take it out before if you don't want to have any problems."

At that time, in a small town in Burgos, young women did not have much sex education. Nor did they have access to contraceptive methods, so they had to be very careful. And pull-out was the most common method in such cases. In the Arlanza Valley, they had not heard of sexually transmitted diseases, but they were very clear on the fact that getting pregnant as teenagers was not a pleasure for anyone.

She even had an erotic dream in which she woke up embarrassed to discover the moistness in her nether parts. Horniness was not Juanito's exclusive property and she knew that, sooner or later, they would both succumb to something that attracted and frightened them equally. She only hoped that Juanito would treat her well and be a gentleman, as she had been told that the first time could hurt and she did not feel like suffering too much.

In any case, María harbored other thoughts in her head, in which Juanito could also have a place, but they were not so lustful that her cheeks turned red when she remembered them. She knew they were just that, daydreams, but sometimes dreams also come true.

The young woman had dropped out of school because she was not very good at it, but she did not aspire to stay in the village all her life, helping her mother in the house or working with her father in the fields. Farming or tending livestock was not her thing, nor was she planning to waste her youth in that kind of life.

María was an intelligent girl, although she was a bit lazy when it came to her studies. School made her tired, and even more so when she had to combine it with housework. However, she was very clear that she wanted to leave the village, leave the Arlanza Valley and go to the big city. She was satisfied with Burgos, which was the nearest city, but she would not mind settling in a more important capital.

She had not yet decided what she wanted to do in life, but it was clear to her that she would not settle for being anyone's trophy wife either. She did not say no to getting married and starting a family, but first she wanted to live her youth in her own way, with a freedom and independence that she lacked under the yoke of Doña Pura, with the iron control from which she could escape on rare occasions.

One afternoon of confidences he told Juanito about it and was surprised to find out that he also wanted to leave Contreras to make a better future for himself than the one that awaited them in his region. The young couple fantasized about running away together to Madrid, or even to some coastal city to start a new life. Neither of them had ever seen the sea and it was something for consideration.

They both knew that it would be very complicated, especially since he was only sixteen years old and had no money to get by with. But the simple fact of being able to share her desires with Juanito brought her closer to him and made her see him in a different way. He was no longer just a young man with raging hormones who wanted to take advantage of her body. He was someone she could trust, someone with whom she could start a new life as soon as circumstances allowed it.

But all that was still a long way off. For the moment María had a closer goal marked on her calendar: to get a whole day off, away from her mother's chains. The following Saturday several young people from the village were going on an excursion to the Mirandilla Valley to see the famous cemetery that was being built for the film, the perfect excuse to get away from home and spend the day at her leisure with Juanito.

The boy had been insisting on the subject for days and María was giving him a hard time because she did not want to get his hopes up. But she was gradually undermining her father's resistance, who was almost convinced. She preferred to tell Juanito the good news as soon as she had confirmation, but for the moment she kept it to herself.

It would not be a trip far from home, but it would be a first step to start a new life. She wanted with all her might to come of age so that she would not always have to abide by what others said, and this excursion would perhaps serve to prove to herself that she deserved another kind of existence.

What she never imagined was that this day would be the beginning of a life journey for which no one had prepared her.

THE CONFIRMATION

Salas de los Infantes (Burgos), early morning of July 23, 2016

We left the monastery in silence and once we were safe, on our way to Salas, we decided to call the Guardia Civil post in Covarrubias. Alberto configured his cell phone so that the call came from a hidden number. He reported that he had found the lifeless body of a person in the ruins of San Pedro de Arlanza and hung up without waiting for an answer.

"I don't know if it was a very good idea, to tell you the truth," he said as soon as he had hung up. "I've tried to change my voice, but I don't know if it will be enough. I know they record all calls at the emergency center, but I don't think they have the same equipment in the barracks."

"Shit, I told you so!" I cried somewhat angrily, "Now they're going to suspect us. How the hell did you know there was a corpse in there?"

"Please, don't make me more nervous. I didn't want to wait there for the authorities, you know: explanations, interrogations, waiting for the doctors to arrive, the judge to remove the body and all the paraphernalia."

Alberto continued driving, while shaking his head in disagreement. I did not want to make him more nervous, especially with him at the wheel. We had left the regional road behind and were already heading towards Salas on the main road to Soria, but I was still uneasy.

"Well, I'll leave you in Carazo and tomorrow we'll see what to do. I don't think we should mention this to anyone for the moment."

"Of course not, that goes without saying. Another thing is whether we are capable of lying to everyone's face. But we have the perfect alibi."

I did not want to take advantage of the situation, nor in those moments of anxiety after what had happened, did I think of anything romantic or sexual, but perhaps it would be our salvation.

"I don't feel like going to Carazo now and waking up the people there up so I can get into the house. I don't have the keys, I didn't realize that when Ana left."

"So?"

"Well, I can stay with you in Salas. Julián will spend the night in Covarrubias and I think your room has two beds. That way I don't have to bother anyone in Carazo and if anyone asks, we left the party early and I spent the rest of the night in the rural house."

"But..."

"Relax, that's not the point. After what we experienced at the monastery, I simply don't want to sleep alone. I'm still on edge. And if the others think it's something else, that's up to them. We don't have to make them believe otherwise."

Alberto looked confused and I felt very strange presenting it that way. It was the most practical thing to do, even though it might have had other consequences. But I thought we had to be pragmatic and deal with what had happened while we still had the advantage.

We entered Salas without saying another word. Alberto was very serious and I was afraid I had messed him up.

After the wonderful prelude at the party, with those kisses that seemed too few for the need I had for him, we were going to finish off the night in the most unlikely way: after finding a corpse in an uninhabited place, now we were going to spend the rest of the night together, but not the way it should have been.

I instantly regretted my decision, but I could no longer refuse. I had only thought about our safety and the best way to get out of that macabre discovery. Perhaps I should have paid more attention to Alberto's ideas, he was the criminology student, but my temperament took over and I let myself go.

It was certainly not the way I had imagined spending my first night of intimacy with Alberto, and even less so after what had happened at the party. But circumstances dictated and we both had to adjust. We parked the car on the side of the country house, next to the main road that split the town in two. We tried not to make too much noise when we got in so as not to wake the other guests.

It was almost four in the morning and I was a wreck. The adrenaline that had driven me had vanished, and the fear that had held me upright in the monastery had slowly settled deep in my soul. Exhaustion took hold of me then and I sighed with the sight of a bed crying out to me in the dark of night.

"If you want, you can borrow a T-shirt of mine to sleep in..."

I had not even thought of that. Alberto had seen me in my bikini, but not in my underwear, and I was not planning on sleeping with my clothes on. I was not about to crawl into bed like my mother brought me into the world, so it seemed like a good idea. I nodded silently and Alberto looked in his suitcase for something to lend me. He then held out a huge gray T-shirt that could double as a nightgown given our size difference. It suited me, so I took it and then pointed to the bathroom.

"Of course, you go first."

I thanked him silently and went into the bathroom. I did not have anything to remove my makeup, so I washed my face a bit so I would not look like a raccoon when I woke up, if I managed to sleep a wink. I stripped down to just my panties and I put the T-shirt on. It came almost down to my knees, so I had nothing to worry about. It was not the most glamorous or sexy outfit for our first night together, but I could not get too fancy either.

I came out of the bathroom a little embarrassed, with my clothes in my hand. Alberto had turned off the main light and only the one on his bedside table was on, but I still noticed his gaze on me. It was not discomfort, but I felt something strange at being exposed in that way before his eyes, so fragile. Then I remembered that I had taken off my bra and prayed that my nipples would not show through the fabric of the T-shirt.

I looked down and was grateful that the dim light of the bedside table did not allow him to distinguish the blush that was gradually taking over my cheeks; something that was too noticeable on the pallor of my skin, so I quickly went to the bed next to the window, as far as possible from the bathroom and the entrance to the room. I removed the quilt and got under the sheet, still hot from Alberto's gaze on my body. I did not want to think about what his mind might imagine under the nightgown I had bought for sleeping. I turned my back to him and snuggled into the sheets, waiting for him to turn off the light.

I thought I heard Alberto go into the bathroom; perhaps he was also embarrassed to change in my presence. It was not the most romantic situation in the world, but it did not matter. We needed to sleep for a while before facing the next day, where we might have to explain too much.

I did not want to think about what I would tell Ana and her family. They would all assume that I had spent the night with Alberto for one reason only. They had set us up after the girls and Julián had run away, and I did not even want to think about the inquisitive faces of the entire Castro family when I showed up at their house in Carazo.

The bathroom opened again and soon all the lights went out. Not all of them, because the powerful spotlight emanating from the emergency light over the door dazzled me if I looked in that direction. I thought I could make out Alberto's silhouette in the shadows, apparently dressed in shorts and a T-shirt, just as he lay down on his mattress.

I began to toss and turn in bed, unable to sleep. The shocks of the last few hours, many and varied, had my mind in turmoil. My body was exhausted and demanded rest, but my neurons were still running at their own pace, bothering me as much as possible.

I felt a blast of cold air inside the room, but it seemed impossible. Perhaps it was a product of the frosty ice installed inside me after the escalation of sensations suffered in that godforsaken enclave. The fear of the unknown gave way to anxiety and then to panic, to absolute terror, as I found myself face to face with death inside the monastery. And this accumulation of emotions had taken its toll on me.

I shivered and curled into a ball, before giving in and throwing the quilt over me. In a rural house located in a region more than a thousand meters above sea level, I was sure I could find a blanket to mitigate the cold, even if it was the middle of summer. But I did not want to move too much or wake Alberto.

And even less so when I heard, a few minutes later, how his breathing was getting deeper and deeper until I knew he had fallen asleep. He did not snore, but his nose made a rhythmic sound as it expelled air that I did not want to think too much about if I was going to get to sleep in that atypical early morning.

I was stunned minutes later: physical exhaustion overcame my brain activity. But a nightmare took over my dream and took me to the moment when we discovered the bloody corpse of that man. The worst thing was that the dream turned out to be too real and in that recreation, events happened that had not actually taken place - the dead man opened his eyes, looked directly at me and stretched out his arm to grab me. I woke up instantly, soaked in sweat, while trying to control my heartbeat after the monumental fright. The experience had been all too real and I knew I would have trouble falling asleep. But not just that night, every night if I became obsessed with our discovery.

We did not even know if the Guardia Civil had heeded Alberto or if they thought it was some prank by someone returning from a party on a Friday night. Perhaps the body would still be there, at the mercy of scavenger birds and other predators, until someone else stumbled upon it in broad daylight. I did not want to be in the shoes of the would-be finder, although I honestly believe it was worse to stumble upon it at night, considering the pressure we were under.

Who had sent Alberto those mysterious messages? Was it the murderer himself, or was it someone on his trail? Too many questions and too few clues, especially at five o'clock in the morning of a night we would never forget.

A strange idea settled in my mind and I wanted to be selfish for once in my life. I carefully got out of bed, walked over to Alberto's bed and crawled in next to him. The sleeping beauty was resting on his side, so I moved behind him and curled up as best I could. I did not want to touch him so as not to wake him up, but instantly I felt his hand, perhaps in my sleep noticing a presence behind his back, grabbing my left arm so that I would cuddle up to him.

I then pressed myself closer to him but without any hint of sexual connotation. My muscles were tense, but I adjusted my breathing to Alberto's and began to relax. His mere presence at my side offered me the calm I needed in those moments, so I ended up abandoning myself. And I did not mind that my breasts, free from the restraints of the blasted bra, rested gently on Alberto's back as my pelvis pressed against his hips.

I do not know how long it took me to fall asleep, but I remember that my fear disappeared and I managed to sleep for a couple of hours without subjecting my mind to the torture of nightmares. It had certainly done me a lot of good to sleep with Alberto, even if it was not in the way I would have imagined for the first night we both spent together in the same room.

I looked at the clock and saw that it was only half past seven in the morning. The sun rays were trying to filter through the holes in the blinds, but fortunately not too strong. I thought it would be a good time to get up and go back to bed before Alberto woke up, but I did not make it.

I had not even noticed the change of position. His arm rested on my side and it would be hard for me to move him without waking him up so I gently slid next to him. But what really shocked me was to feel another kind of touch on my back.

I knew about the famous morning erections of men, and there was one in all its glory, against my buttocks. I got very nervous and did not know how to react, but I tried to calm down before making a fool of myself. Alberto was still sleeping and that was only due to a physiological reaction, nothing more. I am sure the same thing happened to him other mornings and it was not because of my presence next to him.

Hot flashes began to set in and my body rebelled against my mind, leaving behind any hint of shame. I wanted to move as I pleased, to rub myself against him and arouse him genuinely, but it was neither the time nor the place. I managed then to disengage myself from his arm while listening to his grunts and was about to escape from the bed when I heard a few centimeters from my ear:

"Good morning, gorgeous."

His voice, hoarser than usual, gave me a very unwelcome tingle that affected my entire central nervous system. All my nerve-endings went on the warpath and I did not know how to react. I rolled over a little until I was face up on the bed, while my cheeks flushed as I felt myself being examined by Alberto's mischievous eyes. I knew there was no turning back....

A DAY TRIP

Contreras (Burgos), August 1966

María still did not know how she had managed to get her mother's permission, but she had managed to get away from housework at least for that day and accompany other young people from the village, who wanted to spend the day in the Mirandilla Valley. This way they could admire the cemetery that had been prepared for the film, and attend, even from afar, a day of filming in the region.

"I don't want you to come back too late, María. And watch who you hang out with. I'm sure that the son of the Burgos' son is out there. I don't like that kid at all, you know that."

"Don't worry, mother. A large group of boys and girls from the area are going, and then we'll walk back together from Mirandilla.

The girl chose to ignore the warnings about Juanito and pretend innocence in Doña Pura's eyes. She had not lied about the group of local kids spending the day in the Mirandilla Valley, but she did not have to give her mother any more explanations either. She and Juanito would go with the group there, although she hoped she could be alone with him afterwards.

Doña Pura seemed to give in a little and even prepared a satchel with food and water for her to take on the excursion. María thanked her silently, afraid to say something that might spoil everything. She even accepted the hat that her mother had included in her backpack to keep out the sun that had been beating down hard since early in the morning.

"I don't want you to get sunstroke, María. You're very white and it's very hot at noon, you know that."

"Don't worry, mother. We'll stay in the shade of the trees in the valley, we won't be in the sun all day."

"Yes fine, but you put your hat on just in case. I'm sure you'll spend hours watching how they make that movie and I don't want you to end up in the hospital."

María nodded and agreed with her mother, she did not want her good mood to vanish as if by magic. She had no intention of wearing that awful hat, but no one needed to know. She would hydrate well and wet her head from time to time just in case, she did not think she was really going to get sunstroke either. The young woman had other worries on her mind and the temperature outside was the least of her problems.

Juanito had been ecstatic when she confirmed that she would be able to come on the excursion with the rest of the village kids. She had to thank Menchu's mother, one of her best friends in Contreras, who had interceded for her with Doña Pura. After all, almost all the young people their age were going to the Mirandilla Valley that day and it would be very strange if María stayed alone in the village. Doña Pura had finally given in, more for the sake of what people would say than out of firm conviction, but that was all the same to her daughter.

María did not know what Juanito had prepared for the excursion, but she had a feeling that he was not planning to spend the whole day with the group of neighbors from the village. She had prepared herself in case they managed to have some intimacy that day, you never knew what might happen. Yes, they would be in broad daylight, but they could always find a secluded spot away from prying eyes. The Mirandilla Valley and its surroundings were very vast, and the journey was long, so perhaps that day would be marked forever in her life for a reason that made her tremble with impatience and excitement, but also with some fear and anxiety.

They both looked at each other with embarrassment when they found themselves in the town square, next to the church, where they had arranged to meet the rest of the kids for their summer excursion. From there it was a four-kilometer walk to the valley, so they had to get going as soon as possible. It was already hot at that time, her mother was right in the end, so they prepared for another hot day, something they were not too used to in the Arlanza region.

"You'll see when you see the graveyard they've built, you're going to love it!"

Juanito was enthusiastic about the excursion, although they soon separated from the group and continued on their own, a few meters behind the rest of the kids. The boy then dared to hold María's hand, knowing that they could be the object of ridicule from their friends.

She did not push his hand away; she liked the feeling that came over her at the touch of his calloused fingers. She did not know if it was love or what, but she felt very comfortable with Juanito. And she was proud that he wanted to show that they were together in public.

"I don't know, to tell you the truth. I don't like graveyards."

"Relax, silly, it's a fake one. You'll see what they've set up in the valley, you're not going to recognize it!"

The journey was shorter than they had expected and in less than an hour they had arrived at their destination after walking along the forest track that linked Contreras with the Mirandilla Valley. María had not been there in a long time and was surprised by the frenetic activity in an environment where the people of the region normally took their cattle to graze.

As soon as they entered the immense esplanade that preceded the valley proper, with the Carazo rock as a silent witness to their arrival, the young people began to run and jump, surprised at what was before them: hundreds of rows of tombs, placed concentrically around a central circular cobblestone that attracted attention.

"What do you think? I told you that you weren't going to recognize it."

"It's awesome! You were right, I would never have imagined it like this. There are thousands of graves!"

"They're fake, but they're pretty cool. And look at that over there! It even has its own hangman's tree."

María followed Juanito, who was heading towards the indicated place with great strides. The other Contreras neighbors who had preceded them along the path were also approaching. They had not joined them on the way, but now they all gathered around the cobblestone circle as they admired the magnificence of the fictional graveyard.

* * *

The production crew was preparing the scenes for that day and they were allowed to go into the grave area for a while, before shooting actually began. The Contreras kids had a blast playing in the faux cemetery until someone from the production crew called their attention, lest they mess up something in the area and they had to change their shooting plans.

"Come on, kids, get out of here," one of the assistant directors ordered them. "You can stand over there, on that hill, so you can watch the shooting of a very important scene. But I want you to be quiet and still, okay?"

The group of youngsters nodded and left the cobblestoned area that had caught their attention. One of them was carrying a camera she'd borrowed and wanted to immortalize the moment. The whole Contreras gang posed for the photograph next to the hanging tree and several snapshots were taken, some with the burial mounds in the background and others with the circle of stones and the immensity of the valley as a backdrop.

The group stood in the place indicated by the technician, at a good distance from the center of the action, but close enough to be able to contemplate in situ the fascination of a film shoot. A general "Ohhh" was heard when the American actors appeared on the scene and they had to ask them to be quiet from the area where the Italian director was giving his orders.

"Avanti!"

The youngsters remained engrossed as they followed the unfolding action, dazzled as they watched the actors appear before their eyes. The indolent gait of *El Rubio*, a cowboy who must have been almost two meters tall, impressed most of the girls, who smiled and elbowed one another, blushing as they watched the star the whole county was talking about.

The boys, however, preferred to look at the actor they all called *Ojos de ángel (*Angel Eyes*)*, an ill-faced guy who caused awe just by looking at him. Although Juanito's favorite was still *Tuco*, the little Mexican with whom he had already coincided on more than one occasion during that peculiar summer.

The magic of the cinema became a bit tiresome for a gang that wanted to have fun and not spend hours hiding there, standing still, while the shots were repeated over and over again until the director was satisfied. The rumors in the region were not unfounded, and everyone could notice the volcanic character of the director, who shouted at the top of his voice as soon as something did not go according to his indications.

The scene held the young audience spellbound, as it looked like a real three-way duel between the protagonists of the film. In the background, connotative music filled the Mirandilla Valley with different sounds, which in turn helped the film crew to get in the right frame of mind. But the hours went by and the young people decided to spend their time on other things.

They had all brought their sandwiches and canteens to eat in the valley, but once the meal was over, the large group divided into small groups that scattered around all the corners of the valley. Juanito looked at María slyly and saw determination in her eyes, something that pleased him greatly. The young man then took the girl's hand, ready to walk away from Sad Hill Cemetery, with only one idea in his mind.

What they did not know then was that that place would mark them forever.

THE SILENT CYPRESS

Arlanza Valley (Burgos), July 23, 2016

I was already feeling hot enough after the wonderful awakening next to Alberto before confronting the owner of the house. What were we going to tell her? Alberto was supposed to have rented the room with Julián, and now he was coming out with a girl. Maybe she would be amused and not say anything so as not to embarrass us, but I did not want to risk it. I insisted that we sneak out quietly and have breakfast outside.

We got into his car and headed for a café in the center of Salas after a day that I, at least, would never forget. I did not want to bring up the subject, but we could not ignore that it had been an evening of strong emotions: the party, the dance, our first kisses, the direct threats to Alberto, the macabre discovery in San Pedro de Arlanza and the unbeatable way to start the morning in his arms after a night of anguish.

We also discussed the advisability of calling the Guardia Civil, although we could no longer back out. I only hoped that they had not taken the call as a prank, so that the corpse would not remain exposed to scavengers. And we prayed that no camera had focused on us in the vicinity.

"Let's not get ahead of ourselves, come on," I interrupted him. "You enjoy the day's activities and I'll go spend the morning at Silos with Ana. Although I don't know how I'll be received when I get to Carazo, still dressed in last night's clothes.

"You're right, I'm sorry," he said, embarrassed. "What are you going to tell them?"

"I don't know, maybe I'm being silly. I'll say that it was very late, I'd had a lot to drink and I didn't want to wake them all up. You told me that you had a spare bed in your room and that it would be better if I rested there for a few hours before coming back".

I did not know if they would fall for it, especially when I remembered that many people had seen us kissing at the party. I guessed I would have a hard time the moment I showed up there and felt the scrutinizing gaze of Menchu and the rest of the family but I was a free girl and I could do whatever I wanted! Although I understood that since I was staying at Ana's family's house, they would not be too pleased when I showed up like that. The best thing would be not to wave it aside and leave as soon as possible to Santo Domingo de Silos.

"Yes, of course, whatever you think. I know you have a lot to think about these days but I just wanted you to know that tonight was very important to me. We'll have time to talk about it. Meanwhile I will try to find out more about the blog I told you about."

I was pleased with his response and I knew he had feelings for me too. It certainly was not the best situation, the two of us involved in a possible murder plus a strange investigation based on a photo worn out by the years, but we could not ignore what had happened in his room.

I did not want him to be late for the opening of Sad Hill and I urged him to leave, but first I warned him about the dangers that lurked ahead. Alberto promised me he would be careful and I asked him to keep his ears open in case he heard anything about the murder.

Alberto nodded and we chose to chat about inconsequential topics in the few minutes left before we reached Carazo. It was not the right time to delve into our amorous encounter, nor did we want to go on thinking about everything else. He stopped the car a block away from the house, I sensed that he did not want to greet the others. I did not think anything of it; besides, the man was late for Salas. I steeled myself, first to face Ana and company, and second for my next move.

"Be very careful, Alberto," I said and then planted a sweet kiss on his lips that I hoped would encourage him to think of me for the rest of the day.

His smile told me that he liked my goodbye, just as I was opening the car door. He stared at me for a few more moments as I walked towards Ana's house, but he immediately started the car and drove off.

It was already after ten o'clock in the morning and I was showing up in Carazo, in the same clothes I had worn the night before and with my face washed. I had not slept much, but I did not really have dark circles under my eyes either, maybe the morning sex had helped me wake up better. I did not even want to imagine what Ana might say to me as soon as she looked into my eyes. I was going to be unable to pretend even for a second.

I arrived at the house and saw no one outside. I was about to knock on the door, when I saw that it was open, so I just walked in. I called out from the door but there was no answer. I thought it strange not to find anyone there, but then I saw Ana's head peeking out, and she beckoned me upstairs, where our rooms were.

"Where have you been, you bitch? You had me worried."

"Sorry, I didn't realize. I should have texted you or something, it's just that I had too much alcohol last night."

"Yeah, yeah, alcohol... That's what they all say."

“I'm sorry, I really am. By the time we realized it was already four in the morning and I wasn't going to come here and wake everyone up. I don't have keys to the house and it wasn't a good idea to appear drunk in the middle of the night.

“Okay, I understand. My fault for not telling you. Here the door is always open, this is not Madrid.”

“Oh, wow, I had no idea....”

This habit of the villages was something that was hard to understand for those of us who had always lived in the big cities. It was totally unthinkable that someone would leave the door of their house open in Madrid, but in Carazo I could even consider it normal if I thought about it.

“But don't even dream of getting away with it, Sandra. Where did you spend the night?”

I began to blush before I even stammered out the first words of my response. I was unable to hold my friend's gaze and bowed my head as I tried to find the most appropriate words. I hesitated. I didn't know what to say.

“I was in a pretty bad state and Alberto offered me the possibility of going to the country house. Your brother wasn't there and he had a spare bed in the room, and we didn't want to disturb you at that hour.”

“And I was born yesterday!”

“He was a real gentleman - you'd better believe it. I was a little reluctant to wear one of his t-shirts to sleep in, but he did a great job of making the situation not too uncomfortable for me.”

“Really? Come on, I'm not swallowing that you spent the night with Alberto each in your own bed.”

“Yes, we did! Together but not together. It was very strange. I'm not going to deny that. And I couldn't sleep, my head was spinning.”

“Naturally, between the drunkenness and making out, I'm not surprised that your head was going around in circles. And you want me to believe that Albertito behaved well and didn't want to take advantage of the situation?

There are no guys like that anymore. Although what's even stranger is that you didn't seize the opportunity either. What a waste! If I had caught him in those circumstances, the man wouldn't have escaped alive."

"Well, I..."

On the one hand I did not want to tell, but Ana was my best friend and I needed to let it out. Everything that had happened during the night had left me more upset than I had expected and at least I would rather focus on the only pleasant part of the whole evening.

"You really? What a bitch! And I almost believed you!"

I could not hold her gaze, I bowed my head and then I let it all out.

"I won't go into details, but yes, it's what you think. We did sleep in separate beds for a while, that part's true, but then, at dawn we got a little closer."

"What do you mean you won't go into details? Even you don't believe that! Come on tell all."

I was spared the interrogation because Ana's cousin soon arrived to pick us up. She had some errands to run and was planning to drop us off on the way. In the end we would go alone to Silos, although perhaps Raquel or Julián would join us later in the afternoon, since Alberto was busy all day.

We decided to spend the morning visiting the picturesque village of Santo Domingo de Silos. It was quite lively, with hordes of tourists wandering the streets, so we had to make a reservation at a central restaurant to avoid problems at lunchtime. We also booked a visit to the monastery for four o'clock in the afternoon and maybe later, when the heat had gone down a bit, we would go for a walk to La Yecla.

Ana kept trying to make me talk throughout the day to know more about my night with Alberto, although I tried to divert her attention asking her questions about the town and the famous monastery of Santo Domingo de Silos, which we wanted to visit after lunch. And, of course, with so many questions I could not get the image of Alberto out of my head.

I thought of him and felt my cell phone vibrate in my purse, almost as if it were a divine sign. I smiled at the thought that he was also thinking of me and wanted to make me part of his day. Alberto sent me some photos of the inauguration of the graveyard, it seemed that the event was very lively. I showed them to Ana and she waved them off indifferently, she did not seem very enthusiastic about the event.

"Alberto is a bit of a nerd, isn't he?"

"Well, it's just a hobby like any other, isn't it? Some guys like the gym, others like the movies, you know" I said with unease as I remembered Julián's posturing when he used to upload pictures of his routines to the social networks. "By the way, tomorrow we're all going to the field excursion together, right?"

"Ufff, I'm having second thoughts about it. And even more if I have to watch a cowboy movie that lasts almost three hours, lying on the grass with hundreds of people. It will be really uncomfortable, and, on top of that, we're going to freeze."

"Don't be a spoilsport! I'm sure we'll have a good time, you'll see."

"Yeah, sure. You'll get to make out with the criminologist and I'll have to put up with my brother's bullshit, what a ball!"

* * *

For his part, Alberto also had quite an entertaining morning. Along with many other fans of the seventh art, he boarded buses rented by the organization to head for the Mirandilla Valley, the site chosen fifty years ago by the Italians to build what would later be known as the Sad Hill Cemetery.

The criminology student was trying to chat with his fellow travelers on the way to the faux graveyard, but his mind was elsewhere. The conversation was pleasant and interesting, dealing with topics that would have caught Alberto's attention at any other time. But he had many other worries on his mind and did not want his thoughts to prevent him from enjoying a memorable day.

Alberto listened to the comments of his companions, but his brain could not quite assimilate them. The fact is that what had happened during the previous night took precedence when it came to connecting his neurons. Especially Sandra looking like a helpless fawn, that innocent candor that had always dazzled him about this girl, but he had been even more subjugated when he saw that she could also become a very mischievous woman.

The young man loved the languor of some of Sandra's gestures, in contrast to her energetic attitude on many other occasions. Her slim, slender body hid more than one pleasant surprise, not to mention her beautiful face, with hazel eyes that exuded curiosity and zest for life. Her lips were soft but firm and her smile lit up any room, all highlighted by graceful freckles that drew attention to a face framed by her striking red hair.

Alberto came back to reality, unable to forget the corpse they found in San Pedro de Arlanza. He feared that the Guardia Civil would force the bus driver to stop the bus at any moment, moments before a couple from the *Benemérita* entered the vehicle and took him away handcuffed in front of all his fellow passengers. An image that he tried to keep out of his mind for his own good.

On the one hand, his more protective side would rather keep Sandra out of the whole story, but he knew that she would not let him do so. Especially when she heard from his hacker friend, who had sent him a puzzling message.

This looks like a soap opera, man, I'm finding out some pretty heavy stuff. I'll send you more detailed info by e-mail later.

Alberto had thanked him, although at that moment he did not know what the computer scientist was referring to. He did not want to stop to think too much about that other matter either, the priority in his head was still another one. Apart from Sandra, he could not forget that some guy had set him up to deal with the dead man found in the ruins.

Was the mysterious anonymous man himself the murderer? That had neither head nor tail, because if he really was and had something against them, he could have dealt with them the night before without any problem. In the loneliness of that place, under the starry blanket in which the vultures flew over their heads, a criminal of such caliber could have killed them in a heartbeat. He had chosen the place and they had fallen into the trap, but in the end, they had come out of their adventure alive, unlike the unfortunate man they had found skinned inside the ruined monastery.

What if there was another meaning to all this? Maybe the anonymous man was aware of what was going on in the Arlanza Valley and wanted them to find out. Maybe this guy could not go to the authorities for whatever reason and preferred others to do his dirty work for him. That did not make much sense either, if he stopped to think about it, so he ended up dismissing the absurd idea. So many shocks ended up taking their toll and Alberto felt a slight headache beginning to appear at his temples.

That morning's events were open to the public, and not only to those registered for the official symposium, so the atmosphere was less academic than at the talks he had attended at the Salas Casino. Alberto estimated that about five hundred people had gathered there to attend the inauguration, all in a ludic, festive and very lively atmosphere. First came the unveiling of a plaque by the General Director of Tourism of the Junta de Castilla y León before delivering a brief speech. Then, all those present were able to take a tour of the entire location and enjoy the technical explanation given by one of the event's managers.

Alberto noticed that there were politicians and other personalities present who had not wanted to miss the inauguration. He was also attentive to the groups that formed as they walked through the valley, in case someone mentioned anything to do with the corpse found in San Pedro de Arlanza.

The university student from Madrid had made friends during the previous days with some people from the Basque Country who were very fond of *spaghetti westerns*, so he joined them as soon as he spotted them touring the graves. Together they watched the performance of *Il Triello* by a theater company from Aranda de Duero, and Alberto recalled the mythical scene he had seen so many times on the screen. He was right in the place where Leone's film had been shot, a strange sensation that would accompany him for the rest of the tour of Sad Hill Cemetery.

Afterwards, there were musical performances and a small institutional act. The words of the mayors of the area and the organizers of the event put the finishing touch to a morning that was coming to an end. But the surprises were not over yet...

* * *

Ana and I went to eat lunch around two in the afternoon, since we did not want to go into the monastery with a full stomach. I had heard very good things about the local lamb and wanted to try it, so we ordered a quarter of lamb for both of us with some salad. We almost could not finish it, far too much food and of course the meat was delicious, it melted in your mouth.

We left the place around half past three, with time to digest the meal while we waited for the appointed hour to enter the monastery. We then headed towards the church of San Sebastian and waited with other tourists who were already standing next to the visitors' entrance.

Thanks to the guide we learned the curious history of Saint Dominic, when he appeared in the region in the 11th century. At that time the monastery, then called San Sebastian, was in a deplorable state. Saint Dominic managed to build one of the most impressive Romanesque churches of his time, although unfortunately this construction had been destroyed by several fires.

I was amazed to see the chapiters, each one with its peculiarities and an incredible level of detail considering the time they were sculpted in. Even though practically none of the original colors, which had embellished the stones, remained.

We tourists escaped the control of the guide, who was not very strict when it came to allowing us to take pictures of the cloister and the famous Silos cypress that dominated the center of that enclave. We then toured other rooms of the monastery, such as the curious apothecary or the old refectory, where we came across an exhibition of modern art that contrasted with the millenary environment. Although in the end we did not stay to listen to the monks singing Gregorian chant, something that did not appeal much to either of us.

Ana wanted to know if I had liked the visit.

"I loved it!" I replied. And it was true, as a student and art lover I had been impressed with the serene beauty of the cloister of Silos, its chapiters and sculptures, besides soaking in the essence of a building with so many centuries of history.

"It's still early and it is not too hot today. If you feel like it we can take the hiking trail that connects the back of the monastery with the area of La Yecla. You'll love the gorge and it is a very nice walk."

I said I was fine with that.

In the end, Ana's cousin had not joined us during the day either, and we had no news from Julián, so we headed alone to the Yecla gorge along a picturesque path that we covered in a few minutes.

It was surprising to see the contrast in the landscape when I glimpsed the limestone mass that greeted us at a bend in the road. The road went inside the rock wall through a curious tunnel, and access to the famous gorge, drilled into the rock for thousands of years by the action of a humble stream, was through steps that took you into the depths of the geological formation.

The walk inside the gorge was not very long, a few hundred meters, but it was impressive to follow the walkways between the narrowness of the rock walls, listening to the sound of water and sheltered by a refreshing shade even in summer.

We then reached the halfway point, where the vaulted rock ceiling opened up. At that moment you were surprised to discover how the underground way, opened to the outside as a beautiful gallery from which to look on the magnificence of the gorge. It was the right moment to immortalize it with a series of selfies and panoramic photos of the place that I wanted as souvenirs.

After a while Ana called her cousin on the phone and they chatted for a few minutes. After the events of the previous night and without a good nap to recover after eating, the day was dragging on. I did not complain when I found out that Raquel would come to pick us up, so we stayed near the tunnel dug in the rock, next to the limestone mass where dozens of pairs of birds of prey were nesting.

Ana was telling me something about the vultures but I was not paying much attention to her, I had just discovered a message from Alberto, sent almost two hours earlier. I had left my phone silent during the visit to the monastery and then failed to turn the sound back up. All day looking at the damn phone and I forget to do so just when I get his message, I hoped it was nothing urgent.

It had nothing to do with our amorous encounter, nor was it related to the nighttime find. It did not even refer to the Guardia Civil following our trail, but I gasped and stopped dead in my tracks when I read the content of the message. Especially, when I took a closer look at the attachment.

"Are you listening to me, Sandra? You look as if you've seen a ghost", as my grandmother used to say.

"No, yes, sorry...."

I pretended as best I could and was spared from more questioning by Raquel arriving to the rescue. Ana got into the front of the vehicle, and I sat in the back so I could calmly read the information Alberto had sent me again. María Mediavilla's story still had many shades to discover and I was not going to forget about it, no matter how much it cost us.

I'll tell you more about it later. My friend has managed to recover some blog entries, which apparently had been deleted but remained on the servers of the owner company.

I eagerly read his next message:

I didn't think it was appropriate to send it to you by phone, so I've sent it to your personal email account. We'll talk about it later. XOXO.

I hurriedly accessed my private email and with my nervousness I almost dropped my phone.

The two cousins were still blabbing away and did not notice, as I was sitting in the back of the car.

I finally got to the email sent by Alberto, in which he simply told me to read the attached document carefully and that we would talk about it later. I figured that Alberto or his hacker friend had pasted the information extracted from the blog in a Word file, so I started to read the text, apparently a kind of diary. María's words, coming to me in such a strange way, gave me goose bumps as I discovered what that girl had had to suffer in her youth.

At that moment I was unaware of the true motives, but everything that had happened up to that moment forced me to continue with the madness which had encompassed us. I felt I owed it to that girl and her family, so I set out to find out the true story of María Mediavilla.

THE CORRIDOR OF TERROR

Madrid, November 1967

MARÍA

Even today, almost forty years later, a shudder vibrates through my whole body as I recall what happened within those gloomy walls. I thought that, once I had overcome the excruciating pain of my loss, I could try to get back on my feet and move on with my life, but in that prison of the devil it was impossible.

Our jailers, the ineffable little nuns of the Evangelical Crusades congregation, took care of it with all their Christian ardor. I had known religious fervor at home, with my mother, but what I experienced there surpassed all fantasies. We were continuously crushed, from morning to night, and if more girls did not die there, it was only due to our strength and youth, or so I wanted to believe after the years when I looked back and remembered what had happened in Peñagrande.

I must admit that there was a time when I almost threw in the towel and stopped fighting. After what I had suffered months before in my body, besides the continuous humiliations imposed by the nuns, I thought I would never get out of there alive. The system had absorbed me and no one would care about me, I was just another number in that official concentration camp that would last until well into democracy. I thought about suicide, I will not deny it.

A mortal sin that would perhaps save me from the pain that lacerated me inside. Something my saintly mother would never have accepted, although at that point I did not care what Doña Pura thought about anything. For all I cared, she could be rotting in hell. She was responsible for my suffering and I would never forgive her for it.

Many years have passed and all this time does not let me clearly discern what was going through my head at that time. I was a sixteen-year-old girl who had been taken away from her world, locked up in a prison of hatred where you were brainwashed twenty-four/seven. And from what I could gather from talking to other inmates locked up there, it was all because my family had disowned me, had forgotten about my existence and had given my parental rights to the so-called Patronato de Protección de la Mujer (Women's Protection Board).

What a euphemism! They did not protect anyone! We only served to feed a well-oiled machine that brought enormous benefits to many people for decades. I found that out much later, I do not want to get ahead of events, but inside the organization supposedly led by Carmen Polo de Franco, aberrations and crimes against humanity were happening and enriching many of the regime's leaders.

I am beating about the bush- you will have to forgive me. Painful memories crowd my mind and I can still feel the unhealthy cold of that dreary building on my skin, a place that should be considered the particular museum of the horrors of our country, a national shame that Spanish society has silenced for too long. In fact, unconsciously, I have just realized that I have been hugging myself as I relived those days, just like when I wanted to warm myself in that filthy hole and isolate myself from the nauseating smell of fear that emanated from all the inmates.

The foolishness of taking my life passed quickly. Especially when I saw poor Antonia throw herself down the stairwell with my own eyes. They said she had gone crazy and I was not surprised, especially after what had happened to her. The image of her disjointed body, her limbs broken after the deadly blow, turned me inside out and I knew I did not want that for myself.

At that moment I had thrown up what little I had in my stomach - being starved to death was another thing we had to thank the nuns for. They kept us thin as reeds as another cruel form of punishment - if the crust of bread of that morning could be considered food. But something clicked in my head and I vowed that I would get out of there alive and take revenge on all those who had taken away my youth.

I had a goal and I had to fight for it. There were several ways to get out of there, but none of them convinced me. You could end up much worse, as a prostitute or even as a slave for some sadist sympathetic to the regime. I had heard of cases of girls who were taken away from there and returned to the fold weeks later, turned into human wrecks. We found out later that some of them had died or had been taken away, but others, we never knew what had become of them.

I had to remain alert and wait for the right moment, although later it would depend a lot on luck. I did not want to stay in that hellhole a minute longer than necessary, but I could not rush it either. The problem was that I have never been very lucky and time would prove me right weeks later. At the time I was completely unaware of it, like so many other things - I was a country girl, ignorant and uneducated who had been taken out of her natural habitat to be locked up alive- but many years later I saw myself reflected when I read an immortal work that would become my bedside book.

I had no cellmate or Abbé Faria to impersonate, but what I was sure of was that I was burning inside with the same fury that I later discovered had consumed Edmundo Dantés, just before embarking on the revenge he plotted against his enemies.

Would I end my days as the protagonist of *The Count of Monte Cristo*? For the moment I did not know. Captivity had changed me, and I had lost all traces of innocence along the way. And I only wished I could fulfill my promise before I died, so that the culprits would pay for the infamy committed against me when I was just an innocent child from a small village in Burgos.

But before that I still have a lot to tell you. Please be patient, I beg you.

THE DISCOVERY

Carazo (Burgos), July 23, 2016

Reading that fragment of what seemed to be María's diary had completely thrown me. What did she mean when she said she had been locked up in a prison of the Regime? We would have to find out more. Just before entering Carazo, I sent a message to Alberto, I could not stay still after discovering these revelations.

I'm in shock, Alberto, we need to talk. Sorry, I didn't see your messages until now, can I call you?

I checked that the message had reached him, but Alberto had not yet read it. It was about seven o'clock in the evening, so I imagined that they were already in Salas, in the middle of the lectures that were taking place in the town's Casino. A bad time to try to talk to him.

Fortunately, Alberto must have kept an eye on the phone, or it might have vibrated in his pocket and he had noticed it. He answered a few moments later:

I'm in the middle of a conference, I can't talk right now. Yes, what my friend has discovered is very heavy stuff. I'll call you back in a little while, in the break between speeches.

I could not understand how Alberto could remain so calm after reading that little diary fragment. What else would María tell in the blog? It seemed mind-boggling to me that someone had written those things in a kind of online diary and that no one had done anything about the Mediavilla's daughter's complaint.

Alberto had mentioned that it was a secret blog, or that it might only be available on the Net for certain people. I could not know at that moment whether María had chosen to write it that way because she felt more comfortable than simply writing it on paper or if it was for another reason. I was unaware of the rest of the entries in her blog and of whether her complaint went further, whether it detailed the names of those who had caused her misfortune. Leaving aside the irrefutable fact that she had been locked up in some institution ruled by nuns of the Evangelical Crusades when she was only sixteen years old, and it had happened shortly after the picture Menchu had shown me, had been taken - the real reason why I had become involved in that story that was taking on increasingly dark overtones.

As soon as I arrived, I greeted Menchu and then went up to my room to rest, with the excuse that it had been a long day preceded by a night of revelry. I did not want to sleep, that went without saying, and even less so when I felt my mind boiling. Everything that had happened during those days kept repeating itself over and over again in my head, which led to that prison described by María without knowing what to expect.

My body was still reacting in a very strange way to the events that had occurred since I had first set foot in the Arlanza Valley, and the connection I felt with María had been sharpened as I read her own words. It was something intimate, a personal diary that had come to me in the most bizarre way possible, a fragment of the past that had moved me to such emotion. María's tattered soul as she recounted her ordeal had traveled through time and space thanks to the Internet, and although she may not have wanted anyone to read those words for various reasons, our meddling had worked the miracle. Or rather Alberto's hacker friend had.

What was this Patronato directed by Carmen Polo? I had never heard of it in my life and I was not surprised. In my house in spite of my grandparents' rather conservative tendency, I would never have thought they were very much in favor of Franco, I had not heard much about the time of General Franco's regime. And at school or high school they did not tell us much about what happened in Spain during almost forty years. In fact, we studied prehistory, the Middle Ages, the Catholic Monarchs and so on, but at most we got as far as Sagasta and Cánovas, the twentieth century was barely touched; something that I later found out was not something exclusive to the LOGSE (Organic Law of the General System of Education Ordinance), but that entire generations of young Spaniards had not even studied that period of history in their classes. And no one gave a convincing explanation as to the real reasons for such an omission.

I lay down on my bed and searched through the documents downloaded from my phone to read the text written by María again. According to the headline of the post extracted from her mysterious blog, María had written it not that long ago, in 2006. It recounted the events that had taken place in 1966 and I expected her to continue telling what happened to her later, especially the reasons for being locked up in that place, so we were in the hands of Alberto's computer geek friend if we wanted to continue with the story.

I concentrated on the new reading and could almost taste the feelings that María poured out onto the page, or rather the computer screen on which she wrote that plea against infamy: anger, pain, suffering, fear, despair and finally, revenge. I sensed that this text was only the tip of the iceberg, that our protagonist had suffered unspeakably over a long period of time and that only forty years later she could bring it out of her heart and show it to the world, or at least leave it in writing within reach of whoever she chose.

What was clear to us was that the blog was no longer online, so its owner had deleted it completely. We were only ten years apart from the time she wrote it, almost fifty years since she had been locked up in that reformatory institution or jail as she described it. Would María still be alive? Anything might have happened to her since 2006, but in my inner self I harbored the hope of being able to meet her sometime so that she could tell me first-hand what had led her to the extreme situation she described in such a heartbreaking way.

I wanted to make time while I waited for Alberto's call so I opened the browser on my phone to look for information about the religious order that María had mentioned, the so-called Patronato headed by Carmen Polo. I realized at once something that I had completely forgotten: there was no phone coverage there.

In desperation, I tried to find a signal by moving the phone about until I remembered what María and her family had told me. I jumped out of bed as soon as it dawned on me: if I could not look for information on the Internet and I had no coverage of any kind, I would not be able to receive Alberto's call either.

Perhaps he had not thought of that little detail when he wrote me the message either; being interconnected at all times was something that people of my generation took for granted. We carry our cell phones everywhere, it is almost an appendage of our body, and the most hooked on to social media would certainly have a hard time in a town like Carazo.

I did not even know if Alberto had also written down the landline number of the house in his address book, but I was not about to discuss matters with him from the living room, in front of Menchu and the whole family. No, I had to find a quick solution before he called me. It was after seven-thirty in the evening and, if the next conference started at eight o'clock, Alberto could call me at any time.

For a moment I allowed myself to reproach Alberto for remaining in the auditorium of the Salas de los Infantes Casino, attending symposium conferences, instead of being with me. Yes, I knew that he had been planning that weekend for months and that he had been looking forward to the film event, but everything that had happened to us during the last few days seemed a lot more important to me.

Yet I did not want to be selfish: the poor guy was doing enough to help me with my paranoia about María. And I did not know why, ultimately, I had been right, and there was a mystery in the disappearance of the girl in 1966. I wanted to find out what had really happened to her, but I understood that we were going to run into all sorts of obstacles along the way, apart from the considerable number of years that had passed since then.

Not to mention the other adventure which we had found ourselves immersed in. Since the day had been lively in Silos and, besides, I now had something else to think about after reading the diary, I had forced my mind not to go back to the fateful moment when we had discovered the corpse among the ruins. I had not mentioned anything to Ana or her family, and no news about it had reached my ears.

I am a great reader, and I love mystery novels and my conspiratorial paranoia made me think that, perhaps, the authorities had lifted the body during the early hours of the morning with all the secrecy in the world. Yes, I imagined that they were investigating what had happened, and even that reinforcements from Burgos or Madrid would be coming to help in the investigation, but everything was being carried out with the utmost discretion so as not to hinder the investigation.

The Arlanza region was enjoying a weekend full of activities and all the mayors of the region were involved in making the 50th anniversary of the filming of *The Good, the Bad and the Ugly a* success. I knew that there were authorities attending the events that weekend, so I guessed that bad publicity for the region would spoil the congress and drive potential tourism away from the area. And finding the body of a murdered man in one of the most important sites in the region, used in 1966 as a set for several scenes in the film, would certainly not be good publicity for attracting visitors to the region.

I did not want to be distracted by these thoughts, so I hurried down the stairs of the house. Time was running out and I did not know whether Alberto might be dialing my number to contact me at that moment.

I met Ana as soon as I came down and asked her point-blank:

"Is there no cell phone coverage in the whole town?"

"Oh, yes, at the end of the village on the way out to Salas. But you can use the landline if you need to call someone."

I did not want to give her too many explanations, so I told her a half-truth, "Well, it's just that Alberto sent me a message earlier because he wanted to talk to me, said he was going to call me between speeches, before eight o'clock."

"Oh, the lovebirds, how cute!"

Ana gave me instructions on how to get to the spot where there was coverage. I thanked her and frantically ran out, while my friend watched me with a smile on her face. I did not care if she thought it was a call between two lovers, or any other such nonsense. Yes, there was something special between Alberto and me. But the call was of a different nature and I was not yet ready to reveal that to my friend or anyone in her family.

I walked briskly down the road ahead, glancing every two seconds to see if my phone picked up anything, even if it was only one bar of signal. I followed Ana's directions and accelerated my pace, almost to the point of running, when I realized the time. It was already a quarter to eight and I still had no news of Alberto.

I had to ask a lady for my destination and the nice woman looked at me like I was crazy when she saw me desperate to reach a cell phone coverage area. She pointed me to the exact place where young people used to talk on the phone and that is where I headed in the hope of arriving on time. I did not want to miss Alberto's call and have him jump back into the next conference. I thought I had understood that he would be going to a dinner with the symposium participants afterwards, and I did not think I would be able to wait until the next day without talking to him. I had to hurry.

I finally reached the place and was a little disappointed as there was a man there talking on his phone. It must have been the place Ana had told me about; everyone was going there to look for coverage. I needed privacy, but I could not be choosy. I would talk in code or in a low voice if necessary.

I was about to send a message to Alberto when my phone suddenly rang in my hand. I was a little startled, despite keeping an eye on the device. I answered quickly when I saw his name on the screen.

Alberto was upset that I had not answered his calls. I apologized for not being able to talk to him sooner. The damn coverage, I told him.

"Well, I don't know what to say about María's blog, it all seems a bit heavy to me, doesn't it?"

"Yes, we'll talk about it tomorrow calmly, I have to go to the next conference right away, it's very interesting."

Really? I didn't understand how Alberto could be thinking about those lectures with everything that was going on, but I could not hold it against him.

"What do you think she means by the regime's prison, nuns and all?" I asked Alberto despite his haste.

"It's not the time to talk about it over the phone, but I have my own theories. I've been poking around the

Internet for a while, although I'll need some help from my friend to get to the heart of the matter."

"And can't your hacker friend get more diary fragments?"

"Yes, he's working on it. I know he is busy with other things, but he has promised to give me more information over the weekend. As soon as I have it, I'll send it to you, don't worry."

I had a hard time controlling my impatience. Alberto told me he was planning to stay in Salas having dinner with the symposium people. Ana and I had planned to have a bite to eat with some friends from town. But what worried me most at that moment was the matter of the corpse we had found.

"Listen, have you heard anything about the other thing?" I asked quietly, as if I afraid someone might hear me.

"No, not really, and I was surprised. I didn't hear anything at lunch and I didn't hear anything afterwards either. I will inquire tonight to see if anyone knows anything. I find it a little strange that nobody has said anything about...."

"Well, we'd better not talk about it over the phone, you know. I'll see you tomorrow then. How do we organize the excursion?"

Alberto had a full agenda: he wanted to attend the talk with the film's extras and a lecture on Morricone's music. But he intended to get away at lunchtime.

"Shall I come for you in Carazo?"

"Yes, come as soon as you can, I'll wait for you here. I don't know if Ana and the others will want to join us, but I promised to go to the movie screening and I'll be there."

"I'm fine with that. Although it seems to me that your head is going to be somewhere else. And I'm sure we'll find even more surprises..."

We said goodbye. Neither of us wanted to mention the subject of the anonymous letters or remember that there was someone watching Alberto's every move, and perhaps mine as well. Was it the murderer? Or perhaps a Good Samaritan who wanted to help us? The uncertainty was killing me inside, but at that moment we could do nothing but wait and see how events would unfold.

I stood for a moment staring at the phone in my hand, even though the call had already ended. The other person had left without my noticing, so I was left there alone for a few moments, trying to imagine what might happen. I did not even give any thought to the unloving way Alberto had said goodbye to me. I would have time later to worry about those things. Now I had something much more important to think about.

I was still unaware of what fate had prepared for us as the culmination of a very special weekend.

HUMILIATION

Contreras (Burgos), August 1966

Juanito seized the chance to take María away from the group and go to a place he already had his eye on. They went far away from that day's scene and headed up the hill, where the boy knew they had shot on other days that summer.

They spent the afternoon touring other parts of the valley and Juanito showed his friend the places where he had contributed to a great production which all the inhabitants of the region would be very proud of. María listened with rapt attention as the boy told his anecdotes, whether he was shooting or working in the sun on the sets where the most important scenes of the film would later be shot.

"Where are you taking me?" asked the girl in a mischievous voice.

"You'll see, it's a surprise," Juanito answered mysteriously.

The boy smiled, pulled María up the hill and walked further and further away from the main movie set. María was unaware that this was what Juan ultimately intended, to get as far away as possible from the area where they were working that day so that no one would disturb them.

They finally reached their destination. On the hill top they came across a crane and other machinery used in some phase of the shooting or other. And they also found a small shed, a ramshackle construction erected in the area to store material for the movie.

The scorching sun of that day was elusive in the mid-afternoon, and played among clouds too dark to cover the valley in silence. Perhaps they foreshadowed a storm, María thought, something normal in the middle of August after several days with temperatures that hovered around forty degrees Celsius.

However, the young man from Contreras had other thoughts when he noticed the cloudy sky. Perhaps this lack of light would allow them to be more intimate in what he hoped would be a great moment, the two of them together inside the room. Although he was not all sure, he hoped that María would accompany him inside. And then, once they got down to business, maybe the big moment would finally arrive.

"Come, I want to show you something," said Juanito, putting on airs.

"Where are you going, you fool?"

María followed the boy's lead and accompanied him into the building. The door was unlocked and they went in laughing.

"What are you doing? We're going to get caught."

"Shhh! Be quiet, no one needs to know."

Inside, it was quite dark, since the only light filtered through a small window and the growing gloom of that afternoon was not enough. Juanito pretended to be important in front of the girl and showed her some of the things stored there, materials that the movie people used in the scenes of the film.

"Look, María! Here are some of the actors' costumes."

The girl enthusiastically joined Juanito and they rummaged through the props, playing like children. Then the boy chose some clothes from the wardrobe, stored in covers, and placed them on the floor as a makeshift mattress in a clear area he found.

"If you would be so kind as to accompany me, Miss...."

"You're such a dope!"

Juanito invited her to lie down on the clothes and María did not think twice when she saw that her companion was already waiting for her. The girl laid her head on his torso and stayed there, looking at the ceiling, while Juanito gently caressed her head.

"We're going to get caught here and we'll be in deep trouble, we should go."

"Don't worry, no one will come to bother us. The team is much further down in the valley, you've already seen them."

"But..."

"Don't worry, nothing will happen."

Juanito kissed the girl gently, and pushed all her hesitancy away. Perhaps being there without permission, the scent of the forbidden was too attractive for both of them. The magic of the moment made them abandon themselves and not think about the possible consequences. They gave themselves to each other as if they were the only people on the face of the earth.

The young man gazed at María raptly, she looked more beautiful than ever in the dim light that filtered into that ramshackle room. It may not have been the royal suite of a grand hotel, but for them it was enough. The freckles on the girl's face, which Juanito had always found attractive, stood out against the pallor of a skin flushed with excitement. And her pupils, bright and lustful, ended up making him lose his mind in an instant.

They kissed passionately, while his hands got lost in the folds of her skimpy clothes. Juanito awkwardly unbuttoned the buttons of the girl's blouse, and María, solicitous, had to help him when she saw her companion's nerves. The smoothness of her breasts captivated him, and the young man began to explore those incipient hills that demanded his interest.

The moan of pleasure that María let out when she felt his lips on her nipples emboldened the teenager, who sensed that this afternoon could be epic. Juanito sat up for a moment to delight himself in the girl's pleasure and thought he would never forget that moment. Something that was also going through María's mind, although neither of them knew then that it would be for a very different reason.

A dull thud startled the young couple, who stopped their fiery thrusts for a moment.

"What was that?" asked María, frightened.

"I don't know, it must have been the wind."

"It didn't sound like the wind, Juanito. Go on, go and see."

The boy grumbled, as he did not want to lose the progress he had made. They could be cut off and that was out of the question. The interruption seemed to have affected María more, so in the end he had to agree even though he knew it was silly.

"Okay, I'll check."

He did not have time to say anything else, when they heard a bigger bang. The sound came from the door itself, which had apparently been kicked open. On the threshold, a man appeared with a sinister smile that was frightening under that prism of insufficient light.

"Well, well, what do we have here?"

María unconsciously put her hands to her chest and closed her blouse so as not to show her nudity to strangers. Only then did she realize that behind the intruder, leaning against the lintel of the door, there were two other men who were not amused either.

A mighty clap of thunder then rumbled from within the walls of the barracks, heralding the storm that seemed to want to unleash its full fury on the valley. Although the real danger facing the two kids had nothing to do with the forces of nature.

"So, making out in a place that doesn't belong to you, are you? That deserves a proper punishment."

"Excuse me, but..."

Juanito tried to apologize to the strangers as he got up from the improvised bed, but a strong slap knocked him down again and prevented him from speaking. The young boy was startled and began to grumble under his breath as he realized who his aggressors really were, while María looked on in distress at the unexpected visitors.

"*Macaroni*, come here. Get this little boy out of my sight."

"No, I..."

The second man bowed his head and obeyed the leader of the group. He tried to lift Juanito and carry him away, but the boy resisted. The Italian gave him a punch in the stomach that made him double down, eliminating all traces of resistance. It was then that María started to scream:

"Please help!"

The girl had also become aware of the danger they were in. That group was the one they had crossed paths with days before, when Juanito had thrown stones at them in response to their rude comments. And María knew they were going to pay for it in spades.

The ringleader, a young man in his twenties, grabbed the girl by the hair and slapped her, but this did not shut her up. On the contrary, María rolled over, tried to bite her assailant and earned another blow to the ribs that left her gasping for air.

"Help me, Mario. Find something to gag this cat with and come here to restrain her."

Juanito remained in a corner, anguished before the fierce gaze of his nemesis. The Italian was not much older than him, but he was burly and determined. Determination Juanito had lost after receiving the blow in the pit of his stomach. The boy from Contreras could sense what was going to happen next, but he could do nothing to prevent it.

"You're not acting all that macho in front of your little slut anymore, huh?" The leader said as he put his hand to his forehead, where he had got stitches for the cut Juanito had given him.

"No, I..."

"Don't whine like a little girl now. I told you I'd get my payback, didn't I? I always keep my promises."

"Please, you can't..."

"Shut the fuck up! Watch and learn, this is how you treat a little whore like this."

Remorse took its toll on Juanito, who regretted having behaved that way a few days before. He should have let it go, but no, he had had to act cocky in front of María to get her attention. Yes, he had hit the ringleader with the rock and got away with it, but now they would make them both pay. He could never have imagined that those idiots would destroy their lives like that and he was the only one to blame.

The boy looked at the leader of the group again. He was a scowling guy, with a close beard and the mannerisms of a gentleman. It was impossible not to notice him because he had a little squint in his left eye, so Juanito was not surprised by the nickname by which one of his henchmen called him.

"Fuck, Squint, that's enough. Let's get out of here, the kids have learned their lesson."

The thug did not flinch and looked at his friend with blood in his eye. The other one bowed his head and nodded, not wanting to get in his way or make him angry. He knew his mood swings and his bad temper, so he sucked it up and obeyed his orders.

"I won't tell you again. Come here and hold this whore down, she wriggles a lot and I don't want to hurt her too much."

Oh my God, Juanito thought. They were not going to get out of there alive. Suddenly he realized who the cross-eyed man was: he was a neighbor of Hortigüela, the son of one of the landowners of the town. A guy with pretensions who thought he was above good and evil, a known thug in the region with whom they had had the misfortune to cross paths at the worst possible moment.

This guy called Mario gagged the girl and held her arms from behind to allow his boss to stand in front of her. The squint-eyed man put his tongue between his teeth and, after tearing off the girl's few remaining clothes, set about pulling down his pants, while he gazed at María with a wolfish grin.

"You, kid, look here or I'll give you a good beating later. I don't want you to miss the show. Let's see if you're so smart next time."

Juanito had cowered in a corner, hiding his head between his legs at the imminent start of something he was not prepared for. He was a coward for not confronting them, even if he would lose. But María was his responsibility and he could not take care of her, or save her from those vermin. He had to pull himself together and the Italian forced him in a bad way to face the spectacle. Juanito did not resist, upon pain of receiving a greater punishment, while remorse took over his mind.

Meanwhile, María could not believe what was happening. Minutes before she had been enjoying the afternoon with her friend and now, she was suffering in silence, suffocated by the gag that covered her mouth and, above all, by the physical and mental violence to which those men were subjecting them.

The young woman assumed what was about to happen and stopped kicking. She thought that, if she resisted, maybe that animal would hit her viciously and it would be much worse. Her nerve endings were crackling at top speed and her body demanded a fight, but what little sanity she had left in her mind in the face of such an outrage forced her to try to calm down. Maybe, after all, she could get out of there alive if she did not make too much trouble.

The aggressor positioned himself on top of her, with his member at half-mast, and tried to hold her legs while he gained access inside her. María revolted, but did not fight with all her strength. She waited for the unfortunate instant when she would lose her honor forever.

The excruciating pain she felt in her loins as she was penetrated by the rapist was nothing compared to the fear and shame that gripped her muscles. María felt as if she was escaping from reality, as if her body was escaping from there and floating away so as not to be vilified by that apprentice of Satan. She closed her eyes and prayed that everything would end soon, but her prayers did not get the expected result.

The squint-eyed man came inside her with a ridiculous stertor, while he let out an unmanly moan after a few thrusts. Perhaps the suffering was already over, but María did not want to get her hopes up. Even less so when she saw that the infamous man was leaving his place to the other man, who was now looking at her with lust in his eyes.

The young woman did not notice what was happening a few meters away, in the corner where Juanito was lying, forced to look in her direction by the Italian. The Contreras boy could not stand the situation and bile ran up his throat, forcing him to vomit what was in his stomach. María had given up all hope that the boy could help her. She only hoped that everything would be over quickly so that she could pull herself together, if that was even possible after what had happened.

"I think this slut wants more, don't you? Come on, Mario, it's your turn now."

The squint-eyed man laughed to himself, although no one accompanied him in his bravado. The humiliation María felt was growing by the minute and she was unable to bear it, so she decided to fight even if it cost her life.

However, a lapidary phrase, pronounced just a few centimeters from her ear, made her reflect on her bitter situation.

"If you move any more, I'll cut you, bitch. And then I'll slit your little friend's throat before I go to your house and kill your whole family. Is that clear to you?"

María nodded slightly when she felt the edge of a razor on her neck. She knew that this was the end and entrusted herself to the Virgin, the only one who could save her from absolute madness. She tried to abstract herself from the situation and her mind flew to other places in a few atrocious, eternal minutes, in which her body was a broken toy in the hands of those fiends.

At last they left her alone, throwing her like a rag on top of the clothes the kids had placed as a mattress. The cross-eyed man forced her to look at him, and she saw in his satisfied smile that he did not regret his actions. She did not perceive the same in his friend's attitude, nor in the other guy, the Italian, who also let Juanito go as they left the room and left them to their fate.

"Remember I know where you live, redhead. If you or your little friend ever say anything about what happened here, either to the police or to a family member, I swear to God, I'll track you down and gut you like a pig. Do you understand me?"

Juanito nodded clumsily and María, with her head held high after all, challenged him with her eyes before shrinking back. The cross-eyed man spat next to her to humiliate her further, but finally left the room with his friends, leaving behind him a trail of shame and infamy that no one could remedy.

María pulled herself together as best she could and Juanito came to her aid, although the girl slapped him away. She did not want him to look at her that way, she could not bear to see the terror and pity in the eyes of the person she had trusted the most until then. The girl knew it was not Juanito's fault, but she was not prepared to face him, nor did she want to reproach him for not having risked his life to save her. Yes, he had answered back at them that day and thrown stones at them, even cut one badly, but that did not give those bastards reasons to outrage her in such a way. The rapists should be the only ones guilty of such an affront, they were criminals and they would have to pay for it.

Minutes later they left the room in silence, without looking back. Juanito was not able to look her in the face and she did not want to walk beside him, but she could not afford to walk alone from there to Contreras. It was already late and it was a long way home. She did her best and agreed to walk with him while the images of the barbarity repeated over and over again in her head.

THE TRUE REALITY

Salas de los Infantes (Burgos), July 24, 2016

Saturday night into Sunday we did not sleep much either, even though we had gone to bed relatively early. I accompanied Ana and Raquel to another house in Carazo, where some acquaintances of theirs had prepared a small celebration for the birthday of one of the girls. Some snacks and a few drinks to entertain the honoree, but the party did not go overboard.

What was really revved up was my head, which was still going over everything that had happened to us since we set foot in the lands of El Cid. The trigger had been the discovery of the photo of María Mediavilla and her friends, although there were many other details to focus as of that very moment: the strange accident that Alberto and Julián had encountered, the anonymous letters sent to Alberto himself and, of course, the discovery of the corpse in the monastery of San Pedro de Arlanza.

Although I could not forget the visit to the old people's home in Burgos to meet Doña Pura, her strange behavior in my presence and, of course, the mysterious blog in which María had recounted her memories forty years later.

A kind of diary that we would only finish unraveling if Adolfo, Alberto's hacker friend, continued to lend us a hand.

And if that was not enough turmoil in my head, I also had to reflect on what had happened between Alberto and myself. I had too many things to think about and I did not know if, perhaps by focusing on other issues, I was putting my relationship with Alberto in last place. First, we had to move forward with everything we had going on and then I myself would have to reflect on how I felt about my ‘partner in crime’.

Tired of tossing and turning in bed, and not exactly from the summer heat of a tropical night in Burgos, I assumed that I could not stay idle until Sunday afternoon. Between Carazo's bad coverage, the uneasiness I felt about the whole situation and my own fears and insecurities, I knew I had to do my part to make progress in our investigations.

For the time being, I thought, I would call my grandmother early in the morning. I had the perfect excuse, since we had not spoken for several days and, while I was at it, I intended to ask her if she knew anything about some possible relatives we might have in Burgos. I would have to be subtle and attack that flank delicately.

After breakfast, as soon as Ana got up, I was going to convince her to take us to Salas. I had thought of the excuse of visiting the Dinosaur Museum and waiting for Alberto until he came out of the lectures. But, of course, I did not want to have Ana around when I talked to him, if I could get away. I would have to improvise something or lie to her face directly.

I had it! Of course, Ana need not be suspicious if she thought the two lovebirds wanted to eat alone, since in the afternoon the whole group would get together to go to the excursion to Sad Hill Cemetery. I would tell her a few white lies: that I missed him and that we needed to talk about things, nothing too complicated.

On the other hand, I could also mention to my friend another little detail that was on my mind. On Monday morning Alberto would return to Madrid, or at least that was the idea he had, to return to the capital once the congress on the film was over. And, of course, if I planned to stay in the region at least until mid-August, it was going to be very difficult for me to continue my research on my own. And even less so without a driver to take me everywhere. The following year I would definitely sign up for driving lessons, I was determined.

Depending on what I could get out of my grandmother, maybe I could also return to Madrid for a few days. I would accompany Alberto in his car, although I guessed that we would not be alone because Julián was also going back to the capital that same Monday. Unless Ana's little brother wanted to continue fooling around with the girl from Covarrubias for a few more days and so move into the Carazo house from then on.

Ana was going to be angry with me, but I thought I would assure her that I would come back after a few days and we would spend the rest of the summer together, and I would manage to return to the region on my own. And maybe that way, free from some ties and without Menchu's omnipresent presence around me, I could think more clearly.

Yes, I was determined to stay away from the main scenario where all the remarkable events had taken place, but that gave us certain advantages. In the first place, we were distancing ourselves from the mysterious character who had contacted Alberto. Not to mention the murderer, who I guessed would still be in the area. And, of course, we would also distance ourselves from the Guardia Civil, in case they found out that we had been the ones to tip them off about the dead man.

And, since I would be in Madrid, I could better investigate the fate of poor María Mediavilla. In her own blog she narrated her confinement in a kind of women's prison in my city, so I thought that maybe I could find some clue as to her whereabouts. Or at least join the different threads of the skein and solve the mysteries remaining in her story, a story that had accompanied me in sunshine and shadow during the last days.

If that prison was in Madrid, there must be records of some kind that would indicate the fate of María Mediavilla. It was a bad time of year, the middle of August, to begin a task that might involve dealing with different public administrations or organizations that would be either closed or with few people working because it was the middle of summer. But I was not going to back out, and I was counting on convincing Alberto to go ahead with the task. And if his computer friend gave us a hand, or at least showed us the best course of action, we might achieve our goal in a short time.

After a few hours of sleep, I woke up more tired than when I had gone to bed. A restorative shower and a strong coffee were the best medicine for the soul after a sleepless night. The house was quiet when I went down to the kitchen, with all the members of the family still asleep. I then prepared to have breakfast and I must have made more noise than I thought, because Ana appeared a few minutes later with a sleepy look on her face.

"What are you doing up at this hour?" My friend asked yawning.

"I couldn't sleep and thought I'd get up early, the night is very long without sleep."

"Sorry. Well, with your permission, I'm going back to my room for a while. Anyway, we don't have much to do."

"I wanted to talk to you about that... It occurred to me that we could go to Salas later, without rushing. I'd like to visit the Dinosaur Museum and walk around there."

"Yeah, sure, while we wait for 'your husband'," she answered with a wink. "Well, we'd better talk about it later. I don't think Raquel knows it and I was at the inauguration several years ago, maybe it's not such a bad idea. But first things first..."

Ana said goodbye with a yawn, but before she left, I asked her for a favor.

"I'd like to call my grandmother for a moment to reassure her, you know. And since I don't have reception, I was wondering if I could use the landline for that."

"Of course, no problem. Permission granted."

Ana made a very theatrical gesture and went upstairs, more concerned about getting into bed than attending to my requests. I did not feel like asking my grandmother about certain things from that little living room, in full earshot of everyone, but they all seemed to be asleep at that hour and, on the other hand, I knew that everyone in my house would be awake by now.

In the end I persuaded the girls and we headed to Salas in the middle of the morning. We arrived at about eleven thirty in the town, which was already very busy. Raquel parked on the outskirts and we walked to the center of town.

The conversation with my grandmother had not completely cleared my doubts. She was happy to hear from me and, of course, to learn that I might return to Madrid for a few days. She did not insist on knowing the reasons, and I was grateful for that. However, I noticed that she was more suspicious when I mentioned the subject that had been bothering me so much.

"And speaking of Ana's cousins..." I blurted out. "Her aunt asked me if I had any relatives in Burgos. I said no, not that I knew of. Right, *yaya*?"

"No, no, no," she answered after hesitating for a few seconds. "Not from my side and I don't think from your grandfather's either. Why are you asking?"

"I don't know, maybe it's silly. Menchu showed me a photograph she took with her friends in 1966 and there is a little girl who looks exactly like me; I was amazed to see her. And of course, I wondered if she might be related to us or something. It didn't ring a bell, but maybe there was some lost family branch out there that I had never heard of."

"Well, no, child, not really. We don't have much family, and certainly no one in Burgos. It's just a coincidence like any other. Well, and changing the subject..."

I could not see my grandmother's expression as she spoke to me, but the timbre of her voice seemed different. As if a slight tremor had taken over her vocal cords at the mention of the subject. Perhaps I had stirred something in her, maybe some painful fight with a family member that she did not want to remember and that was why she was being elusive. Because what was very clear to me after talking to her was that she had not told me the whole truth about this matter.

We arrived at the beautiful square of Salas de los Infantes and headed towards the Dinosaur Museum. The small entrance, located under the arcades, deceived the visitor. It looked like a very narrow place, but as we went inside we discovered that the place was bigger than it seemed from the outside, and it was full of interesting details.

I had just written to Alberto to let him know we were there:

I am in Salas with Ana and Raquel. We are going into the Dinosaur Museum now. Call me when you come out, please. XOXO;-)

* * *

Alberto was surprised to receive Sandra's message, just as he was about to finish the interesting talk in which some of the local people, who had been extras in the film or had worked during that summer helping in the construction of the set, had been talking to the audience.

What a surprise! Ok, perfect. I want to stay for the talk about Morricone's music that starts at 12, I'll call you later. I have a lot of things to tell you.

Sandra wanted to know more and asked him again, but Alberto assured her that it was not appropriate to discuss it by message, it would be better to talk about it face to face. The information he had obtained about María Mediavilla was very heavy and he wanted to share it with Sandra as soon as possible.

The symposium weekend was coming to an end and, although Alberto had had a great time, he had somewhat of a bitter aftertaste because he had not been able to fully enjoy all the activities. So many events in such a short time were not easy for anyone to assimilate, and least of all when you found yourself involved in some very unpleasant events.

Fortunately, the anonymous calls had stopped: he had not received any more mysterious messages. And the Guardia Civil had not called him about the night the body was found, so he assumed they had nothing on him. He might have to talk to the authorities later, but he did not think it was the right time yet.

In fact, during dinner on Saturday, the news had already spread that a body had appeared in San Pedro de Arlanza. Someone had overheard talk at the *Benemérita* barracks and the rumor had spread throughout the region. Alberto could see that no one was certain about what had happened.

"Apparently, he was a local vagabond, who must have fallen from the highest part of the monastery. I think he was found totally mangled, with his face disfigured by scavenging animals."

Alberto made a poker face at the comment of a young American who was participating in the symposium. He was partly right in what he was saying, but he had not died when he fell from a height, nor could they know for sure that he was a homeless person.

"A vagrant, you say? I heard that the man had been beaten to death, we don't know," said another of the participants, an Argentinian journalist who always asked very interesting questions at the symposium talks.

"I guess the authorities are investigating, and everything is being handled with the utmost secrecy," said one of the festival organizers. "And I'm personally grateful to them for that, because we are not going to launch speculations without rhyme or reason. It is not good for the region that these things happen and least of all in the middle of the congress."

Alberto nodded at the last intervention, although he had his own point of view. In fact, he had entertained the idea that the dead man was one of those registered for the 50th Anniversary, but there had not been anyone missing at any of the different talks and events that had been held since the corpse was discovered. He also did not have the complete list of participants nor did he know all the registrants, but it might be interesting to get it just in case, the Criminology student thought.

It was a cruel murder and Alberto had seen with his own eyes the disfigurement to which the poor man had been subjected. He did not know whether he had been beaten to death or had had his skin torn off, but he had been found in such a pitiful state that no one would recognize him. In addition, the vermin had also been vicious with his hands, so the authorities would have a hard time getting an identification through his fingerprints. A convoluted case of which he wanted no part, but in which he had been unwittingly involved.

Who had sent him the anonymous letters? What did he want from him? He did not know if it helped or compromised him by putting him in the killer's crosshairs. Alberto was more nervous than he cared to admit, and everything that had happened during those days was not helping him to cope better.

And, to top it off, he had a lot of other things to think about. His friend Adolfo had written him the night before with more information about the lost blog, and what he had discovered so far proved Sandra right: there was a lot to find out, the story of that poor girl was unbelievable.

Not to mention his own feelings for Sandra, a wonderful girl he had connected with in a special way. Although Alberto did not know if the noise around them had been the cause of their rapprochement, or it just had to happen and they had both chosen the worst time to hook up.

He had no regrets, that was for sure, but they were in danger, no matter how much they sugarcoated it. And knowing that something might happen to Sandra because of him, or simply for being by his side at the most inopportune moment, made him suffer in silence. Fortunately, the next day he would return to Madrid and get away from the Arlanza region.

Maybe he should persuade Sandra to go back with him to the big city. He knew that the girls intended to spend most of the summer in Carazo, but after what had happened in the region, he preferred his friend to get away from here as soon as possible. He did not know Sandra well enough either, but he sensed that she was a girl who was not so easily deterred and would want to get to the bottom of the matter. The problem was that they had too many issues to deal with all at once.

Like the María Mediavilla issue and all that it entailed. Good old Adolfo was apparently quite upset, the blog had been deleted and most of its content was corrupted or impossible to recover. Alberto had told him not to worry, that he was grateful for the effort made and all the information he could get, but the hacker was no slouch when it came to stubbornness and promised results.

And he had succeeded. Back in his room at the rural lodging he would sleep alone, because Julián was M.I.A. again with his new friend from Covarrubias, he turned on the laptop and found a little surprise. Adolfo had written to his account and supplied him with more excerpts from María's diary, along with a little research he had done by investigating specific data that appeared in the blog.

Along with the e-mail attachments, Adolfo had added a few words of his own. And Alberto had to agree with him on everything.

I don't know what this is all about, it seems very heavy to me. The story is creepy and I wanted to do some research. That information is in the last file, you'll be amazed.

He began to read the documents received and knew that it was going to make a great impression on Sandra. The same impression that had left him speechless when he learned the true story of María Mediavilla.

FORWARD FLIGHT

Madrid, December 1967

MARÍA

No one had prepared me to endure such atrocious physical and mental suffering, stab after stab of pain that eviscerated me every day a little more. The loss of my family, of my nature as a human being and the degradation to which I was subjected, almost finished me off. But I have always heard that weeds never die.

Maybe it was the law of the strongest: pure and simple survival. I would never have thought that I was a bad person, someone selfish who only looked out for herself. Deep down I was just a country girl, a peasant who had been taken to the big city, only to have everything she had taken away from her. But between me and someone else, I would always look out for me.

If that meant picking the crumbs of bread that other inmates despised, either because it was too little for them or because their strength had deserted them, I would have no remorse in making them mine. My survival was at stake and on it alone depended whether I could, one day, take revenge on my enemies and get on with my life.

I had been in Madrid for almost a year, but it seemed like ten. Time passed very slowly and I could no longer even remember, forgotten in the suitcase of my memory like so many other things that would take decades to surface, the precise moment when I was deceived and abandoned like a dog. I would not have been able to treat a poor animal like this and that is why I would never be able to understand what my mother did to me, blood of her blood.

Maybe yes, maybe it was not so complicated to understand her after assuming that I was just another sheep herded by the usual people. I imagined that damn religion and what people might say were the causes of my torment, the real reasons for my descent into hell. It was a doctrine that my mother, and so many other uneducated people far from reason, had been inculcated from religious or secular pulpits to rule our destinies in an unimaginable way. Those champions of the homeland who made you believe in their divine designs with proclamations and chest beating, just so that the common people would bow down before them and would not have to think about the difference between good and evil.

I could understand the shame I could bring on a decent Spanish family. Or at least I tried to understand their point of view during those dark nights when I was looking for a reason for my torment. I could never put myself in their place, even if I tried to empathize with them, and abase myself in a way that exceeded everything imaginable for a human being. But no matter how much devotion or fear there was in society, I could never understand a mother's reasons for disengaging from her teenage daughter in such a way.

If it had simply been that, I might have understood it in a way. The wayward daughter who had strayed from the righteous path traced by an infectious and archaic society whose values were determined by certain men foreign to the true nature of their people and, above all, far from the rest of her European neighbors, who were inexorably advancing towards a Western society that was approaching the 21st century, while in Spain we were parochial and inward looking, closer to the 19th century than to an open-minded society with a future.

I had not lived through the civil war or the hard years of the post-war period, but I had not had a good life either. I was aware of my limitations, but I had never abandoned the hope of improving myself and achieving something in life. Yes, I had given up my studies because I did not like them and I was not very good at them, but I had always had dreams and hopes. Something that had been snatched away from me with the stroke of a pen, a cruel blow of fate that I wanted to amend. Although reality clashed flatly with my innermost desires, locked in a filthy hole from which no one could get me out.

The little hope I had of softening my mother's heart with my supplications and lamentations, repenting of my sins and asking her forgiveness in every way I could think of, always fell on deaf ears. The nuns allowed us from time to time, always under strict control and the censorship of all correspondence, to write letters to our relatives.

I did not even bother to repeat anymore that I was not to blame for anything. I knew it would have no effect on my mother and I would come up against a wall. She never believed the truth of what had happened that afternoon in that damned hovel in the Mirandilla Valley. My mother always blamed it on my adventures with Juanito, whom she had also put in her crosshairs. In my situation I would not even let myself think about my friend, but I knew that something bad had happened to him. He had disappeared from the village overnight, without anyone knowing his whereabouts, and days later my whole family also left the region for Madrid.

Then I would have to change my discourse if I intended to get something in return, although I did not believe that my mother would swallow such a lie. But I did, applying myself in the best way I knew how, although always limited by my sparse cultural background. Yes, I knew how to read, write and the four rules, as they said back then, but my lack of vocabulary and poor spelling were not the best tools to describe what I really felt. To everything that I had already suffered in my particular ordeal was then added my lack of culture, something I was silently ashamed of, but which I had to ignore in the face of the prospect that was offered to me. I swallowed my pride and asked for help to other fellow inmates, since in Peñagrande there were many posh girls who had also been delivered here by their families to redirect them to the right path.

The center was divided into different areas and we had almost no contact with each other. Mothers and pregnant women on one side, the rest on the other. They separated the rebels from the submissive ones; or the humblest ones like me, from the wing where the well-to-do girls lived, those whose families paid for, who lived in better conditions. Although I found ways if I wanted to talk to any of them.

There were other ways to enter Peñagrande. Talking to other inmates I found out that there was a kind of female police of the Regime that looked for wayward minors, of dubious morals or conduct, to admit them into the boarding school. The reasons given by these women sympathetic to the Regime, to identify their poor victims were very varied: from wearing a miniskirt to dancing or going out with boys, kissing your boyfriend in the street, smoking, drinking or expressing some kind of political thought contrary to Franco.

The help of one of the privileged interns was of no use to me, since all the letters I sent to my family were returned unopened. And not because my mother had abandoned me, that too, but because the messenger could not deliver them due to force majeure: unknown address.

Where had they gone? After leaving the village we settled in Madrid, in the district of Puente de Vallecas, in a humble house located between San Diego and Entrevías. Apparently, no one in my family lived at that address anymore and that is why the letters came back to me, a terrible blow to my faint hopes of getting out of there in a short time and recovering what I had lost.

Perhaps it was the definitive incentive for me to consider life in a different way. I had just turned seventeen and had no one to care about me. In the many months since I had been imprisoned in the underworld, I had learned to survive without attracting too much attention, but always with my ears open.

Families could also turn to the Patronato, if they did not approve of their daughters' behavior, and turn the girls over to the system. Coming of age was at twenty-one at that time, but we were in a legal limbo that could be extended to twenty-five, always under the supervision of the nuns.

That was the most curious thing of all and something that, so many years later, I still do not understand. Perhaps lawyers or people who are familiar with the law would not be so surprised, but I was horrified at the time and it still makes me break out in a cold sweat. How could it happen, in the middle of 1967, that Spanish families of all kinds and conditions, from the lowest to the wealthiest backgrounds, could abandon their 'errant' daughters in this way?

The families, as I learned from the dialectic blows of the cruel nuns, renounced the parental authority of their daughters and handed them over to the State. And the crusader nuns, as defenders of morality and in charge of watching over us thanks to the intervention of the Patronato, took it upon themselves to teach us the right path so that we would not sin again.

Fed up with that situation and, of course, unmoved by the siren songs of some evil women who thought they possessed the truth only because they wore the habit, I decided to get out of there and suffer the consequences. I already mentioned that I had two main options, each one riskier than the other, and over which I lost many hours of sleep trying to decide which would be the least burdensome for my livelihood.

Sometimes policemen passed by, telling us with nice words that they could get us out of that hell. I did not want to believe the rumors that ran through Peñagrande, I had not yet completely lost faith in humanity. I refused to believe that all the people around me had such black heart. But once again, I was completely wrong and I paid for it in abundance.

I ended up trusting one of those policemen who visited us from time to time, a certain Antón. When I came out into the street and breathed free air, I thanked him effusively with an innocent hug that perhaps he misinterpreted. Anyway, to be completely rigorous with the truth, the policeman treated me very well during the first hours of my release: he invited me to breakfast in an elegant place, chocolate with *churros*, I remember it very well. An exquisite delicacy after the hardships I had endured at the damned boarding school.

He took me to a boarding house and bought me some clothes to make me presentable. He left me there for a few hours and I thought he had forgotten me, so I tried to leave the room. But the door was locked from the outside, probably in collusion with the owner of the boarding house. In the evening he came back for me and Antón looked me up and down with a rictus of complacency. He made me accompany him in his car, a vehicle that for me was the height of traveling comfort even though he was ranting all the way because of its malfunctioning. We finally arrived at our destination, a somewhat neglected mansion located on the outskirts of the city, in an esplanade at the back of the road.

The policeman rang the doorbell and a man opened the door almost immediately. He led us through a dimly lit corridor and left us alone in a kind of stuffy little room, lit by oddly colored lamps.

"Long time no see Antón!" exclaimed an obese guy, with a huge belly which his t-shirt couldn't cover. "What brings you here?"

"It's been a long time indeed, since we saw each other last, my friend Marcial. You know I appreciate you and I thought of you and that you could meet this beauty first."

I started to get nervous when the lump of suet approached me and looked at me as if he was going to snack on me that very afternoon.

"Mmm, not bad at all, it's true. Natural redhead, I see. What's your name, princess?"

"My name is María and I am from a village in Burgos."

I do not know why I said that, it must have been nerves. Our host laughed, he seemed to be amused by what I had said.

"Very good, María. Are you a virgin?"

"No, Marcial, you know I have a hand in the Peñagrande boarding school. The girl comes from there, I don't think there's need to explain anything else."

"Too bad, that would have been a plus. Although I don't know if..."

At that moment I felt real fear as I watched this man approach and especially when his thick fingers stroked my hair and face. In one swift movement, something that surprised me given his corpulence, he ripped off the top buttons of my blouse with a simple snap. And sure enough, my breasts peeked through the cleavage he had created for the purpose, something that seemed to please this repulsive man.

"I think I can make good use of her- she has nice tits. Great skin: very white, almost milky, but covered with a few small freckles that would drive my clients crazy."

"That's what I was thinking, my friend, you can make gold with this girl. How much will you offer for her? She's a potential goddess, you can't deny it. With a little make-up and the right clothes - she'll wreak havoc with the clientele."

It could not be! That bastard Antón wanted to sell me to that guy. It had taken me too long to understand the kind of transaction that was going to take place there. I had come out of purgatory to get into the very cauldron of hell. They were going to prostitute me and I could do nothing to avoid it.

Fear took over me and I unconsciously moved as far away from the pimp as I could. He smiled again, amused perhaps at my reaction, something he would have seen tons of times on other girls if he had been at it for a while.

"Don't worry, princess, you're going to be fine here. Daddy will take care of you and if you behave yourself you can live like a queen. Right, Antón?"

"Of course, this is one of the best joints in Madrid. The clientele is of high standing, don't worry."

"But I..."

I do not know how I dared to open my mouth, a blunder according to the angry stare and raised hand I got from Antón. My new owner, however, seemed to take it well and even gestured dismissively to the policeman to let me speak.

I chose to keep quiet anyway, I did not want to get into any more trouble. Marcial's smile began to widen and I did not even notice, scared to death, his next move. The pimp had pulled down his pants and underwear, revealing a tiny penis that seemed to hide between the different folds of his bulging anatomy.

"We'll have to test the merchandise, don't you think? If she knows how to do her job, I'm sure I can pay you more money, Antón."

I tried to turn and run away, but the policeman was faster than me. He grabbed me by the shoulders and forced me to stand there, very still, terrified at the prospect before me.

"A little mercy on the girl, don't be mean. I said she's not a virgin, but she's not an expert either."

"Don't worry, Antón, I'll teach her well. Come on, girl, we don't have all day. Give your daddy a treat, let's see how you suck my cock."

And having said that, he grabbed his penis with his hand, at least so that it would not remain half-hidden between the mass of fat that surrounded his abdominal perimeter. A retch came up in my throat and I had to hold back the urge not to puke all over him.

"Come on, María, it's no big deal," said the bastard Antón in my ear. "In the end you'll get used to it and you'll live here very well, nothing to do with the nuns' boarding school."

And having said that, he forced me to my knees, while thick tears began to roll down my cheeks. The disgust I felt when I saw in close-up the pimp's filthy member, which was gradually increasing in size thanks to the masturbation to which its owner was subjecting it, was something I swore I would never feel again in my life. But the worst was yet to come.

"Come on, María, open your little mouth...."

I shook my head, closed my mouth and gritted my teeth with all my might. The pimp tried to open my lips with his filthy penis and hit me in the face with it. The gagging threatened to open my mouth again, but I had to hold back the urge, I could not give in. I knew I had everything to lose, there exposed between two men, but my pride prevented me from surrendering.

Then I felt an unexpected tug on my hair and Antón forced me to lift my head. The pain in the back of my neck was so excruciating it made me scream, the moment that Antón took advantage to introduce the member into my mouth. I could not breathe, I was choking and the bastard was pushing deeper and deeper, into my throat.

"Come on, beautiful, suck for fuck's sake."

I was at his mercy. Antón held me by my hair and shoulders, and the fat man was penetrating my mouth with unbridled lust. On top of that he was choking me and my mind clouded for an instant. I do not know if it was rage, fear or survival instinct, but I did the only thing I could think of at that moment not to die between violent retching.

I tried to mold my lips to his penis and my movement seemed to please the obese guy. I then opened my mouth as wide as I could and closed it with all my might, clenching my jaws with full intention. My teeth clamped down on the delicate flesh and dug in viciously until I achieved my goal: the fat guy came out of my mouth amidst screams of pain.

"Fucking bitch!" He shouted before slapping me across the face. "Fuck, she almost cut my dick with her teeth. Get her out of here right now!"

"But no, this... Come on, Marcial, it can't have been that bad."

"Get out of here, Antón, before I regret it and give you both what you deserve. I never want to see you here again!"

The policeman picked me up off the floor and dragged me out. He gave me a good thrashing on the way to the car, but I was happy. I had gotten rid of that animal, although I was still not safe. I had lost the policeman money, apart from the humiliation he had suffered at the pimp's house, and I did not know what repercussions that incident would have on my physical integrity.

"I should throw you in the river or leave you in the bush, you bitch, with everything I've done for you!"

I bowed my head and said nothing, although the blows to my face did not allow me to speak clearly either. I decided not to further my 'alleged benefactor's' anger and look for a way out of my situation. I still did not know what the policeman had in mind for me, but I would fight tooth and nail for my life if I had to.

This time he did not put me in the car with him, I did not deserve that treatment. He took some duct tape out of the trunk, covered my mouth and tied my hands behind my back. The esplanade near the whorehouse appeared deserted at that hour, so he had no problem taking care of me that way. Then he took me in his arms, put me in the trunk and tied my legs together so I could not move.

The trip in there was horrible and I did not know what my final destination would be. I forced myself not to despair, although deep down I knew there was no turning back. The policeman would kill me and dispose of my body, and no one would care. My family had abandoned me to that 'boarding school' and Antón had taken me away with promises of a new life, so no one would miss me.

I was tempted to give up altogether, although in my heart I still harbored hope. After all, if I had thought of committing suicide some time ago, it could not be so serious now. I only hoped that I would not suffer too much and that I would die as quickly as possible. If Antón did not take his anger out on me, it might be the best solution for everyone.

But my mind flatly refused this and forced me to rethink my next moves. I was bound and gagged, so I could not even struggle. If Antón opened the trunk and threw me into the river like that, I would drown helplessly. But if he removed the gag or the restraints, I would fight with all my strength so as not to end up dead in some ditch.

Minutes later the car slowed down; it seemed we had reached our destination. The trunk opened and Antón picked me up again. He walked a few meters with me in his arms and then put me on the ground, next to the entrance of a building. He cut my restraints, knocked on the door and ran back to his car. He waved goodbye to me and I stood there, dumbfounded, not quite knowing what had happened.

The good thing about this story is that I was alive and had been spared from something horrible. The bad part is that the door to the building opened and then it dawned on me where he had taken me:

"You're here again, you whore, daughter of Satan!" said one of the nuns the moment she saw me. "Come on, get inside, you're going to get what for!"

I had returned to prison and was not even aware of my fate. Relieved, I accompanied the nun into the building without complaining. But my head was already thinking of ways to escape from there. I only hoped I would succeed this time and get my longed-for freedom.

But as I have already said, luck has never been one of my best allies.

THE EVIDENCE OF INFAMY

Salas de los Infantes (Burgos), July 24, 2016

I really enjoyed the Dinosaur Museum. It was very informative. There were also families with their children walking around and I could see that the kids loved the dinosaurs. I was envious to see them jump, laugh and get scared as they tried on virtual reality goggles, and I waited patiently for my turn. When I put them on, I almost died of shock: it really felt like I was walking among huge animals that could crush me with a stomp.

Anyway, I could not focus too much on the tour of the Museum, because a while later I received another message from Alberto.

I'll be out of here in a while, I'll call you as soon as I can. Meanwhile, take a look at the e-mail I sent you to get the picture. I'll tell you more later, XOXO;-)

I logged into my account and saw that I had an email with attachments. I could not just open it there and read it quietly. Not while I was surrounded by happy children interacting with different elements of the visit, apart from the fact that Ana and Raquel were also there. I would have to wait, although impatience was gnawing at my stomach.

A while later we left the museum and headed for a terrace at the end of the arcaded square. There we could have an aperitif while waiting for Alberto's call, although I still had not thought of an excuse to get rid of the two cousins. Not to mention the e-mail I was looking forward to reading with all my might. I do not even know how I could contain myself then.

We ordered beer and *tortilla* from the friendly waiter who served us. I took the opportunity to go to the bathroom while they brought us our order. And hiding there, as if I really had something to hide, I opened the mail and downloaded the first document.

The bathroom light went out every so often, so I had to wave my arms to get it to come on again. The reading kept me absorbed, disgusted by the magnitude of the discovery. María was narrating her ordeal and I felt as if it was happening to me. A madness that I could not understand, but that upset me more than it should have.

In fact, I had not even realized that I had been locked in the bathroom for several minutes. I was snapped out of my reverie by another customer when she tried to access the restroom. I said out loud, 'Busy', sat up a bit, put my cell phone in my purse, and flushed the toilet. I bumped into a middle-aged lady who gave me a dirty look, but I ignored her and went back out onto the terrace.

"We thought you were lost," said Ana jokingly. "Hang on, are you alright?"

"Yes, it's nothing, it's just that it was very hot in the bathroom and I got a little dizzy."

"It's true that you look very pale. Have a sip of beer and try the omelet, it's delicious!"

I tried to concentrate on the girls' conversation, but my mind wandered to María's blog post that I had just read. In it she recounted in great detail the famous day she had gone with a group of friends to Sad Hill Cemetery. What started out as a day out, an excursion with other kids from the village ended up as the worst nightmare that can happen to a woman.

My phone vibrated again in my purse and I took it out to see if I had received any other important messages. Indeed, Alberto was notifying me of his imminent departure.

We're just finishing, I'll call you back in ten minutes and I'll see you then.

I read it out loud to Ana and Raquel, although I was not even aware that I had done.

"Okay girl we'll leave you with your beau. A little bit of fun for the body..." said Raquel giggling with her cousin.

"It seems to me that Albertini has already passed that stage: he has become more than a platonic love or a crush, right, Sandrita?"

I went as red as a tomato and noticed how my cheeks flushed instantly. My emotions were running high, especially after reading María's terrifying story in that dingy little room.

"I, look guys, I'm sorry…"

"Hey, don't worry, take it easy. We'll leave you alone with your 'Romeo', see if you get over the dullness you've been carrying around."

"But then... aren't we going on the excursion together?" I asked blankly.

"Sure, but we'll all meet in the Mirandilla valley," said Ana.

She explained that she was planning to go back to Carazo with Raquel and from there they would go to Sad Hill Cemetery in the afternoon. Julián also wanted to go with his new gang from Covarrubias.

"I'm cool with that, thank you!"

I winked at my best friend and gave her a big hug. She believed that I was happy to be alone with Alberto for a specific reason, which I would not deny at that moment but there were other powerful ones why I preferred to talk about alone with Alberto about certain subjects that I would rather not air in public. And of course, I was grateful to Ana for this, although I felt terrible not telling her the whole truth.

I walked around the square, while I waited for Alberto's call. In my wandering I did not notice that I was approaching the entrance to the Casino, so I was stunned to hear someone calling me. It was Alberto, who was shouting at me from the steps. And I had not noticed.

"Oh, I'm sorry," I said, slightly embarrassed. Neither of us made any pretense of greeting each other more effusively, either with the customary two kisses or in a more intimate way, so I let it go. "To be honest, I was knocked out by what you sent me."

"Have you been able to read it all?"

"Not really, only the first document. My goodness what happened to María near the graveyard with her friend Juanito, that's absolutely terrible."

"Well, I'm sorry to tell you that it doesn't stop there. Adolfo has managed to decipher several more posts, but I think they are not in order. I have also sent you another excerpt in which María narrates how she managed to get out of boarding school the first time."

"The first time? I don't understand..."

"Come on, let's sit on that bench in the shade and read the rest."

We sat, while I racked my brains trying to figure out what Alberto was referring to. What could have happened to María in that sort of women's prison?

When I finished reading the post in which the policeman attempted to sell her to a pimp I almost had a panic attack. I was overwhelmed and started hyperventilating, I could not breathe properly. I was empathizing too closely with María's story. When I read the events told in the first person, I had a terrible time. This was not going to help me much in my search for the truth.

It took me a few minutes to calm down, but I finally pulled myself together:

"This is awful! Jesus, poor girl, what a fucked-up life," I said.

"Yes, the truth is that it is very heavy. And I'm sure we're still missing some things. I hope Adolfo can get more information. Although he has passed me some data that he looked for on his own, regarding this type of institution which apparently were quite common during the last years of Franco's regime."

"We have to do something, Alberto! This can't be. It's terrible."

"If no one has done anything after so many years, there must be a reason, Sandra. We 're not going to be able to change the situation now, least of all, if behind all this there were influential personalities who did and undid things as they pleased."

"But we have to do something!" I cried. It could not be true that all this had been going on in Spain for decades, with total impunity for those who organized it, and nobody had done anything to prevent it. "I understand your position, but I'm going to keep looking for the truth. Will you help me?"

"Of course, you can count on me for anything."

Alberto was not very sure, though and I felt a little guilty for dragging him in that way. We still had many open fronts, each one more complicated and with greater implications, but I planned to go the whole way. I decided to give him a little truce. I did not want to ruin the end of the convention for him.

"Okay then, tomorrow I'll go back to Madrid with you and then we'll see. I'm also thinking about something, I don't know if it's a good idea to tell Menchu about all this. After all, she was María's friend and it was because of the photo she showed me that we had got into this mess."

"If you want my advice, I would wait a bit. At least until we have more information or find some evidence of what we have found out so far."

"Maybe you're right, I'll sleep on it. But until then, let's relax for a while. Let's find a quiet place to eat, continue talking about anything else and this afternoon we'll go on the excursion. Do you agree?"

I winked at him and Alberto seemed pleased with my proposal. We chose a cafeteria where they served a menu of the day and we sat at a back table, away from the rest of the customers. There we talked about other things, although in the end the conversation drifted towards more personal topics.

Trust was growing between us and the events of that weekend were bringing us closer together. We both forgot for a few minutes the trouble we had gotten ourselves into and preferred to focus on something much more intimate and interesting. We did not mind that we were in public, since we did not really know any of the people in the place, so when we finished eating, the intimacy was deeper.

Alberto was sitting next to me on the bench, with our backs to the wall, close together. His hand brushed my leg and moments later his mouth explored mine shyly. I did not want to make a fool of myself in a public place, but I offered him my lips with pleasure, as our tongues twined with delight.

Seconds later we moved away embarrassed, as if a teacher had caught us at fault. We ended up laughing at the absurdity of the situation and enjoyed the rest of the after-dinner conversation as we laughed and bonded over a relationship that I hoped would prosper over time.

The afternoon flew by and we soon had to leave to get to the Mirandilla Valley in time. According to the estimates of the organizers, several hundred people would attend the evening event prepared next to Sad Hill Cemetery, all ready to enjoy a different kind of day and to see *The Good, the Bad and the Ugly* on a giant screen.

"I'm really excited about this evening's screening, I'm sure it's going to be brutal," said Alberto.

"I hope you are not disappointed...."

That was where we headed, more relaxed after the last few hours, but without forgetting the other business we were involved in. I was looking forward to accompanying Alberto during the final day of the symposium, even though none of us guessed at the time the real end of the party we were about to meet.

THE DEVIL YOU KNOW IS BETTER THAN THE DEVIL YOU DON'T

Madrid, February 1968

MARÍA

The short adventure in Antón's company should have served as a lesson to me, but I was still determined. I wanted to leave that filthy place before I completely lost my mind, and I was not going to fool around.

Yes, the experience with the policeman and his son of a bitch friend Marcial was not too pleasant. I had escaped by the skin of my teeth and I did not even want to imagine the torture it would have been to be part of that underworld, to become a sex slave until my body could take it no more or my mind exploded saying enough and I decided to get out of the way once and for all.

Decades later, with the baggage of many years of struggle and suffering as an adult woman, and not as the illiterate and frightened young girl who had been locked up without having committed any crime, I had direct knowledge of the reality of white slavery and all that it entails. Through an acquaintance, who told me about the horror of living through that hell and the suffering endured in the sexual exploitation mafias, I learned that in my youth, I had been very lucky to be spared that living death.

The bad thing was that I did not learn from my mistakes and I made another terrible mistake. I knew that the only way to get out of there before I turned twenty-five was to go away with one of the men who visited the boarding school. And, of course, after seeing the true nature of the men who visited it, it was impossible for me to trust anyone for a long time, and I am still paying for it.

I had to swallow my pride and humiliate myself again to achieve my goals. And our day-to-day life at the boarding school for wayward girls was humiliating enough as it was, from the first moment we stepped inside its putrid walls.

I believe that I have more than paid for all the sins I may have committed in my life, consciously or unconsciously, so I consider that I owe nothing to any deity. I moved away from faith gradually and I have never recovered it completely, until I have become a true agnostic. And so, I continue to this day, although perhaps someday I will try to reconcile myself with the Christian faith, the one that took away so much from me in my youth.

Of course, we were forced to attend mass on Sundays and holy days. But the worst thing happened at the end of each homily. Like an idiot I did my part so as to be included in something that escaped all reasoning, especially when I remembered that this was a western country and we were already approaching the seventies.

Many of the fellow inmates with whom I attended mass were pregnant, and I had witnessed them being led through the choir until they were placed against a wall, side by side. Then the real humiliation began.

Several men appeared in front of the girls, inspecting them as if they were cattle: they looked at their teeth, their asses, their tits, their arms and took their time to make a general inspection of each woman. Something so degrading that it reached its peak when they chose the girl they wanted to keep. Some were put to serve as maids, although I would say more like slaves. And others were taken away to be married, or so we thought in those days.

They say that those bastards paid up to one hundred thousand pesetas for one of us: a real slave trade in Spain, in the twentieth century. It is a total outrage that this kind of behavior was allowed in this country without anyone doing anything to prevent it. But, of course, we did not exist and we were at their mercy; we were in the basement of the system, engulfed by the bureaucracy of a regime that crushed us in a merciless way. And this system lasted for decades, a decadent sign of the darkest Spain.

One of those Sunday mornings I witnessed the refusal of one of the inmates to leave with her buyer, because that is what those unscrupulous bastards really were. We had already heard stories of fellow inmates who were treated like dogs by those men, something we must have considered almost normal or customary if we were to go by the type of man who might go there to buy a wife or a maid. And, of course, when it was the turn of my friend Irene, a young woman from Toledo a little older than me, I knew trouble was coming.

Irene flatly refused to accompany the sadist who had chosen her and I would have done the same. If his gestures, look and attitude were already scary in that situation, we did not even want to imagine what it would be like to live with one of those evil beasts. My friend shrieked and kicked, so the infamous man decided to make things easier for himself and chose a more submissive girl to leave as soon as possible.

My friend had to suffer the punishment imposed by the 'pious' nuns because of her misbehavior. She was taken to a damp room where rats roamed. They rationed her food even more and forced her to perform the hardest tasks, making her life impossible from that moment on. An ordeal that the poor girl could not bear and she ended up killing herself.

We had also seen fellow inmates who came back to the fold, as their buyers returned them as if they were a defective product from a store. Apparently, they were not what they were looking for and were brought back to the nuns as a totally normal transaction. Something insane that still escapes my reason, but it was our daily bread there.

The day I was chosen to do the walk, I decided to shut up and keep quiet, at least until I saw what destiny had in store for me, whether any of those bastards chose me and took me with him after paying the nuns the price demanded.

I did not have to wait long that December morning, in a bone-chilling cold. A short, fat guy who fancied himself a great gentleman began to inspect the merchandise and immediately noticed me. Wish he had noticed his fucking mother! Not sure if you know what I mean.

That human scum, a man with a gray gaze and a nondescript look, subjected me to a good frisk to inspect the goods. I endured lewd fondling on my chest and buttocks, because that is what the scumbag was paying for, and he wanted to know what kind of material he was taking with him. I had to bite the inside of my cheeks until I drew blood, so as not to gouge his eyes out and ruin myself. I could not scream or resist either, so I held on as best I could.

I tried to absent myself in those eternal seconds in which I felt his filthy hands on my anatomy. Still, I had time to notice some details. The little man wore quality clothes, although his ridiculous *Falangista* moustache and his baldness spoiled the outfit. Not to mention his peculiar way of walking, which caused some amusement among the nuns present.

I do not know what my new owner, Arturo Requena, paid for me, but he seemed very satisfied with his purchase. I forced myself to forget that he had bought me, just as the bastard cop had intended when he took me to the pimp, no matter how civilized it all seemed. I thought only of the good part of it all: I would finally leave the walls of the damned 'boarding school', once and for all.

THE EXCURSION

Sad Hill Cemetery (Burgos), July 24, 2016

We arrived at the cemetery around 5 pm, so we had to wait a while to meet up with the rest of the gang. Although it was relatively early for the start of the celebration, we had passed several cars and buses full of people on the way to Sad Hill, whose final destination was also the Mirandilla Valley. A real excursion that promised a good afternoon of fun.

We wanted to arrive early to look at the graveyard in peace, or so Alberto assured me. He was especially excited to show me something he had been telling me about all week and I was curious to see the now famous Sad Hill.

It was much larger than I had imagined. The majesty of that expanse of land left me speechless. We left Clint Eastwood's metallic silhouette behind and headed towards the graves. We passed through several rows of burial mounds and came to the stone circle I had been told about earlier.

“Don't tell me it's not amazing..." said Alberto enthusiastically.

He looked absolutely thrilled and his eyes were shining in a special way. I am a very empathetic person, so part of that enthusiasm reached me too and I could understand the feelings that were bubbling up in Alberto's good nature.

We walked around the surrounding area, but we did not want to stray too far. At no time did it occur to me to walk around the grounds surrounding the valley, not even to make time, for a very obvious reason: I did not want to remember the dreadful scene I had read about a few hours before, when María and Juanito got lost in that area to have some privacy and ended up in the worst possible way, savagely attacked by those three bastards.

Besides, our friends must have been on their way already and the event was already at its peak, with hundreds of people arriving at the Mirandilla Valley. The organizers of the 50th Anniversary had also set up a bar with food and drinks, as well as a small stand to sell merchandising of the event.

I looked at Alberto's happy face and did not want to spoil the moment for him. But my mind was working at full speed, and I could not get what had happened to poor María there out of my head. And, above all, the final consequences of the savage aggression, with the confinement of the young Burgos girl in an infamous boarding school, where she would continue to suffer countless humiliations.

I left Alberto alone for a moment while he talked with other convention participants, and I thought about calling Ana to see where she was. But I did not need to, because a few meters away I saw the whole troop arrive: Ana and Raquel on one side and Julián with his new friend on the other, a very attractive brunette girl whom he introduced to me as Carolina.

"This is awesome, what a great atmosphere!" said Ana as soon as she saw me.

"What a hassle, we got stuck in traffic to get here. It's not like it's Madrid!"

Julián's face said it all: he was not too happy to be there. Maybe he would rather lose himself with his new friend, a limpet who could not take her hands off him. Maybe the girl thought she had to mark her territory in front of me, although the truth was that I could not care less for what those two did.

Alberto also joined the party and we all ordered something to drink while we waited for the evening activities to begin. Julián was already familiar with the surroundings, and Carolina did not seem to have much intention of interacting with us, but Alberto got a little annoying and the cousins had to accompany him so he could give his master class.

"I've been told that there are about two thousand people in the valley," Alberto informed us after chatting with one of the organizers. "It's amazing, I didn't expect so many people."

"You'll be happy then, I think it's a real success," I said.

"Too many people, it's a bit overwhelming," said Julián's girlfriend.

The bar area with drinks and snacks was full with the arrival of so many people, so we moved a little away from there. Afterwards there was a theatrical performance by a small company from Aranda de Duero, which treated us to a recreation of the final duel of the film. Or so Alberto whispered in my ear.

A bit later we were also able to enjoy a small concert at a very different enclave from the places where a music band usually plays. The musicians delighted us with the soundtrack of the feature film and other pieces by the maestro Morricone, according to what Alberto told me. The beginning of the film projection was scheduled for half past nine at night, since the film was two and a half hours long and they intended to end the week of activities around midnight.

"Two and a half hours, you say? I don't know if I'm going to last that long lying on the grass."

Ana's brother was right. We had not come prepared for the occasion, unlike many other participants. There were chairs, deckchairs, mats, sleeping bags, blankets and other items that would make the participants comfortable. In my case I had only brought a denim jacket, so it was quite possible that I would freeze when the night fell, lying under the stars in the middle of a valley in Burgos.

"I have some acquaintances around here who have brought some extra clothes. They will lend us some blankets and mats to make it more comfortable."

Julián continued to grumble, despite his friend's good provision for the movie. There were still a few minutes left before the start of *The Good, the Bad and the Ugly*, so Alberto took me aside and we walked around while we made time. The rest of the group took up positions in the front row, where Alberto had wanted to be in order to see everything in the best conditions. I noticed he was a bit nervous, but I could not guess the real reason. I assumed it was due to something related to the projection but it really had nothing to do with it. That is why he made me accompany him away from the group, because he wanted to tell me something important.

"Sorry, Sandra, I wasn't sure whether I should tell you now or wait until later."

"What's wrong?" I asked anxiously when I saw his expression. "Don't scare me, please."

"Read it yourself."

Alberto placed his phone in my hand, with an open document that could be seen on the screen. I read it with my heart in my mouth, ready to learn about any other kind of misfortune that had happened to our little María.

"Good heavens!"

María Mediavilla's vicissitudes were not over, that was for sure. What seemed incredible to me was that a woman could endure so much suffering, so many humiliations and degradations that continued over the years. And I still did not know the whole story, although after putting all the pieces together I could already see part of it.

After getting rid of the policeman, María had fallen into the hands of another undesirable of the worst kind. And yes, she was finally able to leave the boarding school behind and forget its infamous walls. But perhaps living with Arturo Requena was worse punishment than the most inhospitable confinement cell in the world.

Apparently, Adolfo had sent several documents to Alberto, as he was recovering the old posts from the deleted blog. The first text had left me with the intrigue of her leaving with Requena, but I was still unaware of the rest of the story. María was about to begin a journey in which she would not find happiness either, while her youth was withering away little by little with each misfortune suffered to her flesh.

HOPE HAD A PRICE

Barcelona - March 1968

MARÍA

I never felt at ease with Arturo, even though, at first I tried hard to do so. I knew I should not make faces and I tried to behave well in order to be treated with deference, but it was of little use to me to try, even with all my will. Arturo really disgusted me and I could not hide it, so it did not take long for his behavior towards me to change. And not exactly for the better.

Requena was a small Valencian businessman who had settled in Barcelona, so that is where we headed when we left Peñagrande. I did not even mind moving further and further away from everything I knew. I just wanted to leave all the bad memories behind. I had already assumed that I had been bought for something, so I tried not to think about it and wanted to thank Arturo for his gesture with the best of dispositions.

My place in the house was not very clear from the beginning, but I did not protest. Arturo gave me a maid's outfit and I guessed I would become the house maid. I did not mind, really. That house had all the luxuries: electricity, running water, television, even telephone. A spacious apartment in the heart of the Ensanche neighborhood, with three large bedrooms, two bathrooms, living room, kitchen and a maid's room where I was lodged as soon as I arrived.

Arturo was a widower and lived in that house with his son Luis, a young man of about twenty-five who looked at me with pity. Perhaps he did not agree with his father's decision or perhaps he was bothered by my presence, although he never said anything to me, nor, of course, did he disagree with his father. I only know that more than once I caught him looking at me with a look on his face which I understood as commiseration, although I tried not to make a big deal out of it.

Days later I discovered the real reason why the young man was watching me like that. Perhaps he knew his father's next moves, and did not want to have any part in it. Something I had prepared my mind for in the beginning, not guessing that reality would bury imagination in a corner, forever.

For Arturo I was the house maid, his servant. I washed, ironed, cooked and had everything ready for the smooth running of the household. I was used to helping my mother in worse working conditions so it was not so hard for me. Only at the beginning, until I learned to handle all the household appliances that I lacked in Burgos. But I soon got up to speed and had plenty of time to attend to all the tasks entrusted to me.

There were no livestock to tend, nor did the floors get so dirty. I could forget about chickens and pigs, not to mention helping my father in the fields with the grain. The work was not going to take me away and, besides, Arturo did not mistreat me physically or verbally, so the first two weeks in that house were almost an oasis in my life.

But then everything changed. Arturo thought he had given me enough quarter, and the fifteen-day truce was shattered into a thousand pieces that very night. I had just lain down on the bed when I felt a light rap of knuckles on the door. I pulled the quilt over my bed and said, "Come in," not quite knowing who was knocking at that hour.

Arturo came in and I turned on the light of the lamp on my bedside table. Initially he stood there talking about trifles, explaining some chores he wanted me to do the next day. Then he sat down next to me, on the edge of the bed, I sensed that my luck had just run out. Once again, joy is usually short-lived in a poor man's house, as I had always heard from my mother's mouth.

At first Arturo acted shyly, but he soon became emboldened. I was unwilling to comply but also unwilling to refuse his wishes, I simply did not act and adopted a passive attitude to his clumsy movements. For Arthur did not want a wife, but a maid to satisfy his needs. So, I became his private whore, and what is worse, without any financial compensation whatsoever.

My development as a woman in the affective sphere had been truncated since my youth. I had only had kisses and caresses from Juanito, a memory too painful for everything that the short relationship entailed, in which we both knew sex for the first time. And then, after my traumatic passage through Peñagrande, I found myself with an unflattering destiny: to become the sex slave of a disgusting man.

Arturo did not kiss me, or caress me, or bother to attend to my needs as a woman. I would have given in a little and my body would have relaxed if he had behaved differently. Perhaps not, but if he had acted differently perhaps those nightly encounters would have been more satisfying for both of us.

I did not know whether to consider Arturo as my owner or my boss, since boss was too short and lover or husband too long. I was disgusted by him, although I also felt sorry for the little gray man who only lived for his work. He would come home, have dinner, exchange two sentences with his son and go to sleep. And on Wednesdays and Saturdays, without failure from that first month on, he would visit me during the night in my room to unload his seed.

I did not even worry about getting pregnant, as I had been assured that I would never be able to have children after my time at the girls' boarding school. I just endured Arturo's few thrusts, and he would get on top of me for a few brief minutes, which seemed like an eternity, until he fell defeated on my body after emptying himself.

I became a cynic and learned to live with what I had been dealt. I did not even try to change the situation, nor did I consider escaping from my new prison. I had a house and food, I worked a few hours a day, and I put up with Requena two nights a week, nothing more. It could have been much worse, I thought at the time, so I did not want to risk it.

Maybe Luis would help me escape and could offer me some money to start a new life, either in Barcelona, Madrid or any other city. But after what I had experienced with Antón I could not risk it, my luck could change and I could fall into the clutches of someone far worse. I did not completely trust the young man either, even though he seemed to be less of a scoundrel than his father.

The little gray man started to behave worse with me from the second month of my stay in the city. I had heard him yelling on the phone and even arguing with his son. I thought I understood that he had problems in the company, something to do with imports, which I did not pay much attention to. Of course, his mood turned sour and he took it out on me.

He began to yell at me and treat me worse, even in Luis' presence. But in the intimacy of my bedroom, he stopped fooling around. I had always thought that if he had cared a little about me, with a warm-up beforehand to encourage me to participate in the sexual act, we both would have enjoyed it more. This way, without any kind of preliminaries and with that attitude, I only found a lack of lubrication in my body that hurt me with every penetration and I do not know if it excited him more or not, because he was finishing sooner and sooner.

I missed his previous behavior, because from that moment on he became a real animal. Sometimes he would rip my clothes off and even slap me, as if he needed to hit me to feel more of a man. I am not a psychologist and at that time I was far from being a well-read person, but it did cross my mind that his work problems had repercussions on his masculine vigor. Arturo was starting to have problems maintaining a proper erection, so the encounters became increasingly unpleasant for both of us, as his frustration grew and I was the one who paid for it.

That situation lasted a couple of months, but come spring I noticed that Arturo was happier at home. His visits to my bedroom had become less and less frequent, perhaps to avoid showing me his lack of manhood, until something changed in him from one day to the next.

In fact, he showed up one Sunday night in my room, something totally unaccustomed and out of place. I was already half asleep after a more strenuous than usual day of housework, so I had to wake up to attend to my owner. He surprised me as soon as he walked in, as he addressed me directly and talked to me, something he had not done in a long time. Normally he did not speak and limited himself to a mere physical exchange, so I was momentarily taken aback. Even more so when he asked me if I would like to travel, to get to know other countries.

I stammered like a fool: I did not know what to answer him. I had left the village to end up locked up in boarding school. Then I arrived in Barcelona, although I did not know much about the city either. Some Saturdays I accompanied Arturo to the market to buy groceries and little else: I did not leave the four streets of the neighborhood. On some occasion I thought about running away and getting out of there, but I had nowhere to drop dead, so I decided to wait for a better occasion.

Maybe I behaved like a coward during that time, sometimes I think about it. I have always considered myself a fighter, but in those days, I got comfortable, I let myself go. I will never know if my fate would have been different if I had shown more courage during that season. That is something that no one can remedy anymore.

Life has dealt me many blows, some very hard and difficult to overcome, but I have never given up. I want to believe that at that moment I was just taking a break, assessing my chances, rather than thinking that I had become accustomed to that shitty life. Yes, I had no shortage of food to put in my mouth and a bed to sleep in, but I lacked affection and many other things that make life a fulfilling experience.

I do not want to digress from the main subject, so I will get back to the point. Arturo then looked at me with a different gleam in his eyes, almost as if seeking my approval. He looked happy, or perhaps a great weight had been lifted off his shoulders, something that had been tormenting his soul and preventing him from breathing normally. He did not even look so ugly to me after all, or I was beginning to look at him with different eyes. I could not bring myself to hate him, but I had not expected my feelings for him to go the other way either.

What really threw me off balance the next moment was that he asked me directly what I thought about going to a foreign country. Arturo got up from the bed where he had been sitting to talk to me face to face. He began pacing in circles in the little space left in the room, sharing his thoughts aloud.

"You see, a great business opportunity has come up, and I have to take it before my company goes under. And for that we have to move to Uruguay for a few months. Luis, you and I, what do you think?"

Was he really asking for my opinion? I was in no position to refuse, nor did I harbor any hope that my opinions would influence his decision, if it had already been made. So, I just nodded and blurted out some more nonsense, knowing that my status in the house was not going to change at all no matter how far we went to the other side of the world.

"I'm fine with whatever you decide, Don Arturo."

"Very well then, perfect. I will prepare the tickets and all the necessary documentation for our trip. Talk to Luis for the transfer arrangements, he already knows what we have to take with us."

And having said that, he approached me, kissed me on the forehead and left the room without realizing that he had not exercised over me the right he had acquired when he bought me. His overflowing joy did not allow him to see any further and I thanked him for that! I did not want to get my hopes up about his new attitude, but maybe a change of scenery would do us all good.

I was not even aware of one detail which was not minor. I had no documents and there was no way to locate my parents, so Arturo should forget about finding my original birth certificate or family book. So how was he going to get me a passport to leave the country?

If I thought about it, it was not so incredible. Arturo had acquired me in the way we already know thanks to his good relations with important people in the Regime. From there to asking for certain favors - or maybe collecting them, I never really knew - there was not much of a stretch. It would not be so complicated for him to obtain documentation in my name. Or in the name he was most interested in...

...

I will not bore you with the details of our boat trip to Uruguay, I will just point out that it was dreadful. I was beset with seasickness and Luis fell ill from bad food and Arturo looked like a caged animal pacing up and down the deck wanting to step on land for once and for all.

The beginnings in Montevideo were not very encouraging. We settled in a small apartment in a working-class neighborhood of the Uruguayan capital. Arturo continued with his business meetings and I was still unaware of the real situation. I did not know what was going on, so I had to keep my ear to the ground to see if I could pick up any details in the discussions that father and son were having with increasing frequency.

"I told you it was madness, father! We already had problems in Spain, but now we won't be able to face our debts."

"Shut up and let me think!" Arturo replied in a sour tone. "I'll sort it out, don't worry. These guys are not going to get away with this."

We were getting by on the cash the Requenas had brought for the trip, but I could not see the fabulous business opportunity they had told me about in Barcelona anywhere. Arturo was getting more and more taciturn and no one could guess what was going to happen to us.

The situation in the small apartment was not very different from my stay at the Requenas' house during the months I lived in Barcelona. I was still doing housework, although at least I got rid of the bonnet and the maid's costume, thanks mainly to Luis. Arturo had too many issues on his mind, so he visited me a couple of nights, but he ended up forgetting about me in that sense.

In fact, we looked like an ordinary family when we went out for a walk in the city. I did not want to get my hopes up, but I could perfectly pass for Arturo's niece and Luis' cousin, even though we did not look too much alike. And almost as if they had read my mind, one morning they introduced me that way when we passed the landlord in the doorway of the building where we were staying. I played dumb and said hello politely, because I did not want to get into trouble.

The first month went by without any apparent changes, apart from Arturo's mood worsening, since he no longer spoke to anyone and every night, he locked himself in his room after slamming the door. Apparently, his business was not going the way he had expected and the situation was becoming untenable, from what little I could understand. I could not do much to help either, so I just went about my business, did not look for trouble and waited for events to unfold.

I could never have imagined the outcome that Providence had foreseen for that intermission of the tragedy that my life had become. Overnight my world changed again abruptly and I could not assimilate the new situation.

One night Arturo did not show up for dinner and Luis worried about his father. I thought he was out and about, drowning his sorrows in alcohol, or maybe drowning my frigidness in some real prostitute. But the reality was much more brutal.

The next morning, as we still had no news from Requena, his son called the Metropolitan Police. It took them a few more hours to give us the news, but that same afternoon they confirmed the true reality: Arturo had died.

"But what happened?" I asked Luis when we found out.

"Last night he was stabbed in an alley. The police think it was some petty thieves who wanted to rob him to steal his money. You see, he didn't have a penny...."

The shock had not yet fully affected Luis, who told me about the misfortune in a neutral tone. But he immediately broke down and began to cry inconsolably, hugging me to find some relief.

I do not remember very well my reaction to the unexpected news, perhaps I felt relief. I did not wish death to the wretched Requena, but I was not going to cry for him. Yes, I had nowhere to drop dead and on top of that I was in a foreign country, but I was getting closer and closer to my longed-for freedom. Unless Luis took the role of his father and continued to take care of me, something I was not willing to happen.

But misfortune never comes alone. I thought I would be happy after the macabre turn of events, but the goddess of fortune still did not smile on me. And, of course, everything that does not get better, gets worse, as my mother used to say. Our situation drifted towards catastrophe and Luis told me that he was thinking of returning to Barcelona. He did not have enough money to pay for my ticket and apologized for it, but he could not do much more for me.

"You know I never agreed with my father's way of treating you, and I'm sorry I didn't try harder to prevent it. I am a coward and I deeply regret it."

"Don't worry, it doesn't matter now. I'll manage, at least I'll be free."

"I will send you money as soon as I can raise some in Barcelona. You can't stay here alone. My father is dead and I must take care of your safety."

"You don't owe me anything, Luis, really. You have enough problems as it is. What are you going to do with your father's debts?"

It transpired that Arturo had been ruined in Barcelona and that was why he had fled to Uruguay in the first place, chasing a business dream that turned out to be a swindle. He had been taken for a ride and the Requena family was up to their eyeballs in debt. Luis knew that the creditors would come after him as soon as he set foot in Catalonia. He would have to be very careful.

"I'll sell the house, pay the most urgent bills and get out of town. I'll start from scratch somewhere else. I'll figure something out. And I'll take care of you, if it's the last thing I do."

Nor did these half-baked plans come to fruition, at least at first. One afternoon I accompanied Luis to pawn some of his father's jewelry, a quick way to get cash with which to continue subsisting, and I was distracted for a moment looking in a shop window. The twilight sun blinded me as I crossed the street. I did not realize the danger until I felt an excruciating pain in my legs.

A car had hit me and ran over my legs. I only remember the screams around me before everything went black. The next image that comes back to my memory was of me lying in a hospital bed.

...

The doctors did not fear for my life at any time, but they did fear for my mobility. The brutal hit-and-run had shattered my legs and, when I fell, I had damaged part of my spine by hitting a curb in a bad way. They were not sure if I would end up a paraplegic, but for the time being I would not be able to walk or stand up. At least for a very long time, although first I would have to recover from the rest of the after-effects of the accident.

"I'm sorry, María, but I have to leave for Spain. I can't delay it any longer."

"Don't worry, you've done enough for me."

Poor Luis had spent days and nights watching over me in the hospital, dozing as best he could in a very uncomfortable armchair that he was able to procure in order to be with me during my convalescence. It was he who told me about the seriousness of my injuries and how close I had come to death after the accident, especially during the emergency surgery I had undergone. Several problems had arisen during the surgery, according to what the surgeons told him, and I had been on the verge of slipping to the other side.

"The doctors have told me that it is possible for you to walk again, but you will have a long period of convalescence and rehabilitation."

"Trust me," I retorted," I'll make it. Go on, go now, I don't want you to lose the money for the ticket to Barcelona again."

I did not want to trouble him too much, although he said goodbye to me with tears in his eyes. He was a good boy at heart, although the circumstances in which our paths had crossed were not the most appropriate. Perhaps in another life...

I was left alone with my thoughts, regretting again everything that had happened. I had two options: to give up and let myself die, something that really struck me because of my supervening circumstances, or to fight to recover completely.

The dilemma did not linger in my mind for too long and I decided to go ahead. At least I would not have to pay the huge hospital bills, or so the nurses and Luis himself had assured me. It transpired that a benefactor would pay the full cost of my stay and recovery, and I did not think he was a good Samaritan, so I guessed that the man who had run me over was purging his guilt in this way.

I was not planning on reproaching him for it, even if I never met him. I could only think about recovering as soon as possible to get out of there. Luis had left me some money to get by, so I urged all the atoms of my body to fulfill one goal: to walk again, although Fate, my friends, had other cards marked for me.

THE PROJECTION

Sad Hill Cemetery (Burgos), July 24, 2016

I could not believe that, once again, we were left in the dark regarding what had happened to María.

"And she leaves us like that?" I asked upset as I read the end of the fragment.

"Yes, Sandra for now. Adolfo has come across several obstacles recovering the documents. Some are corrupted and he hasn't been able to decipher their full contents."

"Damn it! Hence the half-baked paragraphs and the jumps in the narrative, what a load of crap."

The hacker had left us feeling cheated. Had María stayed a few more years in Uruguay? Would she have recovered from the accident or had she become an invalid in the end? A whole lot of questions to which I had no answers. We could only wait and pray that Adolfo would unravel the mysteries of María's blog and give us one more chapter, just one more small fragment of this drug to which I had become hopelessly hooked.

"I guess that all this must have really thrown you off. What a story! I think Edmundo Dantés was less fucked up than that poor girl."

"You don't say! I'm totally amazed. There's no name for this woman. Call me naïve, but I think that in the end she must have pulled through and pulled herself together. What we don't know is why she wrote that blog ten years ago, then hid it and later disappeared herself."

"Maybe I did the searches wrong. If Requena got her a false travel document, María's last name would no longer be what we thought it was. And we don't know what happened to her in later years either, maybe she's changed her name more than once."

We still did not know where María was now, and her story had too many gaps. Between the sexual assaults and her confinement, something else had to have happened. And from the 1970s until she started writing the blog there was an even bigger gap that we needed to fill. I felt in my gut that María was well, alive and kicking. I did not know whether this woman, a lady of retirement age, would be living in Spain at that time, but I was determined to find out at all costs.

"I don't want to be a spoilsport, Sandra, but the screening is about to start. I'm going to our seats, are you coming?"

"Of course, I'm not going to stay here alone. Although I can't promise you that I'll be able to concentrate, my mind is elsewhere."

Alberto nodded, understanding perfectly. We returned to our friends' side, who urged us to sit on the floor and not block their view. Five minutes later there was absolute silence and the screening began.

What none of us had expected - or at least I had not, since Alberto had known in advance, as he later admitted to me - was that we would have a very special prologue. Clint Eastwood himself had sent a personal greeting to all the attendees in the form of a video recorded for the occasion. The audience gave him a standing ovation and I felt many people around me moved by the words of this icon of the seventh art.

There were also two other videos, with recordings of Ennio Morricone and the singer/guitarist James Hetfield of Metallica. Alberto explained to me that all the concerts of that group used to begin with a video of the final scene of the film and the artist had also wanted to contribute his little grain of sand to the 50th anniversary of Sad Hill from afar.

The audience was already in ecstasy before the film started, but they quickly calmed down when the credits appeared. I tried to pay attention to the film, I promise, but my mind wandered hopelessly. I began to make my own guesses about María's fate, imagining different scenarios for her next moves. I did not want to be tempted into thinking negatively, but I had to assume that Adolfo might not be able to retrieve any more fragments of the hidden blog, so María's story would be forgotten forever if we could not recover it.

That would never happen! I had already planned to return to Madrid the following day and now I had more threads to pull. My means were meager, but with Alberto's help, and perhaps Adolfo's - if I could not unravel more parts of María's diary but searched his databases - we could locate other characters in this peculiar story. Perhaps Luis Requena could give us some clue about her, if we did not succeed in investigating the boarding school and everything related to her confinement.

Wait a minute, I thought then. We had someone else to turn to, I had completely forgotten about it after what had happened in the last few days. Doña Pura, María's mother, was still in the nursing home in Burgos. I guessed that she was still in a vegetative state, although we had seen her reaction when we showed her the photo of her daughter, so we could not dismiss the idea that she might help us find the definitive clue.

Why had María's family locked her up in that boarding school and forgotten about her forever? It was something beyond my comprehension. I felt that I owed something to that girl who had lost her youth because of the intrinsic evil of men, or perhaps because she was immersed in a corrupt system that only looked out for the interests of a few.

And when she was finally free of her captors, whether they were the nuns, the policeman or the shoddy businessman, María had suffered an accident that had left her bedridden. What else could have happened to her? I did not even want to imagine, given her background up to that point.

Absorbed in my own thoughts, I did not notice that the film was progressing without me paying attention. I guessed that those arid landscapes at the beginning of the film had been shot in Almería, thanks also to recalling some of the many stories Alberto had told us about the movie. But from that part, I only clearly remember a scene in which Lee Van Cleef confronted some men inside what looked like an old farmhouse, and also the complicated relationship between two rogues like the characters played by Clint Eastwood and Elli Wallach, who always escaped the gallows by the skin of his teeth.

I looked around me and saw that most of the attendees were gazing at the huge screen in rapt attention. Some were sitting, others were lying on mats or blankets. The cold was beginning to make itself felt in the foothills of the Sierra de la Demanda, and more than one of them crawled into their sleeping bag or snuggled up next to someone under some thick blankets. Perhaps it was time for me to do the same with Alberto. I moved closer to him on his left side and our bodies brushed against each other. We had a small blanket for both of us, although we could not completely cover each other with it. I played dumb and half-voiced that I was cold, to see if Alberto would react.

He seemed to notice the physical contact, and his pupils were glowing as he watched one of his favorite movies in a magical setting. I did not harbor the same feelings as many of these fans of film, but I could understand their excitement at finding themselves in that unique place, surrounded by hundreds of graves recovered by an association that had done the unbelievable to put Sad Hill Cemetery back on the map.

Alberto pulled me to him and held me by the shoulder, so I ended up curling up next to him. I was very comfortable like this, even though the hard ground of the Mirandilla Valley was not the best of mattresses. The two and a half hours were going to be long for many of us, and I could see that Julián and his little friend had had enough of the movie and were engaged in much more fun activities.

I did not want to interrupt Alberto, but I would not have minded if he had kissed me and really held me in his arms. The cold was becoming more and more unbearable and it was getting into my bones, although perhaps what I had learned a few minutes earlier about the misfortunes that had befallen poor María was not conducive to feeling warm. An uneasy feeling came over me and I shivered from head to toe, although I knew it was not due to the low temperatures of a summer night in Burgos.

Alberto noticed my discomfort and tried to keep me warm. I was not trying to spoil his evening and wanted to accompany him until the end of the projection, although sitting on the ground for so long was becoming very uncomfortable. I did not know what to do with myself so that all my bones would not ache when I got up and I had a feeling that the film was going to be very long. Twelve o'clock at night was still far away on the horizon -we were not even halfway through the film-, so I resigned myself to endure the wait with resignation while disturbing my companion as little as possible.

The film was running with the audience totally engrossed in the big screen. I then recognized the scenes of the Betterville fort, filmed nearby, as Alberto had told me a few days before. Burgos locations that would remain forever in the retina of thousands of moviegoers.

A movement to my right distracted me for a second from watching the screen. In the distance, in the middle of the graves, I thought I saw several people scurrying off. I thought it might be a couple or two who had gotten bored with the movie and were looking for a different place to frolic, at least because of the curiosity of the cemetery. I did not think much of it, especially when I realized that I was not the only one who was uncomfortable.

Julián and Carolina got up and slipped off to the side, after saying goodbye with a brief greeting. Alberto did not seem to pay much attention to them, but Ana came up to me and said in my ear:

"It's open season and I think we're going to leave too. Raquel is not feeling too well, she's cold and doesn't want to get sick."

"Okay, don't worry. I'll stay here with Alberto. I don't want to spoil his movie."

"I'll leave the door open, if you want to sleep at home. Unless..."

"Shut up, get out of here!"

Ana had winked at me when suggesting where I could spend the night. The movie was going to end late and then there would be a traffic jam to get out of the valley, besides Alberto would surely want to say goodbye to some of the people with whom he had shared the whole week of activities. It was likely that we might repeat the experience in the house, especially if we were already in the early hours of the morning and we were too lazy to go to Carazo.

I was sure that Julián would not go to the house that night either, if he wanted some intimacy with Carolina, although we would have to make sure just in case. I was already getting ahead of myself and there was still a long time to go before the end of the movie.

Alberto seemed to be in a trance watching the screen, which at that moment was showing the spectacular blowing up of the bridge over the river. I was delighted to see him so happy, with that goofy smile that never left his face, all because of the experience he was enjoying.

A while later Alberto stirred nervously and I immediately found out why. His phone had vibrated in his pocket and he looked at it slyly, with the screen devoid of brightness so as not to disturb the others. He fumbled with the device for a few more seconds and I thought he might have received another message from his friend Adolfo. Then I was the one who became alert, but Alberto calmed me down with a gesture and put the phone back in his pocket.

One of two things: either it was nothing related to that matter or, if it was, he preferred to tell me about it calmly when the film was over. I was not entirely reassured and did not enjoy the screening as I should have.

The end of the movie was approaching and I already had an idea of what we were going to find after the performance of the theater company, which recreated that mythical three-way duel at the beginning of the afternoon. I also remembered having seen some YouTube video on Alberto's phone, but the feeling of watching it on a giant screen, right next to where that scene was filmed, became a moment that I could not describe well with words.

Morricone's music gave another essence to the film. But the master surpassed himself at the time of the final duel, that *triello* in the center of the stone coliseum of Sad Hill. A scene that held me in a spell, as well as the hundreds of spectators who were still left in the valley. Not to mention Alberto, totally moved, enjoying the culmination of this work in the same place where it had been filmed fifty years ago.

When the film ended, a thunderous ovation was heard throughout the Mirandilla Valley. The silence that had reigned seconds before, at the climax of the film, was broken by the applause that echoed throughout every corner of that magical place. Hundreds of people in perfect communion with nature had just lived a unique experience, something that made the hairs stand on end for many of us, even if we were not big fans of this type of film.

People began to wake up, as some of the attendees had brought their sleeping bags. It was time to break camp, say goodbye to friends and head back to the parking lot so many rushed to get out in the first positions. I had assumed that this would not be our case, but what I would never have guessed was that our delay in leaving the valley would be due to a much more sinister reason.

Alberto was chatting amicably with various groups, shaking hands and even hugging certain people with whom he had made friends during the intense congress they had experienced. And then a murmur began to run through the meadow, a guttural sound that was increasing in volume, almost as if an animal were waking up after a centuries-long lethargy and were threatening us for disturbing it in its eternal rest.

I began to see movement to our left and saw several people running from different points in the valley, on their way to the central stone coliseum. Then I heard a blood-curdling scream of terror, a high-pitched female voice that echoed throughout the valley.

"What's going on down there?" Alberto asked me when he saw that I had been looking in that direction for a while.

"I don't know, but I think we should go check."

Alberto agreed and so did the rest of the people nearby. We began to walk there, first at a brisk pace and then almost running, as we skirted the cobblestone area in fear of falling when we tripped over one of the graves located on that side. The crowd of people was getting bigger and bigger, so we did not see the cause that had caused such uneasiness until it was practically on top of us.

"My God!" I cried overwhelmed at the discovery.

I stood a few meters away and put my hands to my face, unable to believe that the Dantesque image that was laid out before us was not in fact something of fiction, a theatrical display that recreated another scene from the movie. But unfortunately, it was not and shock took over the valley on a night that had not yet ended.

"It's Mario, from Hortigüela," someone exclaimed.

"Somebody, help me get that poor man down!" we heard someone else shouting next to us.

"No, don't even think about it! We can't touch anything! We have to wait for the judge on duty and the rest of the authorities. Has anyone called 112 or the Guardia Civil?"

Alberto was right, and he was able to overcome the horror painted on that unfortunate man's face, a man who showed agony drawn in his gesture of pain. Alberto was studying criminology so he knew the importance of preserving a crime scene so it would not be altered and any important evidence preserved which, if destroyed, might prevent the investigators from finding the culprit.

And I say crime because I did not believe that this man had committed suicide, even if that way of dying was common for some suicides. Our criminal seemed to have become a serial killer and was once again leaving us a poisoned gift, although on this occasion we were not the only spectators of his macabre art. It was logical to believe that the author of such a barbarity was the same savage who had abandoned the body of another tortured in the monastery of San Pedro de Arlanza.

I had not even realized that the two corpses had been left in natural settings where the film had been shot. The horrifying image was too much for me to process easily. I moved a few meters away from the crowd that had gathered up in a moment, while Alberto tried in vain to shoo away the onlookers at the top of his voice.

Hundreds of people milled around the tree, snapping pictures with their phones and forever spoiling the confidentiality of a crime scene. Knowing people, the image of that hanging man would go viral within minutes. I was already imagining the hashtags on the Internet and, above all, the sensationalist headlines in some digital pamphlets.

Before us we had the body of an elderly man, dead by strangulation or perhaps by breaking his neck, after being hung with a rope from the hanging tree. An image that was forever etched on my brain. A mental photograph that would accompany me for the rest of my life. And there were already a few such images in a week that would change my life forever.

LIVING DEATH

Contreras (Burgos), August 1966

MARÍA

I could never fool my mother at any time. The trip on foot from the valley was very long and Juanito and I arrived in Carazo at an hour when our parents were already worried. The punishment was going to be one to remember, although that would not be the worst of that unfortunate night.

Juanito was not able to look me in the face all the way from the Mirandilla Valley to our village. The rest of the gang with whom we had gone to visit the cemetery had left long ago, so we were the only people walking along that road when it was already dark and it started to get colder.

I marched in front and Juanito had my back. We did not talk about it out loud, but we were both afraid of meeting the undesirables who had destroyed my life again. The solitude of the place did not encourage us to feel safer, so we tried to pick up the pace as much as we could. We both had bumps and bruises all over our bodies that prevented us from walking normally, plus fear was still in our veins. In my case, apart from the bruises, I also had an ache in my soul that would not allow me to breathe normally.

I was outraged and degraded. Two savages had raped me mercilessly and at that moment I had not thought of any other possible consequences of their actions, when perhaps they could have given me some disease or damaged me internally. Not to mention the terror that ran through my body when I realized the obvious: if a man ejaculated inside a woman, it was very possible that...

I put those ideas out of my mind and tried to focus on my steps. I did not want to stumble and fall on my face. I was already battered enough. Although the black cloud that had settled in my head threatened to drive me crazy.

The images of the aggression kept replaying over and over in my mind. I tried to push them away, but it was not an easy task, even less so in a state of nerves that forced me to look everywhere as soon as I heard any strange sound around me. It was a dreadful journey on foot, an agony that lasted longer than necessary perhaps because I myself wanted to delay it before the imminent meeting with my parents.

I began to feel guilty, as if I had done something wrong. I did not even want to imagine my mother's reaction when she found out that my body had been stained like that. Although then I remembered that I could not say anything to anyone, those bastards had threatened to kill us. But what could I do?

I had no excuse for coming back so late and on top of that we were arriving in a pitiful condition. I then thought of an alibi that could save us. Perhaps if we said that we had been mugged on our way home, by thugs who ambushed us on the road to attack and rob us, we might have a chance of getting out of the situation safely.

I talked it over with Juanito and he agreed with me. Or so I assumed, because he neither opened his mouth nor dared to look me in the face. He just nodded and I had to take his answer for granted. I imagined that he was totally ashamed over what he had witnessed, or perhaps he was flagellating himself for not having been able to help me, something too complicated given the numerical difference with the bullies. But his worries did not concern me, I had enough on my mind to think about someone else's feelings.

We said goodbye a few meters from my house and I saw Juanito going straight to his. That would be the last time I would see him. I went into my house with compunction and was happy to see my father's relieved face, but my mother's gesture made me get on my guard, and even more so when she asked me in a terse way where I had been to arrive at that hour. She told me she had been about to report me to the Guardia Civil.

I was unable to string two words together and broke down. I began to cry inconsolably and my father came over to hug me, cradling me in his arms as he had done since I was a little girl. His words of encouragement and his stroking of my hair were a saint's hand to my soul, so the unrestrained sobs began to subside into a fainter hiccup, a whimper that did not soften my mother's attitude.

She reproached his attitude towards me and attacked me again. She insinuated that I was late because I had been with Juanito and I could only bow my head. My father moved back a little and looked at me more calmly. He immediately noticed that my clothes were in tatters and that my milky skin appeared bruised like a peach on too many areas of my body that were free to the naked eye: arms, legs or neck. The good man was scared and asked me if someone had attacked me.

In the end I managed to tell the story I had invented minutes before as best I could, but my mother was not convinced by my explanations. She forced me to accompany her to her room and left my father in the living room. I was afraid to face her alone, without the support of my father, the only one who had always defended me.

My father was a good person, a bit weak in his relationship with my mother, who was the one who really wore the pants at home, but he went out of his way for his family. Although he was soft, and sometimes because of being a good person he had had more than one disappointment with neighbors of the town, I knew that if he found out what had really happened to me in the valley, he would stir up hell to give the culprits what they deserved. And I did not want him to get into trouble, even less when I knew what kind of guys they were.

"You don't fool me, you little wall flower. Tell me the truth, what have you done to have your clothes torn and those bruises all over your body?"

"I've already told you," I answered ashamed, unable to hold my mother's fierce gaze. They attacked us and when I tried to turn around, I fell into a rocky area. In the end they left us alone, but we were very frightened".

"And they dared to attack the whole gang of brats you were coming back together with?"

My mother was not a fool and I realized her strategy. It was quite possible that by then she had already been able to confirm that the rest of the Carazo neighbors with whom we had been on the excursion were safe and sound in their homes, so she must not catch me out. I did not have much time to come up with another ruse, so I got out of the way as best I could. I tried to explain that I had fallen behind the main group because my foot hurt and I had to walk slowly. I told him that Juanito was accompanying me.

"I knew it..." she smiled with satisfaction. She had me where she wanted me, or so she thought. What I could not imagine was what her next move was going to be.

"I already knew that whelp was involved in this story. Come on, get undressed."

"But I..."

"No buts! Strip right now or else…," She demanded.

I was unable to refuse and obeyed. I took off the few summer clothes I was wearing and immediately noticed that the bruises were becoming very visible in too many areas of my body. Even though my mother could not know that my neck and nape were hurting horribly from the rapist's hair pulling. Not to mention my insides and, of course, the irreparable damage my soul would carry forever.

I kept my panties and bra on, but my mother insisted. I was already very embarrassed to undress in front of her, especially since I had become a young woman, but the situation got worse from that moment on. I wanted to turn around, but she would not let me, so I stayed naked in front of her, with my arms covering my breasts and crotch in any way. Something the matriarch of the family was not going to consent to either.

"This is the last time I'm telling you, María," my mother's unmistakable voice thundered.

I was scared to death and embarrassed, I listened to her instructions and slowly withdrew my arms. I was then aware of the numerous bumps and scratches on my chest, but I missed something fundamental, a small definitive detail for me, the beginning of the end. My mother's triumphant face gave me no advance warning, but I knew something bad was about to happen.

"And what's that down there, you bitch?"

"What do you...?"

Confused, I bent my head to look at the spot my mother was pointing to. I had not noticed until that moment, but then I could see a trickle of blood running down my thighs from my crotch almost to my knee.

"It's not time for your period yet, so there's only one explanation left. Have you been a whore, María? Have you committed a mortal sin with that bastard Burgos?"

I tried to explain myself, but she would not let me speak.

She forced me to wash myself from top to bottom, as if the trace of ignominy could vanish with soap and water alone. I was aching inside and out so I did not do my best, but her orders were not open to discussion. In the end she snatched the washcloth I was trying to clean myself without hurting myself too much and rubbed me with all her strength, with a roughness that forced me to complain loudly.

"And now, get dressed and get out of my sight. You will stay locked in your room until I decide what to do with you. No daughter of mine is going to put me to shame in front of the whole town, least of all by sleeping with a son of Satan."

I implored her but she kept her word and left me locked up.

For a second it crossed my mind to tell the truth, even if it meant endangering my family. But everything happened too fast and I could not even protest. Perhaps it was better that all the blame fell on me, although I knew that my mother would not stay still. Poor Juanito was going to suffer the consequences, and the wrath of my parents would fall on him if I did not prevent it. How could I warn him?

...

The worst came ten days later, when I did not get my period on the dates my mother calculated. She gave me a margin of three days, just in case I was late for other reasons, although I had been quite regular since I was thirteen, but I did not go free. At the end of the week I had to accompany her to a doctor in Salas, who confirmed our worst fears: I was pregnant.

My mother took me by the ear to the village church. I thought her intention was to make me confess in front of the priest, but she had other ideas that she did not share with me. What she did do was regale me with a wide variety of insults to make me see how ashamed she was of her wayward daughter, a woman lost in the eyes of the Lord, who needed to purge her sins.

My mother locked herself in the sacristy with Father Cosme. She stayed there for a long quarter of an hour talking to him, while she forced me to remain on my knees, praying in front of the first pew facing the main altar.

When they came out they were talking as if they were lifelong friends:

"Thank you very much, Father, I can't thank you enough."

"Don't worry, my good woman, I'll take care of it. I'll make a couple of calls and confirm what we discussed as soon as possible. Although these arrangements take time, of course."

My mother nodded and I was left wondering, not knowing what they had been talking about. What I could not imagine was the betrayal that had been forged behind my back without me being able to do anything to prevent it.

Before leaving the church, I was forced to confess my sins in front of the priest. I was solicitous, but I quietly asked my confessor for a small favor: I would be much easier if my mother was not present, so that I could confess all my sins freely. The young priest accepted my request and ordered my mother to wait for me outside.

In the end I confessed everything that had happened to us, without leaving out a single detail. Nor did I specify too much, although the priest insisted, perhaps eager for morbid details. I even noticed some anxiety in the imperative tone with which he exhorted me to let go, and free my soul as I confessed my sins, when in reality it had been others who had sinned against me.

I knew the secret of confession and trusted that the Contreras parish priest would respect those limits. I hoped that the whole story would not reach my mother's ears and, of course, that none of the aggressors would ever know that I had told anyone about what had happened in the vicinity of the graveyard built for the film.

I was absolved of my sins after fulfilling the penance imposed by the religious. I walked away from there with a circumspect gesture and my face looking at the ground, self-conscious and ashamed of the situation. I was pregnant by one of those wretches who had soiled my body, but my mother blamed me and, above all, poor Juanito.

I turned my head for a moment before leaving the temple and I seemed to distinguish a different gleam in the parish priest's eyes, a not too beatific smile that even then, did not make me suspect the true intentions of the strange couple who had conspired against me. Later, I would understand the fundamental role that don Cosme had played in my subsequent misfortune.

I got out of there and my mother held my arm firmly, just in case I thought of running away or something. The way home was very tense, and the looks from our neighbors when we passed them did not help my mother to calm down. On the contrary, some of our neighbors rebuked us which enraged my mother further.

"Jesus, Pura, what are you doing to your little girl now. Too bad you didn't look after her so well before, you know what they say...."

"Mind your own business, Agustina's. And don't let me know that you're going around spreading gossip if you don't want to deal with me."

"Oh goodness, you scare me!"

The town's *comadres* laughed at the gossipy neighbor, and I picked up my pace to get away from there. I would rather be locked up back in the house than get into a fight with other women in the village on account of what had happened to me.

Because there had already been some rumors going around Contreras. Some people have bad intentions and must get bored too much. Something that my mother was not going to allow, that was clear to her.

I was also worried that I had not heard from Juanito for days. I was aware that he had been wandering around all the towns in the region, especially since the movie people had arrived in the Arlanza area, but I feared for his safety. My father had already threatened to break his neck as soon as he found out about my pregnancy, especially since he believed all the bullshit my mother had told him about it.

The confinement ended abruptly and it was not because my punishment was lifted. Overnight, out of the blue, we began to pack our things to leave town. Supposedly, my father had found a job in the city and we were all leaving Contreras. My family would rather leave than be the talk of the town, especially when my belly started to grow. What I never imagined was that the move would not be to the provincial capital.

Our real new destination was the biggest city in Spain: Madrid. And that is where we headed, with all the belongings we were able to gather in such a hasty move, while the neighbors murmured around us as they watched us close the Mediavilla family home.

I could not say goodbye to my friends, and I did not even hear from Juanito until much later, as it took me a long time to find out what had really happened to him. The cursed day we decided to approach the Mirandilla Valley had transformed the lives of several local residents and that infamy would forever haunt all of us involved.

We settled soon after in the big city, in the San Diego neighborhood of Madrid, just behind the church of the same name. We became new neighbors of Vallecas, a working-class area of humble people that was growing a lot in the south of the capital. But I did not have time to get attached to the new neighborhood, because the definitive setback came to put an end to my meager hopes.

I did not want to have a baby at sixteen, but as the weeks passed the little seed began to germinate in my belly, and my feelings towards a creature who had no guilt about its infamous origins gradually changed.

I was not prepared to raise a child and take care of it. I was a brat whom life had put in an untenable situation. I did not even know the meaning of the word abort, which I had heard on occasion from my father's lips, but I knew that my mother was not going to give in.

"You're crazy!" my mother had yelled at him when he brought it up. "That's even worse, a greater sin than what the girl has committed. Not to mention the danger to her life or the money it could cost us."

"But Pura..."

Arguments ensued, but in the end my mother got her way. I was unaware that we had left with the clothes on our backs and that we had settled in a humble house thanks to my father's savings. The poor man did not even have a job to feed us, so he got up early every day in search of our livelihood, unable to get a decent job in the big city.

The bickering in that tiny apartment was constant, but then my mother changed her sour expression - she had heard from the village and seemed happy. I tried to find out what was going on, but I could not get anything out of them.

Weeks later there came a turning point in my life for which I was not prepared. I fell for it like a fool when my mother asked me to accompany her on a cold November afternoon for a snack. She was meeting someone she knew. I was very surprised to meet Father Cosme in a cafeteria near our home, never suspecting his true intentions.

I remained attentive to the conversation between the two, but their sentences were too cryptic and I did not understand a thing. Even less so when sleepiness took hold of me, with drowsiness I was not used to at that time of the afternoon. I began to feel sick and almost threw up the glass of milk with *churros* that I had ordered for a snack, courtesy of our visit that afternoon.

Everything became foggy around me and I was not aware of what was happening. I must have lost consciousness and when I woke up the real nightmare had just begun: my mother had locked me up in Peñagrande.

THE MURDERER'S MOTIVES

Sad Hill Cemetery (Burgos), July 25, 2016

The Mirandilla Valley had become a hive of people, people running in all directions after the discovery of the man hanging from the hangman's tree. The murderer was playing with us, or maybe just with the authorities, recreating scenes from the movie *The Good, the Bad and the Ugly*, but this time with real dead people.

Alberto and I discussed this theory, but we could not agree. He told me that Clint Eastwood's character had almost died at the San Antonio Mission, and that *Tuco* had also escaped death's clutches on more than one occasion after being sentenced to hanging. In our parallel reality two men had died in two of the main locations where the film had been shot, so he maintained that the whole criminal plot had to do with Leone's film.

Neither of us could forget that a few days earlier an Italian who had participated in the movie had also died. However, we could not be sure that it had been premeditated.

"I think the criminal has seen a lot of thrillers, and wants to drive the investigators crazy by leaving clues related to the movie."

"Or maybe it all has to do with something that happened on the set, fifty years ago now. I don't know the actual age of the individual we found in the monastery, but I'd swear he was also quite old. Three men dead in strange circumstances, and all over seventy years old. It can't be a coincidence..."

"Are you saying that...?"

"I'm not saying anything, but there's something fishy going on here, don't you think?"

The uproar created by the macabre discovery transformed the cemetery into a real chaos. The few civil guards sent to the scene were not able to control the masses, much less secure the perimeter of the crime scene to preserve possible evidence left by the culprit.

Many people decided to leave the place before the authorities cut off the different accesses by car and did not allow them to leave the valley. All of us present might be witnesses to a crime, although apparently no one had seen anything. And, in addition, to make the work of the Guardia Civil even more difficult, there were many other participants who had left the Mirandilla Valley long before the event.

"We should leave too," I suggested to Alberto when I saw that he was heading straight to talk to the head of the *Benemerita*.

"We can't do that, Sandra."

"Really? Would you rather give them your name and tell them that you witnessed this crime, not to mention the discovery in San Pedro de Arlanza. And let me remind you that they also have your data as the discoverer of the car accident in the Carazo curves."

Alberto agreed with me. I had been too sarcastic in my intervention, but he did not take it personally. I was the first one who wanted to find out the truth and feel safe when the Sad Hill killer was put in jail. But we were getting nowhere by staying there all night, sleepless, waiting for the authorities to question the hundreds of people still left in the valley.

So, many of us had the same idea and the different vehicles started leaving the parking lot improvised for the occasion, to the despair of the civil guards. They had asked for help from their headquarters, but the scarce forces would still take a long time to increase enough to be able to carry out a task of such magnitude.

"This is getting out of hand Sandra, the Judicial Police in Madrid will also have to come. The department here doesn't have the means to solve these crimes."

In the end I convinced Alberto and we left the valley around two in the morning. The stream of ambulances, civil protection vehicles, police and civil guard left a curious picture in a bucolic environment that we could never again consider as such. A violent death and more so in the circumstances, in which it had occurred, would have a negative influence on the whole region. Or perhaps the morbid attraction of the hanged man would add a touch of legend to Sad Hill, a fictional cemetery that had become the real tomb of a man who was apparently well known in the Arlanza area.

Alberto's analytical mind continued to unravel details about the situation that I had not realized at that point of the night. Exhaustion was taking its toll on me, and even though the adrenaline shot after the discovery of the dead man had made us draw on our reserves, my body was asking me to rest so as not to collapse. That is why I did no t pay much attention to Alberto's next words: I switched on the autopilot and let myself be carried along those dirt tracks, on my way to civilization.

"The guards have a tough nut to crack. The murderer might have participated all afternoon in the different activities and left halfway through the film. Nobody noticed that a guy was hanging from the tree, who knows how long he had been hanging there." I nodded silently.

"He may not even have needed a car to escape from the crime scene. By car you can access the track from Contreras or through the curves around that rock to Silos. But apparently there are other roads that link the valley with towns like Carazo and that can be done on foot. Remember María's narration."

"Aha," I answered while trying not to close my eyes.

"Not to mention the difficulties to make a complete list of the participants in the excursion. I guess that the organizers of the festival have registered those who have signed up for the conferences, but no one asked for tickets to enter the valley. And here today there must've been about two thousand people, a hell of a lot."

"You're absolutely right, and that's what the murderer must've done," I said a little clearer, although I couldn't help yawning.

"We should have stayed at Sad Hill, although then we wouldn't have been able to leave tomorrow for Madrid. I guess they'll find me as soon as they check the list of participants in the convention, although it will take a few days while they sift through all the information. It will be impossible for them to find any decent clues at the crime scene. Hundreds of people have been there and then people have gone crazy about the dead man."

"I'm telling you; I even saw a van from a local television station in Burgos. And I'm sure the nationals also show up before they cordon off the area. Look, it's on Twitter: the murder is already trending topic.

At that time several hashtags having to do with what had happened between Contreras and Santo Domingo de Silos were trending topic in the province: #SadHill, #Hangman, #Cemetery, #Silos and of course, #ClintEaswood or #Leone. The social networks at the service of the news, although in reality it was the morbid and the television carrion that sold at that time.

"Shall I take you to Carazo?" Alberto then asked me. "I don't think they'll have heard anything, especially if there's no cell phone coverage there."

"I don't feel like explaining myself now and spend the whole night talking about it. I want to rest and get up early tomorrow to go to Madrid."

"As you wish..."

His half-sideways smile told me clearly that Alberto did not mind me spending the night with him, even though I did not have anything romantic in mind. Least of all after facing my second dead body in less than a week. Although, after what had happened with the discovery at San Pedro de Arlanza, I was not going to put my hand in the fire for anyone.

"If you don't mind, I can sleep in your quarters, but each of us in our own little beds," I replied as I winked at him.

"It's fine with me, no problem."

Julián was still not showing up in Salas, so no one would bother us. I thought we could get up early the next day, go to Carazo to pick up my things to leave early for Madrid and tell Ana's family what had happened in the cemetery after our friends' departure. But fate had not finished playing with us.

THE PUNISHMENT

Peñagrande Maternity Hospital (Madrid), autumn 1966

MARÍA

After waking up in that hell, I could not accept that my family had locked me up in that women's prison. Peñagrande was supposed to be a boarding school and maternity home for unmarried mothers, but the bars I encountered as soon as I entered the building bore witness to the true function of that institution: to keep the poor wanderers who did not comply with the precepts ordered by the Regime in the custody of the nuns.

When I arrived at Peñagrande I was almost four months pregnant and my stomach was starting to show. My thinness did not help to hide the pregnancy, so at that time I only had belly and breasts, which had also begun to grow during the last few weeks.

Whore was the nicest thing our jailers called us, those little nuns of the devil who made our lives impossible for so many months. They wanted to drown you, undermine your morale, and the beating was systematic from the very first moment. The role of each one of us in that representation of terror was clear from day one. We were not even allowed to raise our heads and look them in the eye, because we were a disgrace to society. But I had always been argumentative at home, so I refused to bow to their demands and paid for it with various punishments throughout my captivity.

I saw real barbarities with my own eyes. Like a poor girl who was there because she had become pregnant by her own father, who had systematically raped her since the onset of puberty. The nuns had taken it out on her from the very first moment and the poor girl could not take it anymore.

The worst came when this girl, a few months after giving birth, became pregnant again. The only time she left Peñagrande and had any kind of contact with a man was when her father got permission to take her out of there and take her with him for a weekend. You can imagine the string of insults that the poor girl received when they found out that she was pregnant again. Whore and bitch were understatements for her, who only wanted to fornicate with any man who crossed her path, always according to the nuns.

Our day started early, around seven in the morning. As soon as we got up, we were already working: each intern took care of different tasks that were entrusted to us, whether it was cleaning or in the kitchen. And all this without breakfast, so that we would learn. At that time there were no mops, so you can imagine how hard some of the tasks were, like scrubbing the floors on your knees with the nuns shouting because you were not doing it to their liking. And all this with an increasingly bulky belly.

Then they would deign to feed us a frugal breakfast so that we would not faint. Following that we would go to 'workshops', which were nothing more than manufacturing work for big brands. I am not going to mention these companies, but for decades hundreds of inmates worked there in subhuman conditions while sewing labels, making repairs, assembling boxes or any other tedious task that needed to be done. Real labor exploitation for which, to this day and as far as I know, no one has apologized or explained what actually happened there.

I hated saying the rosary, an activity we were forced to do twice a day. If at home I did not enjoy accompanying my mother in her prayers, I ended up getting a real grudge after my experience in the religious boarding school. I have not been to church for years and sometimes I regret it. But I think that, if God really exists, I will never understand why life has treated me so unfairly.

We endured continuous daily humiliations, insults and more humiliations. We were evil personified, sinners who had become pregnant as teenagers, only because of our desire for fornication, as Sister Brígida used to say. If we had been able to beget a baby out of wedlock, we had no right to have a full and happy life. Nor, of course, could we ever aspire to marry a normal husband who would love us and treat us well.

Later I learned that the state paid the religious order a generous monthly amount for each of us, but this did not result in improvements in our daily lives. Food was scarce and we wore increasingly tattered clothes, which we sometimes inherited from each other. Not to mention the lack of hygiene or medical attention, essential for pregnant women or those who had already given birth and were living there with their babies, all of whom were in rather deplorable condition.

The nuns took advantage of us and beat us mercilessly in our weakest moments. They repeated the same litany to me since I entered Peñagrande, assuring me, that a wretch like me would never be able to raise a child. I did not even have a family. I had been disowned - as my beloved crusader nuns kept telling me - and I had nowhere to even drop dead. How was I going to survive outside those walls, and with a child on top of that? The best thing would be to give her up for adoption and let a decent family take care of her upbringing and education in the firm Catholic principles.

Between insults and reproaches, as I had already heard from a colleague who had gone through that ordeal, you were forced to sign the adoption papers in the delivery room itself, if you had not done it before. While you were suffering from the pains of childbirth, screaming like crazy in a room that did not have adequate hygiene measures, the midwife would say: "You weren't screaming so much when you were under him". Of course, in those conditions, you would sign whatever was necessary to put an end to so much bitterness.

The truth is that at the beginning I only thought about ending the pregnancy, because I did not want to have the fruit of a rape inside me. But as time went by, I got used to my belly and I even talked to my baby and sang a lullaby I had heard at home in a low voice at night:

"Sleep, my pretty girl. The Virgin is with you..."

I did not know the sex of the baby, and I remembered the song that way because I had heard it from my mother. But deep down I did believe that I was going to have a girl, a precious baby that I grew more and more fond of as I pushed its true origin from my thoughts. For that reason, and even though I knew I could not get by with my child, I refused to sign the adoption papers for several months.

We were not allowed much joy, but the inmates managed to talk to each other. Ultimately, I learned the true nature of that maternity ward, which had become a gigantic money-making machine for a few.

A newly delivered co-worker was told that her baby was stillborn. The girl wanted to see her offspring, but was prevented from doing so. She never saw the baby's body, nor was she given a death certificate or anything like that. In fact, the nuns told her that the baby had been buried in the garden next to the main building of Peñagrande.

Another intern told me what she had heard from the mouth of 'Scalpel' the midwife famous for slitting all of us without any consideration:

"Don't worry, your child will be in the best of hands. A good Catholic family, who has made a generous donation to the cause, will take care of adopting him. Then he will be able to grow up in a real home and not be the unfortunate son of a whore like you."

The moment of delivery was dangerous because you could easily be tricked, but there were other women who lost their children months after birth. If the children got sick, they were taken to the *Botiquín* (dispensary), a place that began to be feared throughout the compound just by naming it. And it happened that apparently healthy children did not return alive from there, either because they had been sold or for other reasons that escaped our reasoning. Then their mothers would also disappear, like a conjuring trick that kept those of us locked up, alert at all times.

We all knew the place where the newborn babies were kept, placed in their baskets in a room with windows, so that the families who came to Peñagrande could choose the desired merchandise. According to rumors, up to three hundred thousand pesetas were paid per baby, at that time, a real fortune. A real market of children that took place there as something totally normal. Crimes against humanity that have never been judged, to the shame of several generations of Spaniards.

We came to believe that losing our babies was not the worst thing that could happen to us, since the adorable little nuns were also doing business with us. And I do not mean making money with our slave labor, which they did too, but the very fact of selling us wholesale, as if we were just another commodity. Many pregnant women suffered this in their own flesh, but I was spared in my gestation period because I had several medical problems during pregnancy. My time would come, Sister Brígida's disdainful smile seemed to say.

I had tried to raise my awareness throughout those months, but when my time came, I was not ready. My water broke and I went into labor one spring morning in mid-May 1967. The contractions became more frequent and painful, so I cried out for help. The nuns treated me terribly and forced me to walk to the delivery room, while they searched for the midwife without much interest.

When I was already on that rack, they spoke to me again about adoption. I screamed and cursed because of the intense pain. I just wanted my suffering to end. I cried and said no, shaking my head while thick tears rolled down my cheeks. I saw the icy stare of the nuns, immune to the pain of others, and I could not understand the lack of empathy of women who were supposed to serve God.

At the end they brought me some papers and I do not remember well what happened. I am not aware of having signed anything of my own free will, but in the haze of that moment of blood and pain I think I have a glimpse of iron hands grabbing my arm, placing a pen in my hand and forcing me to scribble on a piece of paper. Sister Brígida seemed satisfied, looked at me with contempt and made a gesture to 'the Scalpel' before leaving that filthy room. And the slaughterer began to do her work.

They did not trick me with excuses that the baby was stillborn or that they were taking it to another room to put him in the incubator. They just took my baby away from me, without even allowing me to see or hold it, I had already signed the adoption papers. I never knew if it was a boy or a girl, although in my heart I kept thinking that I had given birth to a beautiful little girl. A baby girl that I would never cradle in my arms, and my soul was hopelessly broken as I realized the truth.

I screamed and kicked, I did not want them to take my baby. But every effort was in vain and I could never ever recover what had been taken from me with such viciousness. I wanted to take it out on the first nun I came across, and as soon as I recovered a little, I insulted all the architects of that robbery, ranting loudly while I was spouting blasphemies of all kinds. And, of course, I took my punishment.

First, they forced me to wash with cold water the very sheets that I had stained with blood during the delivery, assuring me that I would spend a long time in a punishment cell for my dirty mouth. Adrenaline had tugged at me at the sight of losing my baby, but immediately my body reacted to the real botched job that 'the Scalpel' perpetrated on my body, and I passed out on the spot. When I woke up hours later, I knew I had lost everything.

During my pregnancy I had only put on a couple of kilos due to the poor nutrition that prevailed in Peñagrande, although the baby seemed to have been born strong and lush. At least I had heard its cries and they sounded powerful, with great character. A distant cry that I would hear in my sleepless nights for a long time.

But in the weeks that followed, I lost even more weight because I refused to eat. I shut myself in my solitude and refused to fight, oblivious to everything. I did not want to go on living, not after assuming that what I loved most had been taken away from me, the baby born from my womb that I could never cradle or breastfeed.

A breast that had been bandaged as soon as I gave birth so that my milk would not come, but which plunged me into an even deeper depression because of what it meant. At least I was not forced to be a wet nurse to other children, as had happened to other fellow captives.

My ordeal lasted several weeks, but the nuns would not allow me to starve to death. They forced me to eat and kept me alive, when all I wanted was to leave this miserable world. It took me a long time to come to my senses, but in the end, I slowly climbed out of that pit, not knowing that later I would fall into others just as deep and dangerous.

THE TRUE RAISON D'ÊTRE

Salas de los Infantes (Burgos), July 25, 2016

The night had been very long and not precisely because Alberto and I had devoted ourselves to the amatory arts, although we woke up again sleeping in the same room of the rural lodging. The events at Sad Hill Cemetery upset any plans we might have had in mind, but the early morning also left us with a new shock in the form of fragments received from María's diary. What it told was terrible. The news of the post-rape pregnancy left me very shaken.

"Wait, there's still another post to read," Alberto told me.

If I had already been blown away by María's account of how she found out about her pregnancy and how she had been tricked into being locked up in Peñagrande, the following text completely knocked me out. It could not be! María's baby had been taken away from her and an inconceivable idea began to take hold of my mind.

"It all makes more sense now. Wait a minute... You don't think you...?"

My neurons were working at full speed, even though minutes before they had been threatening to shut down completely. The shock of reading the last fragment of María's diary had left us speechless for a few moments. But I quickly pulled myself together and assumed what Alberto was trying to insinuate. Anything was possible. I was María's spitting image, as I had been told in her village. I could not rule anything out.

"Yeah, I know, it's very heavy," I said to Alberto as he looked at me without hiding his astonishment,

"My mother is María's lost daughter. And that means that my mother was a stolen baby, or that my grandparents adopted her through the boarding school in Peñagrande".

"You'll have to talk to them to find out …."

I nodded silently, pondering the true magnitude of such a serious event. I did not know if I would have the strength to face something like this: to confront my grandparents and find out the best kept secret in the family. Before falling asleep, I had time to imagine the conversation with my grandmother, where I would have everything to lose if it came to that.

The next day we decided to leave the lodge early and have breakfast in Carazo. I had discussed it with Alberto and he supported me with some reluctance, but it was the best decision: we would share all the information with our friends to unburden ourselves and ask for their advice. Minutes later we arrived at our destination and Menchu and Monica were there to greet us outside the house. They invited us inside for freshly brewed coffee and we gladly agreed.

Monica instructed us to sit on the bench in the living room while she prepared us a good breakfast, after learning that we had not eaten since the night before. We then had to endure the direct interrogation of Menchu, who seemed to suspect that this was not a courtesy visit.

I did not know where to start and Alberto came to the rescue. He encouraged me by holding my hand in his and intervened as a prologue.

"Did you hear about what happened last night at Sad Hill?"

"No, what happened?" asked Monica. "Don't scare me anymore, please."

At that moment, Julián's sleepy face appeared on the stairs, and he seemed surprised to see so many people gathered around the main table of the house. He waved to us and went to the kitchen to get a glass of water. We all fell silent and stared at him, waiting for an explanation of his presence.

"Yeah, I spent the night here, okay? I had an argument with Carolina and I decided to come here. I didn't want to bother the lovebirds."

"Oh, man, you should've warned me," answered Alberto. I did not even have time to blush at Julián's affirmation, who was absolutely right. "You haven't heard anything either?"

"Heard about what?"

The noise coming from the first floor of the house ended up waking up the only two tenants still in bed. Raquel and Ana also appeared minutes later, and I made up my mind.

"Hey guys, come down as soon as you can, this will interest you. We need to talk to you and I'd rather you were all present."

"Are you getting married or what?" asked Ana jokingly.

"I swear this is very serious. And a very long story that we have to tell you. We need your advice and your help. This is beyond us."

Menchu must have realized that I was serious and took charge of the situation, a detail for which I was grateful. Her attitude had changed and now she was looking at me with a hint of curiosity, perhaps trying to guess where things were going to go. I do not think she really had the slightest idea what we were planning to tell her next.

"Well, folks, first we'll tell you what happened at Sad Hill at the end of the movie screening."

Everyone was nonplussed at Alberto's tale, and he was peppered with questions during his speech. I tried to help him as much as possible, but nerves began to surface in the room and Menchu had to bring order.

A few minutes later I took over Alberto's place, standing at the head of the table. It was my turn to speak. I began by talking about the accident that Alberto and Julián had witnessed, but our friends did not understand why I was bringing it up again.

I asked them to be calm, everything in its own time. My nerves were on edge, but I had to continue. Alberto intervened to help me and managed to dazzle them with a story typical of the suspense genre. Without going into amorous details, he narrated our trip in the middle of the night to the monastery after receiving those mysterious anonymous letters.

Everyone scolded us for having been so reckless, but I could no longer stop my storytelling. I needed to let go and tell everything that was tormenting my soul. I asked for their patience again so that I could explain what had happened during the last week. The part about the murders had not been easy, but now it was really complicated. I explained the investigation of Menchu's friend María, and her family in her presence, with a story that had upset us for many reasons.

"You see, it all started the same day I arrived here...."

I explained my feelings at the sight of the 1966 photograph and all that it entailed. Ana already knew about it, but the rest were very surprised to learn that Alberto and I had tricked them in order to go visiting a senile old lady in a nursing home in Burgos.

"So, Doña Pura is still alive?" asked Menchu with surprise.

"Yes, but she couldn't clear our doubts."

I told them what María's mother had told us in detail and how those words of hers had led us to discover the hidden blog of her lost daughter. Menchu was thrilled to hear from her old friend and wanted to know more.

"Did you find her?" She asked excitedly.

"No, not so far, although we are working on it. If you will allow me, I am going to tell you what we have discovered in the same order in which we have been finding it out. Although it is not a linear account, you will see that it all makes sense."

Initially, I was interrupted with questions here and there, but, in the end, everyone remained silent, absorbed by my narration. I felt more and more comfortable, perhaps liberated by talking about something that had been gnawing at me for days. A catharsis that encouraged me to tell everything, including the final discovery, the last post read a few hours before.

They all looked at me expectantly, assimilating my words and I guessed that they had reached the same conclusion as we had. Then Menchu got up from her chair and came to embrace me with a special affection. I took refuge in her arms and let myself be cradled, while my muscles, contracted by the accumulated tension, began to loosen. I relaxed and let go after the effort, letting out a sigh that I did not mind sharing in front of the group.

"My girl, I already had a feeling that you belonged to that family," Menchu said with a much sweeter expression on her face. "You know I was shocked when I met you, it was like reliving my youth and being in front of poor María again."

"We don't know for sure yet," I replied. "I'll try to talk to my grandparents today and see what they tell me."

"I don't know what they will tell you, child, but you are María's granddaughter, I have no doubt now. I didn't want to burden you with my ideas, but I had already thought about it before. And not only for being the spitting image of my childhood friend.

"What do you mean?" I asked.

"This, irrefutable proof of your true origin."

Menchu approached me, asked permission to move my hair away from my neck and pointed to a spot just below the nape of my neck.

"What's going on?"

I did not understand anything, especially when I realized that the rest of the people in the room had remained mute, examining the back of my neck.

"Now I understand," I replied as it dawned on me. "Yes, I know, but it's not that unusual either. I have a heart-shaped birthmark on my neck, but a lot of other people have birthmarks too."

"That's all very good, Sandra. The problem is that María had one exactly like it in the same place as you. Doña Pura didn't have it and your mother, I've no idea but María did and so do you. It seems that the birthmark skips a generation and is passed down from grandmother to granddaughter."

I could not suppress my emotions and had to sit down on a chair. I covered my mouth at the discovery, still unable to assume the consequences of the finding. Menchu had just confirmed that I was María Mediavilla's granddaughter and the shock left me bewildered. It was hard for me to react, troubled by the implications of something I had been thinking about since the early hours of the morning. Although in my inner self I had already felt, for several days, that I was related to that lost girl who had suffered so much in life.

There was silence for a few moments in the room and I was grateful for the deference of those present. It is not the same to have suspicions as to have something confirmed, news so devastating that it forever changes your view of the world. Who was I really? And why had I ended up in a beautiful house in the Arganzuela neighborhood instead of anywhere else?

The vicissitudes of María's life, my real grandmother, had affected me more than usual throughout such an intense week. Since we began to receive loose fragments of her personal diary, I knew there was something more to it. It was not normal for me to be so shocked to learn of that girl's odyssey, no matter how empathetic I thought I was and no matter how heartbreaking her story was. No, her unfortunate misadventure affected me on a much more intimate and personal level.

María's story would become my own story, the narration of a life of suffering and pain that changed the personality of a poor girl forever. Adversities that forged the character of a person I wanted to meet with all my strength, a fighter with whom I totally identified.

I could never avoid the connection I felt from the first moment with something that should not have moved me in that way. Something ancestral, mythical, that came from the gut. During those days I did not want to stop to think about it carefully and the maelstrom of everything that happened did not leave me a second of peace, so I could only go forward with everything that was happening to us.

But from then on, nothing would be the same. I had to assume that my life had changed, and although I would always keep my current name and surname, I needed to know everything about my origins. Maybe I would never find María, or maybe she had already died, and if the rest of her family had passed away and Doña Pura was in the last part of her life's journey, I would be orphaned again, as when I lost my real mother. It was too big a setback that I did not intend to accept. Hence my determination to find María, the heroine of this whole plot, at all costs.

"Come on, child, that's enough," Menchu told me gently. "We all support you, but now you have to talk about it with your family."

"Yes, I'll do that as soon as I get home," I replied a little calmer.

"Forgive me for interrupting," said Alberto, more cerebral than the rest of us. "I don't know if the story we told about that day in the valley and all that followed corresponds to your memories."

Alberto had addressed Menchu directly, and the good woman still took a few seconds to answer. She seemed to reflect on the question or perhaps she was trying to dig into her memory of the events of fifty years ago.

She then told us a story that left me somewhat confused, perplexed by some details I still did not know about what happened in that summer of '66. The rumors about María's pregnancy, the fate of Juanito or the inexplicable disappearance of the Mediavilla family from the village overnight added more discordant elements to an already very complicated equation.

The story was beginning to take shape, although there were still many shades to be discovered. We had come a long way but I was not a conformist person. I had already drawn up a short list of tasks in my head for when I returned to Madrid: to investigate the Peñagrande maternity ward, to visit the neighborhood of Vallecas where the Mediavilla family had lived in case anyone remembered them and, above all, to lay my cards on the table at home.

I had to make sure that this whole story was not a huge fabrication of mine, to verify that my mother really was María's illegitimate daughter, although I was very afraid, really panicked actually, of running into more unpleasant surprises. The dice were cast and I could not let go.

I had to get going as soon as possible. We concluded the conversation - at least on my part, as I went upstairs to gather my things, since the others continued to talk about the subject in the meantime – so as to return to the capital with the greatest speed. I heard some loose snippets of conversation from the room, while Alberto gave some small instructions to our mutual friends.

“And remember, if the Guardia Civil asks you, you don't know anything.”

“I don’t think they will come here to ask,” Raquel answered. “In any case, we left early and didn't see anything, so we wouldn't be able to tell the police much.”

“I also left before anything happened” Julián assured. “I don't think they are looking for us, it will be more normal for them to try to talk to you, since they have a better idea of where you are because you actively participated in the activities of the congress.”

“Don't worry," Menchu said. “The secret will be safe within these four walls, no one will talk about what we have learned here today.”

I was not present when she said this, but I understood that Menchu's word was law and no-one there would say a word. None of us had committed any crime, although we had come across a corpse in a strange way, but there would be time to clear it up with the authorities. I had other priorities at the time and everyone seemed to understand and support me in my difficult decision.

I thought about suggesting another visit to Doña Pura to Alberto before returning to the capital, but in the end, I did not do it. We said our goodbyes, promising to return to Carazo as soon as possible, and set off for Madrid.

The most difficult day of my life had just begun and I was afraid of what might happen when I held my grandparents up to the mirror of their past performance. I did not want to prejudge them or criminalize their behavior, but I would need some very convincing explanations to understand why they had done what they had. But above all, why they had kept it from me all that time.

ISOLATION

Contreras – end of August 1966

María Mediavilla and her family were the talk of Contreras during those days. The rumors ran from house to house throughout the town, and nobody knew for sure what was happening in the heart of that home. The only thing that seemed clear was that Doña Pura had punished her daughter, who was locked up and not allowed to see anyone.

Young Menchu learned this firsthand when she tried to visit María. Doña Pura flatly refused to let the girl into her house and would not allow her to hear from her friend. She admitted that her daughter was grounded until further notice, but would not explain any more. She begged her please not to insist, she was not going to give an inch.

Menchu was not deterred and tried to find a solution. She even went so far as to harass poor Jaime, María's little brother, to see if he could tell her something about her friend. But as soon as Doña Pura became aware of the situation, she also forbade the boy to go out on the street alone so as not to give more fuel to the gossips.

Other friends tried on different occasions, but the result was similar. During the following weeks they did not manage to see María again, except for the day when Doña Pura dragged her to the church, to the mockery and derision of everyone. Half the town witnessed the unpleasant argument between Doña Pura and other neighbors of Contreras, although in the end there was no bloodshed.

Nobody thought of asking don Cosme, the town's parish priest, in case he could shed some light on such a lurid matter. They knew that the young priest would not break the secret of confession, plus the gossipy neighbors preferred to continue to speculate at their own pace, with increasingly imaginative ideas about the situation at the Mediavilla home.

Menchu recalled a few days later what happened on the excursion when she met one morning with other friends in the town square. Dolores, the owner of the camera with which they had taken pictures in the valley, met with several of the girls to give them a copy of the images of that day.

"That's a great picture!" said Menchu as she saw one taken with many of her friends next to the Sad Hill hangman's tree.

Many other neighbors of Contreras appeared in the image, among them María and Juanito. And, of course, the conversation between the girls drifted towards what happened to the young couple, the subject of whispers in most homes in the town.

Menchu had not spoken directly to María about the matter, but through her friend Carmen she knew that the girl had been involved with Juanito for some time. In the group they sensed that they were going steady or something like that, so it had seemed normal that they were walking all day together in the Mirandilla Valley. Someone had noticed that in the middle of the afternoon the couple slipped away on their own, but they thought it inconsequential.

Later, Menchu had returned to Contreras in the company of other boys and girls from the village, although not all those who had left from the church in the morning were present. Among those absent were María and Juanito, but no one made much of it, they would return at their own pace when they wanted to.

Hours later, Doña Pura had gone to some neighbors' houses to ask if all the kids had returned from the excursion and to see if anyone knew the whereabouts of María. Her friends covered for her as best they could, although the news that Juanito was also missing from his house spread quickly. María's mother tied up the loose ends and exploded.

Evil tongues had a feast during the following days, with more and more implausible stories about what really happened. The town's gossips took advantage of the occasion to vilify María and take revenge on Doña Pura, who was not exactly the most beloved woman in town.

Menchu did not want to pay attention to the gossip, but in Contreras they only talked about María's possible pregnancy, the main reason why the girl could have been locked up, separated from her boyfriend and her friends. Someone who knew the doctor in Salas that the Mediavilla family visited confirmed the rumor and the *comadres* were furious against the poor girl.

Meanwhile, Juanito preferred to sneak out of town and also avoided going near the Mediavilla's house, just in case. María's father had sworn in front of witnesses to deal with him, and the boy was not about to allow himself to be beaten mercilessly. Although it was of little use to him to take so many precautions.

Days later a hunter found his body in the river, half eaten by the vermin of the mountain, very close to the gorge of La Yecla. The authorities said that he had fallen and broken his neck in the fall, with the fatal result. His family cried foul, but no one lifted a finger to investigate that misfortune.

The news fell like a bucket of cold water among the small group of young people of the town, although they soon forgot about it. Everyone had heard about Eusebio Mediavilla's threats against the deceased young man, but no one investigated the case. And, in addition, days before the macabre discovery, the Mediavilla family had vanished from Contreras overnight. That smelled rotten, but nobody seemed to care.

The memory of the Mediavilla family faded with time in the imagination of the neighbors of Contreras, who only from time to time spoke of that strange situation. Months later new news arose about them that nobody could corroborate: some said that they had emigrated to America, others that they were in Galicia. However, no one ever heard anything about any member of that family again.

THE CONFRONTATION

Madrid, July 25, 2016

The trip from Arlanza to Madrid was shorter than I expected. At first, I shared my impressions with Alberto, as we talked about the conversation we had had earlier at Carazo's house. Neither of us knew if we had done the right thing, but at least we got rid of a great weight that was weighing heavily on our souls.

Once we passed Aranda de Duero, Alberto put on the radio and left it at a discreet volume on a classical music station. Perhaps he thought that I needed to calm down in the face of the painful prospect looming in my immediate future: the confrontation with my grandparents.

My whole vision of myself, my family and life in general had gone down the drain from one day to the next. What I had known at home, with my family, was nothing more than a lie, a vulgar hoax that now showed its mouth ready to devour me mercilessly. The fire I felt in my gut was eating me up inside, but at the same time it gave me the strength to find out the true reality that enveloped me.

I did not want to get riled up beforehand. I did not know why they had adopted a baby - if that was the right term to describe what had happened to my mother, taken from María's arms when she was just born, although that in itself was not unethical or unlawful. I could also understand that they wanted to protect me, believing that it would affect me to know that my mother was adopted and not blood of their blood.

This information was not essential for me. Perhaps my mother had known everything and had assumed it naturally, although one would suppose that the truth she was told had been somewhat sweetened. The memories of my mother were buried in my memory in a diffuse way.

I was still very young when she died, but from what little I remember and from conversations I have had later with people around us, my mother was always a very upright and capable person, an idealist who fought for what she believed was right. And I was very surprised that she had willingly accepted her own sinister origin.

I could not even imagine my grandparents' motives for going so far in such a delicate matter for anyone. I knew of some cases of people around us who had adopted children in other countries after a very painful process, but which had turned out well in the end. If those children were loved in their new home, treated as their own children and raised in a good environment, the happiness of all the members of the family eventually overcame any difficulties that had arisen along the way.

I had even read information about adopted people who were aware of their true origins. Some of them got to know their biological parents, I imagine in a not easy process in which many different factors were involved, but they always considered their adoptive parents as their real family, the one that had raised them and given them the values they carried out their life with.

My case was different, yet similar in some respects. I was not the one to judge a couple's reasons for adopting a baby, but if that fact entailed a type of action that brought more harm than good for the mother who was leaving her child behind, I could not accept it just like that. Even less so after learning about the real suffering of María Mediavilla, a terrible story that I was planning to tell my grandparents.

I imagined then discovering that I was the adopted one and that my birth mother had had to give me up under such distressing circumstances as María had suffered. The pain would have torn me up inside and I might never have been able to forgive my adoptive parents. But the reality was quite different. I was only the daughter of an adopted woman, a woman with whom I could never share my concerns after being abandoned in my youth due to a fatal accident.

I missed my mother more than ever. I needed her by my side. Yes, my grandparents had given me everything, but I had grown up without true references. Not only did I need my mother, but also the father figure loomed large before me when I remembered the bad times I had experienced in my childhood. Especially when I suffered the mockery of my classmates at school, the cruelty of children that marked you with fire at a stage of your life, that you would always remember with sorrow and anguish in your soul.

"Wake up, Sandra," I thought I heard in the distance. "We're arriving in Madrid. Do you want me to take you straight home?"

"Huh? Yes, sorry, I was distracted."

Alberto nodded and continued looking at the road. We crossed the city in less time than usual; the summer traffic allowed drivers accustomed to the chaos of Madrid to take a little license. And a few minutes later we arrived at Toledo Street. Alberto double parked for a second while I got my suitcase and said goodbye to him, on my way to one of the most difficult moments of my short life. I promised to call him later and made my way to my front door.

I rang the downstairs bell and my grandmother opened right away. I stepped into the elevator loaded with my small suitcase, while a jumble of emotions overflowed inside me.

She was waiting for me on the landing and I could not hold back. I dropped the suitcase on the floor and ran to meet her, hugging her, as if it were the last time I would be able to hold her in my arms.

"What's all this about, Sandra!" exclaimed my grandmother.

"I missed you so much," I exclaimed, it was not a lie: the incredible story I had been involved in brought out feelings I had not even been aware of harboring inside me. But what I really felt was a terrible fear, a panic of being left without the people I had shared my whole life with.

"And I've missed you too, honey. Come on, let's go inside."

My grandmother's expression of joy when she saw me changed. I thought I could see a shadow of uneasiness on her face, even though she could not imagine the bomb I was about to drop on her.

"Are you all right, Sandra? You seem upset about something."

"Well, yes, you see..."

First thing in the morning I had not had time to look for anything, between leaving the rural lodging and then the conversation with Ana's family. On the way, before I got caught up in my own thoughts, I wanted to check for myself what they were saying on the Internet about the previous night's event in Sad Hill.

Several digital media echoed the news plus it appeared in the more important newspapers, but not with big headlines. None of them had it on the front page, so I assumed that at home they had no reason to have heard about it. Social media was a different matter, especially Twitter and Facebook, but I was less concerned about that. My grandparents were old-fashioned and did not have social profiles of their own, so there was no need to worry.

I did not know where to start anyway. I had not yet planned my defenses well and I was not prepared for an assault of any magnitude. In my daydreams about how the dialectic duel with my grandparents would go, I had imagined two main options: attack by surprise, as soon as I arrived, to catch the other side off guard (I did not want to think of them as my enemies), or wait, giving myself time until I found the best moment for direct confrontation.

What I had not taken into account was that all the poise I could have mustered to face such a delicate moment would slip through my fingers as soon as I had my grandmother in front of me. Her big almond-shaped eyes looked at me with gentleness, but also with a firmness that made me cringe. Doubts were not good counselors when facing something so delicate, so I decided to face the situation.

Then it dawned on me. My grandfather had not come out to meet me and that was impossible if he had been at home. I did not feel like repeating the torture twice, so I had to ask first.

"Where's Grandpa?

"He'll be here soon, honey. He's gone for a walk and to run some errands. You know he does not like to sit still at home, he needs to get out and clear his head."

I nodded with a sad smile; I knew my grandfather. He did not take retirement well - he was a very active man. He always had something to do, some activity that kept him busy. And that day was to be no exception. At home they ate early, so I figured he would be here soon. I glanced at the clock slyly and saw that it was close to one o'clock. Maybe I would have time to prepare the ground while we waited. I could try, although my grandmother would see me coming before I even tried any tricks. I regretted it as soon as I told her I had something important to tell them.

A look of concern appeared on my grandmother's face. She had escorted me to the living room and I did not even have time to go to my room to drop off my suitcase. We sat on the wide *chaise longue* and she took my hands in hers. I could not break down, but I felt I would not be able to go through with it.

"Let's see... Do you remember what I told you the other day?"

"What do you mean?"

Her face reflected unfamiliarity, but I knew that my grandmother knew how to disguise it very well. Her memory was perfect for her age and I had no doubt: she remembered our last conversation perfectly well. It was another thing if she felt like remembering it or digging into a specific subject.

"What I told you about the photograph they had shown me, the one of a girl from Burgos, a friend of Ana's aunt, who looked a lot like me."

"Oh, that, yes..." She replied dismissively, as if it were nothing important. "Are you still going on with that nonsense?"

"It's not nonsense, Grandma. Look at this."

I then took my phone out of my purse, looked for the image and enlarged it so that she could see it more clearly. My gesture did not admit a refusal, so if she had thought at some point to ignore me, she had to change her mind. She put on her reading glasses and took the phone from my hand. She looked at the photograph with indifference while I watched her reactions.

She was good, I admit it, but her face betrayed her. Her pupils glowed when she saw what I had already told her, and she could not hide that physiological reflex, although she tried to hide it, as best she could. She took off her glasses as she pulled herself together, moments before looking at my face again.

"Yes, maybe, it looks like you. I don't see too well, you know that my eyes are not what they used to be..."

"She looks just like me, you know that. As grainy as the image is, that girl and I are spitting images of each other when I was her age."

My tone came out harsher than I intended, but it was no time to mince words. She acknowledged the blow with aplomb and pulled herself together immediately.

"Maybe, I don't know... A coincidence like any other, I don't know what all the mystery is about."

"That's what I'd like to know, Grandma, the reason for so much mystery. And no, it's no coincidence, it's something much stronger."

My grandmother leaned back on the sofa. She seemed a little upset and, even if that was not my intention, perhaps it would serve to disarm her before achieving my goal: learning the truth about María Mediavilla. I thought about waiting for grandfather, but nothing could stop me now. I noticed a point of weakness in her and I could not restrain myself. I had to use that advantage and, although I felt terrible for manipulating an old woman in that way, I was not going to let her give me any more delays. It was now or never.

"Did you know that this girl's name was María and she was sixteen when she disappeared? Her friend Menchu was speechless after meeting me. She thought she was seeing a ghost..." my grandmother tried to speak, but I abruptly cut her off, "Let me continue, please. Menchu assured me that María had a birthmark on her neck very similar to mine. Is that also a coincidence?"

"It's not so strange, many people have birthmarks."

"Yeah, but that's not the case. I'm just like this woman and we even have the same birthmark. Menchu never found out what happened to her friend fifty years ago, but apparently her family disappeared from the village when the rumor spread that the girl had become pregnant."

"I don't know why you're telling me all this, really."

My grandmother Matilde's facade of indifference had given way to a demeanor that I could not quite define. There was concern on her face, of course, but I also recognized a hint of curiosity. As if deep down she wanted to know what I had found out. It was not the time to let up, so I went back to work.

"Are you familiar with the Peñagrande maternity house? That girl was abandoned there by her family and someone later took her baby away from her."

My grandmother became nervous at the news, as if an imaginary blow had hit her chin. Her surprise was genuine and she could not or would not hide it. The name of Peñagrande was not new to her, and I knew I was close to wringing a confession out of her.

"Well, no, actually, it doesn't ring any bells."

Even she realized that she had not lied too gracefully. But she did not back down and continued with a haughty, proud pose, without looking away. I knew the ordeal went on inside, but it was going to take me a world to defeat her.

"Are you sure, Nana? That's not what I've found out...."

I bluffed and I knew I had hit the bull's eye. To tell the truth, I only had speculation, circumstantial evidence. I had no proven facts to show that my grandparents had snatched María's baby from her mother's arms. But my grandmother's defensive gesture and the slight twist of her neck told me more than her words could ever confess.

She had cocked her head to one side unconsciously, perhaps seeking to check that the evidence was still safely tucked away in her room. And it was in that direction that I caught her looking for a fleeting moment. Almost a flicker, nothing significant, but after all a gesture that did not escape me.

"What are you doing?" she asked anxiously as she saw me get up at full speed and head for her bedroom without hesitation.

"Nothing, just checking that you're not lying to me. I just remembered the scolding I got for rummaging through your room one day when I was a kid. I never went back in, maybe it's time to take a good look in your drawers."

My grandmother stood up and tried to stop me from entering her room, but the emotion of that instant got the better of her. She had to stop halfway and sit down again, with a look of overwhelming panic on her face, a look that she could not disguise.

"Are you all right, Grandma?"

"Yes, honey, it was just a dizzy spell. Go on, bring me a glass of water."

Was she lying to me? It seemed very strong to me that she could be faking an attack to get rid of me in such a way, or perhaps to hide the evidence of infamy before I found it. I was not planning on searching her things without permission, but her reaction to my movements confirmed what I already sensed.

I brought her a glass of water and she seemed to recover her spirits minutes later: her agitated breathing calmed down and the blush rose again to her cheeks. It hurt my soul to see her like that and I did not mean to hurt her, but I was willing to go all the way.

"Grandma, please, no more lies. Trust me, I will not judge you for what you may have done. I just want to know the truth."

"Oh, my child, it's not that easy. Sometimes the truth depends on the glass through which you look at it, you will understand with time."

At that moment I heard a noise at the door and saw my grandfather enter the apartment. He was surprised to see me at home and his face lit up as if by magic, until his countenance turned ashen when he realized the state of his wife. I did not even have time to greet him as he came to help his wife.

"Calm down, Adolfo, it was just a dizzy spell. Don't worry, I'm fine."

"Are you sure?" he asked, unconvinced.

"Yes, really. It will pass in a few minutes it was just a drop in my blood pressure when I got up in a hurry."

"I've told you...."

"Come on, Sandra, talk to your grandfather. I think he can explain it better."

The old lady did not deny the evidence and seemed to want to get out of the way and pass the ball to her husband. I had gone too far, even to the point of upsetting my grandmother, so I could not back out at that point. He looked at me strangely, trying to figure out what it was all about. I am sure the truth had not crossed his mind then. I did not think his wife had told him about my discovery when I had phoned him a few days before from Carazo.

"Will someone tell me what the hell is going on here? And you, Sandra, why are you back so soon? I thought you were staying a couple more weeks at your friend's town."

"Please, Adolfo. The girl will explain everything to you, won't you, Sandra?"

If it had already been difficult to confront my grandmother alone, now the situation became even more delicate with both of them hanging on my words. I sighed inwardly, inhaled as deeply as I could and set about tearing down any defenses that might still remain in the family.

"Yes, I'll explain it to you right now. But first I want you to answer me a very simple question, Grandpa. I just need a yes or a no, okay?"

"Of course, just ask."

"Was my mother adopted?"

The direct question caught my grandfather off guard, he did not know where to hide and looked away instantly. My grandmother's alarmed demeanor told him clearly that he had made a mistake, although he tried to redirect the situation."

"What's that all about, child?"

"Answer the question, please."

"I don't understand why you're asking me that, really. I..."

"I know everything, grandfather. I know about Peñagrande and I have found María, my real grandmother. I need to know what really happened."

My grandfather looked at me with his jaw unhinged and his eyes popping from their sockets. He seemed to ask his wife for confirmation as he silently questioned her with his gaze, and my grandmother's downcast mien must have convinced him of the truth. I took the opportunity to pull out my phone, show him the photo of María with her friends at Sad Hill and explain what I knew.

The old man seemed to collapse, although he soon recovered after he sat down on the sofa. He looked at me with a serious but determined expression, almost as if he was taking a great weight off his shoulders by confessing his sins.

"I don't know what you think you know, Sandra, but everything was legal. It's true, we adopted your mother, but we followed all the correct channels."

"Really?"

My grandmother went to her room and rummaged through the drawers, until she found the documents she had previously feared I would discover. She handed them to me silently and my grandfather nodded to me, so that I could check it with my own eyes. There were various papers there, such as some sort of contract or receipts for the money paid. My adoptive grandparents had spent a whopping three hundred thousand pesetas for an adoption that sounded to me like a common baby purchase. A lot of money for the time, and we will never know in whose hands it ended up.

But what caught my attention the most was the signed authorization from the biological mother, or the supposed letter from María, in which she told her unborn child that she did not love it, that she could not take care of it and that it would live much better with a good family.

"But this is very irregular and you know it. María did not want to part with her daughter, the baby was taken from her in the delivery room."

"Sister Brígida assured us that the mother was a young girl, without resources or family in the world, who could not take care of her daughter. She agreed to give the baby up for adoption to a family who could care for her as she deserved. You have seen her signed consent. We signed all the papers and took the child. We never even heard from the real mother."

"But you paid the nuns for it!" I shouted in confusion at her speech. "You bought a baby, for God's sake! And for no less than three hundred thousand pesetas."

"That is not so, we paid for the mother's care and childbirth and a small amount for expenses, apart from a maternity contribution, nothing more."

"And isn't that buying a baby?"

"You have no right to talk to us like that," my grandmother interjected, offended. "Your grandfather has already told you the truth and you keep insisting. Besides, we never hid the fact that she was adopted from your mother and she took it in her stride after assimilating the news"

I looked at my grandfather and he confirmed it with a nod. I understood less and less, although I could not imagine that my mother had been told in detail about her true origins. Surely they had hidden the letter, in which her biological mother had said goodbye to her, because no one would believe that.

"Besides, you accuse us of buying a baby as if it were nothing. As far as I know, any family today has to pay huge amounts of money when adopting a child in China, Russia or any other country. Do you think that bureaucracy, paperwork, bribes to officials to speed up the paperwork and everything else doesn't cost money? Let's not be hypocrites, that has been happening all our lives."

My grandmother's outburst caught me completely off guard, I had not expected such a reaction. She may have been partly right, but that did not excuse what they had done in a time too dark in our history, from what little I could gather.

"Stop it, Matilde, please," my grandfather pleaded, "Go and lie down, rest for a while before eating, I'll come in a moment."

She reluctantly obeyed and left us alone in the living room. My grandfather became serious and told me the whole story, at least from his own particular perspective.

"We could not have children. Several doctors had already told us that, but your grandmother was determined to become a mother. She became housebound without going out at all, depressed for not being able to fulfill her greatest desire. I couldn't let her become ill and I called on everyone I knew. Sometimes contacts come in handy in life."

"Sure, I can imagine," I said sarcastically.

"There is nothing obscure, I assure you. They put me in touch with the maternity hospital in Peñagrande and I went there one day by myself. I spoke to the people in charge, told them about our situation and they confirmed that they could help us. They explained a little about how the center worked and asked us if we had any preference as to the sex of the baby."

"Oh, my God!" I was shocked, "you could even choose the sex?"

"Please let me finish. We did the right thing, filled out all the paperwork they asked for, made a first payment and waited a few weeks. Then they called us to confirm that a baby girl had just been born and was in urgent need of parents, so we went there immediately. We never met the mother, but as soon as we saw the little girl's face in her crib we fell madly in love with her."

"They lied to you, grandfather. María didn't want to give up her baby, she was tricked in Peñagrande. Not to mention everything she suffered until she got there, including being abandoned by her family as if she was a piece of human trash."

I explained to him briefly, what I had found out, but my grandfather was still in denial. It was not that he did not believe my words, but that it was much easier for him to continue thinking that they had done the right thing. His façade cracked as I told him about the misfortunes María had suffered in her youth, but he insisted that none of it was his fault and he had no way to avoid it.

"We raised your mother as our own daughter. Years later, when she was already a teenager, we ended up telling her the truth."

"But did you register her as your biological child or not?"

"Yes, well... That's what we were advised to do at the maternity hospital after talking to the doctors and the mother superior."

"So, it wasn't all so legal, was it? My mother had been adopted and yet she was raised as your own daughter for legal purposes and I imagine for the rest of the world. I understand that grandma couldn't just show up overnight with a baby when no one had seen her pregnant, right?"

"Well, the truth is that we didn't have to invent anything. Your grandmother had been in a delicate state of health for months and we moved to the house in the mountains so that she could rest away from the hustle and bustle of the capital. When the baby was born, we stayed there for another season, until we returned to this house."

"And, of course, the baby could have passed perfectly well for a biological child, since they hadn't seen you in the neighborhood for months. What a coincidence! Well, at least Grandma didn't have to fake the pregnancy or put pillows under her clothes, as in other cases that have come to light in recent times."

From the first time I had heard about this subject, I was shocked that something like this could have happened in my country. In the context of Franco's regime and the harsh post-war period in many areas of Spain, I could understand it a little better, but it did not enter my head that these criminal practices were still going on in the 1980s in clinics and boarding schools in cities like Madrid.

There was even a TV series on the subject, I remembered at the time. I had wanted to watch it since it was announced, but my grandparents were not very keen on it - I could not understand their reasons then, so I finally watched it later on the network's website on my own.

Several books had been written about the subject and various documentaries had been aired, especially related to a famous doctor and a nun who were being indicted for cases related to this. What I could not imagine was that there were even worse places, such as those reformatories associated with the Patronato de la Mujer, where the practices against those teenage mothers were even more brutal.

"Yes, but we didn't do it out of fear of having committed any crime or irregularity. It was rather to make sure that your mother's life was as normal as possible, that people would not be prejudiced when they met her and that she could have a full development. We certainly did not do it maliciously and I believe we were not wrong in this respect."

"But in the end my mother found out. Although I imagine you didn't tell her about her true origins."

"You don't understand, Sandra, you can't judge us. She asked questions, your mother was just as curious as you, and in the end, we admitted it to her. But she didn't need to know the whole truth. We told her that her biological mother had died during childbirth and that we had adopted her through official agencies, but that we were advised to register her as our own daughter. She was surprised by the story and was a little strange for a few months, but she soon forgot about it. She had enough on her plate as she was going to college soon."

What my grandfather told me seemed incredible to me, as if it was the most normal thing in the world. And the worst thing is that it was so: those methods were the most common during that time, as we learned later. A dark time in which many excesses occurred in this country around the birth of thousands of babies.

My grandparents were one more couple who took advantage of their good position as they moved in certain circles sympathetic to the regime. A well-known psychiatrist and his young wife looking for a baby would have had had no trouble adopting under certain circumstances. As much as it seemed fine to them and as much as it made my guts churn when I learned the history of that adoption.

Yes, my grandparents and other similar couples had been duped by those who ran the show in that illegal underworld. Or they had simply looked the other way since everyone was a winner in that transaction. A very lucrative business that enriched certain characters of distracted morals that had to do with maternity hospitals such as Peñagrande, whose case was not the only one that arose throughout the country. Doctors, nurses, nuns, priests, religious congregations, lawyers and registry officials saw how their bank account increased during a few decades in which nobody controlled something that for me, escaped all reason.

"I want to go to Peñagrande! I need to know that horrible place that María describes in her writings, the prison where she suffered such atrocities."

"Forget about this matter, Sandra, it's better for everyone. Besides, the Peñagrande maternity hospital no longer exists. Its main buildings are abandoned or have been integrated into a secondary school."

"I don't care!" I replied angrily. I did not understand my grandparents' attitude and I was very angry with them. They did not seem to care about other people's suffering and had no intention of helping me in my research. However, I had no intention of backing down. They might think they had done nothing wrong, but I did not agree. "I intend to go and see this sinister place and search through their files if they are still stored somewhere."

"I would be very surprised, Sandra. The nuns were very jealous of their documentation and I don't think you can access it just like that."

"Well, I'll find my own way. I'll find someone to help me, don't worry."

I got up from the sofa very upset and did not even consider that my suitcase was still unpacked in the living room. I needed to think, and the atmosphere in that little room was suffocating me, I was short of breath. I said a curt goodbye and left the place; I could not look my grandparents in the face.

"I'm going out, don't wait for me for dinner."

"But, child..."

"I am neither your child nor your grandchild. Or don't you remember?"

My answer carried a venom that my grandfather did not wish to countenance. I know now that I was a bit unfair at the time; they had raised me and learning of my true origins in this way had turned my world upside down. I needed time to come to terms with it and they had to understand.

"Sit down, calm down. And think on what you are going to do. We will always be your grandparents, whatever you think. And we'll love you as long as we have the strength, that's for sure. Nothing and nobody will be able to prevent that. I only hope you come to your senses and allow us to continue being part of your life."

"I'd rather bite my tongue so I don't say something I'll regret later, really. But if you love me so much, you should understand me, support me in my decision. I need to find María. I know she is still alive and destiny has wanted me to know her story in this unusual way."

"God bless you, child. We'll still be here, you know where to find us."

I did not want to add insult to injury when I heard the name of God on my grandfather's lips. I have never been very religious, even though I was brought up in the Catholic faith at home, but the hypocrisy was getting on my nerves. That religious organizations had been profiting from the suffering of others for decades did not speak well of any of those involved, no matter how much they tried to sell the idea that they were doing it for the good of the poor mothers and their children.

I called Alberto as soon as I was out in the street, mainly to let off steam. He was surprised that I had argued like that with my grandparents, although it was foreseeable. I hoped to redirect the situation, but first I had to settle some matters. Above all, I had to clarify my own ideas on the matter, mixed in a jumble in the cocktail shaker of my mind.

"Come to my house if you want. I was going to make a salad and steak for lunch, do you feel like sharing?"

"I wouldn't want to disturb you, Alberto. Or show up at your house in this state, your parents will think I'm crazy."

I knew that Alberto had offered to help me, not to set me up and introduce me to his parents. We could always say I was a friend from college. He did not have to tell them about ourselves out of the blue - and even less so when neither of us was clear about where we were headed - although his idea was much simpler. The male brain is different from the female's, I always forgot those details.

"Relax, I'm home alone. My sister is in Greece with her boyfriend and my parents are also on vacation in the Canary Islands."

I know he meant no harm, there was no double talk in his offer. Although I did not think it was such a bad idea to have his apartment for ourselves in Madrid.

"Well, give me the address and I'll be on my way."

I went to Pirámides, took a train to Nuevos Ministerios and then took the subway towards Avenida de América. Alberto's place was near there, in the middle of Príncipe de Vergara Street, so it did not take me long to get there.

THE ESCAPE

Contreras, August 1966

The events around Sad Hill that summer shook the foundations of the Mediavilla household. The brutal attack that María had suffered and its aftermath disrupted the way of life of a family that was comfortable in Contreras, but did not want to be the laughing stock of the town.

Eusebio, the patriarch of the clan, was not coping well either. He preferred to get out of the house and take refuge in the fields. There he could be calmer, only worried about harvesting the crops or feeding the animals. He did not feel like arguing with his wife, nor of course feeling the stares of his neighbors when he walked through the village.

The man did not want to make bad blood, but Pura poisoned his head with horrible ideas. She insisted that it was all Juanito's fault and forced him to go to the Burgos' house to ask for explanations. Eusebio and Venancio were not exactly the best of friends, but they respected each other and did not want to get into a direct confrontation. Venancio did not need to cover up for his son, since the young man had not been at home for days for fear of possible reprisals from María's father, reason enough to suspect him according to the Mediavilla family.

The argument between the two men grew in intensity, but in the end Juanito's mother managed to calm things down before they escalated. Eusebio returned home without a convincing answer, and his wife screamed to high heavens. Once again, arguments broke out in a home that was falling apart at the seams.

All those vicissitudes were also experienced by little Jaime, a boy only eight years old. Jaime idolized his sister and had a terrible time seeing her like that, sad and crying almost all day long. The boy did not know what to do to help and felt useless; no one paid attention to him. His parents spent the day arguing and María seemed to be absent, locked in her room without even coming out to eat.

The situation became entrenched over the next few days and Jaime was a silent witness to some events that would change their lives forever. He had not been able to accompany María when Doña Pura took her to the church for confession, but he found out what his mother was planning anyway. The boy, terrified, did not know whether to tell his sister for fear of punishment or even worse, like a beating with his father's belt.

During a meal to which his sister did not deign to appear, he had to endure the reproaches between his parents, until he heard some words that he did not understand at first.

"I won't stand for it, Pura!" their father shouted, very upset. "María stays with us, by all means. And if there's another mouth to feed, then we'll put up with it as usual. It won't kill me to work a little more."

"She'll be fine there, you'll see," Their mother sibilantly affirmed. "The nuns will take care of the child and María will come back as if nothing had happened. It will be like a vacation, just as if we were rich and had sent her to one of those boarding schools. Don Cosme told me that they will take care of everything, we won't have to pay for a thing."

"I said no! I don't trust priests! They always want something in return. Those people don't do favors for no reason."

"Don Cosme has assured me that everything has been taken care of. María will be in good hands and will come back better than ever. It's done, Eusebio, we can't refuse. Besides, you didn't think that bastard was going to live under our roof, did you?"

The child did not understand many of his parents' words, but he grasped the gist of the idea: María was going to be taken away somewhere and the nuns would keep her child, whatever that meant.

Jaime was not aware that his sister was going to have a baby. Yes, he had heard the word pregnant several times, but he did not associate it with María. It was something that did not enter his mind. She did not have a belly like he had seen other women in the village, so it was impossible that she was going to have a child. Besides, María was still very young and did not have a husband or anything like that.

The boy also did not understand the change in María's attitude towards him. He knew she was having a hard time because of their parents' punishment, but he was not to blame. Jaime would have given his life for María and she knew it. They had always got along very well and he longed for those moments between the two of them. So, Jaime ended up being angry too, one more in the Mediavilla family.

On the other hand, his fear of his mother prevented him from telling María what he had found out from listening to his parents. Nor did he tell her that Menchu and other friends of hers had approached him to ask about her, since she was forbidden to leave the house alone or talk to anyone without his mother's presence.

Jaime felt bad, as if he was failing his sister in something important. Although days later he forgot what he had heard when he found out that they were going to move far away, to a place called Madrid or something like that. Their mother was fed up with Contreras and had convinced her husband to leave town. This news he did want to share with his sister, and hoped he would not be punished for it.

Two nights before leaving, something strange also happened that disturbed little Jaime. On a sultry night when it was difficult to sleep, the boy got up to drink water. He heard his father coming home and thought it was strange, it was already very late. His father was very nervous and Jaime heard him mumbling nonsense. His mother tried to calm him down and assured him that no one had to find out, but that they would have to get away. The boy did not understand what was happening and went back to bed not knowing what to do.

They left town without looking back and did not even have time to say goodbye to their friends. Jaime forgot all the things he had been accumulating inside him at the prospect of such a radical change. Even more so when they arrived in the big city, a totally different world for the Mediavilla family.

Madrid puzzled all members of the family to varying degrees. They were not used to so much change. The Mediavillas were lost in such a huge city and missed their things. In the village they had had everything at hand and in the capital, they had to be careful even to cross the street, with that infernal traffic that populated everything.

Eusebio left early in the morning to look for work, since they had left Contreras with nothing. Neither María nor Jaime could protest too much at the sudden decision of their parents. At first the boy did not dislike the move, but as soon as he realized that he no longer had his friends and could not come and go as he pleased as in the village, he changed his mind. On top of that, María was getting sadder and sadder.

Jaime tried to talk to her one day, but the girl ignored him. Perhaps she believed that her brother was still a child and could not understand her, but Jaime only wanted to understand her, protect her and help her in any way possible. He felt helpless in the face of the situation and so he hid one afternoon when his father wanted to talk to María alone. He hid behind a door and listened to the conversation, hoping to shed some light on a situation in which he was very lost.

"Child, you have to change your attitude. I'm sure if you do that, your mother will forgive you and we can move forward. "

"I haven't done anything wrong! I've told you many times, Juanito isn't to blame for anything. I will never forgive my mother! I couldn't say goodbye to him or to any of my friends. I hate her!"

Jaime could not see his father's face from his hiding place, but he thought heard a hint of doubt in his voice as he continued speaking. Eusebio pulled himself together and went on with his rant, while María was becoming more and more hysterical.

"Don't shut us out, child, you have to tell me the truth. If you don't, your mother will do something horrible, I can feel it."

"I can't, Father, I'm sorry."

"It was that bastard who took advantage of you, wasn't it?" Eusebio's tone seemed to be one of justification, but to Jaime it sounded like despair. "In the end your mother is going to be right, we have done well to get away from the village. We couldn't go on being the talk of Contreras that was going to finish us off."

"And this is a solution? I don't want to be here, I'd rather die!"

"Don't talk nonsense, María. We'll get through this, don't worry, and your baby will grow up strong and healthy, I promise."

"I don't want any baby!" she cried disconsolately. "Either you take him out now or I'll take a knife and cut myself from top to bottom any day now."

"Don't talk nonsense, child!"

Jaime was startled by his sister's words. He had understood that perfectly. He slipped away as best he could; he did not want his father to catch him hiding there, eavesdropping on their conversation. But a while later, when María was left alone, he returned to her side to try to talk to her.

"Are you all right, María? I don't want anything bad to happen to you...."

María wiped away her tears and tried to calm her brother, who was looking at her scared with his huge eyes.

"You're not going anywhere then? I don't want you to be taken away."

"No, honey, I will never leave you," María replied, not knowing what her brother meant.

"Will you promise me? I could help, you can tell me anything you want, I would never tell mother. Sometimes, when she starts screaming, it scares me a little."

"Don't worry, Jaime, mother is only angry with me. You are her favorite child, she loves you madly."

"I don't know, I don't like what she's doing. Why did we come to this place?"

"Because I did something wrong, little one. Well, not really. I wasn't to blame for anything, it was some bad boys who caused all this."

"What boys, María?" asked Jaime eagerly.

"Nobody, really. Just behave yourself and you'll see how soon everything will be back to normal."

The boy was not very satisfied with his sister's explanation. But the worst was yet to come. It all started that afternoon when their mother told him she had to go on an errand with María. Their father was still not at home and Doña Pura did not want to leave Jaime alone, so she asked Francisca, her neighbor, to take care of him until her return. When they got together again for dinner, one member of the family was missing.

"Where is María, Mother?"

"She's going to be away on vacation for a while. But she'll be back soon, don't worry."

"Don't lie to the child, Pura!" exclaimed Eusebio. "What you have done is unforgivable, locking the child in that place. Tomorrow I'm going to take her out of there."

"You won't be able to, everything is already arranged. You shouldn't meddle in the Lord's designs, the path for María and her bastard is already defined."

The next morning Jaime accompanied Eusebio to a strange place where his father claimed María was. The boy was happy to know that he would be able to see his sister, but disappointment struck them mercilessly. They were not even allowed access to the building where the girl was, even though Eusebio presented himself there with the family book to prove that María was his daughter.

"I have already told you that nothing can be done, sir," a very unpleasant nun answered him bitterly. "You have given María's parental authority over to the Patronato and now we are in charge of her care and protection."

"But this can't be! I demand to see my daughter right now or I will call the authorities right away."

"Do as you see fit, but this is completely legal. And don't waste my time, I have a lot of things to do. Good afternoon."

With that said, the nun had shut the door in his face. Eusebio began to bang viciously on the sturdy wooden door, while tears ran down his haggard face. Jaime clung to him, frightened to see his father like that, and asked him to return home because he did not like that lady in black. The boy had not understood all of the woman's words, but he did not like her tone or his father's reaction to hearing them.

Jaime was slow to understand what had happened to his sister. But he took Eusebio's side when the arguments at home increased in category and intensity. His father threatened to go far away and take Jaime with him, and his mother did not stop him, so months later he began a new journey with Eusebio in a distant land.

The poor boy felt terrible, even though his father tried to calm him down. He had lost his sister and his mother in a short time, leaving behind everything he knew in life. And on top of that, he carried with him a terrible feeling of guilt, as if he could have done something at his age. This feeling would stay with him throughout his life, a sense of failure that would keep him from being happy throughout his existence.

THE FRUITLESS SEARCH

Madrid, July 25, 2016

It was very hot in the capital. The summer was still raging there, and the temperature at night was not going to drop as sharply as in the Arlanza Valley, so I prepared myself to take the heat of Madrid as best I could.

After telling my sorrows to Alberto at his house -he had a lot of patience with me, he was earning a place in heaven with my neuroses- we were looking for information on the Internet with his laptop. It was impossible to go out at that time of day, at almost forty degrees, so we postponed our excursion until mid-afternoon.

I wanted to see the Peñagrande maternity hospital from the outside, even if we could not enter or see too much from the outside.

“No problem," Alberto told me, "We'll drive over later. I don't think we'll see too much traffic -everyone is on vacation. Although we could go somewhere else first, if that's okay with you.”

“Where to?”

“Why don't we go to Vallecas? María said in her writings that they went to live there, near the church of San Diego if

I remember correctly, when they left the town. Maybe someone still remembers them. It is a neighborhood where many old people still live, lifelong neighbors, and if they had contact with the Mediavilla family, they will surely remember them."

I thought it was a very good idea but we did not have time to put our plan into action, at least not until a while later. Alberto received a call and asked me to wait for a second while he took it. Maybe it was something important. When he hung up the phone a few minutes later, he took a moment to react, as if something did not quite add up.

"What's wrong?" I asked scared. I didn't want any more shocks in my life, I just hoped it wasn't bad news.

"Nothing, it was Adolfo. He's still there trying to decipher the rest of the blog posts, but he's having a hard time."

"We're so close Alberto. It's a pity, we almost have the whole puzzle. We're only missing a few small pieces."

"Yes, that's why I also insisted to my colleague. I know I'm taking advantage of his good will, but really, deep down he gets off on this geeky stuff. It's a kind of challenge for him, he likes to push himself to the limit. And he's also been captivated by María's story, he says that the poor thing has had a life like a movie and he wants to know the end of it."

"So do I, but do you have anything else?"

Alberto smiled mischievously. I already knew he had gotten something else, if only to taunt me. The former hacker had also become obsessed with the subject that I could not let go of.

Even though Adolfo had been about to throw in the towel when he could not get more information from María's blog. Besides, he was very busy with other issues, but Alberto managed to get another promise out of him: to help us find the archives, or find out more about the practices at Peñagrande. Or, at least, something related to the mysterious Patronato de la Mujer.

But until then he would keep trying to unravel the missing parts of María's complicated life. Apparently, he had managed to rescue, one more small fragment, one more shot of that drug we needed to keep breathing. It was not the solution to our problems, but it would have to do for now.

"And what are we waiting for?" I asked eagerly. I needed to read María's words, to know what had happened to her in those dark years of which we still ignored everything."

"Don't worry, he's sending it to me in the mail right away. Or so he's told me, don't be in such an agony."

The end was near, I sensed it. But we still had many surprises to discover. María's life had become the only thing that mattered to me. I would think of nothing else until I solved the mystery.

There it was again: a fragment of María's life, a brave woman who had faced the world in an all-out fight. An unequal duel in which I was immersed as if I were at the very center of the battle, fighting side by side with the person who was telling me the story of her life.

THE FINAL DEFEAT

Miami, year 2006

MARÍA

This may be one of my last posts on this blog, we'll see. But there is still a lot of work to do and I do not know if I will have time....

I do not think I had told you at the time how I managed to get out of the hospital where I was bedridden after my accident in Montevideo. After many months of surgery and long rehabilitation sessions, I had not achieved my goal of walking again, so frustration took over and depression knocked on my door.

The efforts of the nurses and, above all, of Dr. Grandinetti as the doctor in charge of my rehabilitation, put some sanity during that painful process. I had the immense fortune of dealing with an excellent medical and human team that made my life more bearable, although I never thought it would be to that extent.

Antonio Grandinetti was an eminent orthopedic surgeon and traumatologist, or so the nurses assured me when he took over my case. He was a handsome young man in his thirties, who had already received several academic distinctions despite his youth, and had published numerous articles in the most important medical journals in the world.

At first, he took me as just another patient in his care, although the complicated circumstances under which I had arrived there made him put a little more effort on his part. I never liked being pitied or patronized: the poor 'little Galician girl' who had no money and no place to drop dead, so my first reactions to his unexpected interest were generally rather cold.

My natural reserve towards men, especially after the setbacks I had suffered throughout my short life in my relationship with them, did not allow me to let my guard down at any time. And that is why I was more surly than usual with a doctor who only wanted to cure me. But the operations followed one after the other, the rehabilitation with the physiotherapists went on for long weeks and the results were not as satisfactory as we both longed for.

I took it all out on him and ended up refusing to be operated again. Every time I went to the operating room and put myself in the hands of the surgeons, under general anesthesia and the risks derived from any surgical intervention, the less I felt like repeating the experience. The day came when I put my foot down, much to Dr. Grandinetti's chagrin, and refused to be operated on again.

The doctor had taken my case as something personal and the relationship between the two of us had developed, at least in the human aspect, since on the medical side, he had not achieved the success he was looking for. I had already resigned myself to my fate and told him that I wanted to get out of there, even if it was in a wheelchair.

He tried to convince me not to leave the hospital just yet, but I was not about to give in. I had spent the most of my life locked up, whether in Peñagrande, with Requena or now in the hospital, and my body demanded some freedom for once in my life, so, I became stubborn and, in the end, I got my way.

I believe that at first Antonio did it out of pity, or if you want to call it that, out of Christian charity. The same charity that neither the nuns at the reformatory nor my dear mother, who had thrown me out like a dog for being a sinner, had for me.

The thing is that Grandinetti knew that I had no financial means or family in Uruguay, so he offered me to stay at his house for a while, at least until I could fend for myself. I was worried, but I had nothing to lose. I chose to swallow my pride and accepted his proposal, although I swore to him that I would pay for my living expenses by taking care of the housework.

He smiled and did not take me up on it, knowing that in my condition, prostrate or in a wheelchair, I would not be very useful with household chores. Besides, Antonio had a housekeeper in his huge house and his only intention, according to his words, was to follow my evolution closely and help me start a new life.

...

I will not bore you with romantic stories, it is not my intention at all. In fact, the discovery came to me out of the blue and it was quite a surprise for me when I realized the truth, since I assure you that I did not have it in mind at that time. Familiarity breeds love or contempt, or so they say, and in the end our doctor-patient relationship underwent a big change, months after I had left the hospital. Antonio said he had fallen in love with this little Galician girl and I appreciated him very much for all he had done for me, even though at that time I did not feel so strongly about him.

We were married in 1970, just after I turned twenty. Antonio was twelve years older than me, but it was not an insurmountable difference. He knew that I would not be able to give him children due to the destruction that the midwives of Peñagrande had wreaked upon my uterus when my baby girl was born, but he did not mind too much. We became husband and wife, something I could never have imagined.

...

We enjoyed more or less happy years, although the social environment was not the best to develop our incipient relationship. Antonio had more and more work and rarely stopped by the house, so I was bored out of my mind. There came a time when my improvement slowed down and I could no longer go beyond a certain point, so I ended up getting tired, overwhelmed by so many rehab sessions. And, of course, it was totally impossible for me to start walking by myself again.

After the coup d'état in Uruguay in mid-1973, Antonio decided to move to another country. We settled in Argentina and could not stay there for long either, since in 1976 the military also took power in the country, controlling the entire South American Southern Cone.

In the end we arrived in the United States, and after a few months of hardship, we managed to form a more or less stable home in Miami, where there was an important colony of expatriates from many Spanish-speaking countries. A new beginning that was not easy, until Antonio managed to open his own clinic and begin to prosper.

...

We overcame a multitude of problems and life went on. I came to forget all the people who had hurt me in my life, I just wanted to wipe the slate clean. I promised myself one day to return to Spain, especially after Franco died and the country began to see the light when democracy was restored years later. But I dismissed the idea when I realized that I would never walk again. Besides, I had no one left there except my brother, whom I had not heard from for years, so I buried any thoughts of my country of birth in the recesses of my memory.

And then, when I was not expecting it, magic happened. You know that the circumstances of my existence have not made me a faithful devotee, nor have I ever had an unshakable faith in God but when I heard the news, I wanted to believe that there really was someone up there and finally a small miracle had been worked in my life.

I will not be hypocritical: at that time, I was living in conditions I could never have imagined. Antonio was a sweetheart and took care of me like the most precious treasure on the face of the earth. Never ever, in my childhood and teenage years in the village, would it have crossed my mind to suppose that I would end up being the wife of a reputable and wealthy surgeon who gave me everything. But something was still missing.

That something was the possibility of walking again. There was a small rift between us on that matter, since Antonio would blame himself for not having been able to cure me, with all the similar cases he had been able to solve. And of course, at the slightest opportunity, in the event of a couple's argument, I would pull out the heavy artillery and jab him with his uselessness to heal me as a battering ram.

I would be lying if I told you that I fell madly in love with Antonio. I loved him in my own way, that is true, and I gave myself to him to the best of my ability, even though physical relations with men were never satisfactory for me.

Perhaps my body rebelled and kept in its genetic memory the infamous way in which I had been outraged by two criminals when I lost my innocence in that shabby shack near the Mirandilla Valley. After that I had only been intimate with Requena, so sex was not exactly one of my favorite activities. Something I would also have to 'be grateful' to my rapists for, they had cut off any possibility of being a complete woman after that episode which I tried not to evoke in my mind.

I did not pay much attention to my husband when one afternoon he came in all excited, shouting at the top of his lungs all over the house, mad with joy, because he seemed to have found a solution to my problem. And thank goodness I listened to him, because that time he was right. He had heard about the studies of a neurologist from

California who had cured people in my situation and who wanted to study my case thoroughly before giving us a final verdict.

It had been many years since I had lost mobility in my legs, and science was advancing at lightning speed. I gave in and let myself be driven to California. I met Dr. Mathew Collins and he was immediately enthusiastic about my case. It would be a challenge for him to cure me, so he assured us.

The tests performed were initially positive and we decided to stay in Sacramento, the city where the neurologist had his office. I underwent a risky operation, one more, knowing that I could even become a quadriplegic if the doctors lost their pulse. But I had had enough of the wheelchair, so I took a gamble and the coin came up heads.

Antonio had to close his practice for a few months, although he made continuous business trips from California to Florida, two states bathed by the sun that I had always loved. After having lived all my childhood in the harsh Castilian plateau, with freezing temperatures most of the year and snowfalls of more than a meter during the winter, I was in paradise enjoying the warm winters of Sacramento and Miami.

Once again, I found myself immersed in hard months of rehabilitation, with intense sessions that made me cry from pure pain. But the goal was there, within reach, and I was even promised that I would never have to undergo surgery again. Neither Dr. Collins nor my husband gave me any respite, determined that I would achieve what I had been longing for, for so many years. And in the end, I did it: I could walk again.

A wonderful experience that I still cannot quite put into words today, the feeling of leaving the damn wheelchair behind and being able to stand on my own two feet after such a long time. I would have to use a cane forever, but I did not mind. Eventually I got used to the object, almost an accessory in my daily attire, and I even developed a certain affection for it.

It was time to return to Florida. But fate - or whoever is pulling the strings of this world - had another unpleasant surprise just around the corner. It has always been said that God writes straight with crooked lines, or so I had heard from my 'saintly' mother. And the devastating blow sank me again when I was just beginning to poke my head out of my shell.

Shortly after we moved back to Miami, with my husband working again at full capacity and me still immersed in adapting to my renewed status as an autonomous walker, Antonio had to stop his infernal rhythm because he started to feel sick. I got worried and forced him to have a check-up. Doctors have always been very bad patients and I had to argue with him many times to make him listen to me.

...

Those were very hard years, in which I took care of him as best I could while I felt how the cancer consumed him little by little and extinguished the flame of a man who had shown me the goodness of the human being. In the end Antonio could not stand the pain any longer and took a lethal dose of his pills, ready to stop the suffering, to go to the other world when it seemed right to him. A brave decision with which I agreed, even if I doubted that I would be able to repeat it, and which, on top of that, was frowned upon and could even be considered a crime. But nobody found out the truth and Antonio could finally rest in peace.

The loneliness affected me more than I would have guessed. Once again, I found myself without anyone in the world, but the circumstances had changed. I could walk again, although always supported by my beloved cane. As a bonus, I had a more than comfortable economic position with Antonio's inheritance, so I would not have to worry about money for the rest of my life. I had just turned fifty and I had not yet said my last word.

I could not be idle, I needed to occupy my time so as not to go crazy. I wanted to travel, to see the world, after so many years as a slave to a wheelchair, which I threw away as soon as I knew I would never use it again. I set out first to get to know the United States from top to bottom, a fascinating country in many ways, full of its own contradictions.

I was a rich widow, who still retained some attractiveness despite the hard blows received and the ailments of age. But my heart harbored no romantic intentions, so I pushed away any suitors who approached me.

Sometimes I fantasized about returning to Spain and going for a day trip to my old town, perhaps driven by a chauffeur in a high-end car. But I immediately lost the desire, I had not lost anything in the old Castile and I was not thinking of ever going back. Even though gloating, and passing one's triumphs in life before people's noses, has always been a sport practiced in my country since time immemorial.

I signed up for various activities so that the house would not suffocate me when I was not traveling. I joined a book club in Jacksonville where I met other women my age and enjoyed their weekly meetings with a child-like enthusiasm.

I had not studied much as a child and Antonio knew I was ashamed of my lack of culture, so throughout our marriage he helped me to educate myself. My husband hired a private tutor to give me classes and recommended certain readings that I devoured at night. Just another example of all I have to thank him for in this life, one more of the favors I could never repay him for.

I became an enthusiastic participant in the book club and there I also learned how to create a blog on the Internet, in which we would talk about the books we liked and share our opinions with the whole world through the Net. The world had changed so very much and everything was accessible at the click of a mouse. I had not thought about it, but then the thought settled in my head - of course, curiosity got the better of me and I started looking for information about the people I was interested in.

I did not find any remarkable information about any member of my family and I was a little disappointed. On the other hand, I did find information about the closure of Peñagrande in the eighties, something that surprised me. That damned institution was still open when Spain had already been a democracy for several years, maintaining its abnormal operation in a first world country without anyone preventing it. A crazy idea that I did not want to think about.

The problem was that one thing led to another. And then I learned about the horrific case of a girl who was also savagely raped by a group of young men near Miami. I imagined the horror the girl must have suffered and the ordeal that awaited her for the rest of her life. I vowed to try to help women in her situation and began to think of a harebrained idea that settled in my head.

Thanks to Antonio's estate and my stubbornness, I opened the Grandinetti Foundation for women who had been sexually assaulted. A non-profit foundation in which I hired the best professionals (doctors, nurses, social workers, psychologists and anyone who could lend a hand), ready to help a larger group than I could have ever imagined.

It was an occupation in which I was able to fulfill myself as a person, helping victims in a situation I knew all too well. But the hard work, although demanding and very rewarding, did not chase away the ghosts of my past. On the contrary, nightmares returned to my dreams and I realized that I was not able to erase from my mind the happy afternoon when I had gone to the faux cemetery with Juanito and the others.

Anger then took hold of me and I wanted to tell my story. I talked it over with Yanet, a very outgoing Cuban woman with whom I had become friends at our book club meetings, and she encouraged me to give it a try. But maybe I will tell you about that in my next entry, if I have the strength left....

THE PIECES OF THE PUZZLE

Madrid, July 25, 2016

Once again, we were stymied, although we had made progress in our investigations. María had told us what had become of her in those unknown years when we had lost track of her, but the most important thing remained: to find out where she was right now, what had become of her life in recent years.

We decided to continue with the idea we had had before Adolfo's last interruption: to visit María's old neighborhood in Vallecas and try to get the definitive clue.

It did not take us long to get to the neighborhood of San Diego, between the area of Entrevías and Puente de Vallecas. We did not even have to consult the navigator, Alberto had a friend who lived nearby and knew how to get there without any problems. We looked for a place to park and headed to the entrance to the church of San Diego, located on the avenue of the same name, an ideal place to bump into elderly people from the neighborhood who had just attended mass.

I had passed Alberto the photo in which María appeared with her friends in Sad Hill via WhatsApp. That way,

Alberto and I divided the work asking anyone over sixty years old that we found in the area. Some looked at us strangely or were even wary and quickly walked away from us, but we managed to talk to several people although without any positive results.

Until one man seemed to remember something when Alberto told him about the family and showed him the photograph. The good man tried to remember, but his memory failed him and he could not give Alberto concrete information. Alberto called me and I approached from across the street. Then suddenly, the old man's countenance changed completely.

"Oh my God, now I remember!" he exclaimed as soon as he saw me. "The girl looked so much like your friend. It's come back to me all at once. They lived at the end of that street, near the railroad tracks."

The old man's reaction to seeing me was not the same as Menchu's, but my appearance also had an effect on him. I had not even considered it - I did not want to upset any elderly person. Apparently, I was just like my grandmother, something I had not forgotten and which made me even more eager to finally meet her.

We took the perpendicular street that came out of the main avenue, called Alfredo Castro Camba, and we headed towards its end, almost reaching Entrevías Avenue. We began to knock on the houses in that area without finding anyone who could give us news of the passing of the Mediavilla family through the neighborhood. We only found young or middle-aged people, mostly foreigners, who could not possibly have lived there for more than fifty years. Until we ran into Doña Francisca.

"Oh, child, that was many years ago. But yes, that family was my neighbor around the time you tell me. They weren't around much, but that little girl attracted attention wherever she went. Just like you, beautiful."

I blushed at the old lady's compliment, happy in any case to find someone who had information about the

Mediavilla family. The good lady insisted on inviting us for a snack and we accepted to chat with her. The woman had been widowed a few years ago and was still living in the same neighborhood where she had been born, almost eighty years ago.

In any case, we did not get too much out of it. Doña Francisca remembered the arrival of the family to the neighborhood and the problems of the Mediavilla family. Eusebio was looking for work in a difficult time for everyone and María was arguing with her mother in the street to Pura's embarrassment.

"Shortly after that I stopped seeing the redhead in the neighborhood. People talk a lot, you know, and they said she had gone to London to have an abortion. But that family had no money, I can tell you that my parents tried to help them."

"Do you know where María went?"

"No, child, no idea. The parents argued a lot, I could hear them from here. The poor little boy cried and cried, and said he wanted to see his sister. But a short time later, the father also left taking the little boy with him."

"And what became of the mother?" I asked.

"Well, now that you mention it, I don't remember well. It was said that the man had found a job in Bilbao or Galicia, I don't know for sure. She stayed here alone for a while, but she had no money to pay the rent and no job to get by with, so she also left a few months later. They were never heard of again. I'm sorry."

We said goodbye to Doña Francisca after thanking her for the information, although it was of little use to us. We did not know what had become of Pura afterwards, even though now we had her located in the residence in Burgos. It was a pity that dementia prevented her from talking to us properly, although I was not throwing in the towel and I still had it in mind to pay her another visit.

Anyway, I did not think María would have contacted her after what we had read in her online diary. Maybe

Adolfo could give us a hand in finding the father, but it would most likely lead to another dead end. I could not think of any other thread to pull, until Alberto told me some good news.

"Well, Adolfo 'the geek' comes to the rescue again. He has located the telephone number of a historian who has delved into this issue. It turns out that she has been researching the Patronato and its practices for years. Shall we call her?"

"Of course! I think I should be the one to talk to her, if you don't mind."

Alberto agreed. He passed me the number and I dialed it from my phone as we walked back to where we had parked the car. I moved a few meters away from him, preferring to have some privacy to make a call that was not easy for me.

Soledad Acosta, that was the historian's name, was reluctant to talk to me on the phone and even more so when I told her that I had got her number through a friend, without specifying anything else. But when I told her María's story and that I was the granddaughter who wanted to find her lost grandmother, one more of the hundreds of women who suffered the unthinkable in Peñagrande, she agreed to talk to us.

"Fantastic!" said Alberto when I confirmed that we had an appointment with the historian the following morning. "Come on, I'll buy you a drink to celebrate."

We had a drink at a nearby terrace and a while later we were on the move again. Alberto kept his promise and we drove through the surroundings of Peñagrande, although we had little idea of the area after the changes suffered in recent years.

Anyway, something made me forget about the building altogether. Alberto's phone vibrated again and his face lit up as he read the message.

"I think we should find a quieter place to read this. It looks like Adolfo has sent us more excerpts from María's diary."

I agreed with him and we headed back to his house. Twilight was falling over the city and I did not even realize that I had not returned home and had not mentioned that I was not going home to sleep. I had already decided to stay at Alberto's house, if he let me, since I was still very angry with my grandparents.

But if I harbored any intention of taking advantage of the situation with my host, the two of us alone in that apartment in Príncipe de Vergara, I had to dismiss it immediately. My body was reacting in a way I already knew from being close to Alberto, but my mind was wandering elsewhere. Even more so when I learned the nature of the texts Adolfo had sent us.

We were in front of the last salvageable post of María's blog, the one that would give us the definitive clue about her true intentions. And that was more important than any other matter at that precise moment. Although I was unaware of the nature of the passage, it was a part of her diary that would leave me marked forever.

THE WEBLOG

Miami, year 2006

MARÍA

I finally made my mind up, a little over a year ago. That is how I started my own blog: This is Your Home, where I began to tell my misfortunes since that fateful summer of '66, when I was just a child.

I have never been much of a techie, so I needed Yanet's help to get up to speed with the Internet. Besides, I was too embarrassed to expose my inner self in public, and even more so in a medium where anyone with Internet access could know my story.

My friend helped me set it up to be private or have restricted access, with users that I authorized to enter. That way I began to feel more at ease and I noticed how I was loosening up as I wrote - it also served to exorcise my own demons, the same ones that from time to time harassed me at ungodly hours.

...

It has been a little over a year since that shaky start, some of you may still remember. At the beginning I limited myself to writing occasionally and shared it only with a few people in my inner circle. Some of my friends, knowing the ordeal I had gone through and knowing what we were doing at the Foundation, urged me to take the leap, even if only temporarily. Initially I refused, knowing that if I made my diary public, there would be no turning back.

I finally yielded and gave it a try, just a couple of months ago. The Web is immense and has millions of Web pages, although you never know who will find you surfing cyberspace. I have not advertised the blog anywhere in particular, as I have not been interested in reaching too many people, but Yanet convinced me to link it to the Foundation's new website. And, above all, to include some specific tags in the writings I post, something I do not quite understand.

You will think: what does this crazy woman want to tell us now? Be patient, I beg you, you have little time left for putting up with me in this aseptic and impersonal medium, although it can be quite the opposite.

My friend continuously monitors the traffic of the blog and has assured me that these changes have helped us to have virtual visitors from all over the world, more and more, in a proportionate rise that has surprised me. I am not lying, there you are to corroborate it, right?

The thing is that in a short time this has changed so much. From those first hesitant writings, without anyone reading them or just a couple of visits during a whole week, I have gone to something that I almost cannot control. In the last few entries, I have already found myself answering comments from women all over the world, and just the other day, I was able to chat with another girl who had suffered in an institution similar to Peñagrande, a reformatory in Toledo that was also controlled by the damned Patronato.

But what I am going to tell you now is a real scoop for almost all my visitors, the real architects of the space in which I have arrived.

Well, here goes: what never crossed my mind when I initiated this was that one of those visitors on the Net would be my own brother Jaime, whom I had erased from my mind many years ago. I could not believe it!

I have never signed the articles with my real name, but someone has read all my misadventures and thought they knew me. His cryptic message left me speechless a few weeks ago, and I did not know how to react at first. It was too much of a coincidence, but deep down I sensed that the comment might be true: my brother had found me after such a long time. His message read as follows:

I am Jaime Mediavilla, a native of Contreras (Burgos, Spain) and now I live in Argentina. If you are who I think you are, please write me without fail to this address: jmediav58@yahoo.com.

That was only seven weeks ago, I have it written down in a calendar. One of the greatest joys of my life has also been the cause of a deep uneasiness in my spirit, the same one that seemed to have found peace after so many disappointments throughout my life. But destiny has a final twist in store for me, as you will soon find out.

I hesitated quite a bit to respond to that email, but in the end I could not resist. There he was, my little brother, alive and kicking. We started exchanging e-mails and, in a few days, we even spoke on the phone after overcoming the natural reluctance after decades of estrangement.

During this time the poor guy told me how bad it had been, when my mother locked me up in Peñagrande and his tantrums, when he could not manage to visit. I have now learned from him, that my father had flatly refused my confinement, and that he even tried to reverse what my mother had done, but it was impossible. She had given over my guardianship to the Patronato and there was nothing to be done, although my father fought tooth and nail to get me out of that hell.

My brother has also told me the rest of their story, something that has always bothered me because I did not know what had become of them. After what happened at the end of 1966, they left Madrid for good, for Galicia. My father ended up working on a fishing boat while Jaime grew up. Until a storm in the Bay of Biscay wrecked the boat and no one could ever find the bodies of the fishermen, swallowed by a criminal sea that did not take prisoners. My little brother was also left alone in the world and ended up enlisting on a merchant ship, in this case one that was on its way to Mexico. Another one that has been stumbling around America in the last decades, and it seems he is now in my old adopted homeland, Argentina.

He did not know or did not want to give me any news about my mother, nor did I ask too many questions. Jaime was very young, just an eight-year old boy, who did not understand what was going on. He had been forced to leave his village overnight to come to the big city and a few days later he had lost his beloved sister. The boy had had to overcome all these changes and then go far away again, to the other side of the country, accompanying his father while he wondered why his mother had broken up the family forever.

...

In those first days of contact, we promised to see each other soon, but we knew that our respective obligations and the distance between us would prevent a quick reunion of the Mediavilla siblings. And then fate, capricious as ever, has once again acted against us.

...

I am going to tell you the truth, the real reason why I say that this is the last entry of a blog that I have become so fond of. Your comments, your unparalleled support and the strength that you have given me throughout all this time have been my engine, the nurture that has made me keep fighting for everything I believe in. But there comes a time when the strength fails, the body says enough and there is nothing we can do.

Here it is, dear friends, the news I never wanted to tell: I am dying. My continuous headaches made me go to the doctor again, something I swore I would never do after the suffering which I have lived with most of my life. My trusted doctor did not make too much of it and prescribed me some pills, but one day I got really worried when I momentarily lost the vision in one eye. I knew then that something was wrong with me and I underwent a whole battery of tests, including a brain scan.

And there was my new enemy: glioblastoma. The specialists I have seen have not given me much hope: I have only three months to live. The monster in my head will start to affect different parts of my brain little by little, hence my need to write the last lines before I lose my sight, my reason or any other side effect of the damned tumor that is going to end my life. A bastard that is advancing at great speed, like a downhill train, with no brakes, that will undoubtedly finish me.

I have spoken to Jaime, and he has promised to come and visit, but I have told him not to. I do not want him to see me like this, like a drooling vegetable, so I have expressly forbidden him to. But I have asked him for one last favor before I die.

I have told him to look after this blog when I am gone. I want him to close it for good after a reasonable period of time. Perhaps many of you will think that I could leave my writings here as a legacy, but there is so much pain inside me, the physical pain that attacks my skull and the moral pain that destroys my soul when I remember all my experiences, that I think the best thing for everyone is that it disappears with me in the immensity of cyberspace.

I am becoming dizzy, I can no longer see clearly, and I am even beginning to suffer from terrible tremors that leave me feeling sick. The doctors cannot do much more for me, and I have refused to go to a hospital for palliative care, I prefer to die peacefully at home. I am not afraid of death and I have no regrets about anything I have done in my life, although, if I could go back I might change a few of my past actions. Like my relationship with Juanito and my trip to a place I should never have visited.

I am having a hard time closing this post, but you deserve one last effort. But first, if the convulsions that drive me crazy allow me, I will leave my epitaph written in the form of a grievance, the ignominious list of the people who ended my youth.

* The damned cross-eyed young man and his friend Mario, the two bastards who raped me savagely in a dingy little room and took away my innocence forever.

* His Italian *compadre*, Arrigo I think his name was, for having allowed the sexual assault while holding my friend, Juanito.

* Father Cosme, for listening to my mother and helping her to lock me up in Peñagrande.

* My dear and adored mother, Purificación Castroviejo, for getting rid of me as if I were a piece of broken furniture. She destroyed my life and that of the rest of my family, and gave legal custody to the Patronato so that they could finish me off.

* Sister Brígida and 'her army', the nuns of the Evangelical Crusades, for making my life impossible inside Peñagrande. And of course, 'the Scalpel', for destroying my insides by butchering me with that c-section. What a midwife! Damn her and the whole system for taking my newborn daughter away from me like that.

* The policeman Antón, for deceiving me in that way to get me out of Peñagrande and selling me to the owner of a brothel.

* The pimp Marcial, for wanting to buy me as if I were a piece of meat, raping me first to test the merchandise and then trying to prostitute me.

* I would include the wretched Requena, but he already had his just punishment.

I can no longer take revenge on these people, nor give them what they deserve for the crimes they have committed. Maybe some of them have been pushing-up daisies for a long time, like Requena, but I do not care. I do not care if they all burn in hell.

I have never been a vindictive person, but I do feel hatred and resentment towards those people which I have tried to purge from my mind, especially so as not to end up consumed by something beyond my control. Maybe now the tumor is pressing on some part of my brain that forces me to say what I really feel: yes, I admit it, I would love to finish them all off with my own hands. But that will no longer be possible, dear friends.

I only hope that if there really is a God in this universe, he will not let them end their days peacefully in bed after life-long happiness. I want them to suffer and die knowing what they have done to other people. And since almost all my enemies seemed to be pious people, I hope their Creator sends them an Exterminating Angel to bid them farewell from this world.

My fingers stiffen and I can no longer write well, and my vision blurs at times. I think the time has come to say goodbye to all of you, the virtual friends who have accompanied me throughout all these months.

Thank you again for your support and patience in putting up with the ramblings of this woman, who, in the end, only wanted to try and die at peace with herself.

Farewell.

THE HISTORY OF THE 'PATRONATO'

Madrid, July 26, 2016

I could not hold back the tears, which were cascading down my cheeks as I tried to fully assimilate the information: María had died and I would never be able to find her or embrace her.

It seemed totally unfair. A woman with a big heart, who had suffered unspeakably throughout her life, did not deserve to end up like that, when she still had so much to offer. I felt terrible and a rage came over me, knowing that there was nothing I could do about it.

Alberto tried to cheer me up on a miserable night when I needed all the support in the world. I knew he had the best of intentions, but grief had taken hold of me and I ended up cursing fate for having robbed me of my real family again, without even giving me the chance to meet María in person.

"It's a tragedy, I can't see it any other way. We were so close, this has left me stone cold. I still can't believe it."

"I understand, although I can't put myself in your shoes or imagine what you're going through right now. Maybe it would be better to cancel tomorrow's meeting with the historian."

"Are you kidding? No way, I need to talk to her and find out what happened there. If I can't meet my grandmother, or avenge her in the way she truly deserves, the least I can do is find out the whole truth and report it."

"All right, I'll come with you. If you feel like it, we can return to Carazo in the afternoon," Alberto said surprisingly.

"How come? Don't tell me something else has happened that I haven't heard."

"Nothing, I got another message from Julián. It would seem that the authorities are making enquiries, just beating around the bush. The Guardia Civil is questioning everyone who attended the conference, so I imagine it will be my turn soon. Maybe it is better that I go directly to the barracks and get ahead of the game."

I thought Alberto was hiding something else from me, but I did not want to insist too much. Sometime later, I would understand that he also spent a sleepless night, just like me, but for other reasons that had kept him thinking for hours.

"But are you going to tell them everything we know?"

"I think so, Sandra. We'd better talk about it tomorrow. If you agree, we'll discuss it with the rest of the group when we tell them the end of María's story. Let the authorities handle it. I've lost the urge to play Hercule Poirot."

It was not very clear, but perhaps Alberto was right. A murderer was at large, and the authorities should know about the anonymous letters and the fact we had found the body in the monastery.

"I don't know, we'll talk about it. Come on, let's go to sleep, it's been a long day and maybe tomorrow will be a repeat. I want to rest, although I imagine that María's death will get into my incessantly spinning brain."

Alberto had prepared the guest room for me and neither of us was in the mood for anything else, so we slept in separate rooms. A night in which the memory of a young and vibrant María, running around the Mirandilla Valley, hailed me from the depths of my subconscious.

The following morning, we went to a coffee shop downtown, where we had arranged to meet Soledad Acosta. I still could not believe the fatal outcome of a story that had completely entrapped me. Rationally, I should forget about it, there was no solution, but my heart refused to give up.

From the first moment I was involved, I felt a special empathy with the protagonist. No doubt it was because, in reality, María was my real grandmother, but there was something else. I could not put my finger on it, a special connection, a chemical current that had united our souls forever. Her death should have buried that feeling, but on the contrary, I felt closer to her than ever.

We went downtown via public transport and met our appointment. She was a middle-aged woman, well dressed and lightly made up, who was rifling through some papers she had just taken out of a folder. We introduced ourselves and Soledad got straight to the point, "Tell me what you know."

I told her everything that had happened to María in Peñagrande and emphasized that I had just found out that she was my real grandmother, without going into too much detail. I did not confirm her death, I refused to admit it, I just mentioned that I was investigating her life and had encountered many obstacles. I needed to know more about the institution where she had been locked up, and the historian was the ideal person to clear up any doubts.

"Well, you see," she began, "I have been digging into official documentation for a long time and I have also talked to affected women. Peñagrande was a horrible place, but it was only one part of the Patronato de Protección a la Mujer, a euphemism for an institution at the service of the Franco Regime to control thousands of women who, according to the regime, did not conform to the required standards.

Rage began to take over me as soon as Soledad began to describe the barbarities that were committed against those poor women.

"Between 1941 and 1985, thousands of teenage girls were locked up in religious centers under the auspices of the Patronato de Protección de la Mujer, the institution that supposedly controlled the morals and good customs of women during the Franco era and even beyond this, as I have been able to verify first hand. Whether they were handed over by their parents, denounced by relatives or even ex officio, the Patronato assumed the guardianship and parental responsibility of thousands of girls who were locked up against their will without trial."

Alberto and I looked at each other in amazement, unable to believe what Soledad was telling us. Apparently, in those institutions they locked up any woman who strayed from the rigorous canons established by the Franco regime. It did not matter if she was a lesbian, a prostitute, a raped woman, a rebel or a communist. They did not even have to have sinned, because they included those who were 'at risk of falling'.

"There were police raids, but you could end up in the clutches of the Patronato in various ways. Many families gave up their daughters, but the poor girls could also be denounced by a neighbor or any fascist acolyte. The Patronato relied on wardens - women of irreproachable Catholic morals and principles akin to the Movement, who visited the 'hot spots of sin': movie theaters, discos, swimming pools, nightclubs and such like. If they saw something untoward, they informed the police and the poor girl they had singled out was lost in the gears of the system without knowing why."

The historian was quite shocked that so many families willingly gave up their daughters and relayed that in some cases it was viewed as a kind of punishment - they believed they were being sent to a boarding school or reformatory where they would be straightened out, even paying to send them there. Others did it consciously, to get rid of a rebellious daughter or a girl who had become pregnant. And of course, when some families wanted to regain guardianship of their daughters, once they knew the true extent of having given them up they ran into numerous problems.

"It was normal for these misguided girls to go first to an observation center that existed in Arturo Soria. There they did virginity tests, because of the stigma of the teenage single mother. In their report they would put 'Complete' or 'Incomplete', depending on what they found.

"That's outrageous!" I cried.

She told us there were several religious orders that ran institutions similar to Peñagrande throughout Spain: the now sadly known Evangelical Crusades, the Adoratrices, the Trinitarians or the Oblates, which were among the harshest. In these boarding schools the girls suffered all kinds of humiliations: cold showers, head shaving, insults, degradation, and confinement in unhealthy cells for any kind of rudeness, forced labor or lack of good food or adequate hygiene.

"There they could only do three things: scrub, pray and sew. They spent a large part of the day working in the workshops, sewing pieces for large multinationals or making clothes for the families of the wealthy. A generalized exploitation for which the inmates were not paid a cent, when the nuns received from the State more than two thousand pesetas per woman per day of work at the beginning of the seventies, a small fortune."

Soledad told us about the centers that every inmate feared, such as one in Jaén to which they threatened to send the most rebellious ones, or the sadly known asylum of Ciempozuelos in Madrid, where they could end up depending on their behavior and mental evaluation.

She also explained in more detail what we had already read in María's diary, the incredible way in which they were sold almost to the highest bidder, exhibiting them as if at a cattle market. Many of these women ended up as maids, sales clerks or housekeepers for hire, although some managed to escape. Many ended up committing suicide.

"Peñagrande, and other institutions, were at the center of the stolen babies scheme that rocked Spain for decades. The infamous doctor, who is to be tried for this plot, was also the gynecologist at Peñagrande. You get the idea. "

The most mind-boggling thing was that this institution continued to operate until the mid-1980s with the same guidelines, when the Patronato de Protección a la Mujer was supposed to have been abolished in 1977.

"The maternity of Peñagrande, officially called Nuestra Señora de la Almudena, was run by the Evangelical Crusaders until they abandoned this center. Oddly, this congregation continues to run two centers for needy mothers in Madrid and Salamanca, with public subsidies. And they have more schools and centers all over Spain. Naturally they do not want to talk about Peñagrande and I have had no response from their current leaders."

A few minutes later Alberto received a message on his phone, read it with studied interest and apologized to us. I would ask him later what all the mystery was about.

The conversation with Soledad went on for almost an hour and a half, and we promised to keep in touch. My hair stood on end as I learned the ins and outs of such a monstrous system, something impossible to conceive, and above all to find out that it had lasted almost to the present day, many years after Franco's death.

It was already mid-morning and we were still in the center of Madrid. I had to go and pick up my things at the apartment if I wanted to go back to Carazo, so I arranged to meet Alberto later.

I took the subway back home, unpacked the suitcase I had left behind, and filled it again in a hurry to leave. My grandfather was not at home and my grandmother did not want to say anything to me when she saw my angry face, but in the end, she could not hold her tongue.

"How long are you going to go on without talking to me, Sandra?"

"I don't know, Grandma..." I stopped at the end. "I still have a lot to think about. Give me time. I'm going back to Burgos for a few days, we'll talk when I get back."

"Of course, honey. I'm not one to meddle in your things, but you may end up hurting yourself in the long run. It's better to leave the past behind, forget it and look forward."

"I see. Better to bury it all so it won't affect us, right? Like they buried poor María in life, locking her within the four walls of hell on earth before taking her daughter away from her."

"No, I didn't mean to say...."

"Did you know that your beloved little nuns allowed a corrupt policeman to take María from the reformatory so that he could resell her to a pimp?"

"No, I..."

"No, of course you didn't, how would you know. Nor that your dear little daughter, my mother, was the fruit of a multiple rape that poor María suffered."

"Jesus, Mary and Joseph!"

"I'd better not say what I think about those three. It was a religious institution, sponsored by the powers of the State that brought María down. When she got rid of the policeman and the pimp by pure instinct, she returned to a place where she was continually harassed. And finally, she was sold as a slave to a businessman sympathetic to the Regime."

The old woman pretended to be shocked, but I thought she was only doing it to ingratiate herself. Perhaps I was being too cruel, they had no reason to know the tortures to which these girls had been subjected to in the homes of the Patronato. My foster grandparents had just wanted to have a baby, they pulled the right strings and took my mother without worrying about the backroom of what was really going on. The good families, like mine, looked the other way and got on with their lives.

I put a halt to the conversation I did not want to upset my grandmother again. I told her I would call them in a few days, when things were calmer, and I left the only home I had known since my mother died.

Alberto was already waiting for me, double-parked. He must have seen the angry look on my face - he did not say a word to me. He just put my luggage in the trunk and set off. As we entered the organized chaos of the M-30 traffic, he queried,

"Is everything all right, Sandra?"

"Yes, well, no... I ended up arguing with my grandmother again and I had to leave before it escalated."

"I understand, I really do. But think about this for a moment: María would have suffered the same whether your grandparents intervened or not. If the nuns had decided to do business with the baby, they would sell it to anybody and María's fate would not have changed if your mother had come to any other home."

"We don't know that for sure. If the baby had not been taken from her or if her family had intervened more insistently, maybe everything would have changed."

"You don't know that, there's nothing you can do about it anymore. All you're doing is hurting yourself and two old people who would give the world for you."

"Okay, maybe you're right. I'll see what I do in a few days, but first I want to focus and close this circle."

Alberto nodded, hopefully agreeing with me. We continued our journey and I did not remember to ask him if his mid-morning call had had anything to do with our investigation. Maybe it was something personal or some other matter unrelated to what had happened during the last week, so I forgot about it as we approached Burgos.

"I noticed you haven't brought a suitcase. What are you planning to do?"

"Nothing, I'll drop you off in Carazo and go talk to the Guardia Civil this afternoon. I'll see if I spend the night there in a pension or go straight back when I'm done."

"That's a lot of driving, I'm sure there's room for you at Ana and Julián's family home. They have plenty of rooms, I don't think they would mind putting you up for a few days."

Halfway there I called the landline at Carazo's house and spoke to Menchu. I told her that we would be arriving around three in the afternoon and she seemed pleased with the news. She assured me that we would be expected for lunch.

We arrived a few minutes later than expected, but nobody seemed to mind. It was hot at that hour, although at the foothills of the Sierra de la Demanda the sun was a little less intense than in the center of the capital. We were surprised to be greeted by the whole family, including Julián. After the usual kisses and hugs, we all went to the living room. The eight of us fitted in perfectly well and we all sat at the table while Menchu acted as hostess: she told me that she already had the room ready.

I was partly over my annoyance with my grandmother and I decided to let it go. Besides, Menchu's attitude towards me also seemed to have changed, something I was also happy about.

"And you, Alberto, didn't you bring a suitcase or did you leave it in the car? I hope you're not going to Salas again, there's plenty of room here."

He stood still for a moment, not having expected Menchu's intervention.

"No, the truth is that I didn't bring a suitcase. I'll go to the station later and return to Madrid. I have things to do."

Menchu insisted that he stay.

We ate in a relaxed atmosphere, and enjoyed some anecdotes told by Julián and his cousin Raquel. We did not want to spoil the after-dinner conversation, but when Menchu brought us some coffees she was the one who decided to put her finger on the sore spot.

"Well, Sandra, I think you have some news about María, am I wrong?"

It was hard to start. Anguish gripped my chest and prevented me from breathing normally as I remembered the last text. Alberto helped me get started and then I continued solo, telling everything we had found out the night before.

"I'm so sorry, honey," Menchu gave me a heartfelt hug that comforted me for a few moments, although the pain was still visible. "I would have loved to meet my old friend again, but fate has not allowed it."

I nodded in turn, still anguished as I recounted the last words of my real grandmother. I then went on to tell them briefly about the meeting we had that morning with Soledad Acosta, and everyone was aghast to learn some of the more lurid details of the Peñagrande reformatory and maternity home.

"Jesus, what a bunch of bastards," Julián said indignantly.

"Poor María, all she had to suffer," Menchu interjected. "And all because of her mother's stubbornness. How obtuse that blasted woman was...."

Alberto glanced at me with a strange expression on his face - very focused. He seemed about to speak, but could not quite make up his mind. I gave him a look of incomprehension, in case he needed prompting, and then he intervened.

"Forgive me for interrupting. Sandra, could you read aloud María's last sentences?"

"You mean the list of people?"

"Yes, that's right. If you think it's too hard for you or you don't feel up to it, I can do it. I want us all to consider one detail."

"No, don't worry, I'll look for the file right away."

I had no idea what Alberto might have in mind, and the rest of the group stood by, oblivious to our conversation. No one knew what list we were referring to, so there was silence in the little room while I fiddled with my phone. Luckily, I already had the document in downloaded files, so I located it without any problem.

I cleared my throat a little before, hoping I would not make a spectacle of myself by getting too emotional as I recited that infamous list. I began - there was a deathly silence in the house:

I *am having a hard time closing this post, but you deserve that last effort. But first, if the convulsions that drive me crazy allow me, I will leave here my epitaph, in the form of a grievance, the ignominious list of the people who ended my youth.*

Everyone gawped at me when I uttered the list of shame, struggling to get to the end.

My *fingers stiffen and I can no longer write well, and my vision blurs at times. I think the time has come to say goodbye to all of you, the virtual friends who have accompanied me throughout all these months.*

Thank you again for your support and patience in putting up with the ramblings of a woman, who, in the end, only tried to die in peace.

Farewell.

It was Ana who hugged me then, she knew I needed comforting - a tactile response to leave behind a trance that was too painful for me. Even Menchu wiped away the tears that had slipped down her cheeks, while the rest of the group seemed stunned. Until Julián uttered one of his comments, while Alberto was still pondering, ruminating on something that was gnawing at him, as far as I thought.

"Fuck, it sounds like Arya Stark's list."

"What's that? asked Raquel.

"Yes, man, *Game of Thrones*. Haven't you seen the series?"

"No," Ana, Raquel and I answered at the same time.

"Let's see, I won't explain the series now, don't look at me with that face, it's not something for geeks. It's known internationally, you must be familiar with it, based on the books by George R.R. Martin's.

"If you say so..."

"Okay, whatever. I meant that one of the main characters spends half the series reciting a list of people she wants to take revenge on for what they did to her or her family. Those named fall one by one..."

"That's it!" exclaimed Alberto, as if he were Archimedes himself shouting *Eureka* upon discovering the principle that bears his name.

I looked at him blankly, waiting for an explanation. He waved a local newspaper he had found in the driveway in front of my face and I did not quite know what he was referring to.

"The blasted list!" said Alberto, while we stared at him.

"What do you mean?" asked Menchu.

Julián was strutting around, although he had no idea what Alberto wanted to tell us either. We all waited for his answer, which came a few moments later.

"Damn it, it was right under our noses!"

"Alberto, please," I tried to calm him down, "We're not in your head, explain!"

"The list, that was the key. The list of revenge, those who must die for what they did in the past. It's all related. From the beginning, we have been blind."

"Man, get to the point," said Julián in confusion.

"Here, in the local newspaper, they have identified the hanged man as M.H.S., sixty-nine years old and a resident of the county."

"I still don't understand anything, Alberto," I assured him.

"When they discovered the guy hanging from the tree, someone shouted: 'It's Mario, the one from Hortigüela'. Don't you remember?"

"Yes, but I don't know what that has to do with..." The gears in my brain spun at full speed in search of a solution. First, they stopped when they recognized that Mario's name matched perfectly with the initials in the newspaper. But there was something else... Wait a minute! The pieces then began to fit together, but Menchu beat me to it.

"It's the friend of the cross-eyed man, María's rapist!"

"It can't be..." I whispered as I realized the implications of the discovery.

What if the dead men of the last week belonged to María's famous list? The Italian was seventy years old and the hanged man was sixty-nine, besides, his name was the same as that of one of the rapists. In terms of age, the two could match perfectly, two young men in their twenties in 1966 who had met their death fifty years later.

"Holy shit!" Julián exclaimed. "Someone has listened to María and is killing all the guys who screwed up her life."

"I think I remember a gang of kids, local bullies, who were looking for trouble during the festivities at that time," Menchu recalled. "Yes, maybe they were from Hortigüela or Hacinas, I'm not sure."

"And was there a cross-eyed man among them? Or a Mario?" asked Alberto.

"Maybe, I don't know. I seem to remember that the leader of the group, a small-time thug, was called Chema or something like that. He was the son of someone important, I don't remember well."

"I knew it! It's them, no doubt about it."

Alberto told us that he had spoken to his friend Adolfo -Julián, Ana and I knew perfectly well who he was, but the rest of the group did not - and he had informed him of an important detail. Apparently, a certain José María Hernando had been missing from his home in Valladolid for a few days. A man from Hortigüela, seventy-one years old, who was also a member of the regional parliament of Castilla y León.

"Do you think that individual is the one they found skinned in the monastery? From what we have heard, it has been impossible to identify him."

"Yes, it is likely. The deputy's wife raised the alarm after his disappearance a few days ago and the authorities are not ruling anything out. They are apparently checking dental records to see if they match. It was impossible to get anything clear from the deceased's fingerprints and that is the next step. If it's inconclusive, they will have to do a DNA test."

"But has that man been here all this time?"

Menchu's question was quite pertinent, although we did not know how the murderer acted. Perhaps he had murdered his victim far from here and then deposited the body in San Pedro de Arlanza.

"Yes, his wife assures that this José María was planning to visit Silos for the inauguration of the Sad Hill cemetery. He had been invited by the General Director of Tourism and, as he was a native of the region, he couldn't refuse."

No one asked how Alberto's friend had accessed confidential information that belonged to a police investigation.

Meanwhile, my mind was racing at full speed trying to piece the puzzle together. If Alberto was right, someone had taken justice into their own hands to avenge María Mediavilla.

According to his list, the first three had already fallen: the two rapists and the Italian, if indeed, the one who had crashed, been pushed into the ravine by the criminal was the one we were looking for. Although no one could assure us that this Arrigo Ambrosini, assistant cameraman in Leone's film, was the man who had held Juanito's hands in the vicinity of Sad Hill while his friends abused María.

"You have to go to the Guardia Civil and tell them everything," said Ana.

I agreed with her, but we were not going to be taken seriously. The story was too far- fetched, even if it made perfect sense to us. We had no conclusive proof, nor could we tell them about what we had discovered through the hacker. Alberto would have to come up with a strategy.

There were too many inconveniences and too little gain to be made.

The only thing we really had at that moment was a concrete motive for the murders: revenge. And, of course, we had yet to know the avenger, although one person had all the cards to become the ideal candidate, the number one suspect. It was Julián who gave me the cue to verbalize it out loud.

"If María died several years ago, who is avenging her death?"

"Her brother Jaime," I stated, just a second before Menchu answered.

"I was going to say the same thing. Jaime was very young when they left town, but he was always very close to his sister."

We were all silent for a moment, sensing that we had reached the solution to the mystery. I did not think that any Jaime Mediavilla would appear among the attendees of the film symposium, but the murderer must have been in the area for several days. And there were still other possible victims to attack, according to the list written by María.

"Alberto, does this ring any bells? From what you have mentioned, this Jaime has lived in America for many years. Maybe he has passed himself off as a Mexican, Uruguayan, Yankee or some other nationality."

"I don't know, there were people from all over the world at the conference. No idea, it could be anyone. If he participated in the activities, maybe he just went on the excursion and got the guy from the monastery somewhere else. We can't tell. This is frustrating."

We still had too many uncertainties and too few concrete facts. The best thing to do was to let the real professionals take care of it.

"We have to go to the Guardia Civil right now, Alberto," I urged him, noticing another detail. "Doña Pura is still alive and she is one of those who also appear on the list. They have to put her under protection right now."

"It's true, you're absolutely right. Come on, let's go to the station."

It seemed very perturbing to me that Jaime would murder his own mother, but worse things have happened. If the avenger had a plan and intended to stick to the list of shame, Doña Pura was the next candidate.

Then I thought about the rest of those pointed out by María. Both the policeman and the pimp were probably already dead or very old, as were the nuns of Peñagrande. Perhaps Father Cosme was likely to be next, although we had no more information about him. I asked Menchu just in case:

"Excuse me, Menchu, do you remember Father Cosme?"

"Vaguely, I didn't go to church much at that time. I seem to remember he was a young priest, who had some trouble in the village and left a few months later".

"From what we've seen, I'm sure he ended up as a bishop or worse."

Julián was absolutely right, that was the way the world was built around us, and we poor mortals could do nothing to prevent it. Good people struggled all their lives to get ahead and there was another type of people, born with rotten souls from birth, who prospered at the expense of others.

"I'll try to find out more about the priest," said Alberto. "Wish us luck, guys."

THE END OF THE ROAD

Madrid, July 26-27, 2016

So many years of effort and sacrifice were about to culminate in a resounding success. It had taken an immense sacrifice to find all those involved, he had very little left to give but needed to sleep peacefully at night again, if he was not caught, of course. In a few hours he would give the only two missing people their fair dues and María would rest in peace forever. Edmundo Dantés would be proud of the two of them: the revenge would have been executed.

Jaime Mediavilla had not lived a life of luxury since he was parted from his sister. After his mother's unilateral decision and his father's inability to rescue María from the reformatory, they left Madrid behind, not to return for a long time. He did not want to lose his sister or the family to break up, but he preferred to accompany his father rather than stay with his mother, who seemed to have lost her mind.

The beginnings in Galicia were not easy and young Jaime had to learn to survive, since Eusebio spent long periods of time away, fishing on the high seas. The owner of the boarding house where they lived took care of him from time to time and turned a blind eye, but the boy was never very sure of where he stood.

The years went by and Jaime's character soured over time. The circumstances of his life were not the best for the development of a teenager, he ended up getting into much trouble. He was on the verge of ending up in a reformatory himself, but Eusebio supported him during a period he spent on the mainland in the Galician Rías Baixas, and managed to keep him from being taken away by the social services.

Jaime became a quarrelsome young man and did not seem to learn from the problems he had dealt with. On the contrary, he began to associate with certain elements that led him astray. Especially when he met some boys who were involved in tobacco smuggling in the docks.

After Eusebio's death at sea, the young man from Burgos completely lost his way. He believed that the police, were about to arrest him as they did to some of his Galician friends, he thought it time to leave. He ended up as a stowaway on a merchant ship that docked weeks later in Mexico, the land that nurtured him during the following years of his life.

The young man became an adult and managed to carve out a future for himself. He changed his name. No more Jaime Mediavilla; and he swore to himself to leave behind any memories related to his homeland, Madrid or Galicia, where he had only encountered pain and suffering since his childhood.

His character did not mellow with the years, nor with the blows life kept delivering to him from time to time. He married twice and had two children, one with each wife, but he never found true happiness. An inner pain, a voice from the past that tormented him at night, prevented him from enjoying a full life.

He bounced around half of America and, ultimately, ended up in Argentina. He had just divorced his second wife, who demanded alimony for their young son, but he was completely disengaged and put thousands of kilometers between them. Separation had come after numerous quarrels, including a complaint from her for abuse, so in the end he gave in.

In the midst of his fifties' crisis, already settled in his new adopted homeland, by chance Jaime found an article on the Internet that caught his attention. He did not quite know the protocols he followed, but one website led him to another, he clicked on different links and ended up stumbling upon a blog that caught him unawares.

Minutes later, after reading all of the entries, he knew that fate had intervened and wanted him to find his beloved sister.

The joy was immense for both of them to hear from each other. However, it pained his soul that he had not been able to prevent the suffering his sister was put through and the loss of her baby, a niece he would never know, but they both agreed to forget about the past and make up for lost time.

He was unable to travel to Miami to visit María, but promised himself not to delay too long; they had been separated for many years. She could not leave at that time either. Her obligations in Florida were growing, so they continued to chat almost daily, enjoying each other's company even at a distance.

That was why Jaime could not bear it when María gave him the bad news. It could not be true, there had to be a solution. It was not fair that such an aggressive cancer would attack her brain now, just when they had rediscovered each other.

"Don't suffer for me, little brother. I'll finally rest in peace, don't worry. But first I want you to take care of one thing."

"Whatever you want, María, you know that. But please, I want to see you, I need to hug you before you leave."

"It can't be, Jaime, respect my decision. I'd rather you remember me as the big sister who made you mad in

Contreras. Or as the person I became, that happy woman who appeared in the photos I sent you when we met again. But I don't want you to see me in this state, please. The deterioration is grim and it advances inexorably."

"I'll come to see you even if you don't want me to."

"Don't even try, Jaime. I'm locked in the house and I'm not coming out. My housekeeper has orders not to let anyone on the property without my permission, so you'd be making the trip for nothing. Please respect my wishes."

Jaime reluctantly accepted his sister's imposition, but he was not resigned to María's fate. He called in numerous favors, sought help in all the countries where he had worked but he ultimately had to give up: stage IV glioblastoma was inoperable and his sister's end was very near.

Three awful weeks went by during which he had no more contact with María. He was overwhelmed by grief and pain, as well as by the rage of his helplessness to save her and not be able to say goodbye to her. He ended up disobeying her orders and looked for the first flight that would take him to Miami.

What he did not know was that during that time María's lawyer had also continued to search for a solution for his boss, a woman who was no longer struggling to survive but just waiting for the Grim Reaper. The lawyer had consulted with a prestigious neurosurgeon in New York, the doctor gave him the news he needed: there was a slim chance of removing the tumor, but it had to be within the next forty-eight hours plus there were no guarantees.

At first, María refused, when she learned of the risks. It was practically impossible for the operation to be a complete success and, if she did not die on the operating table, she would suffer terrible consequences for the rest of her life: memory loss, blindness, aphasia – she could be left in a vegetative state!

But in the end, she thought, nothing lost, nothing gained. Maybe there was a chance to come out of that experience successfully and for once in her life fortune would smile on her. María did not trust too much to altering her destiny. After all, if dying an appalling death in the next few weeks was the option, it would be better to die on the operating table, oblivious. That would be the best death, sedated and without pain.

When Jaime arrived in Miami, he was unable to find his sister. The house was securely locked and the Foundation in her husband's name had also closed its doors. No one was able to offer any more information and Jaime crumbled: his sister had died and he had not even been able to attend her funeral.

He then remembered one of María's last wishes and logged back into the blog, this time as administrator. It had been a while since he had visited the site and he had missed the last entries. So, when he read her epitaph, he had just found a reason to go on living: revenge.

He did not even enquire further about María's death and subsequent burial. He took it for granted and returned to Argentina, without knowing that the woman, brave to the end, was fighting for life, or death, in a hospital in New York. A real duel in which his sister's willpower won – to which he was oblivious.

María had convalesced for months in the hospital, suffering from various after-effects that had already been predicted. But she managed to pull through and was left with only a slight facial paralysis that she could live with perfectly well. The tumor had been defeated and she was getting ready to start all over again.

One of the after-effects was memory loss, especially in the short and medium term. María remembered her childhood and youth perfectly well, although perhaps she would have preferred to erase that part of her memory. However, she was not aware of having reunited with her brother nor did she remember anything related to her blog. In any case, even if she had, she would never have found him after Jaime had complied with her order to delete it.

A few months later, María moved to Boston, a city she loved. She had endured the heat and humidity of Florida, so she chose a change of scenery for a new stage in her life. After a while she remembered her brother in a vague way, but she had no information as to his whereabouts.

The years passed for the Mediavilla siblings, although at that time neither of them had the same legal surname. Jaime had set out to avenge his sister and spent a long time investigating who could be the cause of all María's misfortunes.

Jaime had several alert prompts in Google to notify him when there was any news related to his town or the region where he grew up. Apart from Contreras he included other place names: Salas de los Infantes, Santo Domingo de Silos, Carazo, Hortigüela, Hacinas, Arlanza, Mirandilla, Sierra de la Demanda and anything else he could think of. And, of course, he would delve into the Internet looking for information on Clint Eastwood, Sergio Leone and the dollar trilogy.

Little by little he obtained significant data. He learned that a certain José María Hernando went from councilman in Hacinas to member of the Diputación de Burgos. An honor for such a small town, that one of its most illustrious citizens had begun to climb the political ladder of the region. And since the last legislature, he had become a member of the Junta de Castilla y León as an autonomous deputy. A real rise to stardom for someone with such a murky past.

Jaime did his own research, but he also hired private investigators in Spain. Thanks to them he was able to find out that His Excellency, the deputy from Burgos, had been a bad piece of work in his younger years. A time when everyone knew him as 'the squint-eyed one' – a condition he had corrected with a simple operation before getting into politics.

One thing led to another, and he soon found a relationship with a certain Mario, a native of Hortigüela. He obtained evidence of the youthful friendship between the two, although apparently the two former *compadres* had eventually drifted apart over an affair of skirts. Jaime did not manage to find any crime or dirty laundry in their files, but he was sure that they were mainly responsible for María's fall from grace. In fact, he had assumed without a shadow of a doubt that they were the rapists who had taken advantage of her.

The film had another pleasant surprise for him shortly after. Thanks to his cyber surfing, he learned of the great event that they intended to organize in his native region on the occasion of the 50th Anniversary of the filming of *The Good, the Bad and the Ugly* in the Arlanza Valley: a unique event to bring together all those who, in one way or another, were involved in the events of '66.

Jaime also investigated the infamous 'Patronato de Protección a la Mujer' and Peñagrande. When he learned that this institution had disappeared in the 1980s and that it was almost impossible to access any kind of record of the center, he decided to focus on other objectives. After all, his sister was right: the nuns or anyone else connected with Peñagrande would be dead or close to it.

He had more trouble finding the Italian who had accompanied the two main criminals that afternoon in Sad Hill. In the end he found out that it was Arrigo Ambrosini, the young valet who had worked for Leone's orders, just at the same time he was witness of his friends' sexual assault. The Italian was living in Barcelona when Jaime dared to contact him with the excuse of being a journalist writing about Clint Eastwood's years in Spain. He managed to inform Ambrosini, about the activities that were being prepared in Burgos to commemorate the anniversary.

The Italian promised to think about it, as the Argentinian journalist assured him that he would come to Burgos next summer. Jaime also contacted the organizers of the event, presenting himself as an admirer of Leone's work, with Castilian roots, who wanted to visit his homeland and, at the same time, enjoy the film convention.

The fake journalist took the opportunity to tell the organizers that he had once met one of the participants in the film, an Italian camera assistant. They thanked him for the information and promised to invite Ambrosini to the convention.

He also found out that the rapists had acted as extras in the film, so he arranged for them to receive an invitation. He imagined that Mario, who still lived in Hortigüela, would attend the event. Something rather grand was being prepared in the region and all the neighbors in the area would participate in one way or another. Perhaps it would be more difficult for the deputy to attend since he lived in Valladolid, but as he worked in the Tourism Commission of the Junta, he was likely to receive an official invitation as well.

The line was cast, all he had to do was wait. He also investigated Father Cosme and found out that he had ended up working in the Vatican. He had had several legal problems there and the ecclesiastical authorities were thinking of sending him back to Spain. Jaime was not very religious, but he prayed that this would happen in the next few months so he would have a chance to give him his comeuppance. Besides, aside from what he had done to María after plotting with their mother, Jaime also had a personal affront that he wanted to collect on properly. Stirring up the past sometimes brings back memories you thought you had forgotten forever.

After months of preparation, Jaime was ready to travel to Spain after so many years away from his country. He rented an SUV at the Madrid-Barajas airport and drove to the Arlanza region. It seemed unbelievable to him to return to his region after so long, but he tried not to pass through Contreras. He did not want to see his house in ruins, or stir up other painful memories, he went straight to Salas de los Infantes. There he had rented a room in a hotel, booked well in advance in view of the avalanche of visitors expected in the area.

As chance would have it, he ran into Ambrosini earlier than planned. He was planning to talk to the former valet during the events, but he was also at the Casino reception when the Italian showed up there for accreditation, claiming to be one of the organization's guests. Jaime blessed his good luck and decided to follow him, just for fun.

He was not proud of what he had done, but neither did he harbor any remorse for causing his accident. He wanted to play with him for a while, get on his nerves, and maybe bitch at him for the next few days until he was ready.

But, in the end he enjoyed the chase too much and over-revved, forcing Ambrosini to his fatal accident. One less on the list, although perhaps he had not suffered as much as his sister would have demanded. It did not matter the guy was dead, he was just as guilty as the others.

That is why Jaime promised himself that the deaths of the two rapists would not be so quick, far from it; he wanted them to suffer for having destroyed his sister's life. An eye for an eye and a tooth for a tooth. He intended to shatter their lives, without remorse.

He was not even surprised to find that he felt nothing when he caused the Italian's death. He did not consider himself a psychopath, or anything like that. Maybe people would think he was in a state of mental derangement, but he did not see it that way. Rather, he was simply in charge of performing a social task: eliminating vermin that were very harmful to the rest of the world.

Jaime was a big man, about six feet two and with a strong build. But he still had to go all out with the squint-eyed guy, who got cocky as soon as he found out he was the brother of the redhead, a girl Chema had not forgotten all that time. He did not apologize or show any kind of remorse, he did not even lie or pretend not to know what he was talking about. In fact, he had licked his lips lasciviously as he recalled the scene and rebuked Jaime, taunting him.

"That little whore enjoyed it like a bitch, don't give me that bullshit now. She's never been fucked like that again in her life, that's for sure."

Jaime punched him brutally in the face and knocked him to the ground. The deputy tried to fight back, but was then hit in the face with a blast of a powerful chemical numbing agent that knocked him unconscious. Jaime tied him up and gagged him so that he would not give him any more trouble, and loaded him like a bundle into the trunk of his SUV.

Fortunately, he had approached him in a quiet place, away from houses or people, just at dusk. He took him to an abandoned warehouse he had seen earlier and enacted his retribution. He was not proud of what he had done to him, torturing him and literally tearing his skin off, but he did not feel he had to apologize for his actions either. He was only fulfilling his sister's wishes, becoming the Exterminating Angel that would put an end to that plague on Earth.

At the time he knew that some kids had noticed the Italian's accident, but he let it go as it did not seem important to him. However, when he heard how one of those boys was asking uncomfortable questions at one of the speeches at the convention, he thought of giving him a scare to frighten him. He had nothing against the young man, but neither did he intend to let him interfere with what he had planned.

He had sent him the anonymous letters and left him the poisoned gift of a mangled corpse in the ruins of the monastery. He thought that this traumatic experience would serve to frighten the university student, but he was wrong again. He did not want to get rid of him, though he would not hesitate for a moment if he got in the way of his plans.

He participated in many of the convention's activities and chatted with several participants from all over the world. In the end, Jaime enjoyed the experience, regardless of the avenging crusade he was on. And, when the excursion arrived, he knew it was the right time to take the next step.

Mario was a poor man, a drunkard who would go along with anyone who invited him for a glass of wine or a drink. Jaime took advantage and plied him with drink during the afternoon before the screening of the movie. He had already spotted him during the week when he had seen him at other activities, so it had not taken much to convince him to have a few drinks together.

When the film began, Mario was already in a pitiful alcoholic state. Jaime stayed close to him, just in case he thought of leaving. But the guy, drunk as a skunk, had the good mind not to take the car in that state. Mario collapsed on the ground anyway and stayed there, half asleep on the side of the meadow, while the film progressed.

Halfway through the movie Jaime decided to act. He reached out to his victim and made him sit up with great effort. He promised to take him home safe and sound with the excuse that he was bored and wanted to rest after a hard day. Mario was not at all suspicious and leaned on him as they walked away from the group of spectators, on their way to the tombs.

"Hey man, where are we going?" the drunk man had asked when he realized that the parking lot was nowhere to be found.

"It's just a moment, sorry. I wanted to take a picture of the tomb I sponsored in my sister's name- the cross must be somewhere nearby."

Months before, when Jaime had learned of the initiative that the association restoring the Sad Hill cemetery was undertaking, he had wanted to do his bit to contribute to the cause. He had gladly paid the subscription and asked them to paint it with his sister's name. María had died there, fifty years before, albeit metaphorically, and this small tribute in the valley where it all began, would be a kind of divine justice to atone for her.

The guy grumbled, but he had no choice but to accompany Jaime to his final destination. When they reached the cross, Jaime illuminated it with his cell phone and showed it to Mario, who looked on blankly.

"Look here, you son of a bitch. María Mediavilla Castroviejo, 1950-2008. R.I.P."

"What are you talking about? I don't understand anything..."

"My sister is dead because of you, motherfucker," Jaime was not strictly telling the truth, but he was already unleashed. "Don't you remember her? Yeah, man, the redhead you raped near here, in that fucking summer of '66."

A flash of recognition fleetingly flashed through Mario's head, but he did not have time to react. Fear took over his actions and he wanted to scream, but all that came out was a babble that his captor cut off in an instant - Jaime put him to sleep with his vaporizer and executed his plan.

He hung him up in the hangman's tree with a deadpan expression as he heard the crack of his neck as it snapped. He turned and stealthily made his escape.

He had his mother located as well, he had already visited her at the nursing home and the old woman had not even blinked when she saw him or heard his voice. Jaime was not sorry to learn that the woman who had brought him into the world had completely lost her mind and could not recognize him after so many years. He had no idea what went through the mind of a person with advanced dementia, he simply assumed she was a complete stranger who should pay for her evil deeds. He would leave her for the bottom of the list; first he would have to take care of another individual far from their homeland.

After dealing with Mario at the hangman's tree, Jaime recovered his vehicle and left Sad Hill. He had not parked in the main parking lot, he did not want witnesses to his escape, it was a few hundred meters to the place where he had hidden the vehicle behind a depression that was not visible from outside due to the surrounding vegetation.

He drove cautiously to Salas, where he arrived well before the end of the film, according to his calculations. He did not know when the body would be found or whether the discovery of the hanged man would force the cancelation of the screening, he did not care. He imagined that there would be a great commotion in the area and he could prove that he had been resting in his room for some time, in case he needed an alibi.

He remained attentive to the events. Around 1 a.m. he finally found a mention of what happened in Sad Hill on social networks, and an hour later there were already several trends on Twitter, at least for searches related to Burgos.

He smiled when he discovered the general chaos that had ensued, the authorities were not going to be able to control it with their limited means. Thousands of people trying to leave in panic while the Police and the Guardia Civil searched for clues or interrogated possible witnesses, a situation he would have loved to see. But it was much better for his interests to rest in Salas at that ungodly hour.

He set the alarm for seven in the morning, ready to get out of there as soon as possible. He slept for a few hours, without any remorse or concern, and left the hotel after paying the bill. As a foreign tourist who had attended the film convention, he was leaving the region after finishing the activities.

He knew that the authorities would have to talk to a considerable amount of people but he felt that no one would show up at his hotel to demand anything from him before eight o'clock; let alone after a crazy night, so he left with all the peace of mind in the world.

He was returning to Madrid airport, but not to take an international flight, at least not for the time being, he still had some tasks in hand and the first of was to take care of

Father Cosme, who now held a much more pompous position than a simple village parish priest, nothing less than cardinal.

Cardinal Martinez had worked for many years in Rome and had reached a very important position in the Vatican's finance department. He had had some legal wrangling over an alleged embezzlement committed in the accounts under his charge, but in the end the case had been dismissed. The Spanish prelate belonged to the very powerful Opus Dei and was able to get out of that mess thanks to his contacts, but he had to leave Rome.

Jaime had been investigating the cardinal for some time and found out other juicy details -he had also been denounced on a couple of occasions for alleged pederasty in the past, and rumors had returned to the Vatican in recent months. Opus Dei and the new pontiff had issues, so the cardinal was banished from Rome, but he was not demoted to a rural parish priest as he originally had been. No, the Spanish prelate assumed a new position in which he would continue to enjoy numerous perks as secretary at the apostolic nunciature in Madrid, the embassy of the Holy See in Spain.

Martinez had been in Madrid for a couple of months, so it was easier for Jaime to investigate him thoroughly. The detective agency he had already worked with in the past, discreet and efficient without going overboard with the bill, prepared a complete dossier on the man of the frock, he had to smile at the document: he thought he had discovered a way to get close to him without arousing suspicion.

The Nunciature is located in the Chamartín district, in the Pío XII neighborhood. An affluent area, with a high level of purchasing power, where Jaime was planning to carry out the next phase of his plan. Cardinal Martinez, sure of himself and without any perceived danger around him, had relaxed the Vatican discipline and abandoned himself once again to one of his great passions.

Jaime found out that the prelate used the services of an exclusive online escort agency. Every two weeks, on a Tuesday night, Martinez dressed as a layman and used a comfortable suite in a four-star hotel near the Nunciature. He did not even stray far from his sphere of action; such was his brazenness and ego that he did not consider his behavior to be at odds with the commandments of the Church.

Jaime prepared to wait for his chance, sitting in the Citroën C4 he had rented that week in the capital. He parked the vehicle in the vicinity of the hotel and remained alert, ready to execute his plan. Minutes later, the opportunity he had been waiting for arrived.

A cab stopped a few meters from the hotel, and a young particularly handsome mulatto man got out of it. He was a somewhat mannered, elegant and well-dressed gent, who hesitated for a few moments before heading towards the hotel entrance. Jaime passed him halfway, and the man was startled.

"Hi there, are you Gerson?" he asked point-blank.

"Yes, who wants to know?" said the boy in a melodious Spanish with a slight Brazilian accent.

"Relax, I'm the secretary of the client you're meeting with. Didn't the agency tell you?"

"Tell me what? What do you mean?"

The young man then looked at his phone and looked confused. Jaime smiled as he assumed that his bosses had sent him a message to cancel the service.

A few minutes earlier he had called the agency with an excuse, pretending to be Mr. Rocamora, a fictitious name used by the priest, which he knew, thanks to the information provided by the detective. Jaime apologized for not having been able to communicate it before and assured them that he would be paid as usual because he wanted him to continue working with them in the future.

"Sorry for the misunderstanding, we have already discussed it with the agency. Here, you have the usual rate for your bosses, and an extra just for you, for the inconvenience."

The mulatto's eyes sparkled at the generous tip that peeked between the fingers of the man who had intercepted him.

"I really don't know. I don't want any trouble..."

"You just have to give me the access card to the client's room, which is 345 in case you don't trust me. And I'll hand you the money, okay?"

The escort boy hesitated for a moment. His bosses had confirmed the cancellation, but this guy did not look too legitimate to him. He thought about calling the agency to ratify it and tell them what was going on, but then he would be left without the bonus. And extra money, without working on top of it, always came in handy.

"Here's the cash, Gerson. Give me the card and it's yours. It'll be the easiest money you'll ever make in your life."

The Brazilian nodded and put the money in his wallet. From there he also took out the access card to the room, that had previously been given to him, handed it to the stranger and left, without looking back. A night in which he could rest peacefully at home, even if he had to turn on the air conditioning to be able to fall asleep.

Jaime watched the young Brazilian walk away, who must have been in his early twenties although his cherubic face did not seem to bear witness to it. The cardinal had always liked pubescent boys, but at least now he did not seek minors.

The quiet surroundings, with office areas closed at that time of night and some residential buildings, facilitated the task Jaime had set himself. A summer night in Madrid, in a neighborhood with hardly any stores or restaurants open at that time of day, was the ideal time to go unnoticed.

Jaime put the key card in his pocket and entered the hotel lobby. He was well dressed and there was no reason to be noticed by the receptionist, an employee who could not know the faces of all the guests staying at the hotel at that moment. He did not hesitate, crossed the hall with a firm step and went straight to the side of the floor, right where the elevators were located. The employee was still concentrating on looking at some data on the computer and did not even notice the man who had just entered.

He pressed the button for the third floor and seconds later walked down the corridor that would lead him to his final destination. Room 345 was located at the end of the corridor, with no other rooms nearby. The cardinal liked discretion and it showed in his choice of accommodation.

Jaime burst into the room silently, ready to catch the cardinal off guard. The surprise, would give him little margin for error to react, so he had to remain attentive to the cardinal's movements. He prepared himself for that moment and reached into his pocket for the vaporizer that had worked so well so far, ready to face one of his manifest demons in the open.

Jaime pushed away an image that settled in his head, it was not the right time to get distracted. He had to concentrate, no mistakes, and execute the plan properly. He could not allow the memories of the past to cloud his mind at such an important moment.

He allowed himself just a second of relaxation, a flash that he recalled to affirm himself in his task. The image revealed him, a boy, seven or eight years old, going to the village church to attend catechism classes. Father Cosme liked to stay a little longer alone with him in the sacristy when the rest of the children had already left, with the excuse of preparing him better for communion.

The flash went away as quickly as it had come, but Jaime did not allow himself to hesitate even for an instant. The cardinal would pay for all his crimes. He had a long record behind him and his continuous abuse of minors had never been punished. Monetary crimes mattered little to him, but he wanted revenge for María and also for what that priest had forced him to do in his childhood.

Something he had never told anyone, a bitter memory buried in oblivion under seven keys. An unpleasant experience that surfaced months ago, just when he had begun to investigate the list of shame that María had left him as a testament.

He carefully entered the room and felt his way through the small entrance that preceded the sleeping area proper. The cardinal was not there and Jaime was startled for a moment, but he soon heard sounds coming from the bathroom and knew where he had to look for the prelate. He had been lucky, perhaps it was easier than he thought.

He entered the toilet and saw a man taking a shower behind a transparent partition. He could not waste any more time. He flung open the door and sprayed a generous stream from his vaporizer in the face of the surprised cardinal. Martinez only had time to let out

"But what the hell...?"

He did not finish the sentence and Jaime took care of his body. He hauled him out of the shower and laid him on the floor, knocked out by the powerful narcotic. He gagged him just in case. He did not want the priest to wake up and start bawling for help before he tied him hand and foot. He had the whole night to enjoy himself, although he preferred to finish as soon as possible.

When the priest came to, he found himself stark naked, tied in such a way to the headboard of the bed that he had to remain face down, unable to move his arms and legs. In that position, forced by the ties, he could only turn his neck a few centimeters to the left, and that is what he did as soon as he opened his eyes and heard a voice beside him.

"Well, well, you have finally woken up, Your Eminence."

Martinez tried to free himself from his bonds and babbled incoherent words that could not be understood with the gag in his mouth. Jaime saw fear in his pupils, and the cardinal could not guess what he had in mind for him. Perhaps his evil deeds over so many decades of depravity would finally find their just punishment that night. No one could know what was going through the priest's mind in those moments of anguish.

"First of all, I would like to introduce myself, I don't want to be rude to such an important person as you. My name is Jaime Mediavilla, does that ring a bell?"

The man turned his head, back to the center, to rest the muscles - the position of rotating his neck was too uncomfortable to maintain. Jaime thought he caught a glimpse of recognition in Martinez's eyes, but he could not be sure. He did not know if he remembered him, or perhaps he had associated his last name with the Arlanza region, but he would find out soon enough.

"No? Nothing in your memory? I am a neighbor of Contreras, the town where you were assigned in 1966. Do you remember me now? Yes, man, I was one of your favorite students in the catechism of that year. At least one of those who received the most attention from Your Illustriousness at the end of the classes?"

As soon as he finished that sentence, he crossed his back from side to side, with the cardinal's own belt. The crack produced a scream of pain in the victim, drowned out by the gag that prevented him from almost breathing. But Jaime had not finished. In fact, he had just begun and he intended to enjoy the moment.

"And you don't remember my sister María? A very cute redhead, who confessed to you what had happened to her that summer in the Mirandilla Valley". The man's terrified gesture left no room for doubt, he seemed to realize what was happening. "Yes, the rape, I see that now you remember my family. I imagine that you will also have my old mother in your prayers, Purificación Castroviejo, the same one you convinced to lock up my little sister in the hell of Peñagrande."

The cardinal perceived his vulnerability, perhaps after realizing that that night he could purge all his sins once and for all. Tears began to roll down his cheeks and he even urinated on himself out of fear, something that displeased Jaime. The cardinal had taken advantage of innocent young people and contributed to bury other people alive without a second's hesitation, but now he was showing not an ounce of pride or courage. On the contrary, his cowardice was coming to the fore as he faced the summary judgment that would bring him face to face with his Creator. Or rather, it would lead him to visit the cauldrons of hell to greet Satan himself.

"What's the matter, Your Grace? Are you not comfortable? As you can understand, I can't loosen your restraints. But if you behave well, maybe I'll loosen them a little and I might even remove the gag for a few moments."

The man shook his head up and down as much as he could, to affirm in his own way that he intended to behave himself if his executioner had a shred of benevolence for him. Jaime consented to check his reaction, but first he warned him in his ear.

"I'm going to keep my promise, don't make me regret it. If you try any tricks or even think of screaming, I'll snap your neck in one move. Is that clear?"

Martinez nodded again and Jaime prepared to remove his gag, focused on his next moves. It amused him to play with this man, a shepherd turned wolf years before to devour the poor lambs in his flock, just to show him that there were worse predators in the world than him.

"Please let me go! I have a lot of money stashed away, I can give you some of it if you let me go."

"Are you sure?" Jaime asked, "Is that how you want to get rid of this?"

The cardinal blinked in confusion. He did not understand what was going on, much less what Mediavilla was referring to. María's brother expected an apology on his part, a confession of repentance for his actions, but Martinez only wanted to save himself by appealing to the greed of his captor. And the executioner, although he had many faults, did not suffer from that one. Money did not matter much to him, and he was not surprised to see that the cardinal confessed to another of his crimes, assuring that he had a lot of money in tax havens.

"I don't know, I don't understand what..."

"Shut the fuck up!" Jaime shouted in his ear before gagging him again and cinching his legs and arms even tighter. "You've had your chance and all you want to do is buy me with your dirty money. If you had at least tried to apologize for your sins, maybe I would have been magnanimous."

"Grrrr..."

"No, it is too late. You have not passed the test, so your death will be slower and more painful than what you could have achieved with a simple apology. And now, be prepared to suffer the same pain that some of your victims suffered."

He had thoroughly searched the room during the time the cardinal had remained knocked out due to the action of the narcotic. Jaime had found various sex toys with which he imagined Martinez intended to enjoy himself in the company of the young mulatto, but now they would serve his purposes.

Jaime had fun with the cardinal for a long hour, but it was time to finish. He did not know if he had taken him to such an extreme that it had caused him to go into cardiac arrest, but he was not too worried about it. He checked that Martinez was properly dead and left him there alone, tied up in that humiliating position.

He left the room and walked down the hallway to the emergency exit. He knew that an alarm would sound when he walked through that door, but he did not care. Seconds later he was in his car and driving away from Pío XII with a smile on his face. Revenge had been consummated: Father Cosme had paid with his life for the sins he had committed.

CONFESSION

Covarrubias (Burgos), July 27, 2016

They arrived in Covarrubias around six o'clock in the evening, asked for the Guardia Civil post and minutes later parked outside the modest building. The activity in the barracks seemed frenetic, something understandable after the events that had taken place in the region during the last week.

"Are you sure?" Sandra asked before entering the official building.

"Yes, there's nothing else we can do. There've been too many deaths and if we're right in our conclusions we can still save some people, more importantly, help catch the culprit."

Alberto and Sandra told the access control guard that they needed to speak to someone in charge urgently. They had very important information to share regarding the murders in the region and time was pressing.

"Very well, you will be seen in a minute," replied the guard with a dismissive gesture. "You can go to the waiting room, someone will call you right away."

The young couple hesitated to obey the member of the *Benemérita*, but in the end they gave in. The man had only done his job, although he did not seem very impressed to hear their explanations either. They only hoped that his superior would have a more flexible mind when they were able to talk to him.

The minutes passed slowly inside the asphyxiating atmosphere of an unventilated room. After half an hour Alberto got tired of waiting and peeked again at the entrance, ready to protest to the ineffective guard. He inadvertently bumped into an officer and apologized instantly. He sensed that this man would be more in charge than the guy at the gate, and he did not hesitate for a second:

"Excuse me, Sergeant, we need to talk to you."

"I'm very busy, talk to the guard at the gate and you will be attended to."

"Yes, we have already done that. But it's a matter of life and death. We have first-hand information about the Sad Hill killer. We were in Mirandilla on Sunday night and we were the first to discover the body in San Pedro de Arlanza."

The sergeant's face changed instantly. He ordered a subordinate to take their details before speaking to them. Minutes later Alberto and Sandra were sitting in the sergeant's tiny office, nervous at the prospect of divulging their information.

"Let's see, this is very serious, don't waste my time. Explain it to me from the beginning with as much detail as possible."

Alberto nodded and Sandra motioned her friend to begin. She would support him in his narrative, but she preferred Alberto to carry the weight of the statement. It had been his idea in the first place and she was still not sure that their confession would not cause more problems, especially when she noticed the grim expression on the civil guard's face.

Alberto started at the beginning. He explained in a few words to the civil guard why they were in the region during those days, specifying their registration at the film convention and Sandra's relationship with Ana and her family from Carazo. He reminded the sergeant that it had been him, in the company of Julián, who had found the accident victim in the curves near Carazo a few days before.

"That's right, I remember now," confirmed Sergeant Ortega, an Andalusian who hated the cold of Burgos and had been stationed in Covarrubias for two years.

The Criminology student continued with his explanation, somewhat closer to an informal chat than an official statement. He then told how he had received the mysterious, anonymous letters during the congress, in the afternoon that proceeded the night-party they attended in Covarrubias itself, with dozens of witnesses who could corroborate it. He had then explained to Sandra what had happened to him and they had both decided to go on their own to San Pedro del Arlanza.

"We will clarify some details later, but at that time you should have called us immediately, without any excuses. Please continue."

Alberto took the scolding as best he could and knew that he was not going to have an easy time with the officer, who was pissed off by the overwork and stressed by an investigation that was getting out of hand. Those in charge of the *Benemérita* had already called in the 'cavalry' and the next day they would be visited by colleagues from Madrid, apparently someone from the U.C.O. (Central Operative Unit) the elite unit of the Judicial Police. The team was headed by a certain Roncero, one of the best investigators in the Corps, according to what the Criminology student had found out.

He did not elaborate too much in narrating the chilling moment of the discovery of the corpse. He only admitted to having seen the body without touching the crime scene before leaving the premises, on his way to Salas de los Infantes.

"I assume it was you who called minutes later to report the discovery," the sergeant said sternly.

"Yes, sir. You see, I..."

"We will come back to that later. Please continue, I don't have all afternoon, as you can imagine."

Alberto then told him that the two of them, accompanied by a good group of friends, had taken part in the excursion to the Mirandilla Valley on Sunday afternoon. This had happened prior to the projection of the film and the discovery of the man hanging in the Hanged Man's tree.

"It was chaos there and we couldn't talk to your men, so we left the valley. Yesterday we had to return to Madrid for personal reasons, but I imagined that you would want to talk to us and that is why we came as soon as possible."

"In the blessed cemetery there were many people and no one seems to have seen anything. But it turns out that you two are the only ones who saw the corpse of a man in the monastery before we arrived."

"Yes, sergeant, that's true," said Sandra, to the civil guard's chagrin. "Don't forget about the accident: it is also related to the other two deaths."

"You're wasting my time and I'm going to get pissed off. What the hell are you talking about, young lady? Get to the point, please."

Then it was Sandra's turn, although the girl did not know where to start. Alberto's narration had her interlocutor's interest from the beginning, since he was a possible witness to a crime, but in her case, it was going to be difficult to introduce everything related to María Mediavilla before getting to the heart of the matter, plus the state of mind of the sergeant, was not going to help matters.

Sandra ignored her relationship with the Mediavilla family and stated that they had found information in an old online diary about what happened to a young girl from

Contreras in 1966. To Ortega's impatience, she claimed that the girl had been raped in the vicinity of Sad Hill Cemetery and that someone was now avenging that affront.

"Unbelievable!" exclaimed the sergeant. "Enough of this nonsense, I have far too much to contend with. Go into literature or the movies. You certainly have a wild imagination."

The civil guard made an attempt to get up from his chair, while he invited them to leave his office in a loud, officious voice. Then Alberto thought he should intervene with some more conclusive information, but he did not measure his words well.

"Please listen to us, lives are in danger. We believe that María's brother caused Ambrosini's accident and then killed the real culprits of the rape, the deputy whose body he abandoned in San Pedro de Arlanza and the man from Hortigüela hanged in the cemetery."

Alberto immediately realized his mistake. Sandra feared the worst, and the civil guard's response proved them both right.

"And how do you know that the corpse in the monastery belongs to a deputy?" asked the sergeant with a wolfish grin, ready to devour his adversary.

"No, I..."

"You see, in María's diary the names of the culprits are specified. She wrote a list of the people who had hurt her in the past, including a priest and her own mother. Mario's name appeared there, as well as that of José María Hernando."

Sandra's quick intervention seemed to calm things down, but Ortega continued to look at them with suspicion. Alberto then put the finishing touch, hoping that the explanations would have the desired effect.

"Of course, we searched the Internet for the names on that list and discovered information about them. It matched the Italian's file and also that of Mario, so we imagined that the body in the monastery could belong to the deputy who disappeared days ago, that's all."

"I'm beginning to be fed up with you two. You don't look like murderers, but I find what you're telling me very strange. I don't believe a word of this soap opera, but I know there's something fishy going on here."

"Excuse me, sergeant, I..."

"I am not finished, young man. You are going to come with me to the interrogation room to talk more calmly. And you, miss, one of my men will take your statement in the meantime."

"Am I under arrest then?" asked Alberto with more aplomb than he would have imagined.

"No, not for the moment, it will just be an informal chat. Unless you would prefer that we call a lawyer."

"No problem, I have nothing to hide."

The sergeant smiled at the young man's mistake. If he really had something to do with the murders, he should not talk to the authorities without a lawyer in front of him. A not so insignificant detail that the civil guard intended to take advantage of to squeeze him until the pips squeaked. Alberto knew all those details, he was a very dedicated Criminology student and a faithful follower of the police genre in cinema and literature, but he did not consider that he was in danger at that moment and wanted to believe that he could cope with the situation.

The afternoon dragged on too long, with Alberto and Sandra in separate rooms, again telling the same story. Both kept to the truth, without frills, the Civil Guards did their best to catch them out, although they realized that the bizarre story they had relayed, was the closest thing they had to a reliable clue.

Ortega prepared himself for a long night; he could not miss the opportunity. The next morning the case would be taken away from him by the smart asses in Madrid and he did not want the embarrassment. If he managed to discover and lock up the culprit of the murders in the next few hours, or at least find out a reasonable clue that would lead them to an arrest - maybe his luck would change. He would gain many points for a possible promotion and, above all, he might be closer than ever to the long-awaited transfer back to his homeland that he had been requesting for so long.

At about ten o'clock at night the sergeant of the *Benemérita* brought the young couple together again, they remained unperturbed and withstood the pressure well. One of two things: either they were two seasoned delinquents, despite their young age; or this crazy story was simply the truth and that is why they were so calm, without any fear of the possible consequences. In fact, they urged him to provide protection for two possible victims of the Sad Hill killer.

"You have to look for Father Cosme, his life is in danger, so is Purificación Castroviejo."

"You don't need to tell me how to do my job," Ortega replied offended. He then called one of his men and whispered some orders in his ear. "For the moment we are going to continue chatting in the hall, we have many points to clarify. And you, Miss, where did you say you were staying?"

"Me?" Sandra asked, surprised. "In Carazo, at a friend's house."

"Very well, one of my men will accompany you. You can rest tonight, but do not move from there because tomorrow we will continue."

"What about Alberto? Are you going to arrest him?" asked the girl anxiously.

"Don't worry, we are only going to go over some aspects of the statement, nothing more."

"So, can we both leave? If we are not detained, I think it's only fair. We've already told you everything we know, it's your obligation to take care of the possible victims and arrest the suspect."

Alberto was startled to hear Sandra's response and hoped the sergeant would not get angry. He knew that Sandra was right and he had perhaps been a fool to have exposed himself to the Guardia Civil in this way. His only alibi was Sandra but it was plausible that her behavior during the last few days might be considered suspicious.

He hesitated spending the night there could also be considered a kind of detention, even if he was not read his rights or locked up in a cell. And, if that happened, it was clear to him that he would shut his mouth and call a lawyer. The bad news was that he did not know anyone he could trust. He hoped he would not have to go to that extreme.

"Of course, you can leave if you wish. But I think it would be best if you listened to me. You stay in Carazo until we call you back and, in the meantime, I will continue chatting with your friend. Is that all right with you?"

They were not fooled by the sergeant's friendly tone: it was obvious what he was trying to do. But Alberto thought they had nothing to fear, they were the heroes of this story, not the villains. They had discovered the murderer and they should be thanked, not treated like that while other people's lives were in danger. He indicated to Sandra to loosen up and assumed that he would spend the night at the Guardia Civil's quarters.

"All right, I'll stay," Alberto replied before turning to his friend. "Don't worry, Sandra, go back to Carazo. If anything comes up, I'll call you. I guess it won't be a problem, right?"

The sergeant's demeanor seemed to confirm to them that there would be no problem, although they both knew he was assuring them with a forked tongue.

"Remember to call the landline," said Sandra before leaving.

Alberto nodded and said goodbye with a short hug to the girl who had stolen his heart. A thought that came as a surprise, something he had not expected at such a delicate moment. Yet, to realize it gave him courage, a sudden burst of endorphins that gave him enough strength to bravely face what was to come.

A corporal of the Guardia Civil then escorted Sandra to the exit. She looked back one last time in anguish; she did not feel like leaving Alberto there alone, at the mercy of a sergeant with a twisted tooth. Although the original idea of going to the authorities had come from Alberto, she felt guilty for having dragged him into the spiral of madness which had gripped them since they had arrived in Burgos. She only hoped that both of them would come out of the situation safely and, above all, that the civil guard would stop being so obtuse, listen to them and take the necessary steps to solve everything.

When she arrived in Carazo it was already close to midnight. Ana, Menchu and the rest of the family were very worried because they had not heard from them since mid-afternoon. Sandra checked that she had several missed calls and messages on her phone, but she preferred to give the appropriate explanations once the corporal had left and she was alone with her friends, whom she needed more than ever.

"Good heavens, girl!" exclaimed Menchu as soon as she got out of the Guardia Civil's car. "You had us worried, what happened?"

"I'll tell you everything, don't worry."

"Where is Alberto?" asked Julián, who had also peeked out of the door.

"He is still at the station, talking to the sergeant," said the officer.

"Aren't you related to the Escudero family?"

"Err, yes... But I don't understand what that has to do with…… ma'am."

"He says, Ma'am, that's funny. Come on, come with us inside and explain to us what's happened while I make you a hot coffee. I'm Menchu, from Contreras. I've been a friend of your parents for many years. In fact, I've changed your diapers more than once."

The Guardia Civil corporal blushed for a moment but quickly pulled himself together. He then seemed to remember Menchu from some family conversation and relaxed a little, following the rest of the group into the house. There was still a long night ahead of them.

A ROAD OF NO RETURN

Carazo (Burgos), July 28, 2016

The dark circle concealer I borrowed from Ana's toiletry bag was of no use to me on that occasion. I had been suffering from too many sleepless nights.

We had been talking in the lounge until the small hours of the morning. First with the civil guard who accompanied me, while Menchu subjected him to a third degree that the officer endured as best he could. I think he allowed it because she was an old friend of his parents, although the corporal did not seem comfortable with the interrogation.

When the member of the *Benemérita* left, it was my turn to explain. The whole group, Ana's entire family including Julián who seemed to have settled permanently in Carazo, harangued me with questions about what had happened at the station. I began to feel overwhelmed, especially after a few intense hours in which I had been subjected to the same torture, this time by the authorities.

"Guys, guys, a little peace and quiet. Let Sandra explain herself, if you keep going like that we'll never find out."

Menchu's intervention seemed to calm things down and I thanked her with a nod. I continued with my story, interrupted here and there by remarks.

"Have you called the residence in Burgos?" Ana wanted to know. "I hope they believed you and haven't left that poor woman unattended.

"Yes, I insisted before I left. The corporal called in front of me to reassure me. He spoke to the nurse on duty and she assured him that the residence was locked up tight, and that Doña Pura was resting in her room. No one is going to enter at this hour without permission."

"I can't quite believe that Jaime has committed so many atrocities and that he is also going to end his own mother's life," Menchu interjected. "Although I think it's good that they are taking it seriously and are keeping an eye out for him."

"They do not have enough means, so they've spoken to the Burgos Police. From the capital they have been assured that they will send a patrol to control the area. I don't know if that will be enough," I replied.

There was a small discussion among the attendees of the night's council in the following minutes. Some agreed with Alberto's attitude and others stated that such behavior would bring him more trouble and complications than anything else. In the end, after becoming completely exhausted, I decided to go to bed and call it a night.

"Yes, I think it's time," said Menchu. "Everyone to bed, tomorrow will also be a busy day."

I did not pay much attention to Menchu's farewell, as half asleep I climbed the stairs to the second floor. The funny thing is that her words were almost prophetic after seeing what happened the following day.

I went to bed around two o'clock in the morning, with sleeplessness looming to my despair. I have never liked chemicals for that sort of thing, but if I had had a powerful sleeping pill nearby, I would not have hesitated for a second to take it. I needed to reset and rest, even if it was only for a few hours.

I set my alarm for eight in the morning. I wanted to be ready in case they called me from the station first thing in the morning or came to pick me up. Worrying about Alberto prevented me from falling asleep and I spent a few terrible hours in a semi-catatonic state, when I could not move, but I could not sleep deeply either. I woke up completely shattered, in a bad mood as I glimpsed the lights of the new day coming mercilessly through the window, just before the alarm clock went off.

How had Alberto spent the night? I was in a hellish mood after having listened to him and, above all, after abandoning him like that at the station, even though it was the sergeant's direct orders. I would have rather stayed there with him; at least I would have encouraged him to stand up to the fussy civil guard. At least I had been able to stretch out on a decent mattress, but he must have spent the night in an infamous chair that would make his whole body ache.

Anyway, being fair, I could not reproach Sergeant Ortega for anything. He was just doing his job and had to make sure of every detail before taking any further steps. Our story sounded totally implausible, that was obvious, but if he did not listen to us, and the killer murdered more people, he would never forgive himself and neither would his bosses, that was for sure.

After a shower, less restorative than usual, I got dressed and went down to the kitchen to have breakfast. The funny thing was that with so much anguish and stress suffered in recent days, I had not lost my appetite. On the contrary, at that time of the morning, after a night in which I had only had a sad vending machine sandwich for dinner at the Guardia Civil post, I could have eaten a cow.

Menchu was already up, tinkering in the kitchen. The rest of the troop was still sleeping, so I allowed myself to take a few seconds to watch the movements of my hostess.

She seemed tired too, even a bit worried, although she was hiding it quite well. Everything related to María's story had affected me more than I had supposed, but Menchu was not far behind. Perhaps she thought it had been her fault, she was the one who had triggered such madness by reacting the way she had when she had first met me. That was the precise trigger that had got me up to my neck in the lives of people who had meant nothing to me until the week before. Plus, there was still a long way to go.

We had breakfast in silence, broken only by the chirping of birds roosting in the trees near the house. Menchu gave me a sidelong glance and I assumed she would approach me in some way, but someone came in, bursting in a way that brightened our morning.

We did not even have time to get up after hearing a car park outside in the immediate vicinity of the house. Seconds later there was a light tapping on the door frame and the door opened with a slight creak, before letting our illustrious guest in.

"Alberto!" I shrieked crazy with joy when I saw him on the threshold.

He walked in and stood for a few moments, getting his eyes used to the gloom of the place, very different from the splendid sun, shining outside. I almost knocked over the coffee cup as I stood up abruptly, but I could not help myself. I left the table, staggering, and threw myself into Alberto's arms.

I stayed like that for a few seconds, hugging him, breathing in his scent and happy to have him by my side again. He remained still, perhaps overwhelmed by my reaction, but I did not let go of him. I needed human contact, to feel him by my side, to know that he was well. I had had a hard time in his absence, very worried about what might happen to him, and the relief was so palpable.

I let out a stifled sigh and noticed how Alberto's body relaxed. After so many hours of confinement at the station, harassed by the guards, interrogation after interrogation, the stiffness of his muscles was gradually loosening. I guessed that Menchu's presence before such an intimate scene between the two of us was also feeding his unease, although in the end he also hugged me tightly and stayed that way for a few eternal seconds that did us both a lot of good.

I moved a little away from him, looked into his eyes and could not contain myself. I kissed him with all my soul, without Menchu's presence holding me back. He did not seem to mind either and we gripped each other like two castaways who had finally reached dry land after months of anguish on the high seas. Our lips recognized each other and merged into a singularity, sharing in a long kiss with everything that had brought us to that moment.

"Are you alright?" I asked when I managed to get a little further away from him.

"Yes, very tired, but fine."

"Come on, sit down and rest a bit," Menchu said. "Would you like some coffee?"

Alberto nodded and Menchu went to the kitchen to fetch it. I stood gawking at him, while I held his hands, both of us seated at the table. I had a thousand questions to ask him, but I did not want to burden him after such a hard night.

"We were right from the beginning, even if it pains me to admit it. That's why I was finally released. I thought I was going to be arrested in the end and I was about to call you to get me a lawyer."

"What do you mean?" I asked.

Alberto explained the sergeant's distrust, something almost normal after knowing all the ins and outs of what sounded like a movie plot. The civil guards had spent the whole night checking the information we had given them and following other clues they already had, apart from looking for other characters that belonged to such a complex equation.

"There was disarray over there first thing in the morning. Some guys from the UCO have arrived and have taken charge of the investigation, much to the chagrin of Sergeant Ortega, with whom they have had a hard time. He claimed that he was about to catch the murderer and close the case, although in reality what has happened is that the murderer is very close to closing his circle."

"Is he back in action?" Menchu enquired.

"I'm afraid so, last night. Since I couldn't be involved in the new crime as I was detained and you had nothing to do with it either, they had to surrender to the evidence: Jaime Mediavilla has struck again."

"We were assured that Doña Pura was fine last night," I said uneasily. "Had Jaime managed to enter the residence under police surveillance?"

"No, or at least I hope not. But he has eliminated the priest."

Alberto then told us what he had found out. The sergeant was surprised to find out that Father Cosme had become Cardinal Martinez, former strong man in Vatican finance and current secretary to the apostolic nuncio in Spain. That morning the news had been confirmed to him: the prelate had died the night before, the room service at the hotel where he was staying had found his body first thing this very morning.

"They must have spoken to someone in Madrid and, even if it was in a hurry because of the time constraint, they have taken it for granted. Cardinal Martinez was murdered last night in his room, without anyone seeing anything."

Alberto told us how he had remained attentive to Ortega's conversation on his phone, how he had not even noticed that he was listening in. He was only able to hear the words of the person in charge of the Covarrubias detachment, but it helped him to get a picture of the situation.

"Apparently the cardinal woke up completely naked, bound hand and foot, and his death must have been quite anguished. I think Jaime tortured him, although I don't know the details."

"Mother of God, is this never going to end?"

Menchu's question was thrown into the wind without expecting an answer. I had one, but I did not want to share it out loud. Yes, the nightmare would end in only one way. When Jaime murdered his mother; then the list of shame would finally be closed and the Mediavilla siblings could rest in peace.

Alberto read my mind and wanted to leave immediately for the provincial capital. I thought it was our duty to take care of an old woman locked up in a nursing home in Burgos, but then local authorities were already taking care of her safety, and the Guardia Civil would also remain vigilant, if they ended up believing our story.

"I won't allow it, lad. Go upstairs and lie down for a while, so you don't have problems driving after a sleepless night. Then we'll see."

I smiled at Menchu's comment and agreed wholeheartedly. Alberto grumbled a little, but then all the accumulated tiredness came over him and he struggled up the stairs. I accompanied him to the room already prepared, tucked him in like a little boy and let him rest.

I stayed a while longer talking with Menchu in the kitchen. We did not want to wake anyone up, so we talked quietly, until other members of the family started to appear, and gradually came down for breakfast.

I preferred to go outside, I felt like a caged bird within those four walls after the previous day's oppressive afternoon. While Alberto rested, I decided to take a walk around town to clear my head and put my thoughts in order. I did not know what the next steps we should take would be, although the first thing would be for the authorities to catch the criminal and put him behind bars.

I had no attachment to Doña Pura, even though she was my real great-grandmother, as I did not forget the suffering that she had put María through in her youth.

Something that had determined her life forever, when her baby was taken away from her while she was humiliated in a thousand different ways in the hell of Peñagrande. An event that would mark her forever and from which she never fully recovered, even though she had tried to rebuild her life with Dr. Grandinetti.

My feet took me out of town and I walked aimlessly, towards the foothills of a small range. Then I remembered another hill, the Sad Hill, the place where it had all begun fifty years before and which had led all the protagonists of the story to that very moment. Its very name, gave us the guideline: the sad hill, the same one where a small-town girl had been robbed of her innocence.

And what was to become of me from then on? I was still very angry with my grandparents and it bothered me that I could not break the strings that tied me to them in a more forceful way. First of all, because deep down I knew I would end up forgiving them. They had not behaved well and they knew it, although the real culprits for allowing that baby market would never pay for their misdeeds.

The unconditional love I felt for them had been affected during those days, but they would never cease to be my people, the only family I had ever known. The contradictions in my soul at the thought of their behavior tortured me endlessly and perhaps it would be better for everyone if I wiped the slate clean. If I had found María alive, maybe things would have changed, but I could not fool myself. Besides, what was I going to do if I disowned them? I was still studying and had no income of my own, I depended on them even if only from a totally selfish point of view.

I prayed that the authorities would put an end to the trail of murders and arrest Jaime as soon as possible. We did not know what was going through his mind, also disturbed by a life that could have been different if Father Cosme and Doña Pura had not conspired to imprison María for her sins. A catastrophic event that marked the course of all the members of the Mediavilla family, as time would eventually prove.

I walked slowly back to the house, still immersed in my thoughts. I did not even allow myself a second of reflection to admit out loud what was very apparent: I had fallen head over heels in love with Alberto and I hoped he felt the same way so that we could start a relationship. Perhaps the circumstances in which our love had arisen had not been the most ideal, immersed in frantic days, full of painful events, but perhaps it would help us to create a stronger bond. If together we had been able to fight against everything that had happened, nothing could stop us in the future.

As I walked back to the house, I thought of María and vowed to honor her in some way. Perhaps making her story known was not the best solution. I would have to think it through. But I did want to avenge her in my own way, doing my part so that no other woman would suffer something similar in her life. And, above all, I wanted to help unravel that network woven at state level, a real mafia installed in the system that had played with the lives of thousands of innocent people for decades, profiting from the pain of others.

When I entered the house again, I found Menchu in the living room, accompanied by Ana and Raquel. The three of them were staring raptly at the television screen, which was in a corner of the living room with the volume turned down so as not to disturb the others. They motioned for me to remain silent as they listened to the news that was being shown on a morning program.

I stood next to the table, while also watching the screen to find out what intrigued them so much. I had to put my hand to my mouth as I learned the facts, fortunately only from the presenters' mouths and not from gruesome images that might have been shown on the program. Someone had leaked the most lurid details of the death of a well- placed ecclesiastical official, without specifying his name, and the talk show hosts were allowed to give their opinion on the life and miracles of a man who could no longer defend himself.

I have never liked that kind of programs of what they call 'trash TV', but morbidness has always sold, and that program competed with another similar program of a rival network to win the national morning ratings.

There were opinions on everything. Some reasoned that such a powerful man must have had many enemies. Others hypothesized that it was a drug or money affair. They even said that it could have been an orgy that got out of hand; apparently the deceased used to hire escorts. One of the opinionators also said that it could simply have been a jealous attack and that the murderer had known the victim well. Was it a way of humiliating him to teach him a lesson? Some were sure it had been.

The talk-show hosts continued flaying the dead man, fortunately without giving his personal information, while the presenter tried to control the debate without success. I put my hands to my head at some of the statements I heard from the mouths of those despicable people, I did not understand why such information was given at prime time.

Apparently, the cardinal had been found with two dildos in his mouth, although that was not the real reason for his death. His body had suffered lacerations, blows of all kinds, cuts and even burns, but what was most striking was the presentation of the corpse that the murderer had wanted to leave for posterity: a fluorescent light, perhaps torn from the bathroom, was embedded halfway into his rectum. A brutal rape that must have torn him apart inside, the terrible revenge of a tormented soul.

"What an outrageous thing to do!"

Menchu's words came out somewhat muffled from her mouth, but the echo resounded for a few seconds in the room. We had all been stunned, hooked in a gross way to a program that showed human misery in the worst possible way. The private network that broadcast the program did not even consider that, since it was summer, many children would be at home and exposed to a show that was not suitable for all audiences. Even so, it would surely become the most watched program in the morning; people love morbid content.

The rest of Ana's family members joined the group formed in the living room, so only Alberto was missing. I hoped he was a sound sleeper and could rest for a while, although the decibels began to rise on the first floor with the accumulation of several voices. In the end we ended up waking the 'sleeping beauty', who poked his head out of the stairwell and asked the time in a sleepy voice, without addressing anyone in particular.

"Quarter to twelve, it's still early. Go on, rest a little longer, you've earned it," I answered.

"No, I'd rather get up, I've been tossing and turning in bed for a while. I think I'm going to take a shower to wake up. Julián, can you come here for a moment?"

His friend nodded and went over to him immediately. Was something wrong with Alberto? It immediately dawned on me what it might be. He had not brought his suitcase from Madrid for a quick trip and now he had no clothes to change into.

After a while Alberto came down again and I beckoned him. In the living room there was a heated debate about the limits that could be reached in these programs, about freedom of expression and so on, without reaching a concrete agreement as there were different points of view in the group. I decided to remove myself from the discussion and went over to Alberto, who looked much better than he had earlier in the morning after showering and shaving.

"What are you planning to do now?"

"Nothing in particular, why do you ask?

"I don't know, maybe we could go to Burgos, to see Doña Pura."

"What if we run into Jaime? He might be dangerous so we'd better wait for him to get caught."

"He must have seen the situation. I don't think he's a fool, and if he was in Madrid last night, he may have already boarded an intercontinental flight, on his way to some distant country."

"Are you sure? I asked. "He's not done with everyone on the list yet."

"Yes, but he would only be missing his mother. He's eliminated all those who screwed up his sister's life and he'll be satisfied. Deep down, maybe he doesn't want to kill his mother, it seems natural to me."

"Well, I don't know, maybe you're right," I thought for a moment. What if this was my last chance to get something clear from the cause of so much misfortune? The nurse at the nursing home said that her dementia was severe, but sometimes Doña Pura had moments of lucidity. Something had clicked in her head when she saw me, when she looked at the photo I showed her. I still had that little thorn in my side, having been unable to get anything out of our first visit. "Okay, we could go over now if you want, before lunch."

"Perfect. Shall we tell the others?"

"Better not. I don't want them to worry and start questioning our decisions. Like yesterday, even if they were right in the end."

I was surprised by Alberto's fortitude, my nerves were pounding inside me and upsetting my stomach, but he had handled things admirably, even though he was on the verge of being arrested.

We left and I waved goodbye while the others continued discussing in the living room. Nobody made any comment, we left the house without looking back. We got into Alberto's mother's Focus and headed towards the national highway, on our way to Burgos.

As soon as we left the 'Bermuda Triangle' of Carazo, where technology did not work and we were isolated from the outside cyber world, I was able to connect to the Internet with my cell phone and search for more information about the Cardinal's death.

Details had been leaked that should have remained secret, but if the morning programs opened the door, the rest would follow suit. Not to mention some sensationalist digital newspapers, which speculated about certain aspects of the crime and attributed the barbarities to the suggestion that victim and executioner belonged to a satanic sect and other such nonsense.

Suddenly I felt a prick in my stomach and I had a bad feeling. Alberto noticed my discomfort and I did not hide my uneasiness. Sometimes I felt I had to perform a specific action and if I did not do it, I felt terrible. That was one of those moments and I had no trouble doing it.

"I think I'm going to call the nursing home. I just had a strange feeling - I don't know why."

"Sure, go ahead. I hope it's just a false alarm."

It took me a while to get through to the residence. In the end I was spoken to by a very nice girl and I asked her for Purificación Castroviejo, without specifying anything else at first.

"She is out with a relative who has come to visit her. He asked us for permission to take her out for a walk, and since it's a nice morning, there was no problem. Would you like to talk to her? Maybe a little later..."

"Excuse me, are you new? Doña Pura suffers from severe dementia, I don't think I can talk to her on the phone," I blurted out with anxiety gripping my stomach. It was not normal for the nurse to ask me if I wanted to talk to her: Doña Pura's physical condition did not allow her to take calls. Not to mention the relative who had taken her out for a walk. The bad feeling was starting to become a reality. I did not even let her answer my first question and added one more, in a louder voice due to my uneasiness: "And which relative has come to visit her, may I ask?"

Alberto was concerned when he saw me so upset and was waiting for an explanation. I pointed in front of him so that he would keep his eyes on the road; it was not the best time to have an accident.

"Yes, I'm new, I've only been in this employment for a few days, why do you ask?" her answer also displayed some anxiety. Perhaps she was afraid she had made a mistake. Doña Pura had gone outside with her son, as on other occasions.

"Oh, my God," I exclaimed in horror. "I don't understand what's happened, didn't your colleague tell you anything? That woman is in danger, the police had been guarding the facility since yesterday to prevent anyone from gaining access to that old woman."

"I beg your pardon?" The anguish had definitely settled in the nurse's voice and the words trembled in her throat. Then she seemed to remember the moment of her mistake, "No, the night nurse didn't tell me anything about it. Besides, she was in a hurry because her son was ill and she left here in a hurry, almost without saying goodbye. My God!"

"What is it?"

"I just saw, she wrote it all down on the report. I've been so busy all morning and I didn't even stop to read the night's events. I'm so sorry! What can I do?"

"Call the police at once and tell them what's happened. We're on our way there too. Do you know where they might have gone?"

"No, not really. There is a park nearby where the residents usually go with their families, but they could be anywhere. Doña Pura was half asleep in her wheelchair and I didn't pay much attention to her when they went out. We just told them to return before half past one, for meals, you know."

"Calm down, please, and do as I say," I replied. Then I realized an important detail that we had been unaware of until that moment. "Excuse me, what did the man who took the patient out look like?"

"I wouldn't know, a normal man, I don't know. Well, I think he was tall and appeared well- built, but I didn't look too closely."

"Did he have a particular accent when he spoke? I wanted to know, remembering that Jaime had been living in American countries for a long time.

"No, I didn't notice anything strange. He spoke like someone from here."

"All right, fine. Remember to call the police, we'll be right there. See you soon."

I hung up with a terrible sense of unease in my body. I had not been wrong about my feelings: something bad was about to happen. Alberto had understood the situation perfectly and did not overwhelm me at once, prepared for the worst. He just focused on the road, accelerated the vehicle and we prayed to arrive on time.

"Call the Civil Guard in Covarrubias too," he told me a few seconds later, when he saw that I had recovered from the shock. "Tell them to put you through to Ortega and update him"

"But, Alberto, they are far away from here," I said. "By now Jaime could have already killed his mother and then disposed of the body." It was complete madness. If the Burgos police did not react in time, and neither did we, who were only five kilometers away from the capital, it was almost impossible for the members of the *Benemérita* to arrive in time to rescue her" Alberto gave me an imploring look, "All right, I'll try."

It took me several anxious seconds to contact the Guardia Civil. I do not know if the unfriendly guard who had seen us the day before picked up the phone, but I did not give him the option to reply.

"Give me Sergeant Ortega," I said as soon as he picked up. Then I introduced myself properly and added: "It's a very urgent matter, life or death, hurry up. And don't give me a hard time, I know where the murderer is and I need to talk to the commanding officer."

"Excuse me, the sergeant is in a meeting at the moment and the commanding officer can't come to the phone now either. If you leave a message, I can..."

"You don't understand!" I shouted when I realized that they were not going to put me through to anyone. That idiot was my last hope, I had to convince him of the terrible urgency. "Jaime Mediavilla, the murderer of several people in the last few days, is currently in Burgos capital. He has just kidnapped an old woman in the Residence La Luz with the excuse of taking the patient for a walk. The police are already on their way, but your superiors need to have this information as well. Right now!"

Hysterical, I hung up the phone while Alberto swerved so as not to miss the exit leading to the neighborhood of the residence. The speed of the car was not the most appropriate for that maneuver and we almost left the road. Fortunately, he was able to straighten out and we did not end up crashing into a grocery store by a sheer miracle.

"Jesus, Alberto, be careful! I want to get there in one piece, if we crash on the way we're not going to solve anything."

Alberto apologized with a slight wave of his hand, I let him concentrate on the driving. I began to watch out for any passerby wandering the street, with all my senses on high alert. We parked in the vicinity of the residence, jumped out of the car and rushed into the center before heading to the reception desk.

"We spoke on the phone earlier," I said hurriedly, "Have you seen Doña Pura again?"

"No, they haven't come back this way. I've already called the police, they're on their way. Is there anything else I can do?"

"Yes, maybe. Which way is it to the park you told us about before?"

"You can't miss it. As soon as you come out, turn left then go down a sort of footbridge and at the back of the next block of buildings is the park where the residents go with their families."

"Thank you!"

We were off again, running through the streets of Burgos in search of the impossible. In the distance we heard the police sirens, soon we would cross paths with them. But no sign of Jaime or his mother, it was like looking for a needle in a haystack.

We were not even halfway when Alberto started to grumble and I did not quite understand what he was saying. He stopped for a second to take a breath and I did the same. A little breather would do us both good.

"They are not here. Jaime isn't going to bring his mother to a place where he might meet other nursing home patients and their families. It doesn't make any sense if he has in mind what we think."

"I see, you may be right. But what do we do then?"

We were at the park anyway. We did not go into it but scanned the whole area, assuming that our targets were not there.

We retraced our steps and saw in the distance a patrol car maneuvering to pull into a narrow alley after screeching the brakes. Perhaps they had spotted the suspect in the distance although it was a difficult area for vehicles to access, full of turns and ramps at various heights.

"Let's go!"

I followed Alberto in his crazy race, although the oxygen in my lungs was sparse. I had not done any sport for a long time and I could feel the lack of endurance after running a few hundred meters. We still did not have a specific objective, but the neighborhood we were entering seemed like a good hiding place for a kidnapper and his victim. Jaime would not have an easy time maneuvering around there with a dead weight in a wheelchair, so I thought then that maybe he had already got rid of his mother to escape with a better chance of success.

As we rounded a bend, we saw them in the distance: the unmistakable figure of a large man pushing a chair. I do not know why I did it, but at that moment I shouted to get their attention and he stopped for a moment to see where the sound was coming from. I thought he was surprised to see his pursuers. Perhaps my presence caused him the same disturbance as it did his mother, but the distance between us would prevent him from seeing my features in detail.

We took advantage of his halt and reduced the distance that separated us from him. Jaime checked that he had no escape on that side, turned around and we immediately came to within 30 meters of him. He had to change his strategy if he did not want to be caught. And although we were not the police, we had made him nervous and he reacted in a way that we should have sensed and against which there was little we could do.

"Stop right there, Jaime!" I shouted as I saw him crouch behind his mother, grabbing her tightly from behind while his right hand reached out to the front of the old woman's neck.

"Hold it right there! If you take one more step, I'll slit her throat."

His threat sounded very convincing, especially when I noticed the metallic glint of some kind of knife or cutter he held pressed against his mother's throat. We could not gamble. What could we do then?

"Shit man, I know who you are," said Alberto recognizing the guy. "You are the Argentinian journalist, Jacobo Pavón, am I wrong? We met at the film convention, at the casino in Salas."

"Yes, kid, I've had you on my radar for a long time, too. You're a nosey fucker. And who's your little friend?"

Jaime stared at me as he was able to distinguish my features better. I imagined how startled he was to find the spitting image of his sister, perhaps a little older than the last time he had seen her. He looked puzzled, the ideal moment to attack him on that flank with the unvarnished truth.

"I'm Sandra, María's granddaughter. I'm the daughter of the baby they stole from your sister at the Peñagrande reformatory. We are family, Jaime, it's the honest truth; please, put down the knife and give yourself up. We have all suffered enough, don't you think?"

I appealed to the only thing that could soften him a little, although I might have been too hasty and provoked a reaction for which we were not prepared. The tortured mind of a man like Jaime was impossible to decipher and we were there, unarmed, facing a psychopath who had murdered four people in less than a week.

"I don't understand. I..."

"Release the hostage!" a voice behind me thundered. Several policemen had approached our position stealthily but none of us had noticed.

Several firearms were pointed at the suspect and the one who seemed to be the leader of the detachment urged us to take cover behind them, out of the line of fire. We obeyed while Jaime looked at us with a blank face. His few chances of getting out of the situation safely, threatened to vanish and I could sense how the gears in his brain were searching for some kind of solution to his predicament.

We positioned ourselves next to a National Police van, while another Special Operations team, equipped for the assault, took up their positions. Jaime had no chance of escaping and I feared for his life. The chief had given the order not to shoot to avoid injuring the old woman, but no one knew what could transpire.

What happened then was something no one expected. It did seem more plausible to me that Sergeant Ortega would show up on stage with another team of civil guards, but what no one could have imagined was the special guest who had joined the party. My jaw dropped in astonishment when I saw, but I was not the only one affected.

"Jaime, please let go of our mother."

"It can't be..."

A still very attractive woman, a lady of Menchu's age, with an aura that exuded strength and confidence, began to close the distance separating her from the suspect. Her natural hair, similar in color to mine, appeared dyed in a flattering shade of auburn. But I knew immediately who she was, as did poor Jaime Mediavilla.

"María, is that you? It's impossible, you're dead."

"No, honey, I'm here. I'm your sister and I'm here to help you. Please put down the knife and come give me a hug. I've missed you so much..."

She was alive! María's calm tone seemed to have hypnotized her brother, as well as many of those present. I could not get over my astonishment and Alberto looked at me without understanding anything. But the one who seemed most surprised was Jaime, who was about to throw in the towel. He had relaxed his posture and was no longer hiding behind his mother as before. He was giving the elite shooters a chance to shoot him without harming the old woman, but Sergeant Ortega called for restraint.

María did not fear for her life and immediately made eye contact with her brother. She advanced with an increasingly firm step and posited herself between the shooters and Jaime, something that annoyed the police commander, who could be heard snorting from my position. The siblings remained absorbed in each other, oblivious to everything around them, only focused on one thing.

María finished walking the distance that separated her from her brother. She crouched down beside him, caressed his cheek gently and spoke into his ear. His twitching movements began to soften and his face relaxed completely absorbed with his sister. Jaime stood up, threw the knife on the floor and hugged his María. The big man began to sob like a child, overwhelmed at having recovered his lost sister after so many years.

This was the moment the authorities chose to act. Several policemen surrounded them and restrained Jaime immediately. Defeated, his eyes implored his sister for help, perhaps more affected by being separated from her than by the fate that awaited him as a detained criminal. María tried to intercede with the policemen so that they would not harm him; he had already turned himself in and was not going to cause them any trouble.

Ortega then allowed us to approach, while the policemen restrained the detainee, who was being led to one of the vans with his head down, acknowledging his defeat. Although at least I saw him smile when he realized that miracles sometimes do happen. His sister was still alive and he had been able to hug her, perhaps for the last time.

I was still in a state of shock and Alberto encouraged me to snap out of it. The desperate situation in which we had been involved had been resolved in a peaceful way, something I was grateful for and which I could not have been sure of minutes before. No shots had been fired, Jaime had not used his knife, and a calmness drifted over the scene.

Entranced at the unexpected turn of events, I was unable to articulate a word as I approached the heroine who had resolved the situation. Tears threatened to spill out as emotion overwhelmed me. María immediately noticed my embarrassment and received me calmly, with that innate charisma that had captivated us all as soon as we saw her. I did not even have to open my mouth and she took charge of the situation as soon as she understood the reality.

"You? I don't know... I thought you were dead."

"Shhh, honey, don't worry about it now," she said to me with restraint, while she smiled looking at my face and wiping away a rebellious tear that had escaped. "There will be time for explanations."

"Do you know who I am?"

"Not with absolute certainty, but I can imagine. You are my granddaughter, aren't you?"

I nodded and could restrain myself any longer. I let myself go and hugged my grandmother for the first time in my life, crying with joy and also with sadness, for all that had happened, for the torment suffered so that we could finally meet in this world.

Happiness overwhelmed me and I did not want to leave our little chrysalis, the two of us so close together, enjoying that special connection that I had always felt with María. Now I could live it in my skin and it was something wonderful, a feeling I would never want to lose. A haven of peace that ingratiated me again with life, sometimes so unfair and sometimes so wonderful that it made you want to scream with pure ecstasy.

But then another shock came to jolt us out of our reverie. The paramedics were attending to Doña Pura and there appeared to be some commotion around her. We did not know what was happening, but the woman seemed to need urgent medical attention.

"We are taking her to the hospital!" I heard them say as they loaded her into an ambulance.

That moment of confusion distracted us all on different scales. I then noticed that the policemen guarding the detainee also looked in our direction and Jaime took advantage of the moment. He slipped away from the most clueless guard, turned to his left with an agility I would never have guessed for someone his size, and grabbed the gun from the other cop. He had not been handcuffed on the way to the van, a terrible mistake, that the fugitive used to his advantage. Before we knew it, he was pointing a gun at one of the policemen, whom he was holding from behind across his neck, shielding behind his body so as not to be an easy target.

"Get out of here! Let me escape or I'll kill him."

"Take it easy, buddy, don't do anything stupid," replied the other policeman as he kept pointing his gun at him.

"Drop the gun, asshole! Or do you want me to kill your partner right now?"

The policeman obeyed, placing his weapon on the ground without losing visual contact .By the time we realized what was happening, the rest of the members of the State Security Forces were withdrawing and looking to take up positions to face the new situation. I caught a glimpse of Alberto on one side, and Ortega forced us to join him, away from the danger.

"Stay here under cover and don't move," Ortega ordered us with a serious tone, while he instructed one of his men to follow him and another to take care of our small group.

But María was not about to obey, and I understood her. She knew the police were not going to mess around and could shoot her brother at any moment. And if she had already managed to calm him down once to get him to turn himself in, it did not hurt to try again. The problem was that she did not have time, because everything happened in an instant.

From a distance, I could not make it out well, but the policeman in Jaime's grip, made some kind of sign to his colleagues. The detachment chief nodded and I feared the worst, although Jaime was ahead of all of us.

"I'm sorry, María. I did it all for you, I swear. I love you with all my soul, but I must pay for my sins. Farewell."

I heard a scream of agony next to me and María ran to help her brother. But Jaime had ended his pain by shooting himself in the head and nobody could help him in this life...

A NEW BEGINNING

Madrid, May 2017

My second year in college was coming to an end, with the June exams just around the corner. The academic year had smiled on me and the only thing left to do was to finish it off with good grades.

After a couple of weeks of unsettled weather, spring had finally settled in Madrid, more reluctant than other years. I had arranged to have lunch with Alberto in the cafeteria of his school, located next to mine on the campus of the Complutense University of Madrid, so it took me no more than five minutes to get there.

Alberto was already waiting, having a beer at the bar while I was en-route. He saw me before I could surprise him and gave me his beautiful smile to tell me without words how happy he was to see me. We had not been together for a few days, each cloistered at home to study, and we missed each other.

None of us could ever forget the summer of 2016, a time of many changes in my life for which I had to get used to, little by little. It had its good aspects, such as the beginning of a budding relationship with a wonderful man -

a relationship that was going full swing at that point, it must be said - or the return to life of María, my new grandmother. But also, moments of anxiety, such as the strained relationship with my adopted grandparents, a bitter situation that fortunately had been softening in the months since I learned the truth.

The death toll had been terrible, a tragedy that filled the media, from the old-school news programs to sensationalist shows of the worst kind. The Arlanza Valley and the region of the Sierra de la Demanda were on everyone's lips for quite a while. But as no one is capable of predicting human nature, that trail of violent murders did not keep tourism away from the area, quite the contrary. The locals did not know whether to thank Jaime Mediavilla for the resurgence of life in the region, but certainly visits to the area began to pick up, and they remembered the old days of the Gregorian singing monks boom, in Santo Domingo de Silos.

Excursions to Sad Hill became obligatory and the reconstructed cemetery experienced a new era of splendor. Not only for those nostalgic for Clint Eastwood, Sergio Leone or the *spaghetti western,* but also for many others who just wanted to see the renovated cemetery and, above all, take a picture next to the famous hangman's tree.

The forensic tests, both the matching of dental plates and subsequent DNA analysis carried out, coincided with what we all expected: the corpse found in San Pedro de Arlanza belonged to the politician José María Hernando. By the way, the demolished monastery also became a new place of pilgrimage for tourists of all kinds, and the Junta de Castilla y León proposed to restore it and at least avoid its complete collapse, if they could not find enough money for a full-fledged rehabilitation.

After the stressful time in Burgos, there were some details that had escaped us. We learned from the media that an ATM camera had captured the image of Jaime Mediavilla leaving the hotel where he had murdered the cardinal. The Guardia Civil was investigating the list of participants in the film convention, with special emphasis on the visitors coming from American countries, and at last they had found their prize.

The face of the alleged Argentinian journalist Jacobo Pavón, photographed from different locations upon his arrival at Barajas airport, coincided with the one captured in the Pío XII area. The police machinery was set in motion at full speed and they immediately obtained his passport data and found out other details since he had landed in Spain: the cars he had rented under that identity, the accommodation in Salas de los Infantes and other specifics that allowed the authorities to proceed in their investigations.

Above all, by finding a contact telephone number in the rental agency's file, a phone that they were able to track and triangulate with precision, until they had located its owner in a neighborhood of Burgos. That was why Ortega and his team had been able to arrive in time, at the very moment when the Burgos police were cornering the suspect right under our noses.

The presence of María Mediavilla, surnamed Grandinetti according to her official documentation, was fundamental for the development of the events. At the time we met her we did not know how she had arrived there, but we found out days later, when she told us herself.

María was struck by the way we had got involved in her story, after my first meeting with her friend Menchu in Carazo and the very beginning of the investigation. She was also very surprised when I told her all the information we had found out about her life, thanks to the hacker friend who had given us access to a blog that had been deleted for almost a decade. But we had stopped there, with that last post that left me devastated when María announced to the world her early passing.

My grandmother María explained to us everything that happened next: the slight hope that had opened before her eyes with the possibility of life-saving surgery and the whole ordeal that followed. María had lost her memory for a while, completely forgotten that she had been reunited with her brother, and when she had wanted to make amends, she could not find the right way.

"I am a survivor and I had to start over in Boston. It took time and effort, I'm not going to lie to you, but thank God I have never lacked fortitude and willpower. If I had managed to walk again after so many years, I was not going to give up because of a simple life or death neurosurgery operation."

I admired her sense of humor and the frankness with which she told things. Maybe it was her defense mechanism, her only way to face the setbacks that life had put in her way. She had survived everything and everyone, and had risen from the ashes a thousand and one times, without faltering or throwing in the towel even once. She certainly had occasion countless times to give up and abandon everything.

"I had no hope of finding my brother again. I had lost him for the second time and I could never forgive myself. In our conversations during those weeks, I never asked him, nor did he confess to me, the real name he had on his papers. That is why it was impossible for me to find him until now."

By chance, María had stumbled upon a report on American television, in which the vocalist of the group, Metallica was talking about the revival of the Sad Hill cemetery in a rural area of Burgos, in faraway Spain. Everyone knew of the musician's love for *The Good, the Bad and the Ugly*, so it was no surprise that James Hetfield wanted to get involved in the project and support, albeit from a distance, the committed people who had set out to restore such an iconic cemetery for fans of the genre.

That discovery had blocked María for a few moments, overwhelmed by the cascade of painful memories that had invaded her mind: her love affair with Juanito, the brutal rape in the shed and its subsequent consequences. A torrent of images that she could not get out of her head, that hit her again and again without rest and made her relive the most terrible moments of her existence.

When she finally pulled herself together, she had tried to be practical. Thanks to this report, she learned about the deployment carried out in her homeland and looked for more information. She then learned about the activities that would take place in the region to celebrate the 50th anniversary of the shooting of the film in Burgos and was even tempted to attend it herself.

But she immediately dismissed the idea. What for others would be a happy anniversary would only mean more suffering for her. She did not even think of the opportunity that presented itself, since it was possible that many of those who ruined her life would meet again in that area, five decades later. Something that another person very close to her did take into account.

Spite did not feed the heart of this pragmatic woman, and even less so after overcoming situations unimaginable to most mortals. She remembered then her bravado when talking to her brother, when she had assured him that she would take revenge on all those who had put an end to her youth. And, of course, that thought led her to another that caused her dread: what if her brother had also found out about the anniversary celebration and showed up in Burgos as an avenging angel?

She dismissed the stupid idea from her mind and forgot about it, she already had enough to concern her, never mind what was happening thousands of miles away. Even so, she was not completely detached and programmed some alerts in her personal email, just in case there was any relevant news about the film convention and the activities that would be held in the region where she was born.

When the summer of that year arrived, her gut feeling warned her of impending disaster. It was an ailment or an almost genetic virtue, since I had also inherited that strange power of foresight. Alberto laughed at us and claimed that we came from a line of adorable witches, but witches nonetheless. Something that earned him our absolute disagreement, even though he was absolutely right when he said it.

"And then I saw the terrible news about the hanging at Sad Hill, I think it was Monday night. I did some research on the subject in Spanish digital newspapers and found out about the series of strange events that had occurred in the region during the days of the symposium. I knew in the depths of my soul that my brother Jaime was the cause of so much misfortune."

María had hurriedly packed a suitcase and headed for the airport, ready to board the first plane to Spain. It was already early in the morning and no flight would be leaving for a few hours, so she had dozed off in an uncomfortable waiting room.

After an exhausting journey that included a transoceanic flight and a rather surreal cab ride from Madrid to Salas de los Infantes, she arrived at her destination on July 27 at night, with time to stay in a hotel in the town and contact the Guardia Civil in Covarrubias before the end of the day on Tuesday.

"We were at the station that night!" I exclaimed in astonishment.

"Maybe that's why I didn't get to talk to anyone in charge. I got a rather surly guy on the phone and I couldn't get him to understand the urgency of my call."

"That rings a bell..."

"I tried a couple more times, but I was exhausted and ended up falling asleep without solving anything. I woke up totally exhausted a few hours later, with fatigue and gripped by jet-lag. But I couldn't waste any more time. I got ready in a few minutes, had a quick breakfast and asked again for a cab to go to Covarrubias."

"And in the end, you were able to talk to Sergeant Ortega."

"It took me a while, believe me. They told me that the investigation was being handled by some people from Madrid who couldn't speak to me, but I insisted at the control desk. In the face of my vehemence, I ended up talking to an officer, who in turn called the sergeant. When I began to tell him my story, he thought I was making it all up."

"Of course, it's normal," I remarked. We had told him something very similar the night before and he would think we had agreed to make fun of him.

"He left me alone in his office for a few minutes and went off to make some calls. When he returned, he had changed his attitude and seemed to have given me a vote of confidence. That same morning reports began to come in about the death of Father Cosme and corroborated the identity of the dead man in San Pedro de Arlanza, so he had to believe me. Your urgent call when you were approaching Burgos strengthened his position and the sergeant decided to take charge of the case. He ignored his colleagues from Madrid, assembled a small platoon of his trusted men and invited me to accompany them to the city. The rest you already know."

"What an odyssey!"

Our efforts were of little use. We only saved the life of Doña Pura, who managed to recover in the hospital from the emotions she had experienced. In any case, she was almost ninety years old, with severe dementia and a multitude of other pathologies. The woman returned a few weeks later to the nursing home and María visited her a couple of times, but she was unable to talk to her, as she was in a near vegetative state.

In the end, after talking to the people in charge of the geriatric center, we found out that the person who paid Purificación Castroviejo's bills, the man who had institutionalized her years before, was Jacobo Pavón himself, from Argentina. In other words, Jaime Mediavilla, her son, was the only one who had cared for his mother's welfare in her last years, even though he already knew all the suffering she had inflicted on his sister.

"I didn't know that until now, that's why I hesitated when I saw Jaime threaten our mother. I saw him capable of anything after committing such atrocities. He had completely lost his mind. I managed to save her, the person who really destroyed my life, and yet I couldn't save my little brother."

María invited me to accompany her to the residence on another occasion, although it caused me some discomfort. My grandmother thought that perhaps Doña Pura would recognize me better, seeing me so young and so much like her daughter at her age, than coming face to face with a sixty-six-year-old woman she had not seen in five decades. But the plan did not work. The old woman's mind had vanished forever.

"If I had known before, the name Jaime had adopted in his new life, I could have saved them all. And he kept the same name, he only changed his last name."

"What do you mean, the same name? Jaime and Jacobo only start with the same letter, nothing else," I affirmed with some doubt.

"Jaime, Santiago, Diego, Jacob or Jacobo and some others like Yago or Tiago are different variants of the same name of Hebrew origin. My mother was a very religious person and she gave us both biblical names. My brother knew this fact and used it to his advantage, changing his name but ultimately not really doing it."

"You'll never go to bed without learning one more thing, as my grandmother says."

I immediately realized that I had made a mistake, although I had not really said anything strange. It was an expression I had always heard at home, from the mouth of the one I had always considered my grandmother, although the reality was quite different.

I did not try to force the situation. It seemed to me in very bad taste to force María to meet my grandparents.

Perhaps I wanted to think that they were not to blame for what had happened, that they were just another link in the chain, but also deceived by the real architects of the baby-buying and selling mafia. But I understood María's position: for her, that couple had taken away what she loved the most and she could never get it back. Anyway, they did not intend to fraternize with the biological mother of what they considered their legitimate daughter, so everyone was happy. At least they did not put any obstacles in the way of me deciding what kind of relationship I was going to have with María.

María was delighted with her new-found granddaughter and we got along great, but I could see a slight shadow in her eyes when she spoke of my mother, her lost daughter. At the mention of Sara her eyes saddened, no matter how much she tried to light up her face with the most beautiful smile I had ever known. María had retained a serene beauty, that still turned the heads of many men when passing her in the street and I was very proud of her.

When she learned of my mother's death she cried silently, one more loss in her long-life experience. Her happiness was not complete when she met me and she missed the possibility of embracing her own daughter, so one day I wanted to give her a little surprise.

I continued to live in my usual home, although sometimes the tension there became unbearable. The curious thing is that I argued less and less with my grandfather, the real architect of the irregular adoption of Sara Millán, a repentant man who had apologized to me on many occasions, but the quarrels with my grandmother did not diminish. Perhaps because she was more stubborn, she would not give in even if you had the evidence she was wrong, and she would insist with me that they had not committed any crime, nor had they offended God or man. When those moments came, I preferred to disappear and not argue, because it was quite impossible to make her reason. I would have to love her as she was, in her usual way and manner, because she was not going to change at that stage of life.

One afternoon when I was alone at home, I looked through my mother's photo albums. I found some from when she was a little girl and others when she was a teenager, even from her university days. Also, the one from my parents' wedding and some others in which I also appeared as a baby, although the era of digital cameras soon arrived and the habit of treasuring developed photographs went out of fashion.

I chose the three albums I thought were the best and took them to María one afternoon, so that she could at least see photographs of the daughter she would never hold in her arms. The good woman was very happy to see my gift, but melancholy took over her face as she turned the pages, after contemplating the images of someone who had disappeared forever and had left us both orphans in a way that only we could understand.

María returned to America for a few months, ready to settle all her estate there in order to return to Spain and live here permanently. She did not feel like living in her village and she was not sure about Madrid either, although she looked for a rented apartment in the capital while she was getting organized. That way we could get together whenever we wanted, something we both demanded frequently after so many disappointments.

After the events in Burgos the previous summer, there were still some surprises in store for María. The reunion with her old friend Menchu, an emotional and touching moment in which I preferred to stand aside and let them make up for lost time. If Ana had not invited me to spend that summer with them in Carazo, I might never have met María, thanks to Menchu's invaluable intervention in the beginning; the beginning of my obsession for a story that had pushed me to the limits.

I even accompanied them one day to their old village, Contreras. María was moved when she came across her old home, a half-ruined house that she promised to rehabilitate, although she was not sure she would ever live in it, not even to spend a summer there. Nostalgia and pain, mingled in her soul, mixed feelings that she could not separate when she contemplated the place where she had grown up as a child.

I knew that she would also want to visit Peñagrande, even though she knew that this building had nothing to do with the hell where she suffered some of the worst moments of her life. I put María in touch with the historian who had helped us and they immediately became great friends. Thanks to Soledad, she made contact with other affected women who lived there at the time and with others who suffered the same in similar places all over Spain.

María wanted to help Soledad in her work and joined her crusade. They gave lectures throughout Spain, providing documentary evidence that the historian had been collecting for years and, above all, the first-hand testimony of women like María who had suffered.

But their work did not stop there. They formed an association of those affected, with hundreds of cases spread across numerous Spanish provinces, and took their case to the courts, as well as to the press and television. They wanted justice and for the real culprits to pay for crimes against humanity, in addition to seeking reparation that no one seemed to be able to offer them. Decades of opprobrium in which the institutions had turned a blind eye to abuses that were part of the system itself, without anyone owning up. A titanic task that they faced with practically no help, in search of a success that was very difficult to obtain, they would always have my full support.

I admit that since the previous summer I had been looking at the world in a different way. I have never been too much of a complainer, and I had grown up as a privileged girl in an environment where I lacked nothing. But like any girl my age, I had always wanted more. The reality check I suffered when I came face to face with the stark story of my real grandmother was a definite eye-opener.

The life lesson taught to me by María, a fighter who had overcome a multitude of problems over several decades, in Spain and in America, made me realize how unfair life is for some people. Small differences, the flutter of a butterfly in the wrong place, and your life can take a radical turn. From heaven to hell, from nothing to everything, we find ourselves at the mercy of elements we can never master. There is no such thing as free will, and maybe there is no such thing as manifest destiny, but someone is playing dice with us and the consequences can be terrible for the less fortunate.

María could have given up halfway, she had plenty of opportunities to stop fighting and give up. No one could have blamed her, especially after the sacrifices she had to make to keep going. My empathetic vein sympathized with her epic life without seeing myself able to match what this incredible woman had accomplished. If I had been in the same situation, even if it were current, with the consequent advantages that the new century has brought us, I would never have been able to accomplish even half of the things she had achieved with her enormous willpower.

Nobody had given her anything and her irreproachable tenacity had made her overcome a thousand and one adversities. Perhaps she had never dreamed of taking real revenge on the people who ruined her youth, or it was simply a mental exercise that served as an escape while she thought about how to make them pay for so much suffering, but in the end, Jaime had freed her of those people in a cruel way. Neither of us brought up the subject and we tried to avoid commenting on it, but deep down, as good a person as she was, I think María felt that those people had deserved their end. I was not going to hold it against her, far from it, because at the end of the day we are all human.

The experiences of last summer and everything I had learned in the following months had made me mature in a way I could never have imagined. I was still studying at university and had not yet decided what to do with my life, but I would now always have a role model, a mirror to look into when my strength faltered and I ran into difficulties. Nothing is impossible in this world, or practically nothing and I had seen it with my own eyes.

That turning point had shifted my world upside down and made me realize how lucky I had been. I began to worry less about trifles and to enjoy a full life, knowing that there is still so much good in the world. I knew that maybe someday I would achieve fulfillment in the company of the people I loved the most, whether they were family, friends or Alberto.

In the end, María decided to buy a country house in a small village in the municipality of Llanes. She would be able to see the sea from her window and the Asturian mountains, a desirable place to live her last years. She was tired of big cities and did not want to suffer the rigors of the harsh Burgos winter or the excessive heat of other latitudes. Of course, she invited me to visit whenever I wanted.

I already had a place to spend my vacation when I finished my final exams. I only hoped that this time, and without setting a precedent, I would be able to enjoy a quiet and uneventful summer. The eastern coast of Asturias seemed a quiet and idyllic place, the ideal place to rest and leave behind the stress of the big city.

I had heard very good things about the region, endowed with exuberant nature: a region with beautiful places, friendly people, sustainable tourism and a rich and varied gastronomy. I was looking forward to the end of the school year to visit my grandmother and forget about the usual issues.

What I did not know at the time was that the council of Llanes had also acquired fame as a film set for several productions, thanks mainly to its unbeatable natural environment. A disturbing combination after the experience of the previous summer, but I was not going to let that little detail ruin my vacation.

The saying goes that man is the only animal that stumbles twice on the same stone. But in this case, it seemed totally impossible. I just hoped that I would not stumble, or regret my choice of summer destination...

AFTERWORD

THE ORIGIN OF THIS STORY

Let me now tell you briefly how I developed the idea for the novel you have just read. I had the idea a long time ago, in the spring of 2018, but a series of circumstances prevented me from entertaining you with this novel until now.

A few months prior, my novel, *The Scent of Fear*, had just come out. This was a police thriller that took place on the coast of Valencia. And I already had in mind the first draft of what would become *The Shepherd*, the novel I published last year that takes place in New York, with the duel to the death of an ex-police detective and a dangerous terrorist. But I wanted to write something different and chance intervened, to suggest the idea that triggered the spark.

At the time I came across several articles about the Sad Hill Cemetery in different newspapers and other sources. I was unaware of the story and I began to investigate. I soon discovered the amazing work which the Sad Hill Cultural Association was carrying out to rebuild this mythical place, famous for having been the site of the epic and iconic final gunfight of Sergio Leone's movie, *The Good, the Bad and the Ugly*, which starred Clint Eastwood.

I am an admirer of Eastwood's cinema, especially as a director over the last twenty years, with such magnificent movies as *Mystic River, Million Dollar Baby or Gran Torino.* I have also seen some of the movies of his *Dirty Harry saga*, but I have to admit that I only remembered fragments of his spaghetti-western trilogy. So, I watched again as if it were the first time, one of the most valued movies of all time.

Until then I had always thought that the spaghetti-westerns shot in Spain had been done in Almeria, I had no idea that part of *The Good, the Bad and the Ugly*, had been shot in Burgos. But that was not the only surprise fate had for me as the cogs started to turn in my mind, thinking that from all that, a different novel might very well emerge.

Apart from the trouble of rebuilding the cemetery, with its thousands of graves which could be 'adopted' by people from all over the world, I found out that the Sad Hill Cultural Association celebrated the 50th anniversary of the shooting of the movie in the Burgos region of Arlanza, in 2016, with a cinematographic symposium with a great number of activities which drew my attention. A wild idea began to settle in my mind.

The final piece came when I found out that my wife knew part of that story, since she had spent many Summer and Easter holidays at her cousins' house in Carazo, wandering the area of the Arlanza with them and other friends. The story of the shooting of *The Good, the Bad and the Ugly*, in the area was not news to her. Therefore, I had no choice but to travel around those landscapes which had been re-made into movie sets whose story had surprised me so.

In May of 2018 we rented a room at a country house in Salas de los Infantes, the biggest town of the area and the site of the celebration and film convention in 2016 for the 50th anniversary of the film. We arrived there ready to travel around some of the places that had served as sets for the movie, but I also wanted to see other villages of the region and get to know a bit of the character of the place, considering that it had been quite some time since Leone, Eastwood and the rest of them had landed in Burgos.

We went to the ruined monastery of San Pedro de Arlanza, but were unable to visit because of restoration work. Very near was the Blue Fountain, another spectacular place I had read something about and which I wanted to visit for myself. We lost ourselves in the little streets of Covarrubias, the village where the actors and most of the shooting crew had stayed. But there were other locations which were equally important.

We went through the village of Contreras, which would become very important in my novel, and we headed to the Mirandilla valley along a stone path. There is the restored Sad Hill Cemetery, a magical place I recommend you to visit. As soon as I saw it, I knew it would have to become a fundamental part of my story, while the ideas began to settle in my head as various plots were beginning to manifest.

Arantza, my wife, was as surprised as one of the characters of the story when we went into the valley. She already knew the place from the nineties, as a grazing area for cattle, with the mass of the Carazo Boulder dominating the horizon. The 1966 cemetery disappeared shortly after the end of the shooting, and, until its restoration many years later, the Mirandilla valley was only frequented by cows.

We continued along the forest trail to Santo Domingo de Silos, where we toured the quaint village and visited the famous monastery, with one of the best kept cloisters in the world. And by chance, we came across some relatives of my wife's cousins, who were spending the weekend in Carazo. We also wanted to see the Gorge of La Yecla, a unique place that would later serve me as a set for the beginning of my novel. We did that with them and I told them what I had in mind and tried to elicit any details that might be useful for my project.

We went into the family home, which I have recreated freely as Menchu's home in the novel and there I was able to chat with several members of the family who had actually taken part in the shooting of the film in 1966, as extras, and they imparted very valuable information for which I am very thankful. Anecdotes, memories, and details of daily life in the 60s which helped me figure what it was like, and I knew I had to write the story, which would straddle two eras.

Once back home I began the task of documentation - I read Carlos Aguilar's essay about Clint Eastwood and also found Francisco Reyero's fantastic work: *Since my Name Defends Me.* I found out many curious details about Eastwood's and Leone's wanderings around the Spanish territory, which I decided to use in my story.

I also delved into the story and work of Sergio Leone and Ennio Morricone, two giants who would also be important in the story I wanted to tell. I read other non-fiction books along with newspaper and magazine articles, and watched videos regarding the issues I wanted to deal with in the novel.

The juicy anecdotes about the shooting I mention are absolutely true or as true as the telling of what happened there in 1966 can be. What happened to the Mediavilla family at that time is pure fiction but used within the context of real events that occurred during that summer in the Arlanza valley and beyond.

As for the plot set in 2016, I used some of the actual events that took place during the film conference organized in Salas de los Infantes, mixing it with the fictional part of the college students looking to spend a different weekend, with the murders on the movie sets and their precarious investigation, parallel to the discovery of what happened to María Mediavilla throughout the years.

I also knew that the documentary, *Sad Hill Unearthed*, was being shot too, about the wonderful adventure that drove the association founding members to rebuild the cemetery. When I watched it later on Netflix, with my first draft already finished, I was pleased to see that I had recreated the events at the Mirandilla valley authentically, as the last feature of the film conference was the screening of the film in that unique environment after the surprising message from Clint Eastwood for his fans. I did allow myself to introduce a 'small change' to end the evening, the macabre finding at the hangman's tree. I hope you will forgive me for it...

I still had to determine one of the most important plots of the novel and make it fit into the frame I was creating. In many of my novels there is a component of social criticism and here it was going to serve me to tell the story of the Patronato de Protección de la Mujer, an organization of the Franco era that was practically unknown, and which made my hair stand on end once I discovered what went on within the walls if those institutions.

Years ago, I was in touch with an association of victims of the plot of stolen children in a clinic in Madrid, so I had first-hand knowledge of what had been going on over several years in our country with those babies, stolen from their mothers. The story made some waves for a while, but in the end, no-one paid for those abject crimes. But it is what I found out about the Patronato as I was researching, that was even worse.

Everything I tell in my novel, what happens to María Mediavilla or her fellow inmates at the maternity of Peñagrande, is based on real events, the same as what the historian tells Sandra and Alberto. Some readers were surprised to know the truth, since they believed it was my own fiction, but you simply have to type 'Maternity of Peñagrande' in any web searcher to reveal those atrocities.

I have used details of what several women have lived through in order to recreate the anguishing moments suffered by María and her fellow inmates. Stories as chilling as the slave work, physical and psychological torture, or the sale of both the children and their mothers, all this happened inside these centers of 'reeducation'. Facts, not as well - known as the network of stolen babies, I wanted to denounce in some way with this story. I simply cannot wrap my head around the fact that this was happening in our country well into our democracy.

Toward the end of 2018 I had the first draft of the manuscript ready, but I still had much work ahead of me. After a few months untouched, came the stage of revising and editing before I put the final full stop to the story. The novel went through several redrafts and then the pandemic arrived, which turned everything upside down, including in the publishing sector. As a result, it was not until spring of 2022 that I decided it could reach my readers. And for this to happen, I have counted on the help of other people I would like to acknowledge for their invaluable collaboration, therefore I dedicate this novel to:

My beta readers for their priceless comments about this first draft and for the pleasant conversations about the sub-plots of the story.

Luis, for his wonderful work in editing the manuscript in Spanish and advising me on all the little things to polish to improve the work.

Friends and relatives in Burgos, for their help in planning some details of the story and for their support all along the process.

Sergio and the rest of members of the Sad Hill Cultural Association and their wonderful disposition to help me in everything once they knew of this project set in the emptied Spain.

Christy Cox for her advice and comments and Carl Rigby for his editing work in English, thank you.

And last but most important, I dedicate this work to Arantza, my significant other, my companion, twin soul every person looks for. She is a fundamental part of all my projects and her contagious enthusiasm helps me try to be better every day. In this case, it was she who made me discover some amazing landscapes I could use in the novel. But she also helped me with the research, we toured other possible real sets that I later recreated in the book. She revised the different versions of the manuscript, always bringing her interesting points of view, as well as getting involved in marketing and logistics matters. She is always there as a support to overcome adversities, something fundamental to bringing projects to fruition. The writer's work is hard, requiring much sacrifice and sometimes very lonely, and without my own personal muse I would not be able to see it through. Thank you from the bottom of my heart, for everything.

And of course, you, dear reader, because without you all this would make no sense.

Printed in France by Amazon
Brétigny-sur-Orge, FR

14263267R00239